The Course of Fortune

A Novel of the Great Siege of Malta

Volume 3

Tony Rothman

iBooks

Habent Sua Fata Libelli

iBooks
Manhanset House
Shelter Island Hts., New York 11965-0342
Tel: 212-427-7139
bricktower@aol.com • www.ibooksinc.com

Library of Congress Cataloging-in-Publication Data

Rothman, Tony.
The Course of Fortune, A Novel of the Great Siege of Malta / Tony Rothman. —
1st. American ed.
               p. cm.
  1. Siege of Malta, 1565—Fiction. 2. Malta—History. 3. Religion—
Christianity—History. 4. Fiction—Christian—Historical Fiction.
               I. Title.
         PS3569.A6887R8 2011
         813' .54—dc20

Volume 1: 978-1-59687-427-5, Hardcover; 978-1-899694-24-2, Trade Paper
Volume 2: 978-1-59687-428-2, Hardcover; 978-1-899694-25-9, Trade Paper
Volume 3: 978-1-59687-429-9, Hardcover; 978-1-899694-26-6, Trade Paper

July 2024

The Course of Fortune

A Novel of the Great Siege of Malta

Volume 3

Tony Rothman

CONTENTS

Map illustrations by Renee Zhan

Sicilia

Malta

Pozzallo

Cape
Passero

lgarr

Birgu

Mdina/
Città Notabile

Zurrieq

ITERANED

Tripoli

GREAT PORT~MALTA
1565

Gallows' Point

Fort St. Elmo

Castle St. Angelo

Marsamxett Harbor

Guiral's Post

Mt. Sciberras

Post of Sanoguera

Seng

Porto

Marsa

Fountain

Grand Master's Garden

Book V

de Valette

While the Ottoman army was camped at Zemun, where Soliman had received John-Sigismund and promised him all the lands between the Tisza and Transylvania, word came that Count Nicholas Zriny, Lord of Szigetvár, had ambushed one of His Majesty's dignitaries, killing him and carrying off much booty. Soliman ordered a march on Szigetvár at once. Again we crossed the Danube, the Sava and the Drava. Again the rains were torrential and the crossings of these rivers on makeshift bridges treacherous. The oxen got mired in the mud, the artillery stuck and soldiers attempting to free the pieces as well. When at last the Sultan, carried in a litter when the roads proved impassable for his carriage, reached Szigetvár, his army was waiting, one hundred thousand men and three hundred cannon.

Count Zriny had bedecked the city with red banners to honor so great an enemy but had no intention of surrendering. He set the old town ablaze and placed cannon on the smoldering ruins, then fired on His Majesty's troops. Soliman found the strength to mount his horse and ordered the siege to begin. While his slaves attacked Szigetvár, Soliman retired to his tent and ordered me to take up my narration of the events leading to the descent against that accursed island with no name.

His Majesty, appearing weary and exhausted, all the while in extreme ill-humor, warned me that my admission to having been a spy and even having carried news of the descent to the infidel *bey* was no trifling matter. Had I revealed such immediately after the defeat, he would have had me beheaded—no, quartered—on the spot and, unless I could show myself to be more than an accursed agent in the pay of the Grand Master, he would certainly do so now, even as he'd blow up the citadel and decapitate Count Zriny by placing his head before a cannon's mouth. I had no need to recall the parable of the fox, the ass and the lion to understand that Soliman had merely to raise a finger…

Seventy-Four

With the morning Angelus I was up an hour before dawn and, as I had for the past days, dressed myself in the leather jack or brigandine most of the common soldiers wore. I threw the bandoleer over my neck, grabbed my wheel-lock and morion and went across to St. Angelo, where I would be stationed at the fortress arsenal and on the gun platforms. As I passed the powder stores below the Palace and barracks, Commander Francisco de Guiral asked for help to bring more gunpowder and balls to his post. Several men grabbed kegs from the store house and carried them down, out thro' the main gate and along the trench that had been dug to Guiral's Post, as it was already known. The Commander and his men had built the gun platform at the very tip of the castle, next to the big capstan. It stood just fingers above the water, directly atop the stone apron girding St. Angelo itself, and its purpose was to protect the chain and entrance to Galley Creek. The post was well fortified with nine pieces pointing through firing holes to the mouth of the Great Port and, in the other direction, toward the Marsa.

Having brought down the kegs, we went up for more and had just reached the store house when agitated shouts came to us from above; the alarm bell atop the fortress began to clang. Every man glanced at his nearest comrade and sped upward. I raced to the top of the cavalier itself, but even before I gained the summit, I knew the hour we had so long anticipated and dreaded was upon us.

At dawn a small haze cloaked the horizon. Those keen-eyed sentries were doing their best with little success to make out the indistinct forms they had discerned emerging from the whiteness. Slowly the sun climbed into the eastern sky and burned away the haze, leaving a sea that shimmered with a dazzling brilliance. With the proud flag of the Order flapping above them, men gathered 'round the sentries and shielded their eyes. There could be no doubt. Atop the glittering blue expanse, a host of minute, ill-omened silhouettes had spread into a great crescent, which heartbeat by heartbeat advanced inexorably towards us.

This was no repetition of the spectacle that had greeted our eyes during the summer of the *razzia* or at Djerbé. This was something of another magnitude. I know not what thoughts coursed thro' the minds of the others standing upon the cavaliers of St. Elmo and St. Angelo, but even I, who had seen the Turkish fleet being readied, had not entirely imagined this force. Every man crossed himself. Some whispered, "Madonna." One of the sentries ran to the Magisterial Palace below to alert the Grand Master, who had already been meeting with the Council for hours, and encountered him climbing the steps to the cavalier. de Valette stood with the rest of us watching the fleet, yet five leagues out. The crescent advancing on Malta spanned the entire eastern horizon.

"How many?" he asked.

One of the sentries answered: "Two hundred."

At that moment two cannon shots from Fort St. Elmo across the harbor reached us, the signal that the invasion had begun. The Monsignore nodded, the signal was repeated at St. Angelo, and when the sound carried to Mdina, thence to Gozo.

I ran down thro' the town to the landward ramparts, where I found Balthazar fully armed with his comrades at the Post of France, between the two bastions. He had heard the signal and merely nodded on my approach.

"Two hundred ships," I said. "We don't yet know the number of galleys."

The Chevalier hardly paused. "Methinks the number is far more favorable than the thousand the face of that woman caused to be launched against Troy."

"As you know better than I, Balthazar," I answered, "that fleet was but a tale."

Balthazar smiled, asking me what day it was. I replied Friday, the eighteenth of May, and returned to the fortress.

Immediately upon hearing the signal, Romegas and Captain General de Giou manned two galleys of the Order and, with pennants flying and trumpets blaring, sallied forth from the mouth of the Great Port to meet the enemy. Those of us watching from St. Angelo could scarce credit the

bravado wherewith these Commanders so brazenly confronted the foe, as
were they pissing in his face, but de Valette had cautioned them not to
confront the Turk, merely to measure him.

It was well the Grand Master had issued such an order, for Romegas,
on the poop of the *S. Gabriele* with a new monkey upon his shoulder,
snorted to engage. As the enormous fleet loomed before him, he turned
to Vergã with his hand trembling and said, "Hah! How many of them do
you think we could take, Vergada?"

"We could no doubt take half," replied Vergã soberly, "but let's save
our skins today so that we may take them all tomorrow."

For the first time in his life Romegas agreed to withhold an attack. He
and de Giou remained out of range and counted. In the crescent that
embraced the sea and which with each splash of the oar was converging
on Malta, they reckoned one hundred ninety vessels of size, and fifty or
even one hundred smaller ones following. Of the full number, one hundred
thirty were war galleys, many triremes among them, another thirty
galiots; the remainder great galleases, towed barges with supplies and
ships of adventurers who had come for plunder.

As the enemy fleet got close enough to see the fortifications and the
men on them, it slowly began to change course southward. "Eh!" shouted
Romegas, punching Vergã, "two galleys of the Order is enough to frighten
them off!"

Both knew this was unlikely the truth. Plainly, the enemy had decided
not to risk a direct assault on the Great Port and intended to anchor at a
large bay a few leagues to the south—Marsaxlokk the Maltese called it;
the Knights named it Marsa Scirocco, for it was a haven against all winds
but for the Scirocco. Romegas followed until he was convinced that the
Turks were indeed heading to Marsaxlokk, then returned to the Port to
inform de Valette.

Not long after the warning guns sounded, Dr. Jean and a small group
of Knights followed Camillo Rosso, the Order's Protomedicus, on
horseback out of the Birgu gates with a donkey cart behind them. Finding
some irregulars on the ridge, Rosso waved those men along, saying the
time had come: The Grand Master had commanded the big spring in the
Marsa to be poisoned.

They marched a league to the Marsa, a small inlet at the inner extremity of the Great Port. En route, they passed through a tiny village where the Grand Master had built a good house for himself, surrounding it with a spacious walled garden. Some tall poplars stood therein, Vigo noticed, some of the few trees on the island. When the band reached the spring on the other side of the village, a spring so plentiful that it supplied all Birgu, they began the work. The doctors had brought sacks of arsenic from the pharmacy. That went into the big stone well first. Not being at all assured the quantities were sufficient, they added hemp and poison herbs, and for good measure the men gathered up everything they could find around the village and hurled it in: flax, wheat, animal dung. Once they believed they had killed the spring, they rushed back to the Borgo, knowing that but for what had already been stored in the cisterns, the town and Senglea would now have almost no drinking water. Vigo, for his part, lost no time in getting back to the Sacra Infermeria. He had many preparations ahead of him.

With Lady Emilia so ill, Isabella decided to leave her in Mdina under the care of the servants and doctor, while she returned to Birgu and Giansevere. On the second morning Isabella departed early with a servant and was already on the road when she heard the muffled cannon shots from St. Angelo, then, moments later, the louder echo from the guns atop Mdina's bastions. Like everyone else on Malta, she knew precisely what the signal portended, and a shudder ran thro' every limb of her body.

She hesitated, for a moment being unable to make up her mind to go onward or return to Notabile. With a deeper shudder Isabella saw that earlier day when she had been one among thousands trapped in the Old City. She forced herself to return to Notabile for her mother, but now made her way against crowds pouring out of the city. A woman she knew by name, Marietta de Modo, stood against a wall wailing that the Turks should enter the city. Her son had become a renegado and she prayed only for his safe return. Isabella listened to the woman's lament with astonishment and disgust, pressing her horse on. Inside, Emilia refused to quit her bed and Isabella, turning every way, grew angrier moment by moment.

"Mother, let me learn what is transpiring and I'll return this eve or tomorrow," she said at last.

"Begone!" Emilia retorted irritably, with a wave of her hand.

Again Isabella departed. By the time she passed through Notabile's gates, the countryside had come alive. From behind every stone wall and wall of prickly figs, a man sprang up, as from the ground, to begin rushing in the direction of the Port, often with his family and stubborn livestock behind him. With each of her horse's step, the sea in which she found herself trapped became more chaotic. Two-wheeled carts, four-wheeled carts, donkeys laden with sacks, goats with bells tinkling, dogs running this way and that as they barked and fought, men carrying scythes, women with babes in arms; everyone who remained on the island was making for the Borgo, the birds overhead as well. Isabella perceived exactly that she was only among thousands who had failed to be sent to Sicilia, and she hoped that this knowledge would temper Parisot's wrath, the thought of which set her trembling, even as she recollected her dream of a collapsing mountain, which set her trembling for another, not lesser reason. A woman begged Isabella to take her baby, but she could not find the heart to choose this one over another and spurred her horse on, against the sensation that she was drowning.

On the outskirts of the town, pure bedlam greeted her. *"Mur tnejjek!"* *"F'ghoxx ommhok!"* peasants shouted in their strange language at the lines of halberdiers and arquebusiers who held them at bay.

"You dare speak to us like that! We'll take your heads!" the guards retorted. "Stand back, you hear!"

In the midst of the shouting and shoving, a hundred Knights thundered forth on horseback, followed by what seemed to be a thousand more Knights and foot soldiers. The Knights made a splendid sight in their armor overladen by brilliant red and white sopravests, but so violently were the people pressing the guards to reach safety that they hardly stopped to regard or cheer this column making a stately and orderly advance to the south.

When the soldiers finally disappeared over the hillcrests, a full stampede erupted. People in front were crushed by those behind, run down by carts and donkeys. The halberdiers, fearing for their own safety, grew violent and wielded their weapons as they would against an enemy host. Isabella watched with incomprehension a small battle erupt before her eyes. Finally, the guards managed to restore some order and sent half the throng on to Senglea, where there was more space. One of the guard blocked Isabella's entry, but she told him who she was and to her relief he allowed her to pass.

But the streets were already thick with people and she was forced to shove her way through to her house. Inside Giansevere asked what all the commotion was about.

"This day your master Soliman has invaded the island," Isabella replied through one of her slaves. "May God have mercy on all of us."

Giansevere's dull eyes momentarily brightened. "Good," she smiled. "Now I can die in peace."

Isabella caught her breath and regarded her, thinking however her death would be, it would not be in peace.

Pietru had been among the infantry leaving Birgu under old Grand Mareschal Copier. They marched along the south coast following that astonishing fleet from the cliffs, each man exclaiming over and over again that this must be the greatest armada the world had seen since Creation, all of them wondering how many men it conveyed and why the Turks weren't putting in at Marsaxlokk. They weren't. They continued to sail up the coast to the far end of the island. Some said it was because of the Greek wind; others said the enemy was reconnoitering the island. Whatever the reason, as the sun climbed high into the sky, the men marched. And they marched all day in the warmth, seven or eight leagues, until part of the fleet anchored off the village of Mgarr and the rest of it in the channel between Malta and Comino, the tiny rock halfway from Malta to Gozo.

As Balthazar could see no reason to remain at Birgu and owned a horse, he obtained leave from François de la Beissière *dict* Caruan, in charge of the Post of France, to ride with the cavalry under Captain Melchor de Guaras. Tho' Balthazar, like me, had had a sense of the size of the force Malta would face, he too could not but wonder at the fleet sailing along the southwest coast of the island. The bright sails and gay flags passing by in a studied contempt proclaimed a blunt warning: Surrender to the Crescent forthwith, or die. Only one hundred ships, Balthazar recollected, had sailed for Rhodes. As for the numbers of that legendary siege, they had always been disputed. He doubted these would be much less.

When toward sunset the enemy anchored off Mgarr, Balthazar rode up to Colonel Mas at the head of his company of foot, saying that should the

Turks truly anchor in the north, then Mdina would be the first city to come under attack. The same thought had occurred to Mas and all the other Knights. As night fell, Copier ordered the men to march back two leagues to the Old City. They did so, leaving scouts and guards along the way.

By the time the army reached Notabile, many of its citizens had already fled, and when the news the soldiers brought got around, others quickly departed. Yet people enow refused to move and the ring of armorers' hammers was heard into the night. Balthazar happened across Pietru, who sang to himself as he crouched outside the town wall with the other arquebusiers, and asked after his feet.

"Not bad," replied Ix-Xabaw in Italian, taking off his boots, "only ten leagues today, maybe eleven." He offered Balthazar a skein of wine, which the Knight gladly accepted. He had always liked Pietru, tho' in truth he had little in common with the simple farmer, except for fond recollections of their shared exploits.

"I remember when we sailed with Strozzi," remarked Balthazar, "all the time searching for your wife. Now by God you have her. Are you happy?"

Pietru grunted. "We say *Il-mara tilbes minn rasha u r-ragel minn saqajh.*"

Balthazar, who remained standing in his armor, laughed, telling Pietru to speak Italian.

"A women puts her clothes on from her head, and a man puts them on from his feet."

Once more the Chevalier laughed. "That will always be true. Have you sent her to Sicilia?"

Pietru looked into the distance, shaking his head. "*Le.* She was at our village. I told her to go to Birgu when she heard the signal. Lord Balthazar, you are a lettered man. Do you think we can fuck these Turks? We are only six or seven thousand and the Turks have never been fucked, not in a hundred years."

"Knowing that you are fighting at my side, I have few worries that we can fuck them," replied the Knight, "but tell Zaifi the armorer in Birgu that I want him to make you a cuirass." With a tap to his own breastplate, Balthazar moved on. He found Mas resting not far away against a stable wall, dropped his helmet to the ground, unbuckled his sword and sat down next to the Colonel, wincing for a moment at the pain.

"What is it?" asked Mas.

"Gelves."

"Yes," the other nodded. "I remember. I remember that day when your friend wounded Dragut and we carried you to safety. God that he would have killed him! I remember five thousand brave men being starved in a fort and I remember spending two years as a hostage in Constantinople. I'd sooner die than let it happen again."

Balthazar hadn't known Mas before Djerbé, but the slightly older man with a sharp beard was regarded as one of the most dedicated of the Knights, rivaling Romegas in contempt of danger. "It will be worse here, you know," said Balthazar, stretching out. "The enemy force is so much larger ... But everyone salutes you for raising a company ... "

"I wish it were five times the number. You know your friend Barai worked for the Turks in Stamboul."

"What of it?" asked Balthazar, frowning.

Mas shrugged. "Vergada was asking."

"Truly?" Balthazar couldn't disguise the abrupt alarm in his voice. "What did you tell him?"

"That there were rumors Barai had turned. Renegados can burn in Hell for all I care, but I never saw him there. I hold no grudge against your friend. Men do what they must to survive, don't they?" He gazed at Balthazar with a certain importunacy in his eyes.

"They do, and God forgives them."

"Damn the Turks," Colonel Mas agreed and together they leaned against the wall to catch what sleep they could.

That evening on the way to my room I passed Flaminia's house as she stepped onto the street. "I told you to leave, you stupid whore!" I erupted the moment I saw her and slapped her soundly across the face. "Do you have any idea what is happening?"

Flaminia's hand went to her mouth, from which I had drawn blood. "Don't beat me, Francisco! the Turks have come. Where is the talisman I gave you?"

"*Pezzo di cretino!* " I roared, furiously, "do you believe a stone will protect you from what has arrived this day? *Por la Santa Trinidad!*" Thereupon I let forth a string of Spanish, Italian and Turkish oaths with such vehemence that Flaminia could hardly comprehend a word. Only after some moments did I find my senses, clasping my head between my hands. "By the Lord Jesus, have you filled your stores with food and water?"

Crossing herself, Flaminia nodded. She had not been so stupid as to forget.

"Go, pray!" I ordered, naught else coming to my lips. "God save you, Flaminia. God save us all."

I pushed on angrily thro' the streets thronged with people, thinking that if Flaminia had failed to leave, perhaps Isabella had as well. To be sure, at the Guasconi house I found her sitting with Giansevere, who stared upward with a contented expression on her ancient, toothless face. Upon catching sight of me, Isabella ran and grasped me by the arms, but I cast at her only a hard, burning gaze.

"Do not reproach me, Francisco!" she cried. "I intended to leave yesterday, but Mother is terribly ill. I did not know what to do ... Come, I require every strength to face Parisot."

She threw on a *faldetta* and we walked silently the short distance to Parisot's home, through the streets that were already becoming ripe with flies and every evil smell. Parisot, tho', was nowhere to be found and we crossed the moat to the fortress, where at last we caught sight of him in the upper garden, having just come out of Council. When he caught sight of his ward standing before the nymphaeum, he froze, much as I had. Isabella at first lowered her eyes, then raised them slowly to meet his, full of wrath and sorrow. He ordered his Seigneurs away and I removed myself to the side.

"You have disobeyed my orders!" he thundered.

Isabella nodded quickly. "Forgive me, Parisot. Mother is very ill and cannot travel to Sicilia."

E'en at hearing those words, a sensible grief flashed across the Grand Master's visage. "Where is she?" he asked, thunder silenced.

"In Notabile."

The Monsignore glanced away, crossing himself, then fixed on Isabella that deep gaze of concern reserved for her and her alone. "Isabella, I have told you nothing would grieve me more than if you came to harm, nothing in the world. I believe Città Vecchia will be safe. Go there at once and remain out of danger."

"There is the nurse."

de Valette now shook his head, as if such matters were both beneath his contempt, at this moment especially, and beyond his contemplation. For a moment he fell silent, inwardly reflecting. "Do you have food at your home, stores, provisions?"

Isabella nodded again, saying nothing.

"Go then. We will speak again, should God permit it."

As we left the garden, Isabella sighed deeply. "I was prepared for worse."

"He has an infinity of matters weighing on him," I answered, the Grand Master's reproach tempering my own, "and, it is evident, he loves you very much."

Isabella smiled faintly and when we reached her door, bid each other good-evening as stray dogs yelped in the darkness.

Seventy-Five

Early next morning, well before dawn, Balthazar felt someone shaking his shoulder and awoke to see Colonel Mas above him. Balthazar took a moment to void himself against the wall, they downed some wine with a little bread, they helped with each other's armor and mounted their horses. It was yet quite dark, with only the faintest glow in the east and the morning star bright in the sky. Scouts had come with the news that thirty-five enemy galleys had weighed anchor and were stealthily creeping back along the southwestern coast of the island towards Marsa Scirocco. The Grand Mareschal decided to reconnoitre.

Horse and foot went out of Notabile in the direction of Mgarr village, stopping after about half a league on some heights whence they might observe the fleet. Shadows were indeed traversing the bright water. "We must know what they're about," the Mareschal said as much to the wind as anyone. Then he turned to Captain de Guaras and told him to take his cavalry onward to Mgarr. "See if you can capture a stray hen and get the Monsignore some information."

With a caution of prudence and sixty horsemen behind him, the Captain reached the village in good order. Mgarr lay only a few steps from the coast and if Turks were coming ashore, it would surely be here. By now it was light; they looked around. The villagers had fled and the place was empty but for a forgotten cow wandering freely about, bell tinkling, and some falcons sitting motionless on the roofs of the huts. Balthazar could hardly imagine a more forlorn place.

Seeing no one here, Guaras ordered the young French Knight Adrien de la Rivière to go on a little further down the path to try to capture someone. Balthazar was among the eight or nine who accompanied la Rivière past green walls of India figs, whose leathery skin and thorns only added to the desolation around them. When the party got within sight of the water and the fleet, they espied a line of Turks climbing up the ridge.

A few of the Knights were chomping at the bit to engage but la Rivière held them back. "Remember our orders. We lay in ambush for a stray goose and that's that. Quickly, behind that wall."

His men obeyed. They took up position behind one of the innumerable stone walls crisscrossing the farms of the island and waited. Turks were now coming ashore, but only scouting parties. Even so, the dozens of men they discerned upon the ridge far outnumbered them. For two glasses la Rivière's party didn't stir, hoping for a goose or a hen, when without warning one of Guaras's own men from the village appeared from behind, galloping furiously in their direction.

"By Jesus, who's this?" la Rivière exclaimed, watching the dust fly up everywhere about the horse's hooves.

"Vendo de Mezquita," somebody answered the question la Rivière didn't ask. "Fra Pedro's nephew."

Everyone was puzzled. Old Pedro de Mezquita had been appointed Military Governor of Notabile. "He must be warning us about something," la Rivière said. "I'll go."

"Don't—" Balthazar held up his hand.

Too late. la Rivière had mounted his horse and rode out to meet de Mezquita in the open. Immediately the Turkish arquebusiers spotted him and opened fire. la Rivière turned, facing an entire company of janissaries on the ridge beyond, and suddenly, without signaling to anyone, let out a yell and charged with Mezquita at his side. The janissaries fired again. la Rivière's horse went out from under him and the Knight flew to the ground. At the same instant, Mezquita was hit and fell. This Portuguese, seriously wounded, crawled behind the nearest wall as the Turks ran toward la Rivière. The Knight scrambled to his feet, took up his sword and faced his attackers, but another ball caught him in the thigh and he collapsed onto his knees. Before anyone knew what was happening, Grand Viscount Bartolomeo Faraone sped forth from the wall—and an instant later he was down beside la Rivière. Things unfolded too quickly. In the next moment the big Maltese horseman Mikiel was out in the open. He managed to grab la Rivière, hoisted him onto his shoulders and ran back toward the wall, but the Turks were after him with arquebus and scimitar, so close on his heels that Mikiel had no choice but to drop the Knight. "Forgive me, Sir, I can do no more," he said and scrambled to safety as

Turks captured la Rivière and Faraone, and forced them back to their own lines.

The Knights called out for Mezquita without getting an answer and someone crawled far enough to see him slumped against the other wall, a pool of blood about him. The Turks seemed content with their captives and when they had retreated back toward the ships, Balthazar led the remaining men back to the village.

"What happened?" Melchor Guaras immediately wanted to know.

"Perhaps you could best tell us," replied Balthazar to the older man. "Why was this boy Mezquita riding down so furiously in full view of the enemy?"

Guaras shook his head. "Stupid ass. He wanted action. He ran off without orders."

So, it has already begun, thought Balthazar.

"What's happened to him?" the Captain went on.

"He's dead. la Rivière and Faraone are captured."

"They'll be tortured."

"Of course," said Balthazar.

"What does la Rivière know?"

"Everything." la Rivière had been a page and confidant of the Grand Master.

God, tho', had woven a more intricate design. de Guaras led his horse back to Mareschal Copier, who was anything but pleased to hear what had taken place. While they were deciding what to do next, a messenger from Fort St. Angelo rode up at full gallop, telling Copier that the Grand Master ordered the infantry back to the Borgo, while the cavalry, under pain of holy obedience, was to go to Notabile, where henceforth it would be stationed. Balthazar, deciding he must return to his post, accompanied Colonel Mas and the Mareschal.

South of Birgu, not far from the village of Zabbar, the company encountered Captain General de Giou. With a company of fifty arquebusiers de Giou had also been reconnoitering the enemy. Yes, he reported, thirty-five galleys had by now put into the small bay of St. Thomas, about a league closer to Birgu than Marsaxlokk, and were disembarking men. They were making camp at the nearby villages of Santa Catarina and San Giovanni.

"What is their plan?" the Captain General asked without hoping for an answer. "Will the attack come from the south or the north?"

"If they have enough men, perhaps both," Copier replied.

While the Knights stood on this open rise, trying to divine what the enemy was about, five of de Giou's arquebusiers ran up thro' the shrubs and wildflowers, leading a Turkish prisoner. No, he spoke perfect Neapolitan. "You're a renegado," de Giou said.

The fellow said he had only turned because he'd given up trying to secure a ransom in Constantinople, but had never given up hope of escape. He had just managed to elude the Turks at St. Thomas Bay.

"Very well," said Balthazar, gazing at the first of the many, "what can you tell us about the armada?"

"He could be a spy," de Giou cautioned with a raised hand.

The prisoner glanced nervously amongst the three men, but Copier nodded for him to go on. "You cannot imagine the force sent against you," he continued in Neapolitan.

"We will imagine," barked Balthazar. "You shall tell us."

With the fear of God in him, the renegado told. "The Sultan's orders are to take Malta. The Pashas think this should be a simple task and expect to be done in a week. After, they'll go on to la Goletta."

"How many men?"

"Fifty thousand fighting men. Ten—maybe twenty—thousand oarsmen can be used as sappers."

A silence descended upon the circle surrounding the Neapolitan. His was the first report of the numbers facing them. Whether the renegade knew what he was talking about was another matter. de Giou motioned for him to go on.

"One of the biggest ships sank on a clear day in Nauplia channel. Six hundred spahis drowned and much needed munitions were lost. I think it was sunk by the Captain himself to harm our enemy. They still believe they have supplies for sixth months and have brought much heavy artillery. This includes two enormous stone-throwers, the likes of which you have never seen." One I have seen, thought Balthazar, one I have seen. "But," the prisoner added, "the Pashas are not in harmony and the troops regard this as a bad augury."

Having heard him out, de Giou told his men to send him back to the Turks, but at this the fellow pissed in his pants and the Knights decided he had been telling the truth.

"We'll take him to the Monsignore," said Copier, mounting his horse. Better for him the Monsignore than the Inquisitor, reflected Balthazar.

Throughout the day of the nineteenth the Turks continued their disembarkation, overrunning the whole island south of the Borgo while they set up their first camps at S. Giovanni and Sta. Catarina—a place the Maltese spoke of as Zejtun. As night fell, de Valette called to the Magisterial Palace Rafael Salvago, the same Genoese who had been looking after the powder works until about a week ago when we moved them inside the walls, and he went to Sicilia. Salvago found the Grand Master alone in his study as the pages were lighting candles, but de Valette waved the boys away, leaving only the oil lamp flickering on his writing table, by the quill and inkwell. The young man was exhausted. He had returned from Sicilia with supplies two days ago and had eaten almost nothing since, as he had set off at once with the infantry. None of this concerned de Valette, who handed him a ciphered dispatch for the Vice Roy.

When Salvago glanced at it in the fading light, the Grand Master told him its contents were quickly summarized: "The invasion has begun. The enemy has two hundred ships. We await troops from Illustrissimo."

Salvago was to depart again for Sicilia immediately and return the moment he had had delivered the message. Romegas, who had taken charge of defending the Port, would ferry Salvago to Marsamxett, where the Order's swiftest galley, the *S. Giacomo*, awaited with a picked *ciurma*. He would travel under the Grand Master's nephew de Valette Cornisson, who would remain in Sicily to raise troops. E'en as the Monsignore gave Salvago his instructions, Romegas himself arrived from the Towers with his monkey on his shoulder. The first words from the Commander's mouth were: "la Rivière has been captured."

de Valette slammed his fist on his table. la Rivière had been his page; he held the young man in great affection. Worse, no one needed tell him what Mustafa would do to get the information he wanted. Did they have a better estimation of the enemy's strength? de Valette wanted to know. Lescaut shook his head; most of the Turks had yet to disembark. However, Knights had been answering the *Citazione* until the last hour. Perhaps six hundred brethren now stood shoulder to shoulder, and with the Maltese who had suddenly flooded Birgu and Senglea, Romegas reckoned they might muster eight thousand men at arms, even a few hundred more. That included ... everyone.

Everyone, de Valette repeated, but God. He waved Romegas and Salvago from the room. From Kalkara Creek below the two took a *fregata* to Marsamxett, spying no enemy ships. On the far side of St. Elmo, Salvago boarded the *S. Giacomo*, where Cornisson was waiting, saluted Romegas and set sail.

Once the infantry had returned, Pietru had wandered about Birgu trying to find his wife. He was certain she must be somewhere, but she had disappeared like a gopher. Ix-Xabaw came running to the arsenal at St. Angelo where I had been making liquid a mixture of sulphur, oil, saltpetre crystals and egg yolks to use in *granadas*. We had not left them in earthenware pots under manure for a month as some alchemists advised, for I hadn't found that to be of value. Pietru asked me to help find Grezz. As I had been at it all day, I agreed.

"Don't worry," I said, leaving the work to others, "this time she can't be far."

We searched every nook and cranny in the Borgo, took a boat to Senglea. Work on the ravelin at Fort St. Michel and on the walls hadn't ceased and we watched men raise heavy guns to the platform, but we could not find Grezz. "She'll turn up," I assured Pietru again, putting my hands on his shoulders, and I returned to Birgu to learn how Isabella was faring. A strange tension filled her sitting room, where Isabella's slave fed the old nurse yoghoort in candlelight and silence while Isabella looked on, grasping her necklace. Giansevere had resumed her airs, cackling haughtily that in a few days the Turks would destroy the Knights and every one us would be taken into captivity.

"How is it," I said, disgust at her words filling my voice, "that this great descent comes about for such an ugly old crone. Not Helen of Troy." I turned to Isabella. "Why don't you be done with her? Throw her on the dung heap and we'll make gunpowder of her."

Isabella found no amusement in either of us. "How might you feel in her place?" she demanded.

"You forget, Señora, I have been in her place."

Señora Guasconi swallowed, then, looking at me with sorrowful eyes, she said, "Cannot you see, Francisco, she is but an old, old woman, confused and frightened?"

"She is an infidel."

"Francisco," Isabella said, shaking her head with a greater exasperation, "once Fra Balthazar told me in admiration you were a man who learned from his travels. What have you learned?"

Little, I answered. Apart from making guns, I had learned only that God's earth could not hold both the Christian faith and the Mahometan. "As those tens of thousands massing beyond these walls prove beyond doubt."

With some resolution Isabella put her hand on my chest. "These months I have refused to believe you a cruel man, Francisco. More than once you have revealed to me your heart. You have been in San Marco's."

I nodded slowly. I had been there and I had wept.

"So, a heart does beat. And in Constantinople, did no one treat you with kindness?"

"To a degree," I admitted at length, thinking of Abdallah al-Waryagli and e'en Yakhshi. "To a degree."

"Then let it be so," replied Isabella.

"What will you do to your slaves when they run to the barbarians?"

Isabella gaped at me in an unexpected horror, then croaked, "They must be hanged," and having uttered these words, she spun around and said in a voice as merciless as Parisot's, "Yes, we must fight with every strength in our souls and bodies. Our lives and faith depend on it." Hereat she froze, fully sensing her divide. "Francisco," she looked on me again, "those years ago you spoke of your master-at-arms who admonished you to fight the opponent without heat. Can you, w—we fight the Turks this way?"

I scoffed. "Not a man on this island can fight the Turks as you suggest. Nor would it help."

"Are you certain?" she went on, pursuing her confusion. "Balthazar can tell you of the Spartans—"

"Stop, Isabella!" I shouted. "Listen to your foolishness! These are not ancient times. Believe me, the Turks will show us no mercy. Spartans ... " Now it was I shaking my head in disbelief at the useless discourse. At this juncture, tho', Giansevere herself interrupted us in her cracked, sharp voice.

"What is she saying?" Isabella asked.

I was as puzzled as she. "She says, 'If I die, you are my killer, O merciless, infidel woman.'"

Isabella couldn't understand what the witch was at and so I put the question. Giansevere replied that it was from a love poem written by her master, Soliman, to his beloved wife, Hurrem, who came from Rus', where she had been called Roxelana.

"I also write verses," said Isabella to the nurse, sitting beside her as the heat passed. "Perhaps you would recite more of Soliman's poetry to me."

I left the two women in their places, knowing Isabella's slaves could not speak Italian well enow to render verses, e'en bad ones.

All night long they had moved ships back from the north end of the island to the bay Marsaxlokk they had passed on first arriving at Malta. Once the entire fleet was anchored there, Mustafa Pasha ordered two strongly fortified platforms built at the harbor entrance to protect it. While this was going on, Mustafa had decided to establish the main camp at this place the infidels called Marsa, at the inner extremity of the big harbor. It was a pleasant spot, thought Yakhshi as he watched from horseback his *yenicheriler* erect their tents. There was a big house nearby with some trees in the garden, drinking water from a big square fountain too. Somebody said the house belonged to the barbarian master; Vizier Mustafa intended to use it as his headquarters.

Yakhshi was grateful that as a *Boluk-bashi* he had a horse. This island was warm, and he knew in the weeks ahead it would become like Africa. By then he hoped to be gone. He was beginning to wonder, tho'. They'd wasted a few days while Mustafa and Piyale argued about where to put the fleet. Piyale was worried about the Greek wind in this Marsashlok— the name itself meant Harbor of the Hot Wind—and so they went up to the north end of the island, only to find that place more exposed. So last night they turned around again and headed back. The wind at Marsashlok wasn't strong, but Piyale continued to moan he wanted a better anchorage. Commanders, I spit on them. Actually, Piyale was insisting on the harbor near where they were setting up camp now, Marsamshett, but to get into that road they'd first have to reduce the fort guarding its entrance. These *Pashalar* were like dogs sniffing at a bitch in heat. While they sailed from Constantinople, Mustafa revealed to Piyale a secret *firman* the Sultan had given him, bestowing on him powers above those of the *Kapudan*. Yakhshi shrugged. Everyone knew Mustafa was to be in command, but this *firman* only infuriated Piyale, increasing his envy.

Many were convinced an omen lay in this, but things really weren't going badly. The enemy had picked off a few *azablar* who'd strayed from their companies and succumbed to rape and plunder, and as they had begun setting up the main camp, some infantry ran up the long hill from that fort to harass them. Yakhshi couldn't understand those dogs. Their numbers were so puny that they only managed to annoy the Sultan's men, like the flies buzzing everywhere here, and the *spahiler* chased them away. By now Mustafa had landed at least twenty thousand troops. Tents were going up as far as the eye could see, flags flew gaily and the men had already taken out their instruments and were filling the air with pleasant and sparkling sounds.

As Yakhshi leaned over his saddle bow and battle mace watching the spectacle, one of his men ran up, saying the *Boluk-bashi* was wanted by Mustafa Pasha *Hazretleri*. He rode over to the house, where Mustafa had already established himself, looking askance at the strange and rigid furniture abandoned there, and he told Yakhshi to collect his century. Under torture the knight la Rivière had said interesting things about the fortifications and now he wanted to take this Knight and see for himself.

For some years, since Flaminia had grown wealthy enough to employ servants and own slaves, she had slept later than the Angelus, often until sunrise, which she knew to be sinful. But no one had slept much last night with the Turks visible from the city walls, and when she heard the church bells ringing for Sunday Mass, she breathed to herself in surprise and amazement, "Madonna." She decided to go and put on her best dress, which was quite as splendid as any of the noble ladies'. Readying herself, she donned a *faldetta*, took her rosary in hand and made for the Church of San Lawrenz.

On the way, neighbors told her that the Grand Master himself had ordered services to take place as always. Surely, with altar boys carrying tapers as tall as they, and the priest sprinkling holy water on everybody nearby, the Monsignore in his black habit led a great procession of Knights into the church. So many townspeople were flooding in behind them that most were forced to go to the other churches nearby. Flaminia managed to get into S. Lawrenz.

Even in the summer of the *razzia*, she had not felt such dread among the people, or such a sense of purpose among the Knights, all kneeling with the Grand Master in their bright armor. After the priest celebrated Mass, the Monsignore came out onto the church steps, where he was besieged by every townsperson and villager who had fled to Birgu. Wailing and crossing themselves, they knelt in supplication, and the nearest cast their arms around his legs, entreating Eminenza for some assurance they were not all going to die.

As he had faced the Knights a few days earlier, he now faced the people he owned. For as long as she could remember, Flaminia had dreaded the Grand Master, knowing what he could do to anyone on the island—what he had done. He had also made life harder for the *quiracas*, telling the Knights they should live in one part of town even as he regularly visited the Guasconi; she spat on them. Now, he was the only one to turn to.

"At Rhodes," the Monsignore said, as if he understood her thoughts, "when the Knights were confronted by the same tyrant and a host no smaller than the one he has brought against us this day, Grand Master l'Isle Adam said to those gathered about him, 'A glorious victory must be the reward of our valor, or else Rhodes, the strongest rampart of Christendom, must serve as our grave.' Whenever he met townsmen and inhabitants he said to them, 'Never forget that besides the defense of the faith, you have taken up arms for your country, for your wives, your maidens and your children. Fight gallantly, friends, in order to rescue them from the infamy that the barbarians threaten them with. Your blood, your honor and your fortunes are all in your hands, and depend on your bravery.'

"Those words of my great predecessor, who lies buried not many steps from here, are no less true this fateful day. We cannot pause in our labors; an infinity of work remains to be done if the Holy Scriptures are not to submit to the Alcoran."

At that, Parisot assumed his practical air and told everyone to go knock down the houses outside the gates, even his own stables. They should bring the stones and dirt inside where they would make a second defense, behind the city walls. Flaminia did as she was told, thinking the Grand Master must be right.

Later in the day I found her in a torn dress she might have worn years ago in Zurrieq village. She, her parents, hundreds of other men and women, carried baskets of dirt and pulled carts of stone from the houses that swarmed around the Post of Castille, cut down a few mean trees there, all to clear a place for battle.

"A fine Sabbath this has turned out to be!" she moaned faintly, wiping her forehead with a dirty arm. "Working, milking goats, violating every sacrament! We'll all be struck by lightning from a clear sky."

We already have been, I thought, lending Flaminia a hand. "You are no longer accustomed to working on two feet, are you?" I said, to which Flaminia was forced to agree. "Come, I'll give you a lighter profession." I took her to the armory in Birgu, behind the St. James bastion, sat her on a stool and told her to shred the old ropes we had piled up there.

"What is this for?" she asked, wrinkling her nose.

"You will learn soon enough."

At about the same time, Mustafa Pasha with the shackled la Rivière behind him, climbed up the hill at the end of Kalkara Creek to survey the fortifications. Not in vain His Majesty has written, "Everyone aims at the same meaning, but many are the versions of the story." We never discovered exactly what la Rivière told Mustafa. A renegado came into town, saying that under the bastinado, the fearless Knight cried out, 'What will you gain by torturing me? You'll know nothing from me other than that you will never capture Malta! Not only is it strong and well provisioned, but it is held by a Grand Master with Knights and soldiers so valiant that they have all sworn to die for their faith and their Order before they submit to you."

That much is true. What is also true is that the next day Mustafa attacked Birgu.

Seventy-Six

At dawn Pietru set off to work on his gun platform, glanced up and knew at once he would lift no stones today. Above him, their shadows long in the climbing sun, thousands upon thousands of Turkish troops mounted the ridges south of Birgu town. He grabbed his wheel-lock and morion, which hadn't left him in the past days, and ran back to Birgu. Balthazar caught sight of the enemy at about the same moment. He had slept on the ramparts at the Post of France, feeling some fond recollection for his campaigns in Italia, and rose with the morning Angelus. When the light became bright enough, he too discerned the lines of headdresses rising above the southern hills. The sentries atop Auvergne, Castille and Provence were already beating the alarm, and in less time than it took to kiss a whore, all the soldiers and irregulars were running to their companies.

Balthazar attempted to count without success. Since Friday, scouts reckoned, the enemy had landed forty thousand fighting men. That included six or seven thousand janissaries, nine thousand spahis, ten thousand azabs and at least four thousand religious fanatics dressed all in white with green turbans, who desired nothing more than to be sent to Paradise. Balthazar was prepared to oblige them. Beyond those were the followers of Assur; Thracians had come, Macedonians, Bulgarians, Thessalonians ... The Grand Master's scouts hadn't e'en thought to count the oarsmen and camp followers, who must have easily numbered another twenty-five or thirty thousand. Nor had the corsairs arrived. Balthazar, natheless, was happy that the Neapolitan they had picked up on Saturday seemed to have exaggerated.

Grand Mareschal Copier soon climbed to Auvergne, and before long the curtain and bastions were bristling with arquebusiers determined to show the enemy our strength. Verily every man in town was there. I pushed my way thro' the crowds on the walls, found Balthazar at his post, tightened his cuirass. We surveyed the horizon. From the Santa Margarita hills toward the west, running east to Mt. Kalkara and Mt. Salvatore, stood an unbroken line of Turkish troops. The *spahiler* paraded at the wings on their caparisoned steeds, many brilliantly bedecked in gold and jewels, stately plumes rising from their heads. Their bows were hardly visible at a distance, but before my eyes that Constantinople archer again put six shafts into a target in the time I could load a gun. The *azablar* out front made no less a spectacle of themselves, dressed in colorful animal hides and carrying strangely-shaped shields decorated with fantastic claws, wings and eyes. Then there were the fanatical *iayalarlar*—called for the strange cries they made while attacking; the air was already filled with their unnatural warbling, which might have come from a swarm of locusts. The Turks had also brought out banners of all sizes and colors, and for a long time they entertained us with their gay music, which they played on horns, bagpipes, drums and cymbals. I remembered this music as well, from Constantinople and from Djerbé, and I shuddered.

"What do you think?" Balthazar asked.

"Beware their archers, Balthazar," I said humorlessly. "They miss only by accident. I wish you wore a full suit. Beware also their musketeers—" I tapped his cuirass—"This Milanese sun god might save you from an arquebus, not from a musket. God, I wish you'd bought German ... " Then: "What do you think?"

"I think they have many men," he replied, glancing at the foe without undue concern, "four thousand or five on that ridge, but they haven't brought up their siege guns and we have walls to hide behind." He smiled. "The advantage is ours."

At that moment a whisper ran along the ramparts as the Grand Master appeared atop the Post of Provence, not far to our right. Seeing the vast forest of flags waving against us on the hills, he ordered the men to stand our own banners on the far side of the ditch, and then he ordered the trumpeters and drummers to sound their instruments. At once some men ran thro' the portcullis with all the flags of the langues and the Order and planted them on the counterscarp outside Provence. The heralds put spirit into their task and the air instantly became filled with such a racket that the Devil would have taken to his heels.

The enemy didn't.

I no longer looked at the hordes arrayed against us with that childish awe I felt fifteen years ago. They were a foe to be reckoned with, mercilessly. Natheless, words are too weak to convey the sense of anticipation that swept over those bastions. The men's breathing became shallower, faster. Cheers went up all along the walls:

"Auvergne!"

"Provence!"

"Italia!"

Soldiers brandished their arquebuses and swords, which blinded the eye. Above all, a sensible exaltation encompassed those gathered under the vault of heaven. More than at any moment since the Grand Master had announced, "Tomorrow we begin," strength seemed to spread forth from his person, infusing every man's soul with an adamantine determination to triumph or to sacrifice his life in the defense of Christendom. Some swore they saw the Crucifix in the sky. Balthazar and I embraced and ran down to join those poised behind the gates.

As the sound of the infidel drums reached his ears, Yakhshi gazed down from the hill on the garrison below. He could hardly believe Mustafa Pasha *Hazretleri* had been tricked when the dog Rivière screamed out that the post at the southeastern edge of the town was the weakest spot of the fortress. Yesterday, when they took the prisoner to the top of that hill nearby, Mustafa saw with his own eyes the post called Castille, its towers, the casemates, the heavy bulwarks and the ditch, and all the pork-eaters knocking down houses by the walls. One glance was enough to show any fool that the enemy had been strengthening the place for years. Mustafa *Hazretleri* was no fool. The Pasha at once knew his prisoner for a liar and rightly ordered him beaten to death.

But Mustafa went ahead and decided to attack Castille today, as well as those other posts. Yakhshi reckoned he just wanted to show the enemy that their position was hopeless and give them a chance to surrender honorably. The faithful were in high spirits. The storytellers had all night been singing the exploits of the great warriors of heroic ages; the *imamlar* had been raising prayers to the Sultan and exhorting the troops that those who fell in battle today would open their eyes in Paradise. Now the *mehter takimi* was marching around, making its joyful noise on its instruments, and everybody was cheering. The *iayalarlar* had been smoking *afione* and were letting out their throaty trills as the pulse of the drums and cymbals picked up. It was a good time to begin.

Yakhshi was a little worried about Piyale. Before they left camp, Mustafa had the imperial letter of command read out to everybody and he bestowed many favors on the soldiers, giving out silks and skins and promising them *timarlar*, but the *Kapudan* frowned. Yakhshi also worried about all the cannon the infidels had pointed in their direction, about twenty pieces of various sizes, as far as he could make out.

It started as I expected. Mustafa, watching from San Salvatore, sent down some *akinjiler*. These were raiders, lightly armed horsemen from Rumelia, mostly, whose job was to lead the poor irregulars into battle. And they did. The *azablar* came running and shrieking down the slopes into the field, waving their spears and swords like madmen. de Valette wasted no time in ordering the cannon to open fire, and in rapid succession the guns atop Provence and Auvergne lit into the enemy. The deafening volleys sent those pigs scattering in all directions and the battery on St. Michel opened up on them as they ran in that direction. At the same time Castille began hitting Salvatore itself, but Mustafa didn't walk away.

Seeing the enemy put into such disarray, those on the curtain let out a great yell, but the *akinjiler* weren't going to let the *azablar* go anywhere and began rounding them up on their swift steeds, whipping them into formation again. There were so many, that when they regrouped, we saw no diminution of their numbers. de Valette ordered a second salvo but our men were so anxious to get into battle that there was nothing for it. Eight hundred pikemen and arquebusiers, under Mas, de Giou and Medrano sallied forth from the gate, cheering and screaming for blood. Among them were plenty like me who were not part of a company, but who had no intention of being left behind. To be sure, the Grand Master held another thousand men in reserve behind the gate, but so many people were running out in complete disorder that Parisot himself descended to the streets ordering the gate shut, and at last stood by the portcullis with a lance in hand to prevent the reserve and townspeople from streaming out behind us. Afterwards, against the wishes of his pages, he climbed back up to the Post of Provence, whence he could observe and direct the battle.

We were all there outside the walls. Romegas, Balthazar, Pietru, Vergã, me. The Knights ploughed into the ranks of the *azablar* as were they reaping grass. Wielding his two-handed scythe, Balthazar took a head at once, then another. Cries of "Gelves!" and "Gozo!" rose all around. We first took over the ditch, which we used as a shelter. Mas and Medrano, along with some of their men, reached the chapel of Sta. Margarita on the slope, holed up in it and began firing from its windows. The cannoneers and musketeers on the walls kept up their fire and you could hardly hear the man next to you. We slowly moved forth from the ditch. So much smoke was filling the air from guns all around that you could hardly see— or breathe—and everyone was coughing. Mustafa then sent in the janissaries.

Their aim was better than ours, but it hardly mattered. They came down the hill like a screaming wall and so there was no possibility of missing. "Just load as fast as you can!" I shouted to those nearest me. "Their guns are longer and take more time to load."

Vergã, not far off, glanced at Isabella's kerchief tied to my arm but only smiled amusedly. We kneeled, fired, reloaded. The mailed, helmeted cavalry waiting on the hills was what I feared most and I looked around to see if our pikemen had come up. Balls whizzed everywhere. One glanced off my morion and knocked me to the ground. I got to my feet, crossed myself. A Turkish musket ball felled a Knight nearby, putting a hole thro' his chest plate. An *azab* charged Pietru with a raised spear, but Ix-Xabaw managed to club him with his gun. As he fell by me I impaled him. My new rapier had tasted blood.

In the midst of this chaos, the Spanish Knight Sésé, who was in charge of Bormla, was issuing powder to his men from a cask they had brought out on a cart. One of the idiots got too close with a lit match and the whole thing went up with a tremendous explosion. Sésé and ten of his men were killed instantly.

Yakhshi was leading his men on foot with his prized wheel-lock in hand. This first clash was not going entirely as he had expected. The pork-eaters hadn't turned tail and run. *Hiyer*, they were putting up a stiff fight, considering their puny numbers. Yakhshi wasn't too worried, tho'. Mustafa held thousands more *yenicheriler* in reserve, and the Pasha hadn't even thrown in the cavalry. This was hardly more than a skirmish, just to get the blood going. But he didn't like the way the *azablar* were scampering around like goats, and he didn't like the way the enemy could reload their arquebuses so fast. He ordered his men to stay out of range and pick off the *kafirlar*. Nearby, an *orta* of *yenicheriler* was advancing on a tiny church where some of the enemy had holed up. The *yenicheriler* took up positions behind some rocks and after some hot exchanges, drove the foe from the place and took it.

When old Melchor de Guaras in the Città Vecchia heard the cannon salvos from the Borgo, he knew the fight was on, and immediately ordered his sixty horse out of Notabile. They charged forth at full gallop, racing toward the Port, not entirely certain what they were facing. They learned soon enough. On the outskirts of the town, a company of Mustafa's *spahiler* and *azablar* rode out to greet them. The Captain and his men quickly saw they were outnumbered, five or ten to one.

"For Malta! For Christ! For the Religion!" Guaras shouted, raising his sword, and they charged.

The skirmish was hot. Only one or two of his men owned wheel-locks or pistols, which one could use on horseback. Otherwise, it was lances and swords. The enemy had bows. Arrows flew with hard accuracy, glancing off armor. Somehow, it seemed to Guaras that the foe was merely playing with them, riding in circles to test their foe's mettle. By God, he was not playing, and he charged the nearest horseman. He was met by an enemy mace, broke thro' it with a scream and managed to off his opponent. Near him, del Bene Florentine wasn't so lucky and a battle axe caught him in the neck. de Guaras regrouped his men and charged again. And again. The enemy could hardly believe the ferocity of these horsemen and retreated more than once.

They fought for several hours, charging, retreating. Forty *azablar* and *spahiler* had now been killed by these madmen. Forty was enough. The *spahiler* lost their patience and charged with renewed determination. de Guaras took an arrow in his leg, let out an oath and met the oncoming cavalry. His men were behind him, but this time they could not resist the onslaught and he ordered them to retire. The enemy gave chase almost to the walls of Notabile, but the guns there scared them off and the cavalry gained the Old City without further losses.

We'd been at it five hours. de Giou, Romegas and Mas led some men and managed to retake the small chapel of Sta. Margarita. Vergã was in that number who again holed up in the place. A lot of us were not too far below, arrayed in the ditch or in some houses that yet stood, and together we held out against repeated attacks by the enemy. They seemed to send a thousand men down each time. The gun and musket volleys from our walls lent their strength, but for every man we killed another took his place, like those ancient demons. A Tunisian Moor named Abazar, who the Grand Master had given a good horse, kept riding out by himself into the thick of things, showing a complete contempt of danger, and each time he rode back he tossed two or three heads to a friendly slave standing by gate. The slave would run into town and soon the heads would appear on lances atop the curtain. One of the Knights captured a Turkish standard, which quickly found a place near the heads.

de Valette, tho', would not cease exposing himself above on Provence and it was only when his own page, a few steps from him, took a ball in the neck, that he finally ordered a retreat. As the enemy cheered and continued to fire, we gathered up the wounded and helped them back into the Borgo. Then we collected the rest of the Turkish heads we had taken and staked them on the walls with the others. Fra Antoine de Morgut Navarroys was showing off a gold bracelet from a richly dressed Turk he'd killed. The Arabic letters inscribed on it said, "I have not come to Malta to gain gold or honor, but only for my zeal for the True Faith." From then on, Fra Antoine wore the bracelet constantly.

God was with us this day. By some miracle we only lost twenty or twenty-five men, tho' the number of wounded was nearly ten times that number. We killed over one hundred Turks, including a Sanjak-Bey and some other high officers; at least we judged this by the care the enemy was taking to retrieve the bodies. Throughout the entire battle, the men and women of Birgu had not for a moment ceased their work on the defenses. Catching sight of them inside the walls, I froze. Darting to and fro between their legs, carrying scoops of dirt with their hands, as if they were playing some sort of game were—children. The evident truth only then struck me between the eyes: These urchins had not been sent away and would be trapped here with the rest of us. As I stood motionless, Flaminia passed me, carrying a basket full of dirt, and for a moment we regarded one another.

"Why are you not at the armory?" I said, but she only glanced at the dirt she hauled and shrugged.

"How did you fare?" said Balthazar as he came up behind me and put his arm around my shoulder.

"Just scratches today. You?"

"The same."

With stray dogs nipping at our heels, we went together to find some bread and wine. Food prices in the town were already going up.

Watching the wounded being carried into the Sacra Infermeria, Dr. Jean understood at once that should this siege persist for any time, the Hospital would be unable to cope. He remembered with clarity the scene five years ago—fourteen thousand Christian sailors waiting on Malta to oust Dragut from Tripoli. Suddenly petechiae and other pestilential fevers were racing thro' the lot of them. His Eminence commandeered the parish of Birkirkara for the sick soldiers. The thousands of Maltese living there went sullenly into the countryside, but the Order's physicians performed miracles, supplying the sick with fruits, eggs, fowl, and vegetables. They scrubbed the galleys with vinegar, and de Valette fed the soldiers from his own hand. At last the epidemic abated, with two or three thousand dead, and the armada set off for disaster.

Vigo knew they wouldn't be so lucky this time—whither to send the wounded? E'en today, he and his colleagues were treating the leprous and scrofulous with milk and broths; here a pox-ridden man sat on his bed inhaling mercury vapors; there crutches given out for hunchbacks and other incurables. This morning, the renowned cataract operations of the Knights were taking place in the surgery below.

Now, the first clash and ... five physicians, five surgeons and one hundred wounded. The special ward on the top story reserved for soldiers already overflowed. Standing amongst them, Vigo saw the familiar lacerations from arrows and spears, sword gashes; broken arms, legs from clubs and maces; of course punctures from arquebus balls. Blood covered the floor and he immediately ordered the Serving Brothers to wash it with salt water and vinegar. The Infermeria was sacred to God and cleanliness essential to the probity of the Order. He glanced at the ceiling, black with candle soot, and thought something must be done about this.

The doctor walked down to the surgery to lend a hand. How he detested surgeons! Ignorant butchers! There was nothing for it. Every skill would be summoned in the coming days, each hand.

As he passed the front entrance of the Hospital a voice called out to him. "Dr. Jean!"

He turned to see a woman parting her veil beyond the door, Isabella Guasconi.

"*Sì*, Signora," he said, stepping into the street against all those struggling to enter and bowing to her.

"Dr. Jean, allow me to help," she said. Before he could object she added, "I have cared for the sick in Firenze, and you employ women here."

"Well, yes ... a *few*, for tending orphans and feeding the poor."

"I am the ... goddaughter of the Grand Master of the Hospitallers and you will need every hand," Isabella said, simply.

That Isabella Guasconi lived in the shadow of the Grand Master made little impression on Vigo, but he could hardly deny his own words. "I should seek permission from the Grand Hospitaller, but he is ... absent." It suddenly occurred to Dr. Jean that, after his recent promotion, he was one of the Hospital's chief physicians. "Well, come, we shall see." He told the guards at the door to admit her and they stepped aside. "How have you, umm, fared today, Signora?" he asked as she signed the registry.

The question caught Isabella by surprise. Throughout the day, she realized, no one had paid the slightest attention to her. She had sat at home with old Giansevere, unable to conceive that the Turkish army was amassed just beyond the town walls. When the cannon unleashed those never-ending volleys that shook the entire Borgo, she swallowed in terror, and believed it. The acceptance only increased her fear. She told Vigo of her dreams of moving in leaps and bounds.

"Be careful, Isabella," said Vigo, "*adversarius vester Diabolus, qui tanquam leo rugiens circuit quearens quem devoret.*"

"Parisot would agree," she answered. "But, Doctor, how are we to ... ?"

"Soldiers become hardened to such things," Vigo said.

"So I have learned."

"Francisco?"

Isabella nodded. "He fights courageously, but part of his soul has been torn from him. What saddens me the most is that he well knows it."

"It happens to all of them," the doctor said. "Pray it does not happen to us."

In the Hospital courtyard, so many people were running this way and that, that few glanced at Isabella, who had again drawn her veil. Vigo stopped in the surgery and bid her wait at the door. Amputations were proceeding. Vigo held a sponge full of mandrake and belladona under a soldier's nose to put him out while the surgeons sawed. He screamed at the top of his lungs anyway, so they tried the hammer-stroke: his head went into the padded helmet; Vigo picked up the mallet and whacked. *Clunk*; the fellow was senseless. Now blood gushed forth from his leg all over the surgeons, who shoved their hands into the stump, attempting to find the veins and tie them. Another surgeon removed an arrow with the surgical crossbow: he pulled the trigger, the string snapped and the arrow tied to it was yanked from the patient's thigh bone as the soldier let out a scream that could be heard by St. Peter and his blood spurted all over the surgeon's face.

Watching this scene from the door, Isabella nearly fainted. She clasped her stomach and turned away before she retched. "Perhaps it would be best if I began by serving food to the poor," she said.

"Perhaps it would be," Vigo answered.

For a time she tended to the orphans. As she clothed and fed the infants, she held back tears, asking silently, What Knight was your father? What abandoned woman your mother? How will you cast off your solitude? Will you find love? Isabella dreamed of grinding peppers and became melancholy, but at least she knew her half-brother in France, whom she had never met, prospered.

They worked into the evening, until the light began to fade and the serving brothers lit candles. After vespers, priests arrived carrying tapers and chanting the prayer to Our Lords the Sick that dated from the time of Acre:

Seigneurs Malades, pries pour pais que Dieu la mande de ciel en terre,
Seigneurs Malades, pries pour le fruit de la terre que Dieu le multiple
en telle maniere que saincte eglise en soit servie et le peuple soustanu ...

Shortly after, de Valette himself appeared. He did not notice Isabella giving out food to the hungry poor at a side door of the Hospital. He went upstairs to the wards full of wounded, took the silver service from a Knight of Germany's hands and went about feeding his men who had endured injuries on this first day of battle.

Later, de Valette went to pray at the small chapel of St. Anne atop St. Angelo. As he passed the Magisterial Palace, some Grand Crosses standing in the garden informed him that during today's battle a Greek renegado, Baptiste, went over to the enemy—the same Baptiste de Valette had released from prison a few months ago.

"The one who was circumcised?"

The Grand Crosses nodded. They could see Eminenza cursing himself for trusting a circumcised renegado.

"Otherwise," said one of the Crosses, "we have done well today. Few dead."

de Valette nodded heavily. Should as many men be wounded each day as had been today ... He decreed that there would be no more sorties. "Let us await the enemy's next move."

Isabella halted at the door of the St. Anne chapel. Before her, Parisot knelt with his hands clasped above the crypt where l'Isle Adam rested. Darkness had come; the candelabras cast a soft glow over the stones of this closed place and the mantle of night all but concealed her Godfather, cloaked as he was in his black vestments. Isabella convinced herself that he was speaking to his great predecessor, gathering strength from the spirit of he who lay beneath him. For a long time she watched silently as de Valette carried on this conversation. As the moments passed, Isabella too felt l'Isle Adam's presence above Parisot, ever more strongly, until at last she herself saw him as had it been daylight, and she knew she was witnessing a miracle.

She turned to go, and as she did so, de Valette sensed her standing behind him. The spell persisting, he rose, slowly, and faced her. "He is ... here," Isabella whispered, wondrously, tho' she could no longer see the greatest Grand Master.

Parisot nodded with a visage so transformed that Isabella was uncertain who stood before her.

"Has he told you," she asked, reaching out her fingers and fearfully caressing Parisot's face, "how he held out for six months in Rhodes against a force larger than the one confronting us?"

"He was the noblest of us all," de Valette replied, with the ripple of shadows over his features, "and we have learned everything from him, to prepare for the worst, to rely on spies and knowledgeable men, to lay chains and to dig mines, but mostly we have taken from him his strength. There was never a more ardent heart, tempered mind and iron arm."

"But at last he surrendered," Isabella said, her voice faltering.

de Valette shook his head, even as he took her hand from his cheek and clasped it in his own hands. "Only when all hope was lost, when he knew that to resist further would mean his people would be enslaved and the women ravished. We have not been pushed to that place, not nearly, nor do we have the luxury of a retreat. Rhodes lay in the lap of the Infidel, but should Malta fall, the Order shall be extinguished and the Antichrist shall stand at Europe's portal. For us there can be no surrender."

The two embraced silently in the candlelight before she returned to her home. When Isabella later told me of what she had seen, I knew she was right; she had witnessed a miracle.

Seventy-Seven

Before dawn on Wednesday, Toni Bajada was admitted by old Oliver Starkey, de Valette's secretary, to the Grand Master's study in the Magisterial Palace and offered to His Eminence to discover what was taking place in the Turkish camp. Bajada was a swarthy Maltese who talked a bit more than Ix-Xabaw. We liked each other because we both had parts of our ears taken by the Turks. At least it gave us something to joke about. Usually I met Toni when he was speeding from the Palace on one of his missions, and we sometimes spoke Turkish together to annoy the others around who hadn't been slaves. The thing was, Bajada was the best swimmer on Malta.

When Toni discovered him, de Valette had been up all night. At first Parisot refused to believe that Toni could just walk into the Turkish camp and he scoffed wearily, but Starkey—the last English Knight of the Order and Eminenza's confident—said there was nothing to lose. Starkey called himself a poet, and people regarded him as a bard, but I never learnt English. Maybe Bajada's offer struck his poet's fancy and at length de Valette agreed. So before the sun was up, the cheerful Bajada walked down to Guiral's Post, stripped off his clothes and swam across the harbor, where he changed into the Turkish clothes he kept hidden among the rocks on Sciberras. Then he did exactly what he said he would.

When he returned, Toni and some renegados who had also been in the Turkish camp told us what happened that day among the enemy.

Yakhshi didn't know that the decision he heard with his own, whole ears would be the most fateful of the campaign. The *Boluk-bashi* was in no jesting humor. This Marsa was already proving less kind than he'd first supposed. Oh, the tall grass and rushes near the water were pleasant to look at, fish were plentiful and the meadow provided plenty of space for the tents. The thousands of flags, the music, the dervishes, storytellers singing their epics—all filled the camp with an air of celebration. But only days after their arrival men had begun to fall ill. The Frankish water was bad and mosquitoes swarmed all over the place. Yakhshi's bones told him Frankish air was pestiferous. Like many others, he had quickly taken to wearing amber and lapis to ward off the evil.

The skirmish two days ago had not bettered the *yenicheri's* temper. Hundreds already lay wounded in the hospital tents among the nearby trees. A few in his own *boluk* had fallen. What vexed Yakhshi most was that the *kafilar* hadn't just thrown down their swords. Now the Padishah's army would force a surrender. Yakhshi had hoped to be going back to the lodge within a week, at least on to this other fortress, Goletta. Today it looked like they were going to put up with the Maltese sun a little longer.

A servant was calling him to Piyale Pasha's tent. The *Boluk-bashi* pushed his way past the many men waiting outside. He knew exactly what was going on. Inside the pavilion, the young *Kapudan*, all in sparkling white and wearing a freshly wound turban, greeted him cordially and asked a few questions about the behavior of certain soldiers. Mostly it concerned the *spahiler*: Rustem owned a *timar* in Mughla with an annual income of nine thousand *akcheler*, but he had died in the battle and now Ibrahim wanted it. Yakhshi didn't know about the *spahiler*, but when Piyale asked about his own men, he could tell him who should be promoted to the empty places and who might deserve higher pay.

After the decrees had been made, a big war council was convened outside the infidel master's cottage. One hundred officers attended. As Yakhshi arrived, some slaves were erecting Mustafa Pasha *Hazretleri's* pavilion in the garden. The Vizier was complaining loudly that his back already ached from sleeping on the hard bed inside and would abide it no longer.

When the task was done, Mustafa's slaves put a fine crimson surcoat on him and he turned to the officers around him. Without wasting words, he declared that Piyale should take ten thousand men and ten large guns to the old city and bombard it. "At the same time, I will bombard this Birgu and the *Deghirmen Burcu*—the bastion with the mills. We have enough men and artillery. In this way we will be able to achieve our object and go on to the Goletta as Soliman has commanded."

Most gathered around thought Mustafa's plan a good one that conformed exactly with the Sultan's wishes. But Piyale yet drank his own bile after the insults he had suffered and, listening to Mustafa, his face became almost as red as the sash he wore. To Yakhshi it seemed that Piyale spoke out of spite, not out of sense.

"O Mustafa," the *Kapudan* said with a slight bow, bejeweled dagger gleaming, "he who I am to revere as a father. I remind you that five years ago I crushed the infidels at Djerbé, winning great glory for myself and the Sultan. For this reason, just as Soliman *Kanuni* has charged you with authority over the land forces, he has charged me with the safety of his invincible armada, so dear to his heart. Thro' no carelessness of mine will I risk the fame and honor I have fought so hard to gain, and neither will I risk my head, which will surely fall should this fleet come to ruin. Therefore I say: Unless a harbor is found that is safer from the winds than the one where the fleet is now anchored, I will not leave it for a moment."

Many in the council thought that Piyale had spoken well, that the Greek wind would soon play havoc with the fleet in Marsashlok, but other men who better knew the island said this was all *sachma*, that the wind never blew after April. Yakhshi wondered what had become of Piyale's legendary dash and daring, which had truly crushed the Infidel at Djerbé. Mustafa *Hazretleri* saw through the speech and indeed could hardly disguise his scorn.

"O Piyale," he said, returning the other's bow, "he who I am to look upon as a beloved son, well have I believed in your good will toward me, but now I see my eyes have been clouded. The time for dissimulation is over. I speak of a plan that will bring success for our Padishah and glory to ourselves. You speak of the safety of the fleet and yet not. Well do I fathom your motives. Should we follow your advice, I foresee a great waste of days that could be better employed in reducing the crucial fortifications of the enemy. We will forfeit the Sultan's favor and perhaps our heads. But no matter." He paused for a moment, pulling his grey beard and smiling to the officers gathered around. "You, my son, desire a safe harbor, this nearby Marsamshet. Very well, you shall have it. But to gain for you that road, I shall first have to reduce the insignificant fort on the end of this island, a fort that a child can see is of no threat to anyone except he who intends to enter a harbor we do not need."

Again Piyale bowed. "O venerated father, if this Santarma tower is as insignificant as you say, then indulge my vanity and take a few days to destroy it. Once that is done, we will turn to the other fortifications you so ardently desire."

At that one of the *Chorbajiler* objected, reminding the two Commanders that the Sultan had ordered them to defer to Turgut Reis in all decisions, and that Turgut had not arrived.

"Precisely," both *Pashalar* rejoined, agreeing on at least one thing. "Turgut has not arrived and Allah alone knows when he will."

Indeed, His Majesty's words, "Everyone aims at the same meaning, but many are the versions of the story," were never truer than here. Barelli had told us months earlier in Constantinople that the decision to attack the Santarma fortress first had been made in the Divan. But what I have just related is how Yakhshi heard it on that day in May. He returned to his men to tell them the plans.

"Where do you think Dragut is?" Diego, another gunner posted at St. Angelo, asked me.

"How the Devil would I know?" I answered.

But Diego's question was on every pair of lips, not least the Grand Master's, who nearly a month ago had sent Fra Pierre la Roccalaure St. Aubin to Barbary on the Order's *patrona* to determine what he could about Turgut's and Hasan's movements. St. Aubin had surely learned something, for e'en as Diego and I took our lunch on St. Angelo's ramparts, mere hours after the enemy council had met, the watch on the cavalier above spied the *patrona* plying up the coast toward Gallows' Point. The gunners immediately fired blank charges and fireworks to warn the Commander that the invasion was underway and that the mouth of the Great Port was now blockaded by the enemy.

St. Aubin discerned this soon enough for himself when six enemy galleys took off after him. Romegas, rushing up from the Towers, was ready to jump onto the *S. Gabriele*, manned always and ready in Kalkara, and charge to St. Aubin's aid, but events unfolded too fast. We all watched from St. Angelo in disbelief. The six infidel galleys were hot on St. Aubin's tail as he hauled out to sea, but all but one of them quickly dropped behind.

"That's a Venetian galley for you!" I cried. "Hah!"

Suddenly, so far as we could surmise, St. Aubin commanded the left bank of his *ciurma* drop its oars. Within a boat length, the *patrona* had turned completely about and faced its attacker.

"I couldn't have done it better," grunted Romegas as his hands began to tremble and his monkey began caterwauling. The cannon roar and the smoke puffs told us that St. Aubin was firing at the single remaining foe. Aye, the red pennon flapped briskly as St. Aubin, fire snorting from his nostrils, now charged straight into the Port.

"He's mad!" Diego exclaimed.

"He's mad!" Mehmet Bey aboard the Turkish galley cried.

"He's a Knight of St. John," snarled Romegas, quieting his monkey.

Mehmet Bey turned tail and ran, but too many ships after all blockaded the mouth of the Port and St. Aubin was unable to force entry. Without a moment's hesitation, he turned about and sped northward, on to Sicily.

When Piyale heard what had transpired, he was so enraged at the additional disgrace that had befallen him that he spat in Mehmet Bey's face.

Tho' St. Aubin's bravura raised the spirits of those who had witnessed it, the Grand Master was not wholly pleased. "I must know Dragut's whereabouts!" he shouted to Romegas as night fell, slamming his fist on his table in the Magisterial Palace, "and I need to know when we may expect a relief from Don Garcia."

Romegas had no answer to these questions and an awkward silence ensued as de Valette's lioness lifted a suspicious eye toward Lescaut's monkey. Neither Grand Master nor Commander wanted to say how grave the situation was. Romegas also wished to speak of Notabile, for they needed to make quick decisions regarding the Old City, but in this Romegas was forestalled by a page who announced Fra Rafael Salvago.

As the Grand Master's face brightened, the Genoese entered, disheveled and limping, having this moment returned from Sicilia, where he'd delivered de Valette's first message to the Vice Roy. Too many Turkish galleys had been prowling about the Great Port and Marsamxett, forcing Salvago to leave the *S. Giacomo* slightly to the north, in St. George's Bay. With a small party he circled west of the Turkish camp and made his way to Birgu. Enemy scouts spotted them, tho', killing one of his men. The rest of them ran like the wind but Salvago twisted his ankle and staggered thro' the gate, for which he apologized.

The page, standing by the door, asked whether he should light the candles, but de Valette replied, as he did every night, just one; they could speak in darkness.

"Henceforward," he replied to Salvago, "you must go via Notabile." With a smile distinct enough to be seen in the failing light, the Grand Master then proposed, "Messeri, join with me in thanking God that the Turks have not occupied the north of Malta or secured Notabile. Città Vecchia will serve both as the road to Sicilia and the base for our cavalry. In this the enemy has made a large blunder."

Mention of the cavalry allowed Romegas to remind de Valette that Captain Melchor de Guaras had been wounded on Monday and lay in the little hospital at Notabile. "The Governor, Fra Pedro, is old and infirm and also asks to be replaced or aided."

The Grand Master did not immediately respond and instead asked of Salvago, "What did Don Garcia say?"

"His Excellency," the exhausted Knight answered, "wrote to King Philip in my presence and is gathering a fleet as quickly as humanly possible. He reminds us that since Gelves, there persists a shortage of men, and Eminenza well knows how long it takes to assemble an armada in the best of times ... "

His Eminence frowned. "You shall return to Messina immediately, Fra Rafael. St. Aubin is almost certainly making his way thither and God willing you shall both reach the Vice Roy. Convince him that forty thousand troops have landed and the corsairs cannot be far behind. With luck, St. Aubin will be able to tell him the whereabouts of Dragut." At this juncture, a shade of his unconquerable anger crept into the Grand Master's voice. "Assure His Excellency that we do not have the five months it took Don Sancho de Levya to organize Spain's expedition to the Peñón last year. We need a small, picked force—and we need it at once." Almost as an afterthought he added: "You must also deliver a letter to your uncle, which I shall presently dictate to Starkey."

Of course, Fra Rafael nodded; tho' he'd already wearied of sleeping on the S. *Giacomo*, he should be able to do that. While speaking, the Grand Master had not forgotten Romegas's concern and now declared that Fra Vincenzo di Anastagi should be sent to Notabile to take command of the cavalry. After ordering a page to fetch him, de Valette relaxed for one moment and offered those who stood about him some wine. During the brief stillness that followed, Toni Bajada was announced and entered, water still dripping from his moustaches, with his report of what had happened that day in the Turkish camp.

Those gathered in the darkened chamber together released a disheartened sigh at hearing that the enemy had decided to attack Fort St. Elmo, for the small castle would surely be unable to withstand a Turkish onslaught for long. The candle, tho', revealed in its flickering another smile on de Valette's lips.

"Gentlemen," he offered, "the news is the best we could hope for. Each day St. Elmo can hold out gives us a chance to finish the fortifications in Birgu and Senglea, and for the relief to arrive. This is another sign that God does not wish to destroy us. Had the foe decided to sweep down from the north, all would be lost." de Valette crossed himself. "How many men are in St. Elmo?"

Surely the Grand Master knew this is well as the others, but Romegas answered: "Only Juan de la Cerda's company. Eighty men."

"We shall send reinforcements at once."

They adjourned. After a brief meal, Fra Rafael Salvago eluded the Turkish scouts west of Birgu, retraced his path to the *S. Giacomo*, and once more made his way to Sicilia, bearing a second message for Don Garcia and a first for his uncle the Pope.

Seventy-Eight

The enemy's intention to attack Fort St. Elmo became apparent later the same night, when scouts reported that the Turks had begun to move their artillery from the fleet at Marsaxlokk to their camp at the Marsa. The distance was well over a league across rough terrain. I knew that each of the great basilisks weighed three hundred quintals. Hah. That should keep 'em busy for a few days. We couldn't see what was taking place in the dark, but the sentries on St. Angelo soon spotted torchlight atop Sciberras across the harbor. We had only two guns emplaced on that side of the fortress, but whatever the scum were up to we didn't like it and scared them off with a few salvos from a fifty-*libbre* piece at the tip of the castle.

Balthazar hadn't been on watch and slept in his room that night. The yapping of the dogs after every cannon volley woke him once or twice, but he fell quickly asleep each time until the Angelus, when he was finally roused by a knock on his door. He answered and was surprised to see several of Bishop Cubelles's men standing on the threshold.

"The Inquisitor summons you to the Palace," one of them said.

Immediately Balthazar understood what was afoot, yet he could not loose himself from the impression that someone was playing a coarse jest. "You truly mean to tell me that His Excellency is hearing denunciations in the midst of this great invasion?"

"Yes," came the plain reply.

Balthazar could scarce restrain from bashing these simpletons over the head with his *montante*, but he knew he must confront the Inquisitor at once. He dressed, bit into a fruit and swallowed a half-empty cup of water, fastened on an ordinary broadsword and accompanied the guards to the Bishop's Palace. Even the short walk toward the walls was hindered by all the stone and dirt that had been carried in for the defenses, and the men stepped this way and that to avoid it. Outside the Palace, people on the street paused in their business to stare at the Knight, crossing themselves as their faces unwilling melted into expressions of dread. Inside, Cubelles's servants were hastily packing relics and taking down paintings. Amidst the hubbub, in the antechamber, sat two women: the first an unfamiliar merchantess, the second—Isabella Guasconi. A page soon appeared and took the terrified woman by the arm into the Bishop's chamber.

"Who is she?" asked the Knight. He and Isabella had not even exchanged morning salutations.

"Ma—" Isabella's reply was cut short by the boom of a lone cannon from Fort St. Angelo, which set the palace shutters rattling. "What is that?" she started, fearfully.

Balthazar was yet uncertain. "They're firing across the harbor. It must mean the enemy is on Sciberras ... The woman?"

"Ma ... Marietta de Modo," said Isabella, regaining her senses. "Her son is a renegado in Algiers. Half of Mdina heard her praying for the Turks to take the island so he might return safely. Eccellenza wishes to know why I have not denounced her, I am certain of it ... And you, Balthazar, wherefore ... ?"

Balthazar waved her silent and so they remained, she sitting, he standing, for well over a watch. Eventually, the woman Marietta appeared, sobbing, followed by the Bishop's page, who motioned for Isabella to enter the chamber. She got unsteadily to her feet, whereat Balthazar interposed himself. "Inform His Excellency," he said, "that I must be at my post. I shall speak to him *now*, or I shall speak to him not at all." The page nodded and disappeared for a moment; he reemerged and ushered the Knight inside.

Domenico Cubelles, whose heavy beard seemed to have grayed perceptibly in recent weeks, sat behind the oaken table and spoke to a secretary who was poised to transcribe the session into Latin. The Inquisitor motioned Balthazar to the witness chair, but the Knight declined with a bow, saying that he was pressed for time. Startled at the disrespect, Cubelles repeated the command, whereupon Balthazar lifted the Holy Scriptures that lay upon the table and put them to his lips.

Another cannon shot from the fortress interrupted Cubelles's quickly ascending wrath; he shuddered at the rattling window, collected himself and said, "Why have you not appeared to denounce Francisco de Barai, who has been accused of turning from the Faith?"

"Eccellenza, you hold denunciations while the greatest descent against Christendom is upon us," Balthazar said at the same instant in a damascened voice.

"*Silenzio*—*!*" Cubelles shouted abruptly.

"Justify yourself," Balthazar continued.

The impertinence astonished Cubelles; it was cause enough for hanging. "Answer me!" he shouted a second time.

As another boom caused the windows to rattle again, the Abbé scoffed. "Will you threaten me with the question, when almost certain death awaits every person on Malta?"

"I threaten you," the Bishop answered as he surely answered many who had stood before him, "with eternal damnation of your immortal soul."

There could be no more severe punishment, acknowledged Balthazar, terrifying, unfathomable, but he responded without undue hesitation and with equanimity, "I have sworn to die for our Faith. God Almighty has my life in His hands. If He does not wish my soul, so be it."

Two guns went off together; one of the candles in its stand nearby toppled to the floor.

The Inquisitor discerned that facing him was a man who had made his peace with God, who could not be intimidated by the rack or the horse. Such men were difficult to deal with, impossible. "Fra Balthazar," he said in his hollow voice, attempting a different road, "you believe that the only foe facing us stands beyond the walls. Heresy confronts us everywhere, within the walls as well as without."

"Eccellenza, who has denounced Francisco de Barai?"

"That is not your concern."

The Abbé smiled. "Of course not. Forgive me. Yet we both know exactly who it is and to what purpose. I say this: Each day renegados come to us from the Turkish camp, bearing valuable information. Would you put every one of them to the question?"

Cubelles refused to respond and sipped a cup of water.

"Or what of Andreas, the Gozitan, who after five years of slavery in Constantinople spent four years on the run, posing as an infidel in order not to be caught? Eventually he regained Malta. Do you call this man a renegado?"

"Did he wear a turban while in flight?" Cubelles asked, maugre himself drawn in by the question.

Balthazar shrugged. "Almost certainly." He had no time for this. Leveling his gaze at the Bishop the Knight raised his finger toward him. "Eccellenza, I be no scholar of the Mahometans, but I know that to profess to that faith is a pact made between a man and their God, and that is all. I have no eyes into the heart."

"I do," replied Cubelles dryly. "As Apostolic Inquisitor, it is my sacred duty to see into the heart—"

"This is a ruse, Eccellenza!" Balthazar had had enough. "By paying heed to that soulless confrater, you have fallen prey to exactly what the Grand Master foresaw years ago: base scoundrels thro' *libelli famosi* exploiting your office for their own ends. Blaij Vergã merely wants to be rid of an old rival."

"No one exploits the office of the Holy Inquisition for his own ends," Cubelles replied, offense echoing in that tunnel of a voice.

"Ah," said the Knight with a perceptible scorn, understanding something deeper, Isabella's presence. "Methinks your zeal at this late date has more to do with seeing into the Grand Master's heart than any renegado's, or will you name de Valette a renegado as well?"

Balthazar hit the mark and the Bishop exploded. "de Valette," he intoned, "is sick with the bile of corruption. He has violated every vow he swore to the Order. He has permitted dark emissaries disguised as Villegaignon to pervert the Religion with evil to further his private aims. This day he will release prisoners who have smuggled into the sacred Convent the most obscene filth of Luther, and he will provide these enemies with arms. Tomorrow he will release infidel slaves. The Faith itself is being sacrificed at the maw of his fathomless vanity!"

de Valette had hanged rebels and burned Protestant books. He'd release prisoners today—to save Malta. Yet, as Balthazar stared disbelievingly at the Inquisitor, he perceived that before him sat a man whose faith was, by his own lights, so pure that he regarded the Grand Master as corrupt. No one, the ancients said, is a villain in his own eyes.

A knock on the door interrupted them and a page admitted Thomas de Vio, the Assistant Inquisitor, dressed in travel garb.

At once the Bishop demanded of him why he was not interrogating the Guasconi woman.

"Eccellenza," the agitated de Vio said forcefully, as another thunder clap made itself felt, "it is too perilous to stay on Malta any longer. I intend to return to Sicilia on the next boat." While Domenico Cubelles gazed at him in incomprehension and abhorrence, Balthazar pointed out that passage to Sicilia was no certain thing any longer. "It is surely more certain than remaining here. Messeri," de Vio said, "adieu."

As the door slammed shut, Balthazar laughed and himself stepped out of the Bishop's chamber. Taking Isabella by the arm he said, "I believe, Signora, you have nothing more to fear from the Inquisitor for the foreseeable future."

Thereat, the Knight returned to his quarters, donned his armor and took his post at France, whence he observed in wonder the gunners at Provence and Auvergne firing on the enemy trains as they foolishly passed along the hills, creating no little havoc among them.

As he watched the first of the artillery come into the big camp, neither could Yakhshi understand why they were hauling guns in sight of the town. They might have moved west to avoid fire. He shrugged; with so many men and slaves they could afford to lose a few. All in all, they'd been lucky; the stupid islanders had abandoned many bulls and oxen—just left them roaming all over the countryside. Naturally the men caught them and harnessed them to the wagons.

Lucky or not, moving this artillery was proving to be a gigantic task. The army'd brought almost seventy large pieces from Constantinople. Every one had to be hauled overland, among them the enormous stone-throwers. Smiths were strengthening wheels and carriages with iron, and some of the smaller pieces needed ten or twelve oxen to move them. For the others, dozens of men and ropes. The lines of *azablar*, oarsmen and animals pulling the hundreds of wagonloads of powder and ammunition stretched clear from the camp to the coast. All along those lines, whips cracked, wheels creaked, men sang and grunted, animals snorted. It really was an extraordinary spectacle; Yakhshi had seen much in his day but never anything like this. Those streams of tens of thousands of men reminded him of ants in a great, noisy colony spreading over the entire countryside, bringing it to life. The whole island breathed like a giant monster. The thought pleased him. For a moment the *Boluk-bashi* regarded a team of fifty men trundling one of the middle pieces, eight sticks in length, toward Sciberras and the small fort, then he went off to his tent where some comrades had gathered around the pot to sing and dance.

He didn't get far. The sound of arquebus fire reached his ears from the direction of the island of the Santarma fort, and at once the Soup Master was calling some *boluklar* and *ortalar* together. Yakhshi grabbed his weapon and rounded up his men. Soon they were mounting the crest of the hill, where they discovered that a small infantry had sallied forth from the fort below and was harassing the engineers and sappers who'd gathered there to open trenches and build platforms.

As far as Yakhshi could make out, the infidels numbered less than a hundred, but the skirmish proved to be warm. They traded fire, the enemy scurrying this way and that, taking cover in the grass and behind the rocks. This day the better marksmanship of the *yenicheriler* proved its worth. More than once, Yakhshi knelt, wound the spring on his lock with the key dangling from his neck and felt the fountain of sparks thrown off by the spinning wheel. More than once the weapon cracked, enveloping him with smoke. More than once a careless infidel fell. Birds were screeching all around, taking to the air. A stag bounded away. The fighting went on until the sun was high but at last the enemy dogs had no choice but to retreat back into the Santarma Fort at the bottom of the hill.

From St. Angelo across the harbor we took a potshot or two at the enemy, but stopped when we guessed Juan de la Cerda's company had sallied forth from St. Elmo and that a skirmish was underway. This de la Cerda wasn't the Vice Roy of Sicily who had ignominiously fled Djerbé five years ago. He was merely Captain in charge of St. Elmo's troops, but even as we saw the smoke puffs rise from afar, the Grand Master was deciding who to send over to reinforce the garrison against the onslaught slowly being readied before our eyes.

Vergã came up behind me from the Towers. He belonged to the two hundred Romegas had chosen to guard the Grand Master and be dispatched as a sort of flying *soccorso* whither Eminenza directed. "You know it is a death sentence for anyone sent over there," he said.

"I know."

"Will you go?"

I regarded Vergã. He stood dressed in armor hardly less splendid than that of a Knight's, my companion of fifteen years ago unrecognizable. Not knowing what had transpired this morning at the Bishop's Palace, I shrugged and answered his question with my own: "Will you?"

"If sent."

"What profit in this for a man who has ever fought for profit alone?"

This time it was Vergã who didn't answer. Instead he turned and walked away. At the same moment, Balthazar was making his way to St. Angelo to inform the Grand Master about his meeting with Cubelles, when he passed another Knight who stood at a church angrily ripping a denunciation from its door.

"How dare they!" that one exclaimed aloud, "impugn the bravery of Spanish Knights!" He threw the paper in Balthazar's direction; the Abbé grabbed it and saw that the *libello* accused certain Spaniards of impiety and empty braggadocio, that they could not be trusted with their assignments.

Balthazar's momentary smile vanished when the Knight growled that the defamations must be the work of craven Frenchmen. Hurling the sheet to the ground, Navarre with difficulty recognized the other as the Majorcan Antonio Fuster who'd fomented the rebellion against de Vallier at Tripoli those years ago. "I am surprised to see you here, Sir," Balthazar said gravely. "Where are you to be posted?"

"That remains to be seen," Fuster replied suspiciously. "Romegas will send me whither needed, mayhap to Fort St. Michel. Wherefore your surprise, Sir?"

Balthazar looked onto the Knight with barely concealed disgust. "When St. Michel is surrounded, Sir, will you defend it as valiantly as you did Tripoli?"

"Was it you then, Señor," said Fuster, half drawing his sword, "who nailed these vilifications to the door?"

"'Twas not," answered Balthazar, "but you may be certain, Sir, the image of that day in Tripoli remains bright in my memory." The flash in Fuster's eyes told Navarre that neither could that one have forgotten the Knight's hand around his throat that day. "You sat for a few years in St. Angelo," Balthazar continued, "but I also remember brightly it was to have been for life. Of course, you were a countryman of Juan d'Homedes."

Fuster's face instantly turned a deep crimson. "I resent your imputations, Señor."

With a step backward the Abbé bowed deeply. "Accept my sincerest apologies. My bright memory was treacherously deceiving me. Yes, it was not you who gave over the fort but the cowardly Mareschal. I look forward to witnessing your esteemed gallantry against this far greater host." Balthazar hurriedly moved on, knowing a host of sins were being passed over this day, thinking another miracle would be required to keep this rag-tag army together, certain that he would himself convict Fuster for any further acts of bravery.

A few moments after leaving the square, Balthazar appeared cheerfully at my station by the guns and offered me wine from a bottle, as if his encounter with the Majorcan hadn't occurred.

"Whence these spirits?" I asked, accepting the bottle.

"Niccolò," he replied, gazing across the blue harbor to Sciberras, "once wrote that no great defeat of an army ever took place without being preceded by ominous signs and portents. I have seen none. Therefore our victory is assured."

I glanced at the strangely smiling Knight. "I thought you had ceased to read Niccolò—the Inquisition."

"The Inquisition has closed its doors for the duration of this ... " Balthazar passed his arm across the vista opposite and recounted what had just taken place at the Bishop's Palace.

"Vergã!" I spat vehemently. "*Picaro!* He swore on the graves of his parents that our quarrel was over! All this time he has feigned sincerity. I knew not to trust him ... "

"Francisco, some men have lied so long they no longer perceive the difference between truth and falsehood. I suspect his action was as much due to his great love for me—he knew the Bishop would summon me for failing to denounce you."

"Thank you, Balthazar, " I said, taking his hand, "for saving me from Cubelles."

"Thank the Turks. Luckily, you are not circumcised or I'd be buying you out of the bagno ... Ah, this is my fault for forcing a peace where none was to be had. Blaij Vergã intends to do away with you—and mayhap me—but this siege presses on him as it does on Cubelles, and he needs resort to subtle means. So must we." Balthazar fell silent for some heartbeats. "The scoundrel forgets that Romegas is not the only one capable of writing to the Pope."

Without a word more, Balthazar excused himself and continued to the Magisterial Palace, where he reported to de Valette the morning's events. Despite all else, the Grand Master flew instantly into a high rage. "While the island is under attack he dares! This Bishop has been dogging my heels for years. Must I fight a war against two enemies? Despite everything I have done, he opposes my will! Had we not intervened, he would have burnt Villegaignon at the stake! This putrid sack of bile has denounced worthy Knights and caused them to denounce each other. Look at these!" He shook a sheaf of *scripte diffamatori* before Balthazar's face. The Knight said he was well aware of them. "They are everywhere, bringing dishonor to the revered name of the Order at the very moment when we require honor above all. By God, he would denounce me if he could find his way to it."

de Valette was half out the door, preparing to confront Cubelles, when Balthazar told him to think no more of it. "It is done, Eminenza. The Bishop's fangs have been pulled. Turn your mind to the greater matters at hand."

Later, one of Isabella's slaves sought me out and told me to come to her house for supper when I had been relieved from duty. Isabella stared at her guest, covered from head to toe with cannon soot, and in every respect the circumstance was a strange one, sitting at this table lit with candles and laid with fine silver, even while Auvergne and Provence never ceased firing on the enemy.

"We must try to continue living," Isabella said, staring in turn at her prized portrait by Michelangelo that stared back at her from the wall, and her few other likenesses and paintings done by artists she named: Tintoretto, Bronzino and Vasari. Even as she stared, the paintings shook, and the place settings and glasses rattled.

Each boom of the cannon tested her bravery; with each she shuddered and after the third she inadvertently knocked over her glass. She stifled a sob, then breathed, called for the servant to wipe up the wine.

I laid my hand on hers. "You will become accustomed," I said.

As so often, and especially after her conversation with Vigo, Isabella found my words harsh. "My God, I pray not to!" she burst out, glaring at me. Collecting herself, she said thro' damp eyes that she had spent some hours today at the Sacra Infermeria. "It is not enough, Francisco. Europe must know in vivid words what is happening here. I shall write dispatches for the printers. Someone must take them."

"The Grand Master sends couriers regularly to Sicilia," I replied. "Surely letters are already going, but their fate shall be ... "

"I know, yet we must do something ... everything. I must see Mother in Città Notabile."

Her guest gazed hard on her. "Isabella," I said, "the Turks have not seen fit to guard that city. She is safer there than you are here. Do not think on't."

Isabella fell silent, deciding there was no reason to discuss anything with this person, then told me of her meeting with Balthazar at the Bishop's Palace that morning.

"I know. Balthazar was summoned for failing to denounce me as a renegado."

At once Isabella's face turned ashen. "Vergã?" she finally stuttered.

"I trust it is not you," this one said with a somber chuckle, but Isabella shot at me a glance of pure fury. "Forgive me," I apologized at once, realizing my mistake. "We vowed to put the matter behind."

"As Vergã so vowed!" she cried. "I will tell him to his face what I think of such means!" But thereon Isabella rose from the table, wounded. The wretch before her had not a feeling in his heart. He held out his hand; she shook it off, repelled by the touch of men, and walked into the sitting room.

The old nurse was there, pricking up her ears each time a gun sounded, cackling, "O Prophet, exhort the believers to fight!" Unable to understand the displeasing sounds issuing from Giansevere's mouth, Isabella natheless convinced herself that the crone must be speaking from fear, not wickedness, and sat beside her. But when she took her hands, the nurse shook her away, as Isabella had me, hissing, "For disbelievers is the torment of the fire!"

Isabella, unaware that granny quoted the Alcoran in her very home, persisted in attempting to calm her by asking her to recite some of Soliman's verse. Of course Giansevere understood nothing. "Tell her!" Isabella shouted angrily at the stranger by her, who unable to perceive wherefore she insisted, natheless eventually convinced Giansevere to recite some lines, But now Isabella commanded no less loudly that I render them.

"For what purpose?" I said, bereft of all patience. "I am no poet."

"Do it."

Throwing up my arms, I required Giansevere several times to repeat these stanzas, which I followed with difficulty. At last we gave them thusly:

You might conquer farflung lands and seas and rule them as their sovereign king:
Even if your reign on the imperial throne becomes everlasting,
Don't be taken in; one day a hostile wind is bound to blow and bring
To your land of beauty heaven's misfortune and worst suffering,
Don't blow up your chest like a proud sail; shun arrogance and malice.
If you aspire to God's compassion, kindness should come from you too;
Be sure to offer your benevolence and mercy to people of virtue.
If you hope to reach the gardens of Paradise to find love and grace,
Instead of terrifying destruction when the end comes to you,
Humble yourself like a skirt, bow at the sage's feet and rub your face.

Giansevere crowed with pride at the Padishah's verse, reminding us for the hundredth time he had been an esteemed poet in his younger years. My patience for poetry had always been slight and my single thought was that he would do well to heed his own counsel. I bid the two good-evening.

Seventy-Nine

Juro à Dios, there was no time to lose. By sunrise Friday, those of us at St. Angelo and the spur of Senglea could watch the teams of beasts and slaves hauling artillery from the Marsa onto Sciberras. With more terrible clarity we watched unending thousands of Turks amass directly before our eyes on the slopes of the mount itself. No one needed to tell the men in Fort St. Elmo what this portended.

"*Fuego!*" de la Cerda's gunners cried as soon as the sappers came within distance, and their heavy cannon erupted.

"*Fuego!*" shouted Diego by me on St. Angelo, and our two solitary pieces added their thunder to the salvos from St. Elmo.

"*Fuego!*" Don Sanoguera's men cried at almost the same instant, and now the air was split by volleys from the two forts and Sanoguera's Post on the spur of Senglea.

But Diego cast a despairing eye over the lack of ordnance about us. "*Por los Higados de Dios!*" he cursed, "we might as well be pissing on a beached whale ... To the Devil with them!" He fired again.

With the stubbornness of mules we kept this up for a time, filling the sky with noise and covering ourselves with smoke, but the numbers of enemy sappers was so great the Turks never shed a tear. The Grand Master himself finally appeared and told us to stop wasting powder.

By noon, the air above the docks on Kalkara Creek was filled with the scraping of barrels and the grunting of men.

"Hand it here," I said to Diego, as we loaded boats with gunpowder and *granadas* from the arsenal. The clank of metal rose everywhere on the docks around us. As the booming from Fort St. Elmo rolled across the harbor into the creek, Colonel Mas and his men were piling into *fregate*, skiffs, *luzzijiet*, barques—every boat they had mustered. Gaspard de la Motte's company and one hundred more Knights from all the langues were not to be denied the honor of being first and clambered into the vessels with equal vigor. In the midst of this mayhem stood a gang of criminals too, looking not much better than the rats they'd been imprisoned with until this very morning, when they accepted de Valette's offer of good pay to cross the harbor.

The reinforcement of Fort St. Elmo had begun. While helping load the boats, I spied Balthazar amidst the crowd with his servant, placing his arms into a brigantine. "Balthazar," I said, making my way over to him, "you have volunteered for this?"

Armor gleaming, he nodded.

"The greatest folly of all?"

I could hardly disguise the ruefulness of my voice but Balthazar would have none of it. "It may be folly, but it is our single chance and I go without regret." Well knowing this, I natheless felt a hard lump constricting my throat. I loved this man without bound and could not bear to see him so calmly setting off for certain death. Yet, as he had many times in the past, Balthazar laid his hand on my shoulder. "You and I have been in tight situations often enow and we have ne'er abandoned hope—"

"There has ne'er been ought like this," I answered gravely, not so much objecting as reminding. "They can put thirty or forty thousand men against that fort if they desire. How many do you see here?" I cast my gaze over the scene about us. "Six hundred?"

He smiled. "We must delay the enemy until Don Garcia arrives. Every day means life for Malta, for the Order, for Europe. I can think of no better reason to sacrifice my life ... I say again: We have said farewell before and yet live to tell the tale, so let us get on with it. I know why I fight and you know why you fight, Francisco, and both are right reasons."

The Abbé turned without embracing me and I went back to my assigned task of loading the boats with iron and fire balls. Soon Pietru appeared with his wheel-lock over his shoulder, wearing a sparkling new cuirass. He said he wanted to cross.

"Why?" I asked.

"They say villagers from Birkirkara are hiding there. My wife said she would come through Birkirkara. Maybe she is there too."

My God, I thought, women and children in that fort? I enlisted Ix-Xabaw and before long we were among those rowing the small fleet across the harbor to Fort St. Elmo. The journey took but half a glass and we received no fire from the Turks on Sciberras. Whether they weren't prepared or because we weren't worth the trouble, I don't know. We moored the boats below St. Elmo at a small cove surrounded and roofed by rocks, a sea grotto. It afforded an excellent protection and opened to a back gate of the fort, itself shielded by a wall built across the ditch, a *tenaglia*. Even as la Cerda's cannoneers continued firing at the enemy, the garrison cheered the arriving Knights and sallied forth from the sea gate to meet them. Together everyone carried the supplies ashore, biskets, wine, cheese, lard, vegetables, oil and vinegar and the munitions.

I looked about the star fort I had helped raise thirteen years ago. Today each defect stared us in the eye. St. Elmo's long, narrow arms would catch the enemy betwixt and expose him to fire from every side, and the fort indeed sat on solid rock, making it impossible to undermine. A deep ditch, nine or ten paces wide, was surrounded by a high counterscarp, and the walls themselves were of a good height. But we had built the place in a hurry, and after a dozen years plants protruding thro' all the cracks showed off the masons' work. The large piazza would hold the men, but there weren't enough barrack rooms to shelter everyone and no cellars in which to hide. The major fault, tho', had been visible to all before we set the first stone in place, and was starkly visible at this moment as I gazed up Sciberras to the hordes of barbarians gathering there:

Fort St. Elmo sat at the bottom of the hill.

de Sengle's cavalier facing the sea put some height into the castle, but scarce enough. Worse, that massive, tiered tower stood outside the walls and you needed to cross a bridge to reach it. The new ravelin, built to protect the Marsamxett side, had been finished scant days ago. It sat just outside the ditch and you couldn't reach the platform directly except by another bridge. Worst of all, it wasn't high enough to defend properly and was poorly made. No, the Turks wouldn't need many days, not at all.

Bringing some kegs up to the gun platforms, I glanced into the ditch. Below, hundreds of Maltese villagers huddled beneath the guns, having taken refuge there days ago. Pietru was going among them and, sure enough, found his wife Grezz with their cow. The Grand Master had ordered the women and children taken back to Birgu, but able-bodied men would remain.

Pietru hardly knew what to say to this stranger his woman. They had not had a life together since the *razzia*. She hung around his neck a talisman she had brought from their farm and he gave her the money he had with him. "*X'ser naghmlu b'dik il-baqra?*" she asked.

"*Halliha hawn*," he said, taking the cow's rope. "The men will slaughter it for meat."

Now Ix-Xabaw handed her over to me for keeping. "After so many years apart, I'd think you'd have more to say to each other," I said to him, half in jest. Pietru grunted, not understanding. "Yet you spent years searching for her." He grunted again.

Until this moment I hadn't perceived that Ix-Xabaw intended to remain in the fort. I hardly knew what to say myself. We embraced and I readied to return to St. Angelo. Without success I attempted to find Balthazar among the throngs of soldiers and so I departed with the other boatmen, this time ferrying the women and children away from the great danger. With la Cerda's troops, who had already been there, we left eight hundred men in Fort St. Elmo to oppose the entire Ottoman army.

Sunup next Balthazar stood with Ramon Caravajal atop the interior cavalier, which served as a keep for the fort, and watched the enemy sappers get to work five or six hundred paces above them on Sciberras. The ground was hard, but thousands and thousands of oarsmen and slaves were at this moment taking pick and axe to it.

"*Si, Por toda la Perdition del Mundo te lo juro*," remarked Caravajal as the red-and-white banner of the Religion sent its fluttering shadow across them, "they're like insects eating earth."

"You may be right that perdition is about to swallow us," answered Balthazar. Truly, such was the speed and diligence that the sappers worked that the two Knights watched the trenches wind to and fro down Sciberras while they ate breakfast. St. Elmo's cannoneers weren't about to let them get away with this unopposed and kept up fire. It was useless. The enemy filled the woolen sacks they had brought with dirt from the trenches, fashioning gabions, and these defenses went some way to protecting the sappers from St. Elmo's fire. Worse, they dug on the Marsamxett side to avoid any fire from St. Angelo, and this side was also largely hidden from St. Elmo by a ridge.

Soon Juan de Guaras and Juan de la Cerda joined Balthazar and Caravajal on the cavalier. "How long?" de Guaras asked. The high-ranking Bailiff of Negroponte was Melchor de Guaras's brother. Surely two decades older than Balthazar and dressed in splendid armor engraved with a large eight-pointed cross, he had been appointed Captain of Succours and General for St. Elmo because the Governor, Luigi Broglio, was older still and unwell.

"They'll open fire by tomorrow night if the Devil hasn't taken them," said Caravajal. Balthazar nodded.

At that moment the sound of light cannon and arquebus fire reached them from the Port side of Sciberras. Soon after, men ferrying succours ran through the sea gate. Indeed, by now a constant stream of boats passed between Kalkara Creek and St. Elmo, and its piazza was filled with powder kegs and spits roasting animals. Once again I sought out Balthazar, this time finding him in the company of the Bailiff of Negroponte and de la Cerda.

"The Turks have put some small pieces above a cave on Sciberras," I said, "and their arquebusiers are taking aim at the supply boats, but our guns across the harbor are scaring them off. There is little to worry about. Food and powder will keep coming."

de Guaras nodded at the news I'd brought as another from St. Angelo came up and handed him a letter. "The Grand Master wishes to know what further succours are required," the Bailiff said to those gathered around.

Each man standing there mumbled "a miracle." Negroponte, nodding, turned to the tall, balding de la Cerda and ordered him to return with us to Birgu.

Before I climbed down from the cavalier Balthazar took me aside. "Francisco," he said, "do not think to remain here. Your duties are to supply us with the weapons you have made at the mill and to man the guns on St. Angelo. Do you understand me?"

I nodded and, for a second time, without embracing him, departed Fort St. Elmo.

The Monsignore received Don Juan de la Cerda in the Magisterial Palace, offered him a cup of wine, and with no further prologue questioned him about the prospects for St. Elmo.

For the past days, la Cerda's company had singlehandedly guarded the fort and raided the enemy's main camp at the Marsa. Everyone admired him for that, but now the Captain came close to scoffing. "I declare, Eminenza," he said without hesitation, "Fort St. Elmo is indefensible. We don't have the men, it sits at the base of that damned hill, the mortar in de Sengle's cavalier is crumbling, the new ravelin has been built by monkeys, and at this very moment the Turks are bringing up guns that can move mountains. If you care to look out your windows, Eminenza, you will see them. Eight days—less—and the fort will be reduced."

de Valette could not countenance such language. With an irony not entirely chaining his old anger he answered, "I expect you and your men to carry out their sacred duties to the Order. Supplies will continue to reach you in a timely fashion. The Turks have yet to fire a shot against Fort St. Elmo, but when you are certain the garrison can no longer hold out, I shall come myself to defend it."

He dismissed de la Cerda with a wave but the Grand Master, I think, must have understood the truth in la Cerda's words, for he at once sent for Captain Medrano, a private adventurer known for his devotion to the Religion, and ordered him to St. Elmo with his company.

de Valette walked to the arsenal atop St. Angelo, where I was again making fireballs from the rope Flaminia and others had shredded. The Grand Master motioned me after him and we walked to the edge of the fortress. "You have been to Fort St. Elmo, Señor," he said. "How is the spirit of the men?"

I searched for the proper words. "You could not want for braver soldiers," I answered slowly.

"But?"

"Look there," I pointed across the harbor. The Turks were by now building a platform for one of the basilisks near the top of Sciberras. "There is no defense against that monster. It can hurl a six-quintal stone half a league, believe me, Eminenza." My words could not have cheered de Valette, echoing la Cerda's as they did. "There are also twenty thousand men standing on that hill."

On the near side of Sciberras, the Turkish sappers were also erecting large wooden structures, triangular in form, and filling them with earth— shields for their gun platforms. "They will begin firing upon us here at Castle St. Angelo soon," said de Valette.

"Aye," I nodded, "very soon."

The Grand Master commanded some men nearby to demolish a few small store houses and to bring hither some heavy guns. He also realized that the Order's remaining galleys, sitting uselessly behind the chain in Galley Creek, would soon become targets. "Run down to the creek," he told me, "and tell the galley Captains to moor the *capitana* and the *S. Giovanni* in the moat behind the castle. Tell them as well to allow the *Pisano*, the *Corona* and the galley we took from that corsair Yusif Conciny to fill with water."

I sped down to the embankment with the order. The Captains at first did not credit my words and went to see the Grand Master themselves but, when they received the command from his lips, they did as they were told. They brought the two boats into the moat and moored them there, not far from the *Kapi Agha*'s galleon. As crowds gathered at the docks to watch, the crews removed some heavy pieces from the three other galleys and hauled them up to St. Angelo. When the guns, cordage and masts had been removed, the Captains ordered the boats submerged. The sea monsters slowly sank, water coursing over their decks and into their holds, until at last they sat under Galley Creek, waiting to be called someday to the surface again. The Grand Master had just removed from service half the Order's fleet.

Soon the pieces were in place above St. Angelo and our men began firing against the new enemy gun platforms. At first we did the Turks some harm, but we couldn't make them go away. We were pissing on a whale. Those immense, dirt-filled gabions also hindered us a great deal. We might have done better but de Valette again ordered us to husband the powder.

Later that evening Isabella, having washed, put on a fresh dress and rouged her lips, knocked on the door of Blaij Verga's house in the Borgo. His mistress admitted her with a smile and Isabella, casting a sideward glance at the *quiraca*, entered the dining room, where she found him catching a bite to eat, his morion by him on the table. She'd never before set foot in this well-appointed house, which was full of hides, spears, Levantine icons and other trophies of war.

"To what do I owe the honor ... ?" Vergã said, putting down the chicken leg in his hands and wiping his hands on his pants before he rose.

Without replying she addressed him. "Señor, you swore that your quarrel with Francisco was behind you. You have lied."

Blaij waved away his mistress, a dark Maltese girl who wore her hair in ringlets and who was at this moment learning against the door arch, listening intently. "Señora, do join me," he offered her a chair. "Wine?"

Isabella scoffed, tossing her chin sharply; she leveled her eyes at him and waited silently for an answer.

"I do not know of what you speak."

"You denounced Francisco to the Inquisitor."

"I did no such thing," he replied impatiently. "But Señora will agree, a renegado has much to fear from the Inquisition. This is, after all, why they flee to Protestant countries and become apostates twice."

Revulsion filled Isabella. Vergã was lying through his teeth but every side of the Inquisition was buried in secrecy and to prove anything impossible. "You asked Colonel Mas," she persisted, "whether Francisco had turned in Constantinople. You then denounced him, knowing Fra Balthazar would be summoned as well. You intended harm to both, but Balthazar's honor and the siege upon us have conspired to end your malicious intrigues."

Isabella could not doubt the frown of disappointment that passed across Vergã's countenance. "Do you not find it strange, Señora," he said at length, "that a great siege has begun, the first engagements have been fought, guns are booming—and yet, people walk the streets of this tiny Borgo, eat, gamble, visit their whores. You and I speak of renegados and Inquisitors."

"Life somehow goes on," Isabella answered reluctantly.

"Yes, Señora is right. Life goes on—after a fashion. Loves, hates, rivalries ... " Vergã chuckled. "I see in your lovely eyes that you do not trust me. Does Madame Guasconi wish me to swear by the Sacramental Cloth of Daroca or on the Bible?"

"Does Señor own one?"

Vergã cast about amidst his trophies, then spread his hands apologetically and smiled. "No, I don't." He offered her a human skull from atop a chest of drawers.

Isabella recoiled. "What means something to you?" she asked, anger twining with genuine curiosity.

"A token of your esteem as I go to fight the Infidel would mean something," he replied with evident sincerity, regarding her fine dress.

For a moment Isabella stared at him in disbelief, then she did sit down, with her hands clasped before her, her gaze unwillingly transfixed by this rogue. "Wherefore does a man who fights for profit alone stay on Malta now?"

"Francisco asked me the very question yesterday. Like the other soldiers here, I am being paid."

"It is all the same to you who triumphs?"

Vergã reflected, pouring himself some wine. "I do not flatter myself to think that I will keep my head if we lose," he answered, "but if by some miracle we do triumph, booty beyond imagining will be ours for the taking."

Isabella peered into a deeper emptiness than that which she discerned in Francisco. "You are *captivo*, Blaij Vergã," she said, and glancing at a crucifix on the wall, took his arm. Even as she felt her heart thumping loudly within her breast she said, "I shall pray for your soul," and attempted to force him to his knees beside her.

At first he thought to shake her hand away, then accepted the moist grip. They prayed together, but after a moment he impatiently got to his feet. "If your intent is merely to pray, Señora," he said with a perceptible forlornness, "I would not waste more of your time. My mistress hung that cross there. Remember, like yourself, my father forsook me. We share much."

At Isabella's home the servants were attempting to put her house guest to bed for the night with little fortune. Isabella acknowledged that her patience with the nurse was fast waning. Since they had awakened her long-dormant memories for Soliman's verse, she recited them incessantly. Each time a cannon boomed, she raised a gnarled finger and coughed up something spiteful. "This is what ye are promised for the Day of Reckoning!" one of the slaves rendered. When Isabella finally learned the nurse was quoting the Alcoran, she immediately knelt before her image of the Mother and begged forgiveness, throwing a harsh glance at the old woman, who couldn't see her.

Giansevere's health had certainly turned for the worse. In only the past day the unmistakable odor of approaching death had begun to surround her. She cried, "Feruc! Feruc!" over and over again, but her worthless son had vanished Eastward six months ago, never to be heard from again. Isabella sensed that in the midst of granny's defiance was a dim realization that no one knew she remained a captive in this heathen place or cared. This tempered Isabella's irritation.

Once Giansevere was asleep, Isabella sat down in her cabinet to write letters about what was taking place on Malta. She knew some printers in Firenze who would publish the dispatches, if she could get them there.

Eighty

The salvos from Fort St. Elmo's guns against the enemy pionniers continued much of the night. Balthazar managed to sleep thro' them in fits and starts, assuring himself there would be no assault this day.

With the sun—all was commotion. The watchmen on the cavalier were shouting down to the fort; half the men below dropped any cup or bone in their hand and rushed across the bridge up to the tower, Balthazar among them. Reaching the top, he first glanced landward and, despite himself, caught his breath. The Turkish trenches were at hand—maugre the cannon fire, under the cover of darkness the enemy sappers had brought them over the ridge and close onto the very ditch of the fort. Below the colorful, fluttering banderoles wherewith they had dressed the trenches, the pionniers paused in their labor to regard the knights on the tower and some of the slaves saluted them. A few of the Knights waved back.

But the sentries' attention was not on the trenches. All eyes and arms were directed seaward. Among the multitudes of vessels that had by now spread out along the eastern coast of Malta, four new galleys sailed brazenly in the direction of the Port. For a long time neither Balthazar nor anyone around him could make out whose ships approached, but by the time they finally reached the line of vessels blockading the harbor, the crescents they flew told every man on the tower that these were no friends.

"Is it Dragut?" one of the younger soldiers asked with perceptible alarm.

Balthazar shook his head. "No, those aren't his colors."

Scattered arquebus fire from the trenches suddenly began pinging off the cavalier and all the Knights scampered down the steps for cover, still unsure whose boats were upon them, knowing all the same the corsairs had arrived.

Yakhshi couldn't understand all the portents and auguries that infused this morning's air. Men were grinding their teeth for action, yet as more soldiers fell sick each day, many already grumbled that Allah had cursed the expedition. Earlier, one of his *boluk* had tripped, knocking over the breakfast cauldron, but just now a big bird had fallen dead from the sky.

"It's a falcon," Rustem said and everyone breathed a sigh of relief, for it must mean the knights must fall.

The only augury Yakhshi was sure of was the cannon fire from the Santarma fort a league off, which told him that something must happen very soon.

"You're wanted at the house," said one of his *oda- bashiler* from behind him. Yakhshi turned from the circle gathered around the dead falcon and walked to headquarters.

Mustafa Pasha had summoned the officers to greet Uluj Ali, the famed corsair and Turgut's lieutenant, who'd just arrived from Barbary. Within the walled garden of the infidel bey's house, the corsair and the general exchanged bows and the customary gifts: silks, bejeweled weapons, a handsome boy-slave. That Uluj Ali had arrived was undeniably a good omen, tho' everyone was saying he'd brought only six hundred men.

Mustafa's first question was: "Where is Turgut?"

Uluj Ali didn't know and thought Turgut might be going to the Goletta.

Mustafa scowled but immediately turned his attention to the matter at hand. "Today the assault on the fort will begin. I command one hundred strokes on the stomach for any man who does not take part in the fusillade."

"*Zat-i Alinez*," a *chorbaji* objected with a bow. "One in five of my men is already sick with fever or the shits. They can't fight."

"They are lazy dogs!" shouted the Pasha. "One hundred strokes, do you hear?"

With that, Mustafa dismissed the officers and Yakhshi went over to the hospital tents. Amongst the shrubs and few trees, the *imamlar* prayed and the physicians were making lists of men who died. Yakhshi walked among the beds, taking his own stick to anyone he thought was feigning illness. "But why are so many sick?" he asked one of the doctors.

"We think it is the water," the Jew replied. "We're having the spring cleaned now."

To be sure, Yakhshi walked over and watched men pulling out every sort of debris from the big well. He prayed that would be the end of it.

Not long after, Yakhshi and his men crept down the hill in the trenches, readying to take their places with the other thousands. The Santarma guns were causing some trouble, but the engineers had rightly ordered the trenches dug on the side of the hill where the infidels couldn't see them. By now the *topchular* had emplaced five guns behind stone walls on the Marsamshet side, five in the center of the hill and aimed three more heavy pieces across the harbor. But the enemy gunners on the big castle kept spitting and cannon fire now came at them from both Santarma and across the water. Of a sudden, a large ball hit a rock at one of the platforms and blew it to pieces. Instantly, everyone up the hill was bellowing at the top of their lungs and running about like rabbits.

Moments later, some azab came yelling down to the trenches, "Piyale has been killed! Piyale has been killed!"

The *Boluk-bashi* stood stunned. As he'd be carried to heaven by his forelock, this could mean the end of the entire expedition. Allah couldn't have sent a worse omen, unless it be to strike down Mustafa himself. Yakhshi ordered his men to stay put and climbed up the hill to get instructions.

Halfway to the platforms, he was hearing a different story: "Piyale has been wounded!" When he reached the guns, many men were milling about. *Evet*, a splinter of rock had struck Piyale in the side, and even as Yakhshi approached, they were carrying the brightly attired *Kapudan* from the field.

"Will he live?" Yakhshi asked.

The fellow near him shrugged.

Pietru and some hundreds of his fellow Maltese arquebusiers were positioned behind the parapets on Fort St. Elmo when the fusillade finally began. "They're like skulls!" Leonardo next to him exclaimed. The countless turbans and headdresses lining the enemy trenches leered at them from within easy hailing distance, hardly beyond the counterscarp of the ditch. To Ix-Xabaw they didn't resemble skulls and he wasn't about to have a better look. The day was bright, their marksmen and archers well able to assure any fool of a short life. Pietru found it difficult to get a clear shot. Amidst the constant crackle of gunfire, he knelt, loaded, peaked his helmeted head thro' the opening and fired. He was certain only that if he hit anyone, that man was instantly replaced. The same was not true of the Christians; Leonardo, too curious, stood, took a ball and fell two steps from him.

St. Elmo's cannoneers hadn't thought to rest. Surrounded by stacks of balls, powder kegs and bales of straw, those grimy men worked frantically, ladling powder into the muzzles, ramming down the wads of hay, swinging their pieces into the face of the enemy and—"*Fuego!*" one piece roared, "*Fuego!*" the next, "*Fuego!*" the next. The booming was ceaseless, deafening. Dirt at the enemy scarps flew into the air and fell like rain atop the foe. The gunner nearest Pietru decided to try an explosive ball. His mate lit the fuse; they rammed it into the gun; "There's Paradise for you, dog!" cheered the gunner as half a dozen of the enemy sent their souls to Allah. A moment later his comrade was crying out, "*Mur ghand ix-xjaten!*" as he dropped a ball onto his foot and broke his toes.

Hours later, Pietru realized that the Turkish arquebusade hadn't been doing much damage. Only five or ten men had been hit. Toward evening, everything quickly changed: One of the sentries on de Sengle's tower suddenly raised his arm and cried, "They're clearing the port holes!" The Turks were about to unleash their big guns.

The men were already scampering down into the piazza when the first shots flew over the fort, falling harmlessly into the water. But the Turks soon corrected their aim and, nine days after the descent, iron balls at last began to crash against Fort St. Elmo.

Most of the soldiers quickly took shelter against the interior cavalier or in the barracks, where they'd be safe. Balthazar was sitting with Colonel Mas and Ramon Caravajal in the fading light when the Spaniard carelessly remarked, "As I wash my Hands of Pluto's flaming Mansion, those guns shouldn't harm us. They're mounted at least five hundred paces from here." As if to answer Caravajal's dismissal, an instant later the entire fort seemed to shudder.

"In the Name of the Almighty, what was that!" exclaimed the Knight, crossing himself from top to bottom.

"Oh, probably one of the ten eighty-*libbre* pieces they've brought," replied Mas. "You think those infidel guns are play-things? God help us when they bring them up." He also crossed himself as another ball crashed into the ramparts, sending stone and dust high into the air.

"What are we going to do now?" asked a young Knight nearby, unable to disguise the fear written on his face.

"I suggest we eat," proposed Balthazar, waving away some flies.

The rest agreed that was a good plan and moments later the cooks were scampering this way and that, moving all the kitchen gear and wood to sheltered areas. Soon the piazza was filled both with the smell of roasting meat and the acrid fumes of cannon smoke. The cannoneers on the ramparts made no attempt to dismount the Turkish guns, so far up the hill, but they kept up fire on the trenches, e'en as ball after ball slammed against the fort. Pietru had hardly moved for five hours. The gunners next to him were arguing over whether to try paper cartridges as quicker than ladling powder, but there wasn't any paper about. "I like the old way better anyway," one of them said. As twilight turned to darkness and the stars came out, both the enemy fusillade and St. Elmo's answer continued.

Balthazar and his comrades quickly surmised this was no casual bombardment. Those guns bent on their destruction were firing constantly, the only time between salvos being what the Turkish gunners needed to let their pieces cool. Juan de Guaras ordered some of the Maltese to begin collecting the balls. Others began counting the shots but soon gave up.

"Speaking of Hades," Caravajal finally said, leaning against the keep with a piece of mutton in his fist, "at Gelves, during one of our sorties, I was attacking a Turkish officer with my two-hander—tho' of course not with all my might. I happened to miss my Blow and struck my Weapon so deep into the Earth that it penetrated into the Infernal Regions, scratched the tip of Pluto's Nose and not a little damaged one of his Whiskers."

Everyone laughed thereat, as another ball shrieked by and crashed into the wall opposite, sending splinters of stone onto the piazza. "All these years your prowess has ne'er ceased to amaze me, Ramon," replied Balthazar while the dust covered them. "It is a wonder you were taken on Gelves at all." Before Caravajal could object, the Abbé continued: "As we are on the topic of Hades, let me tell you that on one of my trips to Rome, I was speaking with Pope Alexander, a Spaniard, of course. He related to me that when the painter Michelangelo portrayed His Holiness true to life in his lively picture of the Inferno on the chapel wall, some of his cardinals objected, saying the Pope must be removed. His Holiness replied, 'It is most certain that I have no power to take any person out of the Inferno. Had it been but Purgatory, I could have done it with all the ease of the World."

While the others guffawed, Mas scowled. "Fra Balthazar," he said, "you had years to be born when Pope Alexander died."

"Ah," conceded that one with what in the torchlight Mas took to be a fugitive grin, "these popes replace each other with such rapidity that in my old age I sometimes confuse one with the other."

Everyone laughed again as some enemy fireworks exploded above, illuminating the fortress with a brief, harsh light. Then Mas asked in their native tongue, "The real question, Monsieur, is whether we now sit in the Inferno and or merely Purgatory."

"Certainly only Purgatory at this moment."

"Then we must make a sortie. I could not bear sitting here until the Inferno arrives."

By midnight the bombardment and arquebusade had all but ceased. The stars above were dimmed by a pall of smoke hanging over the fort. Two Italian sentries were wondering if they would ever taste tobacco when they heard someone calling softly from the front gate. *"Che c'e?"* the first replied, cautiously peering into the darkness. At first he received no answer but after the fire had died down a bit more, the voice called out, *"Soy español. Quiero entrar en fortaleza."* Hardly believing their ears, the sentries glanced at each other and ran to find the Bailiff of Negroponte, who told them that under no circumstances were they to lower the bridge. Returning at once to their posts, they instead cast a rope over the wall, soon pulling up first an arquebus tied to a sack of clothes, followed by a young Spaniard.

"I'm called Alfonso," he said as the sentries took him to de Guaras.

Under the sentry's torch, the elderly Bailiff regarded the fellow from head to toe. He was dressed respectably and spoke Spanish like a native.

"For good reason, Señor," Alfonso replied, "I hail from Andalusia. I have been secretary to the Bey Hasan of Algiers and tutor to his son."

"Where is Hasan?" de Guaras asked without waiting to hear a word more.

Alfonso shook his head under the light of another bursting firework. "Have no fear, Señor, he will come." Quickly the renegado added, "I came with other Barbary corsairs but wish to return to my true faith."

With undiminishing suspicion, de Guaras eyed him. "Whose ships arrived today?" he asked.

"Uluj Ali's, Turgut's lieutenant."

"Damn Gian Andrea!" spat de Guaras, hitting the palm of one hand with the fist of the other, for it was the same Uluj-Ali who had escaped Doria at Gelves and brought Piyale down on the Spanish armada. Truly, when the other Knights learned of Uluj-Ali's arrival, they cursed as loudly as Negroponte. "There seemed to be a commotion today on Sciberras," the Bailiff continued. "What was it?"

Alfonso looked at de Guaras strangely. "You have not heard, Señor? Piyale Pasha was wounded by a splinter of rock."

"Will he live?"

Again the renegado nodded. "Yes," he said, "the wound was serious but appears not to be mortal. You should know that both Commanders are very brave and do not hesitate to expose themselves to fire. But there is much antagonism between them and men are falling ill at the camp. The army is already grumbling." The Bailiff was glad to learn that the earlier reports they'd received were true. "Natheless, they have but begun." Now Alfonso pointed to the outside cavalier. "You have a big culverin on the tower. You should move it. The Turks have a good Genoese gunner who intends to dismount it."

"Damn these renegados!" de Guaras cursed again.

"The Turks do pay well," Alfonso remarked as Negroponte ordered that he be taken across to Birgu with the wounded.

Men carried the twenty or so wounded out thro' the sea gate to the waiting boats and not long after, Alfonso was standing before the Grand Master in the Magisterial Palace. de Valette, no less suspicious of him than de Guaras had been, immediately asked him how he escaped the Turkish camp.

Alfonso told how he had put on his best Spanish clothing under infidel robes and that during all the commotion he went over to the cave where the Turks were firing on the Order's boats. "They have," Alfonso offered, "put two more guns there to stop succours from reaching the fort." When the Turkish sentries challenged him, Alfonso replied that he wanted to shoot at the enemy boats. They asked why he was wearing a cloak and he told them he planned to sleep on the rocks that night. "So they let me go. When I got close to Fort St. Elmo, I took off my robes and called to the sentries."

Seeing the expression on the Monsignore's face, Alfonso immediately volunteered to cross back over to the Turkish camp and blow up a big store of munitions. At once de Valette ordered Captain André Fanton to accompany him, instructing Fanton to kill the renegado at the least provocation. The two men set off in a skiff, but enemy fire from the same Alicate cave exploded the water around them; in an instant they were swimming back to Senglea. Still wet, Fanton brought Alfonso again to the Palace. de Valette asked Alfonso if he'd make another attempt tomorrow night, but the renegado refused—by then his absence would have been marked. The Monsignore nodded, deciding the Spaniard had been telling the truth, and sent him over to Fort St. Michel.

After sunrise the bombardment picked up again with renewed fury. Beneath the smoke that drifted down on them, Balthazar saw that Mas and Medrano were chaffing for a sortie. Medrano, who'd brought his company over later than the others, was younger than Mas, boasted fewer scars, and was not a Knight of the Order, but he ceded zealousness to no one. Before breakfast, he stomped over to Negroponte, finding the Bailiff at prayer in the chapel. When at last de Guaras rose, Medrano said impatiently, "Señor, the men don't want to sit any longer in this damned fort. Let us go out. Better to die taking heads than to sit here like geese and be target practice for Turkish gunners."

As they stepped onto the piazza another ball hit the outer wall. de Guaras merely shook his head and said it was too dangerous.

Fuming, Medrano returned to where Balthazar and some of the others were taking breakfast. The booming of the guns echoed about the piazza, producing explosions on every side. The sound was mostly from St. Elmo's own cannoneers, who were again hitting the trenches opposite with everything they had, doing considerable damage to the enemy sappers who were trying to dig away the counterscarp for the assault that must come. Suddenly, as Medrano sat down, the air was split by a shriek such that no man among them had ever heard, as were a banshee flying straight from the Abyss intent on swallowing the entire fort in its infernal, wailing maw.

So it was. Balthazar said it was an instant later, others claimed an instant before, but all agreed that in the same heartbeat the hammer of Lucifer struck the cavalier. Rock spewed a hundred *brazas* into the air, men on the tower were thrown from their feet and the entire castle groaned from top to bottom.

When hearts started to beat again, the Knights faced each other with the same question on every pair of stilled lips. Balthazar knew, tho', that the great basilisk had just hurled its first stone. "Do not worry," he said, attempting to make light of it, "I am told that such is the heat generated by each shot that it can fire only once each hour."

The brethren began counting.

Later that evening I was among those who carried provisions thro' the *porta del soccorso* to the besieged fort, where I found Balthazar speaking to de Guaras in the torchlight. The bombardment had been going on only two nights, but already stone from the walls littered the piazza and the tops of a few parapets appeared ragged. The cavalier had a bite torn out of its corner as if by a big fish. Men ran about everywhere effecting repairs. As the Turks moved their guns down Sciberras, it would get worse.

"What was it Ariosto wrote about gunpowder?" asked Balthazar to the sky.

' ... *base implement of Death*
Framed in the black Tartarean realms,
By Beelzebub's malicious art designed
To ruin all the race of humankind,'

... or words to that effect." He paused as the torches flickered on his weary face. "We believe they fired near five hundred balls against us today. This presents us with no shortage of iron. I hope you brought powder."

At that I was able to nod. I then went off to evacuate the wounded.

Sunrise next, the drawbridge came down over the ditch and Colonel Mas and Captain Medrano sallied forth at the head of their companies. Balthazar could hardly credit the numbers arrayed in those trenches before them, snaking up Sciberras. There was simply no end. But the bloodcurdling screams he and his comrades let out in the charge caught the foe by surprise. Within moments Mas had whipped his followers into a frenzy. The Knights, wielding hafted weapons or two-handers, were soon at the enemy trenches. With the arquebusiers lending fire from the ramparts, they jumped in and were hacking the foe to pieces. The sounds of snapping lances, sword against mail and buckler, filled the air. How many they took in that first sortie, Balthazar had no idea; he knew only that he was splattered from head to toe with blood and brain pulp.

Thereon after things didn't unfold as anyone expected. When the Turks at last got their wits together, the janissaries surged into the mêlée and began to press the Knights back by sheer weight of numbers. The spahis were also charging down the hill and Balthazar saw more than one man fall with an arrow in his side or neck. Mas was yelling for a retreat but the Knight could hardly hear him for all the cannon fire from above. Aye, as one gun boomed after the other, the smoke was settling into the ditch and was rapidly becoming so thick that the men struggling therein couldn't see their own noses. Balthazar, scrambling up the counterscarp, wiped away a tear, just as a mailed spahi reared on his horse at the ditch's edge and swung at him with an axe. Hardly making out his foeman thro' the smoke, the Knight rolled down into the ditch again, grabbed a halberd and impaled the horseman.

Everybody around was coughing his lungs out. Finally they got the Devil out of the ditch and retreated into the fort, but the foe had used the smoke as a shield to bring up more men. By the time it dispersed, the counterscarp was lined with enemy flags and streamers.

"I think we showed them something," huffed Captain Medrano to Negroponte, removing his helmet when they'd gotten to safety.

They all climbed up to the ramparts. "Yes we showed them something," said Balthazar, observing the enemy banners a stone's throw away. "Now the fort is surrounded on the Marsamxett side."

Seeing the circumstance, Captain la Cerda shook his head in disgust. "They can crawl thro' the ditch right to the ravelin. It's too low to be defended. We should mine it before it is too late."

Medrano spat, a sentiment to which de Guaras agreed. He ordered the gunners to clear the counterscarp of the enemy and said they would defend the ravelin if necessary.

Later that evening, Balthazar encountered Ix-Xabaw drawing water at the big cistern. He hardly recognized him for all the grime covering his face. "Pietru," he said, casting his eyes onto the men pressed against the bailey walls, "I do not know how long we shall hold out against the multitudes bent on our destruction, who have not yet thought to make a proper assault. You have deserved more of a life than Fate has granted you. Promise me that when the end comes you will do all to save yourself."

Balthazar was unsure whether the farmer understood him. "Fra Balthazar," Pietru grunted, "my life has been no different than the next man's." He offered the Knight his hand and went back to his duties clearing the rubble.

Eighty-One

Dr. Jean stopped on the landing below the top floor of the Sacra Infermeria, where two colleagues blocked his way. "Messeri, please, I am in a hurry."

They pointed out the open window. Much against his will, Vigo glanced across the harbor toward Fort St. Elmo. He, like they, could hardly believe his eyes. Twilight had fallen. A deeper gloom shrouded the fort; it was the pall of smoke that had hung over St. Elmo for the past few days, a pall so thick one could hardly make out thro' it the Order's proud banner flying atop the keep. Vigo understood that he was gazing onto Satan's kingdom. The sky above throbbed constantly with a infernal glow that surely arose from the lake of brimstone, and the ground trembled with an earthquake that was the hammering of devils. Behind that pall, the thin sliver of a blood-red moon was rising.

"What day is it?" Vigo asked.

"Four days hence is the Feast of St. Elmo."

Today was the twenty-ninth of May, the third day of the bombardment.

"The men who came over last night," said one of the doctors, "say there are seventeen heavy pieces aimed at them—"

"The infidels have brought half down to within sixty paces of the walls," added the other.

"How many shots today?" asked Vigo absently.

"The wounded do nothing but count. Seven hundred, they say."

The inconstant *thump, thump-thump* was deafening enough where he stood to rattle his viscera, the candelabras and all else; Vigo did not think he had the courage to imagine what it must be like inside that fort, but he was certain the seals were being opened. "Messeri," he said, wiping his eye, "we must prepare to receive more wounded tonight. Bajada swam over and said the Knights made a sortie this morn. There will be dozens of … *casualties*."

"Monsieur," the first colleague replied, "if this number come every night, before long the Hospital will overflow. What shall we do?"

Vigo thought a moment. "We shall have to find other places ... I shall speak to the Monsignore." He went upstairs, opening the door to the nearest ward. Lighting the lamp he carried, the doctor surveyed the room. The fighting had scarcely begun, no assault had yet been made on the fort, and the room was crammed with wounded from last week's clash and the present bombardment.

"This is from a rock?" one of the physicians was asking the soldier on the nearest bed, as a Serving Brother stood by with a candle. The patient, one Francisco de Aguilar, nodded, grimacing as the doctor washed the gash in his shoulder with vinegar and salt water, then took a needle to it. Aguilar was a respected officer who served under Commander de Guiral at the base of Fort St. Angelo. The Turks hadn't concentrated all their attention on St. Elmo.

"They've been giving us the Devil's pounding—trying to," he said. "We were hitting their platforms atop Sciberras—it irks them worse than a wasp up the ass. The infidels take pricks up the ass but not wasps—"

"Señor," interrupted the physician, "I remind you that you sit in the Sacra Infermeria."

"*Pardon*, Doctor. Well, the Turks decided to be rid of this little wasp, but our post is at water level and they can't lower their pieces enough to hit it. So they've been pummeling Fort St. Angelo above, hoping to bury us in all the falling rock."

"Yes," Vigo put in, "we have heard." Truly.

The Turks had managed to knock some stone out of the old wall and every day Guiral's men had been clearing away the damned debris. "Today it came tumbling down like shit from God's ass ," Aguilar said. "That's how I got this—but the infidels finally got it into their heads that they'll have to knock out thirty armslengths of rock to bury us. This afternoon they took out their frustration on the windmills on Senglea, but now they're moving all their pieces against St. Elmo. By tomorrow they'll have twenty-four heavy guns on that place. God help the bastards trapped there."

Aguilar crossed himself and everyone briefly fell silent. While the physicians finished stitching him up, Vigo asked whether he wasn't married to a pretty Gozitan woman. That was true. "How is she?"

"A soldier can die honorably in the company of his comrades, but a woman ... Were I a woman on this island, I should think seriously about killing myself before ... " Aguilar's words fell away, and as the doctor nodded after him he went back to his post where he might be buried again.

Vigo walked to the next bed and glanced at the record hanging there. Before he e'en glanced at the patient himself, his nose told him the fellow would soon die. The odor was of putrefaction and sepsis. Dr. Jean removed the wool covering from the stump of the leg that remained after last week's amputation. There could be no doubt. Infection was a normal part of healing, he had been taught in Paris, all doctors had been taught. Why then was it so often accompanied by death? Wondering whether such knowledge would ever be granted medicine, Vigo, seeing no sign of the Grand Master, went to find him. Below, he encountered Isabella Guasconi as she prepared to depart for the night. When she did not know where de Valette was to be found, he inquired after her health.

Unexpectedly she choked, nearly broke into sobs but when Vigo put his arm around her shoulders she said, "Forgive me, Doctor, I do not know what is happening to me ... I burst into tears at the slightest provocation."

"Perhaps that is better than not—"

An exceptional explosion that shattered a nearby window cut Vigo off; the great basilisk had fired again.

"No!" screamed Isabella suddenly, clasping her ears between her hands. "This cannot be!" Vigo watched her stamp the ground like a little girl, or her own mother, but at once the lady made a concerted effort to master herself. When the doctor again approached her, she raised her hand and breathed deeply. "Forgive me a second time, Doctor," she said to the shriek of a lone dog somewhere. "Meseems the girl Parisot raised has not become the soldier he would have desired. Mayhap some of her stole away after all. I have sworn to do better." At last Isabella paused, sighing. "What will become of us, Doctor Jean?"

Vigo could hardly stem his own apocalyptic visions. "I should honestly not be surprised if every one of us ... perishes, but I should somehow grieve less if I knew that this great Hospital would be left behind. Of that I am far from ... certain." Ascertaining that Isabella had taken herself in hand, Vigo went on to find de Valette.

During the same twilight, Flaminia sought me out at the fortress mill where we continued to make combustibles. "I killed my Cesare," she said glumly.

"Who?" I asked, raising my voice sharply above the thunder rolling across the harbor.

"My dog." Knights had come this morning rounding up all the dogs for destruction because the sentries complained they made too much noise and raised continual alarms. They also said they the Grand Master didn't want people sharing their food with their animals. They demanded to take Cesare off, but Flaminia begged to be allowed to kill him herself.

"Good," I said. "Now you will have more food."

"Why do you talk so, Francisco?" she pouted. "This isn't you."

"Look there." I pointed across to St. Elmo, which appeared less a castle than a cloud of smoke. "Seven hundred men sit in that fort where the noise is tenfold what it is here. Every few moments a ball smashes into its ramparts, which are slowly crumbling. With every piece of stone that falls from the walls, each man there is coming to know he is doomed. Yet they stay to give us a chance to live. You speak of your dog? Take yourself in hand."

Flaminia attempted to hold back a tear. "Forgive me, Francisco."

"Why are you not at the walls?"

"I would rather work here. Let me, please."

"Very well." I gave the whore more old rope to shred. Once again she asked what the tow was for and I said simply, "Fire balls. We'll wrap it around rocks or wool sacks filled with gunpowder and soak it with tar and liquid resin."

Few words were exchanged as we toiled, but at length Flaminia said she'd heard talk that I'd turned. Without waiting for my reply she said with urgency, "You weren't circumcised, were you? If you aren't circumcised, Cubelles won't arrest you." I told her I wasn't circumcised and that Balthazar had put an end to the calumny. Flaminia shuddered natheless. "The Bishop questions everyone who comes back from slavery. O Blessed Mother, would he take bribes! Be careful, Francisco, I beg you."

Not wishing to discuss the matter, I asked Flaminia whether in the past days she'd had any customers. To my surprise she answered, "Yes, men need *quiracas* now, more than ever." The whore was undoubtedly but made her observation with a great weariness. "Your Señora will be fulfilling her duty!"

"*Silenzio!*" I shouted. "This whole island feeds on whores' gossip. I'll have none of it!"

For a moment Flaminia cowered under my raised hand, but seeing I would not strike her, asked unexpectedly, "Will you bury me in consecrated ground, Francisco?"

She had made two wishes during the year of the *razzia*, to have a house and to be buried as a Christian. At hearing her old plea, my anger passed. She had a house, at least. "Yes, Flaminia, I will."

With nightfall I sent the rich courtesan home, telling her again to gather her strength for the coming trials. The remainder of us from the arsenal loaded the boats with the supplies; the men who would cross the harbor to replace the wounded clambered aboard and we set off to St. Elmo.

The enemy fired at us from that cave on Sciberras, a few balls splashed into the water showering some boats with spray, but to our great advantage he had yet to make a concerted effort to prevent supplies from reaching the fort, and we gained the *porto del soccorso* without a single loss. The scene greeting us, tho', in no way gladdened the heart. Far out in the harbor the smell of cannon smoke reached our nostrils. The crescent moon swam low thro' the drifting haze, and as we docked at the grotto, its faint, rusted light was too feeble to show much. Now a firework exploded high above to reveal bandaged men repairing damaged parapets and, by them, useless, dismounted guns. Cinders rained down on us as we ran thro' the sea gate carrying supplies, unbalanced by the pounding of the enemy guns. Since yesterday day the Turks had added a platform at battering distance, only sixty or seventy paces up the hill, and the explosions were loud enough to annihilate your thoughts. Worse was the concussion of the air that knocked the holy breath out of you. You crouched like an animal, tho' you didn't need to.

After we delivered the food and succours, I walked through the fort attempting to find Pietru or Balthazar. Exhausted men covered with dirt sat or lay everywhere against the walls, eating, drinking, brushing away mosquitoes. Nowhere could I find Balthazar on the piazza and I went instead to look for Pietru. Among a hundred others I found him sleeping or dead on the ramparts with his arquebus cradled in his arms. I crawled over to him as a ball shattered the top of a parapet nearby and took a gunner's face off in the shower of splinters. "Xabaw," I said, shaking him in the darkness, "are you alive?"

Ix-Xabaw turned his soot-covered face toward me. His head was bandaged, the cloth stained red. "I think so. Cikku," he said, smiling faintly, "is that you?"

I nodded, feeling the bite of the rock shards everywhere under my arms.

"I'm tired," Pietru went on. "The Knights made a sortie last morning and the enemy took some of the counterscarp. You can see there." He pointed over the wall, but I didn't look. "An assault must come soon."

"Yes, you are right. Here." I handed Ix-Xabaw a bottle of wine, slapped him on the shoulder and climbed down. Preparing to depart, I now descried Balthazar against a wall near the chapel, playing cards with Mas and Medrano. "Balthazar," I said, catching sight of his dirty, drawn face in the torchlight.

"Would you like to join us?" he said, making room.

I shook my head.

"It is not as bad as it looks," he went on, casting his gaze about us. "If you remember Gelves, we didn't have water ... and it was hotter. Only seventeen guns are pounding us. The walls we built hold. I say these Turks have no idea of what they are doing. We are indeed fortunate that Turgut has gotten lost somewhere between here and la Goletta."

Despite the Abbé's brave words, the lines of his face told me that three days of relentless battering had taken its toll. "More guns are being emplaced," I said.

The other men were no less exhausted than Balthazar and more irritable. "We should make another sortie," Medrano was saying, throwing a card on the stones. "To sit here is useless."

Mas mumbled his assent.

"Beware of being drawn out," cautioned Balthazar. "Remember how Scipio deceived Hannibal in that regard. Only six hundred of us can stand."

"Shut up, Fra Balthazar!" erupted Medrano. "We must have a sortie. Sitting here means an inglorious death. Let us at least die with honor. The men are already losing their spirit."

Balthazar refused to be drawn in and asked me about the situation at Birgu. "The Grand Master uses every day to build a second wall behind the first, with loopholes and terre-plein; in Senglea barrels filled with earth stand everywhere; new parapets and traverses are going up; people level ground on which to fight."

Balthazar listened with a blank expression on his face, sighed. "I say, the Monsignore is disregarding Niccolò's advice: The Governor of a besieged town should never build interior fortifications too early, for it diminishes his reputation and the spirits of the besieged."

"Shut up, Navarre," Medrano said again. "Play your card."

Balthazar tossed a ten of swords on the pile and got to his feet.

"Balthazar," I said, "let me remain with you."

As weary as I had ever seen the Chevalier, he clasped me by the shoulders. "No, Francisco. We have spoken of this. What is more, tho' de Valette will die before uttering the words, he would Isabella protected. See to your duties."

"Nay, Balthazar," I replied. "That duty is in God's hands."

Without warning, a huge blast threw me to the piazza. The basilisk. With infinite slowness I rose, dusted myself off and helped evacuate today's wounded to the waiting boats.

The next morning the watch on Fort St. Elmo's cavalier was again alive with commotion. No fewer than eighty enemy galleys were sailing from Marsaxlokk north along the coast, directly past the fort. Despite the danger, numbers of men ran across the bridge to the tower to learn what was about. Balthazar stood with Fra Geronimo Sagra, who commanded the cavalier, together watching those colorful sails as each vessel in turn wheeled its forward armaments toward the spur of the cavalier and let off a shot or two.

"Heads down!" cried Sagra.

Everyone took cover as they might, but it slowly became apparent that the ships were not taking serious aim but only mocking the fort with salutations.

"What is this about?" asked Medrano, as a ball from the landward batteries smashed into the tower below them, sending a faint quiver thro' it.

"I don't know," said Sagra, "but let's give them a taste of their own medicine." He had his gunners train the big culverin on the nearest galley and gave the order: *"Fuego!"* The shot was good. E'en from this distance everyone saw the infidel vessel lurch under the impact amid-ship and begin to tilt at once. Infidels dove into the water to save themselves and within moments the surrounding galleys were quickly coming to the aid of the foundering ship.

The men of Fort St. Elmo let up a cheer.

Sagra himself, tho', felt a deep shudder run through the platform as the huge piece recoiled. Tho' this cavalier resembled a small mountain, betwixt its own faults of construction and the shots that had been hitting it, he knew the platform would be too weak to withstand the shock of the culverin's discharge for long. He ordered the gun dismounted and moved to the interior keep.

Meanwhile the other Knights remained puzzled by the procession of ships before them. "What is this about?" repeated Medrano, as they continued to watch the pageant.

At length, one of the sentries stretched out his hand and cried, "Look!"

Meeting the caravan from the north were thirteen new galleys and some thirty smaller vessels. They flew red and white banners with blue crescents.

"Is it Dragut?" the same young soldier asked who had with trepidation put the question the other day.

"Yes," replied Balthazar, "it is Dragut."

Eighty-Two

News of Turgut's arrival spread like wildfire. When Toni Bajada and an escaped negro slave informed His Eminence in the Magisterial Palace, de Valette did no more than clench his fist and wave them off. "At last!" snarled Romegas with a certain glimmer in his eye, which the Grand Master returned with a ferocious stare.

For the Maltese, the news inspired a dread scarcely less than that which accompanied the sighting of the Turkish fleet itself two weeks ago. "Madonna!" cried Flaminia, by me at the mill. "He will carry us all into slavery this time. Have we sinned so terribly, Francisco? Our Day of Judgment has come, hasn't it?"

She prattled on and I made no answer. The revelation of Turgut's arrival consumed me. Of a sudden, that long-dormant sense welled up from my soul, that the corsair's destiny and my own were intertwined and that God had after all chained me to Malta for a purpose. The sense was stronger than on those past occasions, so strong that I, like Vigo, felt a seal breaking, and near toppled into a faint.

"What is wrong, *mio cuore?*" asked Flaminia with alarm, seeing my hand on my forehead. "I'll give you a philtre."

"No—it is nothing, get back to work."

Within a few hours of putting into St. George's Bay, Turgut was striding into Mustafa's headquarters. "Turgut! The Drawn Sword of Islam!" Everywhere cheers rose into the sky as the men made way for the famed corsair. Yakhshi himself had the honor of bowing to the *Beylerbeyi* of Trablus as he entered the walled garden. *Evet*, Turgut was old, eighty summers the *Boluk-bashi* supposed, but none of the other commanders had such experience, such brains or such balls. With each step the corsair took in his green silks, Yakhshi felt the spirits of the men soar higher. Turgut had brought only two or three thousand troops with him, but had he come alone that would have been enough. His presence was truly a good omen. Today things would change.

Aye. Before the sun had moved, word was all over camp: Turgut had at once grasped the situation and demanded of the *Pashalar*, "Why are you wasting the Sultan's time and munitions reducing this small fort, which is of no consequence? A beardless youth would have told you to blockade the north of the island, to take the old city first, then the fortified parts of the harbor." The corsair made no attempt to hide his disdain. "The Santarma fort is a suckling and will die of its own accord once it has no teat to nourish it."

Mustapha shot a cobra's glance at Piyale as both bowed to the Drawn Sword. "Agreed," replied Mustapha, saying that Turgut's proposal was the very mirror of his own, "but my beloved son Piyale demanded Marsamshet harbor for his fleet, so dear to the Sultan's heart."

"By the Truth of the Messiah," those present saw Turgut's lips drip with contempt, "the virgin daughter of the Sultan's twenty-eighth concubine would have known better. What has happened to you, Piyale?"

Unable to hide his shame, the wounded Piyale bowed, red-faced, and removed himself forthwith from the tent.

"God has shed a thousand tears since this bombardment began," the old corsair went on, "but the blunder will be thrice compounded should we withdraw now. Let us reduce the fort with all haste and turn our attention to important affairs."

Pietru felt his heart freeze. Turgut's ships had arrived only three days ago, but already things had changed. The Gozitan and everyone else in St. Elmo's had watched with a deadly resignation as the corsair's men erected a new battery of guns across Marsamxett harbor from the fort. Ix-Xabaw knew the place; it was called the Hermitage of Santa Maria and lay only three hundred paces across the water.

"Four heavy culverins and two sacres," Nardo, the next arquebusier, said after word had come down from the sentries on the cavalier.

With the other pieces that had been brought down Sciberras, since yesterday thirty guns now hammered them. Day and night the fort shuddered with groans exceeding anything of the past week—the Beast of the Apocalypse had grasped St. Elmo's in its hands and was shaking it with infernal fury. After a week the men had become hard to the constant pounding. That was a lie. Ix-Xabaw felt wearier than he had in his life; his very limbs weighed him down; he could not stand, he could not sleep. Now night was falling again. They said today was the Feast of St. Elmo. The Gozitan crossed himself and prayed to the protector of sailors, but the only reply he received was more furious cannonading. Hours crawled by, measured by one deafening crash after another. *Boom boom-boom boom.* How many hundreds? With each, more rock tumbling into the ditch, more dust thrown into the air. The bombardment seemed to slacken toward morning; maybe the enemy needed sleep too, but Pietru was unsure for he could no longer tell the difference between waking and dreaming.

Of a sudden, shouting everywhere; Nardo was shaking his shoulder. Pietru could hardly make out a thing thro' the unbearable ringing in his head. Nardo pointed. Blinking his eyes, Pietru peered thro' a hole, only in the next instant to have a ball glance off his helmet. The instant was enough. The Turks had captured the ravelin.

"By the Lord Jesus!" he shouted, hearing only a muffled voice. "How did that happen?"

Yakhshi was astonished. Two engineers, gasping for breath, had just scrambled over the counterscarp and into his trench, pointing with amazement toward the enemy ravelin. "Take the ravelin now!" the first whispered. "There isn't a moment to lose!"

"What are you blabbering about?" exclaimed Yakhshi.

The same one, Kubad, answered that when the bombardment had slackened, he and Durmush went thro' the ditch to inspect the damage to the fort. Somehow they managed to creep all the way to the ravelin without being seen. "The guards must be asleep," they whispered to each other in bewilderment. Kubad motioned Durmush onto his shoulder, who peered through a port hole for one of the enemy guns. Sure enough, the infidel sentries were snoring away, dead to the world. The two engineers quickly ran back to the trenches and told the nearest *boluk-bashi* what they had found.

Yakhshi saw at once this was their chance. "On your feet, now!" he shouted to his men, waving them forward. "Get going, dog, or I'll fuck your mother on her way to the Ka'ba!" The men cheered and poured thro' the breach they had made in the counterscarp.

Pietru shook his head in disbelief. Before his eyes, the soldiers who had manned the ravelin were hurtling themselves across the bridge into the fort, while the janissaries climbed onto that work and into the ditch around it. Hundreds of them swarmed in, cheering, yelling, screaming.

Sluggishly summoning his leaden limbs to life, Pietru emptied his arquebus into the ditch. The cannoneers nearest to him wrestled with the heavy piece to get a shot at the foe, but Ix-Xabaw knew only moments remained before the Turks would storm the fortress.

The drummers were beating the alarm everywhere. Balthazar saw the fifty men who had guarded the ravelin run across the bridge into the fort and was instantly on his feet. He clapped on his helmet and grabbed his *montante*. Old Juan de Guaras, Bailiff of Negroponte, was already summoning the Knights forward.

"Men, today we sell our lives for Christ! Forward!"

"Allah!" the janissaries' cries filled the air as they stormed the bridge.

"*Alla!*" Pietru cried in return and unloaded his gun again. He ducked behind what was left of the parapet, cursing that there were no traverses on this fort; otherwise he might get a safe shot into the ditch. *Thhppp.* To the crackle of arquebuses, balls and arrows already whizzed in every direction.

Balthazar sped up the rampart and onto the bridge, swinging his sword. He sliced a janissary in half and the entrails flew in every direction as the infidel's eyes continued to stare for an instant in disbelief. With an animal grunt, the Knight took a head from another and a leg from a third. Negroponte and Mas were steps away, doing no less of a job, already covered from head to foot with pieces of flesh, as he was, and the arquebusiers on the ramparts were exposing themselves everywhere to fire. The bridge to the ravelin was thick with foemen: loose-robed janissaries, mail-covered spahis with pointed helmets, bucklers in one hand and scimitars or axes in the other. Below him, the ditch was swarming with the same, and more insects pouring in every moment. Balthazar did not deceive himself that the Knights could turn back this tide. Truly, from the corner of his eye he saw the entire Turkish army in motion. It was as if a sea were rising, swelling, about to inundate the fort, an infinite sea of colors, banners, pikes, lances, archers, horsemen, ladders. The only chance lay in the narrowness of the bridge.

An arrow pinged off Balthazar's breastplate but he hardly paused for breath, pressing forward into the mass. Negroponte was at his side. He shouted something to Balthazar, but he couldn't hear, for at that moment the gunners atop the cavalier let off two shots directly into the ditch. The wall of screams was pierced by shrieks whilst dismembered arms and legs flew into the air as had a juggler tossed them.

They were now twenty or thirty Knights on the bridge, surrounded. The foe ahead of them and in the ditch below; arquebusiers and gunners behind. A galley was scarcely more crowded; where to swing a sword? Balthazar grappled with a janissary, startled him by yanking off his headdress and twisting it around his throat; he lifted that one bodily from his feet and hurled him into the ditch, impaling him on the upright pikes. Negroponte snatched up a short battle axe and with a whoosh split open the skull of his opponent like a melon. Scrapings of steel against steel, steel plunging into flesh, bones cracking. The wood of the bridge had become slippery with blood and tissue.

They made no headway to the ravelin.

"We can't reach it!" Adorno shouted.

"If we can't retake the ravelin the fort is lost!" de Guaras cried and smashed his mailed fist into the apple of a foeman's throat, shattering it.

They fought hand to hand; the sun rose. An hour had gone by. At each moment the old pain pierced Balthazar's side. How can we keep it up against these legions? At once a pause in the fighting opened, spread. The Knights caught their breaths, convinced the enemy was retreating. A miracle, truly. Only moments later did they understand no miracle was at hand: The Turks were only bringing their fascines into the ditch to protect them from the arquebus fire. And bringing ladders.

The storming took up again with redoubled fury.

"Aah!" screamed Negroponte as an arrow hit his thigh and blood spurted over Balthazar. Balthazar put his arm under the Bailiff's shoulder and helped him back across the bridge. At that instant a scimitar came down on his own leg, taking a gash from it. Balthazar swung his arm and clubbed his attacker with his *montante*, caught the Bailiff again; together they limped back into the fort.

Negroponte's wound was serious; he'd be out of action for some time. Balthazar laid him down by the wall, bandaged his own leg and climbed back up to the ramparts. The day was already hot in every respect. By now

Balthazar felt the sweat running down his gambeson and the dirt and blood caked on his face, legs. Each breath seared his lungs but the gods granted no heartbeat wherein to rest. The Turks climbed their ladders now. Balthazar pushed a severed arm from a stone atop one of the crumbling parapets, grabbed the stone and hurled it down; found another. A top of a ladder appeared; Balthazar crouched, put shoulder to it and shoved. A Turk appeared, he snapped the neck with his boot. Moments, hours. Too many bodies now covered the ramparts; Balthazar and his fellows hurled them over.

Not many steps away, Ix-Xabaw lit one of the *granadas* we had fashioned and threw down the clay pot into the ditch. Another and another. The explosions were drowned out by the sacra next to him. Most of the guns by today had been dismounted, but the cannoneers wrestled with them, blocked them up on any stone available until their muzzles were pointed almost straight down.

"*Fuego!*"

"*Fuego!*"

"*Fuego!*"

The cries seemed endless, but Pietru could hardly hear anything now. He stopped his ears with cloth but it only seemed to make things worse. When he ran out of *granadas*, he overturned the pots of flaming oil and resin that others had brought up and watched the attackers' robes burst into flame. He launched the fireworks against the waves coming at him. They sputtered, hissed, they flew in mad spirals. Some hit their mark and exploded in a shower of sparks that briefly glittered in the blue sky. Cinders fell, burning Ix-Xabaw's skin.

Yakhshi had never in his life seen men fight with such desperation. He'd been on the bridge and with his men forced the Knights to give up their hopeless attempt to retake the outer platform, this ravelin. The dogs retreated back into the fort, but that was four hours ago. Since then, with his wheel-lock he'd been taking down any careless opponent on the wall and his men had charged time and again, with spirit, with bravery. *Allah!* Yet somehow they had not gained the ramparts. The day was warm and Yakhshi couldn't understand how those Knights could fight covered in metal, but as he watched the bodies of his men pile up in the ditch below the walls, he grudgingly conceded some admiration for the demons before him. As his throat became parched and breathing labored, he slowly perceived they would not take Santarma today. He was almost relieved when the drummers beat the retreat. The *yenicheriler* had kept the ravelin, and that truly was a welcome sign.

Towards evening, when the men rejoined their *boluklar* and *ortalar* to be counted, Yakhshi was astonished to learn that five hundred *yenicheriler* had fallen and another thousand had been wounded. Mustafa was furious when he heard the attack had failed. "You were to have taken this fort in three days!" he shouted to the officers of *yenicheriler* who had gathered at headquarters. "It is now a week! You call yourselves Sons of the Sultan? By Allah, prove it!"

Turgut was no less incensed but immediately commanded that the *yenicheriler* build up the ravelin. He then raised another matter: "Why haven't you placed guns on the spur south of the big harbor where the infidels hang criminals? Do so, and we can batter the Santarma tower from every side and prevent succours from gaining the fort."

With a bow Piyale opposed the plan. "Turgut, *Hazretleriniz*, should we put guns on that spur, I foresee that each day the barbarians will make sorties from the big fortress to dismount and spike the pieces, and I will have to assign a large patrol of galleys to protect them."

The angry response was swift: "I say to you, Piyale, who has left his daring with a concubine in Constantinople, that as long as succours and reinforcements reach that fort, we will not take it. Mount some pieces on that empty rock."

All the damned smoke despoiled the *Via Lactia*, thought Balthazar as he leaned against the wall of the keep with Juan de Guaras, helmet and sword by him. Everywhere on the crowded piazza men sat—lay— bloodied, exhausted, broken. A trail of blood led into the nearby chapel. de Bridiers had been shot thro' the chest, refused to allow his brethren to waste time tending him, crawled into the chapel and died at the altar. "Don't worry," Balthazar said, glancing at the arrow in the Bailiff's thigh, "you'll soon be at the Infermeria."

Negroponte grimaced, shaking his head. "No, I will not leave the fort."

"I'll be certain a surgeon is sent at once," Balthazar replied, not attempting to persuade the Bailiff.

Truly, Negroponte made no complaint. "We did well today, Navarre. What? Twenty Knights and sixty soldiers. How many wounded?"

Balthazar didn't know. Some hundreds. But they had done more than well; what had transpired this day bordered on the miraculous. Balthazar could hardly understand it himself. By what means had they repulsed those infinite numbers for five hours? His friend Francisco would probably credit armor and the Venetian Arsenale. That couldn't be all, Balthazar knew, that couldn't be all. He also knew that they would needs be summon yet greater strength, for more assaults were assured.

As to confirm his fears, one of the sentries shouted down that the Turks were already carrying earth-filled sacks and goatskins to the ravelin.

"They're building it up to the height of the fort," said de Guaras to Balthazar, then waved at some nearby arquebusiers and musketeers. "Clear them off. Now!" The men hurried to obey.

Shortly the gunfire started, persisted. Balthazar could not discern how successful either side was.

Not long after, another commotion arose—this time at the *porta del soccorso*. Soon, a few guards approached Negroponte by torchlight, leading a Knight with some comrades. When the newcomer neared, Balthazar saw that it was Fra Rafael Salvago, who the Grand Master had sent to Sicily a week ago. He had returned with the older Colonel Miranda, who had been there as a private adventurer raising troops.

"By the Fires of Hades!" exclaimed the Bailiff as the cannonading took up again, "what are you two doing here?"

Glancing about at the state of the fort, Salvago shook his head, bewildered in spite of himself. "We sailed back and forth along the coast," answered Salvago, "but finding many Turkish ships—"

"Turgut has arrived."

Salvago nodded heavily. "We couldn't put the galley ashore anywhere, so we launched a small *fregata* straight for the spur of St. Elmo and nobody noticed us."

"By Jesus!" Negroponte snorted again, "another miracle. Well, the Turks have been distracted today." He told Salvago and Miranda of the battle.

By now the relief boats from Birgu had begun to arrive. Balthazar got slowly to his feet and made toward the *porta del soccorso*. He intended to have his own wound treated at the Infermeria and return later, but the evacuation proceeded slowly. Two hundred soldiers needed to be gotten on those boats and by now the Turks had roused themselves against the nightly relief. I was among the oarsmen and as we rowed furiously across the Port, fire from the cave and Sciberras tore up the water around us. Our haste proved not for nothing and we gained St. Elmo with only one man killed.

I gazed about the fort. It was dark, but as I pressed my hands to my ears with each *thump-boom, thump-thump boom* of the guns, I could see that the Turks had been feasting on St. Elmo. The torches and cresses revealed rubble everywhere, the cavalier battered, parapets knocked thro' with holes. The walls held yet, but with only some store rooms and barracks to shelter in, men had thrown themselves everywhere amongst the mountains of supplies, or sometimes walked about aimlessly, crossing this macabre landscape like the spectres they were to become.

"Balthazar!" I exclaimed on catching sight of him limping toward the sea gate. "Look at you! Let me help."

Reluctantly he allowed me to put his arm under his shoulder. While we got to the boats the he recounted to me what had taken place. I could scarce credit my ears. "People will tell this story for ages."

"The story is not done," Balthazar replied laconically.

Looking into the Knight's dulled eyes, I knew I must do more than I had, but said nothing as we evacuated the wounded under enemy fire.

When in the dead of night the first boats reached Kalkara and we began carrying the two hundred wounded up to the Hospital, Dr. Jean descended to greet us. He stood by the main door holding a lamp, hurrying in the limping soldiers or those we bore on shoulders, planks and blankets. But when his light gradually revealed the numbers, he held up his hand. "Forgive me," he said, "there is no more room. I have spoken to the Grand Master. We shall open the ... auberges. Come."

Thus following Vigo we carried the wounded to their proper auberges and kicked the sleeping Knights out of their beds to make room for those who had survived the day's battle. Physicians, surgeons and the German Knights, who were on nursing duty this day, began arriving at once.

"You are tired," I said to the doctor. "You must rest."

"No, Francisco," he shook his head, "I must learn to live without sleep, for none will be forthcoming. I do not believe e'en that infidel potion coffee is the required miracle."

"What is?" I asked.

Vigo paused, searching for an answer, but found none in his weariness; mayhap none was to be found. He smiled faintly and saw to his duties.

The exhausted Salvago and Miranda found de Valette and Romegas in the Palace sitting at the Grand Master's table. When the Knights entered, the Commander and Monsignore started; de Valette rose instantly with the severest frown.

"Fra Rafael," he said at once, attempting to hide what Salvago had already discerned—that he had been sleeping at his place, "you have returned from Sicilia. The news from Don Garcia?"

Catching his breath, not at the journey but at the force of the question, Salvago bowed. "The Vice Roy promises the relief will sail by the twentieth of this month—and he requests that you send him five galleys."

The glance de Valette cast at Salvago averred someone was mad. "Five galleys!" he shouted, pounding one fist into the other hand and leaving no doubt in anyone's mind that *somnus* was behind him. "The twentieth! Such impudence ... ! Do you understand what is happening at Fort St. Elmo?"

"Indeed," replied Salvago, yet taken aback, "we came by the fort."

It was now Romegas who shot a disbelieving glance at the messengers. But recounting the miracle wherewith they had gained St. Elmo, Salvago and Miranda then told His Eminence that the ravelin had been captured. For a moment they thought de Valette would not stand. He seemed to totter, steadying himself with one hand on the table, and they rushed to put a cup of water to his lips, but he waved them off. "Tell me," he said.

They related what they knew of the day, that his men had fought with valor beyond valor. "But the state of the place," Miranda conceded, "worsens by the hour. Eminenza, you cannot deceive yourself that Fort St. Elmo can hold out for long. Only five hundred men can fight; natheless I am willing to return to see what can be done."

"Good," de Valette nodded, having imposed himself a measure of restraint. "The men revere you greatly, Colonel. Take your company thither at once, take charge of the fort and give me a full report about what further succours are needed. Fra Rafael, you will return to Sicilia this evening. Inform Toledo I do not have one galley to spare, yet alone five, and that we cannot wait three weeks. If St. Elmo falls ... I want five hundred men at once. Bring them yourself if you must—"

"St. Aubin is raising troops as we speak. The *patrona* is available—"

"St. Aubin gained Sicilia then?"

Salvago nodded, sensing the roving eyes of Argos.

"Where is the *S. Giacomo*? You cannot return whence you came."

"No, we told the Captain to wait at Gozo."

"Good. Travel by Notabile. I shall give you dispatches for Vincenzo di Anastagi there."

"You'll need men," said Romegas. "Take Blaij Vergã. He's reliable."

"And your uncle?" de Valette said finally, as to ensure Salvago he had not forgotten.

"His Holiness promises every aid. He will open the stores of St. Angelo Castle in Rome and is raising a fleet."

Hereat the Grand Master's eyes did bore into Salvago. "Who will command?"

"G ... Gian Andrea, almost certainly."

And at once de Valette exploded. "*Doria?* The shit-faced son of a whore who almost destroyed Christendom at Gelves with his cowardice!" He paused for an instant, darkly. "We are doomed."

"Eminenza," Salvago ventured, "Gian Andrea must be anxious to atone for his sins. He is five years older. I believe Don Garcia intends to ask Alvaro de Sande to command the foot."

"de Sande," Valette breathed. "Good. There is hope."

At that instant everyone understood that the ghost of Djerbé had never been laid to rest. Nay. Vengeance is mine.

A silence at last fell and the four turned to the door, where Isabella Guasconi stood, having brought a plate of food for the Monsignore. "Excuse me, Messeri," she said, curtsying, "I could not but overhear. Fra Rafael, would you carry to Sicilia or Rome some dispatches I have penned? Europe must know what is happening on Malta."

de Valette nodded, accepting the plate and giving half to his lioness under the table. "This is a good plan."

Salvago agreed to collect the dispatches at Señora Guasconi's home before his departure at nightfall.

Eighty-Three

What I had seen in Fort St. Elmo hours ago left me beside myself with fury. "How can I watch those men sit in that place as the walls crumble about them and they face certain death at the hands of barbarians?" I said to Flaminia in the morning as we made fire hoops at the St. Angelo mill.

The *quiraca* gazed at me in a forlorn way, answering simply that my post, my duties, were here. I let go the stick in my hand wherewith I had been stirring a mixture for *granadas* in a big pot. Posts? Aye, we'd been assigned posts, but with so few amongst us, every person became three. I prepared weapons, aided the relief of St. Elmo and fruitlessly bombarded the enemy atop Sciberras. Flaminia herself yet carried dirt for the fortifications, tho' more often she was by me, preferring the lighter work I gave her here. Insensible to my distraction and with her words interrupted by the ever-present thunder, she asked me whether it was true that slave girls danced in the taverns of Constantinople.

"Yes, it is true," I said.

Some men began shouting from the harbor side of St. Angelo and I went over to find that one of our pieces had just been dismounted. With guns aplenty the Turks had again trained a battery on this fortress as well as on the platform Don Sanoguera was building on the spur of Senglea. All our work proceeded only because Fort St. Elmo was dying. "What do these duties matter?" I said to Flaminia, returning to the mill. "What do they matter?"

She placed her hand on my arm; I tore it away.

Later, well after complines, I went to Isabella's house. We'd seen naught of each other since that useless evening when she had the old witch recite Soliman's poetry. How long ago it was I already couldn't remember. Isabella herself met me at the door, holding her lamp up to me strangely, as she did not know the grime-covered man standing before her.

Natheless, she bid him enter. Her negro boy-slave was at her side. The sight of this infidel urchin suddenly enraged me beyond comprehension. I picked him up by his neck, garroting him with my two hands, screaming that should St. Elmo fall, I would flay his skin from his body and quarter him with my own knife.

"Stop, Señor, Stop!" Isabella shouted, attempting to wrest me from him.

For some heartbeats we struggled, with this slave-boy yet in my hands. At last I dropped him. With all her strength, Isabella pushed me to the door. "Out of my house, you common brute! Never set foot in it again!"

I staggered off, and for the first time in fifteen years sought out Flaminia to share her bed.

After I'd gone, Isabella collapsed onto the stairs to the upper floor in tears, convulsing. She thrashed about, pounding her fist on the steps, unable to breathe. Her chest constricted as that fury and anger shot up within, at once paralyzing her and causing her to shiver from head to toe. She sat, feeling her brow, her flushed face; a fever must be on her. At each moment the windows rattled; a cup tottered and fell from the board in the dining room, shattering.

"Madonna!" she cried out, "I cannot bear it any longer!" Isabella pressed her hands to her head, certain she was losing her mind. Abruptly rising to her feet, she wandered into the big room and knelt in the corner to pray; horrified, she watched the icon of the Virgin fall from its shelf, breaking in two. With agitation only heightened, she grasped a candle and fled to the cellar, there mindlessly checking the cistern and marking the water level on the long stick. This small act calmed her enough that she breathed again. That it was cooler and the trembling perceptibly less down below stilled her further, enough that she glanced at the mark she had made on the stick. The water, she guessed, would last the household another two months, if it had not gone foul.

Isabella sat in the dark cellar for some time, calmer but not calm, unable to take herself in hand, unable to comprehend why she had left Florence, unable even to remember what life had been like three weeks ago. All she saw were a jumble of scenes: the Hospital, searching the streets for fresh food with her servants, buying beef from peasants who somehow yet brought meat in from the countryside, streets crowded with thieves and beggars, butchers selling dog meat, everyone buying it at prices that were highway robbery. Every tenth word stolen by a roar from the guns, roars that ceased rarely day or night, that continued now: *Thump, thump-thump.*

After some moments Isabella noticed she was breathing again. She took a deep breath, assured herself that she had mastered her wits and went upstairs. Giansevere, as usual, was lying on the divan, below the portrait by Bronzino. The crone slept little, but Isabella was certain that she was determined to fight off the hovering Angel of Death to the last. With ever greater wrath she cursed her worthless son and now babbled about something in tones familiar enough that Isabella could guess.

"She speaks of Soliman," the boy-slave by her said. "Oh, how Soliman loved Hurrem! He married her and had children with her, against all the rules of the Harem! It was true love. Never has a sultan so loved!"

"Still Soliman!" Isabella loathed this old, toothless witch with her hideous gums, no less the treacherous slave who rendered her words. "Do you hear those cannon?" she erupted at both of them. "That is the love of your sultan!"

But the nurse had already passed to some world deaf to the rumbling that swept across the harbor, for she merely asked, "What is that noise?"

"That is our death, granny!"

A smile of serenity crossed Giansevere's face and her contentment angered Isabella so much that she rushed to the cellar once more and sat there for an hour. When, well after *l'hora della ruffiana*, Salvago and his party appeared at her door to request her dispatches, Isabella said abruptly, "I'm coming with you to Notabile."

"Señora," replied Salvago, only dimly perceiving Isabella's state, "that is hardly advisable. The risk is great."

Thereat Blaij Vergã stepped up upon the threshold, equally ignorant of what had just transpired. "It is not so great, Señor," he said pleasantly. "Maltese peasants still roam about the countryside. Señora's mother is in the Old City. Better that we should accompany her than she should travel herself."

"Thank you, Señor Vergã," Isabella nodded curtly and Salvago yielded. Isabella gave terse instructions to her servants that she would return on the morrow and sent one of them to apologize to those at the Auberge of Italy for her absence from the Hospital. She handed her dispatches to Salvago and took another deep breath as the five of them set forth on foot.

They made their way under the lyre and bright swan first south, then west. Salvago commanded everyone to silence, which to Isabella was just as well, for she had no wish to speak and no desire to hear from Vergã's lips the reasons he was so eager for her company. They traveled for an hour under the sounds of distant artillery without encountering a soul. The Turks had seemingly abandoned this part of the island. Not far from the tiny villages where the barbarians had first established camp, one of the men suddenly halted, thinking he spied some shadows stirring in the distance. With a finger to his lips, Salvago ordered everyone behind some rocks and sent two of the soldiers out. A few steps away, one of them paused to remove a burning match from its cylinder and fix it on his arquebus. Descrying this, Vergã grabbed the pike that had been with him and ran into the field.

"What are you doing?" he whispered harshly. "Idiot!"

He tried to snatch the fuse away from the other but—too late. They were spotted. The enemy scouts opened up and an arrow instantly nicked Vergã in the arm. With no more than a glance at it, he tightened his grip on the pike in his hands and ran screaming against the foe. The others followed yelling, not two steps behind. It was a furious skirmish of spears, spears, swords and guns, but it lasted only moments. Vergã ran one of the Rumelian leopard-men thro' with the javelin. Two others went down under rapiers and the last scrambled away as the arquebuses sent balls over him.

"Come, we move quickly," said Salvago when it was over.

"Let me see the wound," said Isabella, discerning that Vergã's arm was dripping with blood. The incident had abruptly carried her far from her earlier humor and she felt fully possessed of herself.

"It is nothing," he replied, "the arrow merely grazed me."

Isabella bound it with a kerchief, wondering that Vergã had likely saved her life a second time. "Here, Messer," she said, finding a small irony in the circumstance, "you requested a lady's token. Now you have one."

Vergã bowed, smiling, and basking in the kerchief's perfume. "Thank you, Señora. Be assured, I shall wear it always."

As it had done before, the evident sincerity in his voice disarmed Isabella; natheless she said, with slightly more gravity, "It is a dressing for your wound, Señor; do not presume to see in it anything more."

Fearing a larger party of Turks might be upon them, they sped along the barren paths, espying nothing more than some hares darting into the brush. Another hour or two passed before they gained the Old City. As they approached the gates a boy challenged them from above and, when they identified themselves, said they might enter. On this rise, nearly three leagues from the harbor, they paused to watch the sky above Fort St. Elmo throb with light; e'en here the thunder was fearful enough to scare away unwary travelers from the island. Otherwise Notabile was quiet in the dead of night but for the subdued conversation of the watch.

"Will you pause at our house for refreshment, Fra Rafael?" asked Isabella, suddenly realizing they had arrived safely.

"With pleasure," the other bowed, "but for a moment only."

They walked the short distance to the Guasconi home. Isabella unlocked the door with her key, only to be met by the loud snoring of men. Instantly the entire household came alive, with candles being lit and soldiers fumbling about for their swords. A servant climbed up from the cellar with a lamp in her hands and Lady Emilia herself appeared at the head of the stairs wearing a night dress. "Who has broken into our house?" she said with alarm, as two soldiers, sleeping on the sitting room floor, got to their feet. "Thieves!"

"Mother, it is I, your daughter."

"Isabella!" Lady Emilia exclaimed, rushing down the stairs and holding a candle up before Isabella's face. "By the mercy of God!"

They kissed and, in the dim light of wax and oil, introductions were made. As a disheveled man of about thirty-five with a full, dark beard emerged grunting from the guest room in back, Emilia said, "Isabella, allow me to present Fra Vincenzo di Anastagi, who has been placed in charge of the cavalry here."

"Señora," that one bowed groggily as Isabella uncertainly extended her hand.

"Fra Vincenzo," Isabella returned, curtsying in the darkness, "I suspect you and Fra Rafael are acquainted."

"Of course," Anastagi grunted. "Salvezza, what news?"

Salvago told him of the assault on Fort St. Elmo and that he was at this moment speeding to Sicilia. Anastagi nodded, replying that there had been a rather large cavalry skirmish yesterday as well. Unfortunately, Salvago could not tarry to hear about it. Isabella ordered the servants to

bring food and wine. Only a few moments after, Anastagi detailed a small
party to accompany Fra Rafael to the coast and the horses were readied.

While the others were talking, Vergã took Isabella aside and said
urgently to her, "Señora, I would save you from danger once again, your
mother as well, if you would accompany us to Sicily. Now is the moment.
Don't lose it."

For an instant Isabella felt the sharpest temptation to flee with him and
gazed openly into those piercing eyes. Nothing beckoned more strongly
than Firenze. Freeing herself with a start, she touched his arm and declined
with the sincerest gratitude. Thereat, the courier and his men vanished
into the night.

At the sun, Lady Emilia served a sumptuous breakfast for Anastagi and
his lieutenants. Rested but alarmed, Isabella took her mother aside.
"Mother," she whispered, "it cannot be wise to be so profligate with food.
Has it not been rationed?"

"Shush," Emilia responded. "Not yet. And for one meal we may pretend
life goes on."

Pretend life goes on. Vergã had said as much, yet, sitting at the table,
Isabella remained speechless with astonishment at precisely how peacefully
life did appear to go on in Notabile. Yes, cannon fire from the harbor
echoed thro' the streets and soldiers clanked by the windows, but the fact
that her mother was serving a proper meal, that the air smelled more of
animals than people, that beggars didn't pound at the door each moment,
that more cows seemed to be slumbering on the squares than peasants—
all this struck Isabella with the force of a wonder. She glanced at her
mother. "Mama, you have made a remarkable recovery in the past weeks.
The country air agrees with you."

"I am feeling very much better, thank you," replied Emilia and asked
Isabella to tell everything that had happened in the Borgo.

"I'd prefer not to," she answered, glancing downward. Instead she
grasped her lute from the corner where she had left it and, as she struck
up a tune, begged Anastagi to speak of the situation in Città Vecchia.

The man sitting across from her exuded confidence surpassing his
middle height, and his reputation for an acute intelligence had preceded
this meeting. "Illustrious lady," Vincenzo Anastagi said with a flourish
to the lightening music, "willingly do I obey your command. As you

know, when Melchor de Guaras was wounded, the Grand Master dispatched me hither to lead the cavalry. I have also relieved Governor Mezquita of many of his duties, as Fra Pedro is old. No one can pretend that the same peril confronting the harbor afflicts us here. As you see—" he spread his hands, adding naught more. "Of course, should St. Angelo and St. Michel fall, Notabile will quickly be reduced to ashes."

For an instant Isabella broke off playing, wishing she had taken up Vergã's offer. "Signore, it is safe here for the moment?" she said.

"For the moment, certainly. Supplies are plentiful; the water is good. A thousand women and children see to our meals and ammunition. We have five companies of soldiers from the parishes sleeping in the stables outside the walls and nearly three hundred horses—far more than the number of horsemen." Anastagi briefly reflected. "That could change."

"I have heard reports of action," Isabella said, hesitantly taking up the tune again, reluctant to ask for details.

Anastagi unhesitatingly provided them. "Every day we skirmish with the enemy." What he described next seemed to Isabella somewhat more. "An escaped negro slave told the Turks that a hundred Maltese were hiding in caves south of here and the barbarians went after them. When de Guaras and I learned this, we at once rode out towards Tartarni. It is true—these Maltese live in caves, hardly better than savages, but the Turks couldn't get at them in that extraordinary warren of grottos and retreated north toward Mosta village."

Isabella found the thought of the Maltese living in caves both curious and repellent. Not for the first time was she struck by how little she knew of, had in common with, the islanders she had lived among much of her life. "Had not de Guaras been previously wounded?" she asked, absently finding a chord.

Anastagi nodded, grasping a cup of wine with one hand. "What do such things mean? We approached Mosta with one hundred horse—all we have—and suddenly find ourselves faced with—four hundred Turks.

"Fortunately Giovanni Vañon and his eighty arquebusiers joined us. The enemy, though, had chained up some prisoners and cattle near a fountain at the village center, and any attack would risk killing the captives and the livestock. We decided Vañon should circle with his men around to the other side of Mosta and creep up on the Turks from the rear.

Vañon's men opened fire, the infidels were pissing into the air—*pardon,* Signora—and retreated straight into the arms of my charging cavalry."

"Then you made short work of the barbarians," said Isabella and put aside her instrument altogether. The harshness of her voice surprised even her.

"Not entirely, Illustrious Lady," Anastagi said.

The fight went on for four hours, arrows and balls whizzing everywhere about the peasants, who cringed by the fountain. Spring had ended and weapons and armor were becoming hot to the touch. Underjerkins, gambesons, were soaked with sweat. de Guaras left the fray after a shaft hit him in his good leg. Anastagi watched a Maltese, Luca, capturing Turks. The exceptional swordsman would feint with his rapier and when the foeman slashed at it with his scimitar, he'd knock him down. Watching Luca, Anastagi wondered whether he had discovered the secret *botta*, the philosopher's stone of all *duellanti*, and thought the fellow might be useful.

"Finally," concluded Anastagi, "the foe withdrew, leaving over eighty dead or wounded. We pursued them to the coast, but saw some Turkish ships putting into St. Paul's Bay, and so we retired hither to Notabile. We lost eight men with thirty wounded, but managed to free the prisoners, and Luca took a few slaves."

"Did you learn anything of value from them?" Isabella asked in the same tone.

Anastagi helped himself to some grapes. "That the Turks are surprised at the resistance greeting them, but that Dragut's arrival has lifted their spirits and that Mustafa is determined to prevail."

"The very thought of Dragut on this island makes me shudder," put in Emilia, actually shuddering. Isabella agreed, saying she wished to see Dragut's carcass filled with sand and nailed to the town gates.

"Truly," chuckled Anastagi, "Dragut is their most fearful weapon. Without him, I have not the slightest concern. These azabs and spahis are the worst sort of rabble who have come only for plunder. With some small help from Don Garcia, I see no difficulty in defeating them. Why no more music, milady?"

Isabella ignored the request. "If no relief arrives?" she asked with rising tenor.

Anastagi shrugged radiantly and gulped down his wine. "We will defeat them ourselves ... Afterwards I shall have my portrait painted. Titian, I think."

Just then a child ran in, saying he'd seen a puff of smoke from St. Angelo. Rising with a bow, Anastagi excused himself to prepare the cavalry to investigate. After he'd gone, Isabella breathed deeply and turned to her mother. "He is very certain of himself, is he not?"

"Yes," said Emilia brightly, "he convinces me everything shall be all right."

For a moment Isabella stared hard at her mother. "Mama, you cannot deceive yourself here in Mdina that all is well. Each of those distant cannon shots is a horror being rained down upon Fort St. Elmo."

Lady Emilia got to her feet, agitatedly. "I have ears. Let us speak of more pleasant matters."

"Mother, are you mad?" Isabella answered with outright disbelief. Yet in the same instant she recalled her panic in this very house fourteen summers ago and, more sharply, yesterday's struggle with that same panic, which she henceforth would never be able to deny, but which she vowed again to banish.

"What news of Parisot?" Emilia said.

Isabella glanced at the bowl of flowers on the table and said, truly, de Valette's strength during this trial was frightening to behold. "God has touched him, but the price will be high—for everyone. You should have gone to Sicilia, Mama."

"You know how ill I was," Emilia returned severely, "but now these few leagues separate us and I can be of no comfort to him. I do miss my crusty soldier. You shall stay here, Isabella. Anastagi has promised to house his lieutenants elsewhere and there will be room enough."

"No, Mama." Isabella glanced about, still unable to grasp the nearly placid scene about her. "I must steel myself and return. I am needed and if you cannot be at my—Parisot's side, I must. I shall beg Anastagi for an escort, that I may return tonight." Ignoring the horror writ on her mother's face, Isabella grasped her lute and walked out into the town. She cast a long, sinful gaze in the direction of Firenze, regarded with despair and loathing a boy-slave who crossed her path, walked on to discover what peace she might for the few hours that she might.

Eighty-Four

As the *S. Giacomo* approached Messina, a weary Rafael Salvago stood on the poop with Blaij Vergã, gazing at the placid, moonlit sea. He did not for a moment gainsay the necessity of his exhaustion. "Every moment I think of those poor souls trapped in St. Elmo," he said to Vergã; the splash of the oars was the only sound to be heard, "and I count myself fortunate."

"Each man carries out his assigned duties," shrugged Blaij.

Salvago regarded this man with whom he was only moderately acquainted. "Carrying out duties will not win this fight," he replied. Then, glancing at the bandage tied around the other's arm, he remarked, smiling, "I think you will carry that token with you long after your wound is healed, eh?"

Blaij chuckled. "I would win Lady Guasconi, why not? She is a great prize."

"Do you wish to win her or to destroy your rival?"

"Barai? I am astounded he still walks. It is his protector, tho', Fra Balthazar, who has insulted and threatened me too often." Hereat Vergã shrugged again. "For fifteen years I have added slaves and booty to the Order's coffers. Why should Lady Guasconi not view me with favor?"

The galley was now sliding into the harbor of Messina and the crew readying for landing. "Yes, I recall you have been offered a Greek bride—"

"Several. An Armenian as well—"

"—and that the Turks have long a price on your head."

Vergã gazed off beyond their destination. "She is an angel beyond compare. When I have saved her, I have felt ... " He faltered. "Worthier. When I am with her I cannot wear my hat, even outdoors."

"All the same," smiled Salvago, "you shall not have Isabella Guasconi, any more than Barai shall."

Thereon Vergã glanced at Salvago in surprise. "Why not, Señor?"

Salvago continued to lean over the side as the *ciurma* raised its oars at the embankment. "Many have thrown themselves at her feet, but she gives her love to no one save her guardian." The Knight now turned, leaning with his back on the rail, facing Vergã. "Orphans are thus, are they not? A thing apart. Their hearts are not to be opened, try as one may, try as they may themselves."

"We have much in common, Isabella and I," Vergã replied. "She desires me; she has prayed for me, you know."

As the *S. Giacomo*'s gangplank went down, Salvago shook his head at his interlocutor and chuckled. "Man's eternal condition is one of delusion. I shall not presume to lecture you, Vergada, but put aside these small matters until the great trial that consumes us is decided. At this moment I'd say our survival is far from assured. Should we emerge alive, you are at liberty to make a buffoon of yourself. Now come, we have no time to waste."

Don Garcia de Toledo, yet in his nightshirt, received them at his residence without delay. Despite the hour Salvago lost not a moment in conveying the gravity of the situation. "Three days ago Fort St. Elmo withstood a Turkish assault. Our soldiers fought heroically, Your Excellency, but seeing the condition of the place and the forces arrayed against it, I cannot but doubt that St. Elmo must soon fall. It may have fallen already. I cannot express to you … " Salvago left off the remainder of his thought and handed the Vice Roy his dispatches. "We must have a relief at once. I repeat, at once."

"I told you by the twentieth," the Vice Roy yawned, walking heavily over to the desk. "And I requested five galleys."

"The twentieth is too late, do you understand me, Eccellenza?" Salvago observed Toledo break the seal of the letters and examine them under the candlelight. "Nor can Eminenza spare a single vessel. The Port is blockaded."

The messages would need to be deciphered, but the expression on the aging Vice Roy's face left no doubt he believed every one of Fra Rafael's words. "Señor," Don Garcia answered, sensibly more awake, "I well understand the gravity of the situation. Do you, Fra Rafael, understand the magnitude of the task assigned me? We have requested an entire squadron of nineteen ships under Alvaro de Bazán en route to Oran for this relief. It must return to Cartagena and ferry men to Mers-el-Kébir before proceeding to Barcelona ... God alone knows when it will get here! The same is true in one hundred other places. Gian Andrea in Napoli, the Lord of Piombino—they have offered seventeen ships." Don Garcia waved his arms angrily toward the harbor. "Do you see a one of them?" He had become heated, Toledo himself perceived, and he halted, daubing his brow with a handkerchief. "I have no ships, do you understand, Fra Rafael? That is the nut of it."

"Do you have men?" Salvago refused to retreat.

Don Garcia as well. "Not enough! Only four hundred have arrived in Zaragoza thus far."

"Is St. Aubin there?"

The Vice Roy nodded.

"Cornisson?"

"Yes, yes, in Zaragoza raising troops." The impatience in Toledo's voice went undisguised.

Salvago was scarcely less exercised. "Permit them, in that case, to ferry the four hundred to Malta and return to Zaragoza."

"Of what use are four hundred troops!" shouted the Vice Roy. "We need ten thousand!"

The Knight regarded Don Garcia now with slightly more calm. "Four hundred soldiers eager to fight are worth ten thousand who are not."

Toledo, tho', put his hands to his head, revealing other concerns. "Sicilia—and Italia—shall lie in the greatest peril should we throw troops against the Turk in drips and drops." He paused, gazing onto Salvago. "I am not an unreasonable man, Fra Salvago. Take them. And please, remember to address me as Eccellenza." Thereat the Vice Roy dismissed his nocturnal visitors.

Once they had descended to the dark street Vergã turned to Salvago. "Do you trust him? I think he is dissembling."

Fra Rafael glanced at his companion. "For what purpose? To gather a hundred galleys cannot be accomplished overnight. In that he is correct."

"Men can accomplish much when they have a will."

The two immediately boarded the S. Giacomo and proceeded with all haste south to Zaragoza. When they arrived the next day, they found St. Aubin with the Grand Master's nephew de Valette Cornisson, as well as the first company of adventurers who had arrived thither for the relief of

Malta. E'en before the two disembarked, Salvago gave Vergã his instructions: "You shall accompany their galleys and the soldiers back to Malta immediately. In the meantime I shall proceed to Naples and Rome—"

"You will speak with His Holiness?"

"Certainly."

"Then inquire after my dispensation, if you don't mind. I have waited far too long."

Salvago merely shook his head, saying that he would mention it should the opportunity arise.

Eighty-Five

We have entered the Inferno. Balthazar thought nothing else as he rowed furiously with Miranda's men across the Great Port in the before-dawn. The entire harbor shook, shuddered as cannon booms rolled over the water in every direction, bouncing from fort to mount to wall and again. The infidels were pummeling Fort St. Elmo from Sciberras as well as from Turgut's battery across Marsamxett. At the same time, Fort St. Angelo and Sanoguera's men on Senglea were hitting the Turkish platforms on Sciberras and—

"Starboard!"

The warning came too late. Spray covered everyone as a ball whizzed overhead, crashing into the water not ten armslengths off the barque Balthazar oared. Staring him in the face not a hundred paces to starboard were the muzzles of the pieces Turgut had overnight placed on Gallows' Point. That battery was not only attempting to send Miranda's company to Poseidon but hitting Fort St. Elmo from the south, while guns from St. Angelo were trained on Gallows' Point too, doing their best to dismount Turgut's new pieces. Another shower of spray; this time Balthazar jerked his head larboard. The light cannon and musket fire from Sciberras and the Alicate cave hadn't ceased either. On every side the flashes were visible, e'en as the sky brightened.

They passed thro' the haze of smoke and dust shrouding Fort St. Elmo, haze that burned the eyes and choked the lungs. Climbing thro' the sea grotto, Balthazar was hardly aware of the pain in his leg, which the doctors at the Auberge de France had cleaned, dressed and sewn in the dead of night. He hadn't slept and he could not remember such weariness. Only yesterday—so long ago it seemed—they'd fought off the Turkish assault for five hours. Only yesterday the Turks had captured the ravelin. Today ... Balthazar could not foresee what would face them. He worked plugs of candle wax into his ears as he stepped into the seventh circle and felt his gut rattle.

Inside, Balthazar at once perceived that no one here had slept either. The constant *crack-crack-thhpp* of gunfire echoed everywhere about the piazza. Soldiers on the Marsamxett side crawled back and forth along the curtain, firing against the captured ravelin. Cannoneers were dragging guns in the same direction. All around, weary and limping men carried stone and earth to terre-plein the walls and repair breaches that had opened. Miranda's company was still passing thro' the sea gate when an eighty-*libbre* ball roared into the cavalier and vomited the newest bite into the air. The Turks would never entirely level that mountain, but it took little to imagine a great tree stump beset by ants.

Seeing Miranda's presence, Mas, Medrano, Caravajal and other Knights came up to greet the famous Colonel, every one wanting to know whether he proposed to take charge of the fort.

"The Grand Master has requested it," Miranda humbly acknowledged against the tapestry of thunder, "but I am too old." He'd already divulged to Balthazar that when Parisot had pressed him, he had recoiled: "God forfend I should accept such a hopeless task, lest afterwards I should be held responsible for the loss of the fort." To those gathered about, Miranda said, "Sound the alarm and let us see the state of things."

Caravajal himself put his hand to the clapper. Those on the wall firing at the ravelin didn't respond. Most of the Knights ran at once for their posts. The common soldiers below scurried this way and that, only to finally throw up their arms, while the men on reserve got sluggishly to their feet and gazed about for the direction of the assault. "Yes," said Miranda. "I see." The tocsin's sharp clang natheless as if foretold that some action was presently to begin. "What's going on there?" Miranda pointed in the direction of the ravelin.

"I'll go," said Balthazar, leaving him with the others. He lumbered over to the Marsamxett side and mounted the steps to the curtain, where he spied Pietru among the line of arquebusiers.

"Lord Balthazar!" Ix-Xabaw shouted, "by God keep your head down!"

Balthazar bent below the crumbling parapets and slowly crawled over the blood-soaked rubble to the gun port where Pietru crouched. Across the ditch azabs were building up the ravelin with fascines and sacks filled with dirt. In a single night they had raised the tower nearly to the height of the fort itself. Dozens of janissaries lurked behind gabions on the work, picking off any soldier who raised his head above what was left of St. Elmo's parapets.

"How are you, Pietru?" Balthazar asked to the *craa—aak thhpp*.

"Better than some—" he pointed to a body nearby, "but when do we get relieved? I see two when I should see one." Now the Gozitan rubbed his eyes, stretched out his arm. "How many guns do you see there?"

Balthazar could make out a pair of heavy pieces sitting beyond the ditch. "Two," the Knight answered.

Pietru sighed. "I was praying I was just tired."

E'en in their exhaustion it took no thought to realize that the Turks intended to mount those guns atop the ravelin and bombard the fort from an armslength away. "Pietru, don't let them."

"Lord Balthazar," he said, shaking himself awake, "I do my best, but look there." Now the Gozitan pointed far off to the left and into the ditch. The wall blocked Balthazar's view, but the ringing of hammers let him decide that the pionniers were pounding ships' spurs into the rock at the base of the ditch—legs for a bridge.

"Pietru, I say again, don't let them." He put his hand on Ix-Xabaw's shoulder. "Remember most of all what I told you—when this fort falls, save yourself."

As they spoke, Mas himself climbed up to the ramparts before the spot whither Pietru had pointed. At once the Colonel saw the infernal scaffold being erected directly opposite his post on the northwest arm of the fort. In the same glance he also saw that the azabs were furiously picking at the walls—those sodomites intended to fix a mine. He didn't have much time, but there were no ports here—and no guns. Brusquely shaking off his own fatigue, Mas yelled for his men to pull down stones opposite the scaffold. At the same time he waved for his gunners to drag the nearest piece over, a demi-cannon.

"Chase the whores away!" he screamed.

The gunners charged the piece with stone and iron scraps, and as soon as the port was made, blasted at the azabs below. Musketeers crowded around too, hoping to cripple the bridge legs with their shot. Roars and crackles of every weapon shrouded the ramparts when a big fellow, Giovanni, brought up from the armory two of our fire pots tied to a pair of javelins and hurled them down at the scaffold. His throws were good and the spears lodged into the supports. An instant later the pots exploded, splintering half the scaffold's legs and the terrified shrieks of azabs added to the cacophony as they ran burning from the ditch. Mas sighed with relief, seeing that the Turks had abandoned their design.

To Balthazar he expressed little satisfaction as together they descended to the bailey. "The only question is, how soon will they be back?"

On the piazza a certain calm prevailed. The soldiers had by now roused themselves to come to grips with the situation and gathered around Miranda in the harsh sun. When Balthazar reported that the Turks would soon be mounting guns on the ravelin, Juan la Cerda, who stood among them, cursed, "I told you we should have mined it! If they mount those guns, we're done for! They'll be firing right onto this square." Vehemently he spat onto the ground. A Turkish cannon roared.

Balthazar could not gainsay the Captain, who had been right from the start. Strangely, most of the soldiers paid little attention. Each had his own complaints and all had one complaint:

"We haven't been paid!"

The shout was drowned out, so they repeated: "We haven't been paid!" In answer, two more great balls ploughed into the cavalier and one into the keep itself. Balthazar thought he saw a sentry atop the cavalier beheaded by flying rock.

Some men protested that the wine was running out.

"They are willing to die," Balthazar leaned over to old Miranda, "but they would prefer to die happy."

It was true. Even as iron now crashed into Fort St. Elmo as rain, day and night, the men demanded their wages. de la Cerda put in that they must be relieved, adding, "We should prepare to blow up the fort."

Mas and others about him nodded assent. Medrano, tho', had other ideas. "Señor de la Cerda is a self-serving coward," he barked. *Craaash*; one of the pieces on the ramparts fell to the piazza. "Anybody can see he just wants to save his skin."

Instantly la Cerda's sword was drawn, but Miranda interposed himself between the two antagonists. As the scene unfolded before him, Balthazar could not help recall Fuster long ago in Tripoli, on a day not so desperate as this one was fast becoming. The Colonel had wisely refused to accept responsibility for the fort, yet he also saw he must do something and now held up his hands before the troops, promising to send word to His Eminence forthwith that the soldiers demanded their pay. "And we will get some wine."

That seemed to satisfy most of these exhausted men. "Who's going to risk crossing the Port and hand such demands to the Grand Master?" one of the Knights scoffed derisively. At that moment, tho', a watchmen from the battered cavalier sped down to the piazza. Something was happening across the harbor. Everyone poured out the *porta del soccorso* to the grotto.

Directly across the mouth of the Great Port, Mareschal Copier advanced at the head of several companies of Knights, horse and foot. As the men at Fort St. Elmo watched, the Mareschal charged against the enemy gunners on Gallows' Point, cutting most of them to ribbons and chasing the rest into their boats.

Everyone gathered at St. Elmo raised what cheers they could and Miranda lost no time in sending a deputy across to the Grand Master.

The shadows in Fort St. Elmo diminished, lengthened. The men propped themselves up against the shuddering walls and caught what sleep they could. Towards evening, some wine barrels appeared at the sea gate accompanied by a priest and a strongbox. On Miranda's orders, the paymaster and the priest at once began distributing money.

"Whence the silver?" asked Balthazar, not believing the Grand Master had any to spare.

"The Bishop and some rich woman donated it."

"Cubelles?"

Miranda nodded and Balthazar crossed himself, knowing that of late God often called for strange bedfellows.

The wine and money did much to raise the men's spirits. Instantly they cleared out two of the store rooms and set up some gaming tables and a canteen within. Since the azabs left off their bridge, the percussion of the air had become constant, but it proved powerless to interfere with the rolling of the dice.

Caravajal, losing at cards, used the opportunity to tell everyone what he'd do when he finally laid his hands on Dragut: "I'll cane him to death, and when he's dead, I'll have him flea'd and his skin curry'd, and I'll make a drum out of it, which I'll beat twenty years after, that Dragut may remember me in the other world." *Boom.*

"Ramon," Balthazar said, picking from his cup the plaster from the ceiling that fell into it, "meseems you made the same threat fifteen years ago on Djerbé."

"Is that so?" returned Caravajal without a blush. "Well, then I'll only beat the drum for five."

The Abbé chuckled softly. For a time he continued to watch the game, uncertain whether he saw a noble contempt of death in these men or such a fear of it they turned the other way. The torches were being lit for the night now and Balthazar went to his post.

Pietru got no rest. All night the crack of musket and arquebus as they traded fire with the janissaries on the ravelin, and with it the sizzle of fireworks launched to make visible their targets. Spitting would have accomplished as much. At dawn Pietru lifted his head with a start, realizing he must have dozed off. Before his very eyes he saw taking place what everyone had most feared. *"Haqq dawk it-Tork jiehduh f'sormhom!"* he cursed to Nardo next to him. "They're pulling those pieces up to the ravelin!" Nardo didn't make a sound. Pietru rolled him over and saw the hole in his forehead.

Ix-Xabaw didn't know what to do. He and the others remaining on the wall kept up fire, but there were just too many janissaries atop the ravelin and in the ditch. "Now you'll see, you *kafirs!*" more than one renegado called out. "It won't be long now!"

The worst thing was, the pigs were right. The ravelin now rose above the parapets and commanded the entire fort. Once those guns were mounted, they'll send us to the Devil. How to stop them? Half of St. Elmo's cannon were by now dismounted, useless. As balls pinged off the jumble of stone, Ix-Xabaw crawled along the eastern rampart, pushing aside a lonely arm that lay across his path, making his way toward the nearest gunners who had a usable piece. They spied him approaching, and saw what was taking place on the ravelin. At once they swung their gun around, desperately dumped powder into its maw and touched the match. Pietru was already crawling back over the cinders to his post and didn't see what happened until after the roar, but when he uncovered his ears and looked up, the enemy guns were in the same place. He reloaded and took aim at the Turkish cannoneers, but only hit the gabions they were putting up.

"May my prick lacerate you!" he cursed. Surely his arquebus wouldn't and he near tossed it away.

His friend Pino stood up screaming, "*Ix-xjaten jehduk!*" and hurled a torch across the ditch. He hoped to ignite the fascines, but the torch fell short and Pino was at once killed by an arrow thro' his chest.

The Turkish guns erupted then, shattering the carriage of the gun that had just fired and knocking it down. Instantly, the splinters killed one of the gunners and the falling piece crushed the other's leg. Other cannoneers around the fort were bringing their pieces into position to take out the enemy guns, but the barbarians had already surrounded them with gabions and planks, making a crude platform atop their tower. The defenders fired. No success. Again they let loose, then the Turks. Again. The *boom boom, boom boom* went on for some hours. By the end of it the Turks had dismounted three more pieces. The barbarians now commanded the fort and hardly any place was safe. To prove it, the Turks sent a ball onto the passage above the canteen.

"The Devil!" cried Caravajal below, throwing down his cards just as a piece of the ceiling crashed about him. "As I abominate the Moors who wander up and down without a King! Now I'm angry!"

The reserves and wounded quickly did their best to move out of the lines of the guns and find places to hide. But that wasn't the worst. Pietru rolled over to his breach in the parapets to take a shot and saw that next to the ravelin the enemy had begun building a second bridge.

By nightfall the Turks had put down supports and laid five or six galley masts lashed together across them. The arquebusiers had tried all day to prevent it and had failed, for the janissaries on the ravelin kept them at bay. Pietru and his comrades managed to toss down some oil and torches onto the bridge, but the enemy had foreseen this trick and foiled it by covering it with dirt. After dark, one of the soldiers who'd taken cover against that wall heard a distinct picking and hammering from the other side. He rushed over to Miranda. "Colonel, they're trying again to mine the wall and undermine the fort."

Miranda perceived at once the foe was using the bridge itself as a shield for the sapping. He immediately called together the Knights in the shadow of the wall, out of sight of the guns. "Men, the barbarians are attempting to undermine the fort. They cannot succeed, for the rock is too hard. But they are also attempting to sap the walls, and in that they may succeed. We have failed to drive them away or burn the bridge from above. I believe we must attempt a sortie thro' the ditch itself and burn that bridge from below before the janissaries make another assault."

"That ditch is filled with azabs and sappers," Mas pointed out as the light from the cress on the wall illuminated the filthy faces under it.

"Yes, let half the men make a false attack on the trenches in front of the fort. God granting, this will divert the azabs' attention and pull them from the ditch. The remainder of us will be able to crawl thro' the ditch and torch the bridge."

The desperate plan suited the men's mood and everyone agreed to it. At once they fortified themselves with food and wine and repaired to the chapel. Commending their souls to God, they armed themselves with their swords, shields, pikes and gave out unlit torches amongst them. Miranda had already ordered the reserve to terre-plein the wall to which the bridge was coming and dig a new ditch behind it, should the sortie fail. The moment the enemy guns stopped speaking, he commanded his men to silence and ordered the drawbridge lowered; two companies of Knights sallied forth. Miranda and Medrano led their men against the trenches, while Mas held back his soldiers within the fort. The plan seemed to succeed. Miranda and Medrano caught half the azabs sleeping at their positions. Abruptly awoken, their screams and shouts brought fire from the janissaries, and the azabs in the ditch ran to their aid.

Mas waited as the fight heated up and for the janissaries on the ravelin to be distracted by it; some even ran down to join the fray. Only then did he order his men out. From the drawbridge, they climbed down into the ditch as cannon balls from the forward Turkish battery crashed again into the walls above their heads. Right under the maw of the Turkish guns, the Knights found the ditch here nearly empty of men and shortly they were around the corner, on the Marsamxett side of the fort. Balthazar had gone out with Mas. Fifty paces ahead he perceived the dim outlines of the ravelin and the new bridge standing this side of it. The dilemma was to reach it before Hell broke loose.

Caravajal stood at his side. "Balthazar," he said, "I vow to God that should Heaven itself fall on us tonight, we shall bear it up with our brawny arms."

To the last, Balthazar slapped Caravajal on the shoulder and smiled gravely, to the last. Natheless, he was not so confident as his comrade. "Ramon, I have said it to you before: Heroic deeds should rather be seen than told to be believed."

With shields raised and pikes amongst them, they pressed forward. The surprise they had achieved gained them only paces before the shouts of the startled azabs alerted the janissaries on the ravelin. Arquebus balls were soon glancing off the shields and every further step became a trial. Caravajal and Balthazar hacked their way forward, treading and slipping on the flesh that squished beneath their feet. More Turks poured into the ditch and for a moment Balthazar was certain they would be trapped. Mas shouted for those carrying pikes to line the ditch, and with diligence they made work of any Turk who climbed down what had been the counterscarp.

Balthazar had taken only an ordinary broadsword, and he lost count of his swings, how many foemen he slew as they labored forward, winning one step, then another, retreating, then gaining one forward step more. Half the night had gone by when they finally gained the bridge.

"Bring that tar!" cried Mas.

It wasn't easy, for the tar-carriers were back ten paces, trapped by azabs from above. Knights went back, surrounded the tar-carriers, and under the cover of the shields, brought them forward, moving all together in a circle thro' the ditch.

At last under the bridge. Balthazar, Caravajal and a few others grabbed the brushes and started smearing the mixture all over the supports.

"Give me that torch!" cried Mas when they were ready and touched it to three of the bridge legs. Those went up at once, but while they were readying to set fire to the others, some janissaries dropped down into the ditch beyond and opened fire. Caravajal was hit in the arm immediately.

"As I defy the Evil Spirit with both my Hands!" he cried, "do you think that will stop me, dogs!" So saying, he took his sword into his other hand and made ready to charge the foe.

The fire was too hot and more janissaries were appearing with each breath.

"After me!" Mas cried and the company retired with shots all around. They gained the fort again with little resistance from the azabs. Balthazar accompanied Caravajal to the keep, where Negroponte lay on a bed, still in a bad way from his arrow wound. A Serving Brother tended the wounded as best he might, and a chaplain said prayers for the dying.

"You'll live," said the Serving Brother to Caravajal.

"To win ever more glory," answered the Spaniard.

"How was it?" Negroponte asked from his bed.

Balthazar gulped down a cup of water from a barrel as other Knights crowded in to the room and the cannonading stepped up. "I don't know. The men behaved well. We have some wounded, not too many. I think Medrano's brother was killed."

At dawn those on the ramparts saw the carnage they had inflicted on the enemy—hundreds of bodies strewn all over the ditch and trenches—azabs and sappers dragging them off. But the bridge still stood and workers were already repairing it.

The assault came at vespers. At the instant the janissaries charged across the bridge, others were climbing into the ditch, and throwing scaling ladders against the walls. Mas's Post bore the brunt of the attack. With his two-hander he lopped off heads as they appeared above the parapets. His men hurled stone after stone upon the attackers. They gored chests with halberds and pikes. The arquebusiers lining the walls let out fusillade after fusillade until smoke blinded everyone, their own morions couldn't be seen and no one could hear through the crackling.

A watch passed, two. Abruptly the enemy retreated. The janissaries scaling the walls gave up their attempt, abandoned the ladders as they fled back across the bridge, climbed out of the ditch. Mas stood on the ramparts, alive and puzzled, so many were the numbers of the retreating barbarians. He doubted he had taken more than fifteen heads himself. By him, his entire company stood along the wall, as baffled as he.

Yakhshi nodded. This is exactly what they had wanted. The *Boluk-bashi*, who had been firing from the ditch, retreated with his men. Now the artillery that had been brought down beyond the trenches opened up, with shot, bits of stone, anything. Nearly every one of the infidels standing exposed on the walls was wounded or killed in the first salvos and he watched them fall in great numbers, dozens after dozens.

Yakhshi yet found himself conceding some admiration for these *kafirlar*. Nearly two weeks had passed and still the dogs were not yelping for mercy. With each day Mustafa's fury grew and by now the *yenicheriler* knew that Santarma would have to be taken at all costs. The *Boluk-bashi* emptied his lungs. Darkness was already falling and both believers and infidels had grown weary. Well, enough. They would take the fort tomorrow.

Eighty-Six

The moon had long set when a page at the Magisterial Palace announced Captain Medrano to the Grand Master. Finding de Valette in the company of Romegas and Isabella Guasconi, the begrimed soldier removed his helmet and lost no time in explaining his purpose.

"Eminenza," he kissed the ring, "eight hours ago we suffered another assault. Twenty Knights were killed and a good part of the garrison wounded." The Captain told of yesterday's failed attempt to burn the Turkish bridge, how guns atop the ravelin were firing into the fort itself, that Eminenza himself could hear the thousand balls now crashing into the walls each day, that the parapets were leveled and that breaches were appearing faster than the soldiers could repair them. He paused, breathed. "The men are united—Fort St. Elmo must be abandoned."

As Medrano finished his speech in the light of the single lamp, de Valette looked onto the armored skeleton. "de Guaras, Mas and Miranda live?" he asked without perceptible emotion.

The Captain nodded.

"They are agreed in this?"

Again Medrano nodded.

"I'll go over at once," Romegas interrupted, stepping to the door.

de Valette stayed him with a motion of his hand. "No, I will not risk you, Mathurin. Dispatch Bajada to the Old City and order Vañon's company of arquebusiers to Fort St. Elmo. That is all."

Medrano's surprise was such that e'en the deep shadows of the chamber failed to disguise it. "Eminenza," he said, wiping the sweat from his brow, "you will not permit us to abandon the fortress?"

"Of course not. Much time remains to make a decision."

Isabella now looked up sharply from the table to regard Parisot, wondering whether he believed his own words. Medrano did not. "Eminenza," he protested, "for ten days this torrent of iron and stone ...

water is short, the guns dismounted ... Troops are refusing to take their posts. You risk a mutiny."

Isabella caught her breath but de Valette's face remained expressionless. "Return, Señor, and tell them we request only that each man among you fulfills his duty to the Order and to God. Thank you, Captain."

As Medrano turned to leave, Isabella asked whether the boats would be ferrying the wounded to the Borgo tonight.

"Señora," he replied, "they have arrived. Be prepared for the worst."

Isabella swallowed, knowing that the auberges would soon be filled.

Once Medrano had gone, de Valette as if collapsed. "We must have every day," he whispered, clenching his fist, "every hour ... What news from Don Garcia?"

"Nothing, Eminenza," said Romegas, "nothing." With a bow he left to find Bajada.

Now de Valette did sink onto his chair. Isabella regarded him as the light flickered over his drawn countenance. At first she thought she looked on a man more burdened by the weight of decision than a mortal could bear. But in the feeble glow she began to wonder whether she deceived herself and that his will was simply adamantine. Looking into her own struggles against fear and night visitors, she could not fathom either possibility. She reached out her hand to touch his arm, but he paid no heed to her or to the food she had brought, and she excused herself to the Auberge of Italy.

The morning Angelus had yet to sound when Medrano gained Fort St. Elmo. Followed by the reinforcements the Grand Master had sent over this night, he skirted the bailey to the side where most of the officers had taken refuge from the guns. Men sat with heads bent, legs and arms broken, bloodied faces. Some walked, staggered, setting rocks on walls that crumbled beneath them. A water boy strayed too close to the line of fire, a crack, he was down, precious water spilling from his bucket onto the stones.

In the warm night air, pulsing in the ear and the eye, Medrano reported to his comrades the Grand Master's reply. Mas was the first to erupt. "Die for the Order each of us is prepared to do! But what sense waiting to be buried in these damned ruins or having our throats cut like beasts? Does Eminenza have any idea of the hordes surrounding this place?"

The others agreed. "We could resist five more assaults—ten—" put in la Cerda, "and in the end it wouldn't make a difference. We are dead men."

"If we could but make a sortie," Miranda said as a piece of the wall above collapsed, "we should at least die honorably."

Then and there the Knights resolved to write a letter to the Grand Master. Balthazar was delegated to pen it. "You know how to write, Navarre," Mas said.

Carefully, the Knights repaired to the chapel where one of them found paper and ink. While dust fell from the stones, Balthazar sat at a bench, holding a quill. For an hour the men raised their voices about what to say, and more than once Balthazar had to begin anew. He wrote with difficulty, as he'd received a hard blow to the shoulder yesterday. The letter belonged to no one in particular, repeated much of what Medrano had already told his Eminence and neither was Balthazar pleased with the style, but under the circumstances it would do:

Illustrissimo, Reverendissimo Monsignore,

When the Turks landed, Eminenza asked we the Knights to defend Castel St. Elmo. This we did with the greatest of good heart, and all that we could do has been done. Eminenza knows this, that we have never spared ourselves fatigue or danger. Now, tho', the enemy has reduced us to such a state that we can neither make any effect on them, nor can we defend ourselves, because both the ravelin and the ditch are in their hands. They have made a bridge with steps up to the Post of Mas and are mining the walls, so that with each passing hour we expect to be blown up. They have raised the ravelin to such a height that one cannot stand at one's post without being killed, and no sooner are sentries sent to watch than janissaries shoot them dead. We are in such dire straits that we can no longer use the piazza of the fort. Numbers of our men have already been killed there, and we have almost no shelter but for the little keep, some store rooms and the chapel itself. Our soldiers despair and even the officers cannot make them take up their positions on the walls. Convinced the fort must fall, they are preparing to save themselves by swimming to the Borgo. Because we can no longer carry out the duties of the Order, if Eminenza does not withdraw us, we are determined to sally forth tomorrow night and die with our arms in our hands. Do not send further reinforcements, for they are no more than dead men. This is the most determined resolution of all those whose signatures Illustrissimo, Reverendissimo Monsignore can read below. We kiss your hands and have taken a copy of this letter.

When he finished writing it out, Balthazar slowly glanced up, "What day is it?" he asked.

"The tenth of June," someone ventured.

"No, I think it is the eighth," Miranda replied as the wall shuddered.

"Let it be the eighth," Balthazar said and added to the letter, "Dated from Fort St. Elmo, the eighth of June, 1565."

Almost all the Knights present lined up and signed the letter, but after fifty-three signatures were affixed, la Cerda said, "Why not you, Navarre?"

"For the simple reason," Balthazar replied, wiping plaster from his hair, "that this letter serves no purpose but to rouse the Monsignore's anger. He is determined to see this place hold out as long as possible and will never agree to withdraw us."

Miranda, considering this, agreed. "E'en were we to be withdrawn, it would merely be to die a few days later at another post."

These arguments failed, tho', to dissuade the majority of the Knights and they dispatched Commander du Cornet with the missive in broad daylight. Balthazar stepped out of the chapel as a musket ball glanced off the stone a few paces away. He watched the Knights disperse, speaking to the common troops. So convinced were the soldiers that upon receiving the letter de Valette would instantly withdraw them, that they at once raised such a cheer as men in their condition were able. Then they lost their minds. Ignoring the danger from the ravelin, many began gathering up cannon balls and dumping them into the big water cistern. "Let's blow up the fort!" a few shouted. Others started to spike their guns.

"Halt!" commanded Miranda, spinning around one of the Maltese who carried a ball to the reservoir, "or I'll have you hanged!"

That one glanced at the Colonel for only a moment, then dropped the piece of iron as his chest exploded under the impact of a Turkish ball. Miranda himself dove for cover into the chapel.

As Balthazar watched all this with disbelieving eyes, the scene from Tripoli again flashed thro' his mind and he vowed not to let it happen here. The Knight cautiously made his way 'round the piazza to some men who were piling powder kegs against the wall opposite the Turkish bridge. "Leave off!" he cried, grabbing one of them. "Are you mad? You have no orders!" Without awaiting a reply, Balthazar struck the fellow across his mouth.

The Maltese merely stared at him in stupefaction.

Truly, these men are more dead than alive, Balthazar thought. He threw the soldier to the ground and took on the others, who put up little more of a fight.

The chaos went on—soldiers destroying munitions, others attempting to stop them, when suddenly—the sound of Turkish instruments drifting over the walls. Beating drums, sounding pipes and cymbals. All signaled one thing.

"My God!" Pietru, Mas, Balthazar and everyone else who could yet walk in St. Elmo exclaimed at the same instant, "another assault!"

The spirits of the men were higher this morning, observed Yakhshi as the band marched along the trenches, playing their gayest melodies. Many of the men smoked *afione* under the bright sun, and the trilling of the *iayalarlar* was serving to put them into the proper frenzy. He had himself taken a bit of *afione* to get ready. The flags lining the trenches fluttered more brightly and colorfully than ever. Turgut and Mustafa had assigned his *boluk* to the bridge, a place of honor, but the assault would be against several places along the walls at once. Those pork-eaters were by now little more than walking ghosts and Yakhshi had no doubt that before the end of the day the Santarma fort would at last be in their hands.

The troops waited for the bombardment to cease. Within the space of heartbeats every gun fell silent and the sudden quiet astonished Yakhshi. Such had been the thunder for nearly two weeks now that each time it stopped before an assault, the hush seemed to him a perfect miracle.

The stillness lasted only a breath before the chanting went up, "Allah! Allahu ekber!" and the brandishing of spears. The drums beat louder and faster now. The shouts and chanting kept pace; always louder, louder, faster, faster. "La ilah illa'llah!" The cymbals were crashing too, dervishes spinning and the horns playing ever more madly as the frenzy spiraled heavenward. "Let the jaws of Hell swallow the Infidel" "The Sword of Islam shall severe the souls of the infidels from their impure vessels!" The fever pitch had been reached, the Prophet's Standard raised, and at last the cry came: "In the name of Allah! Forward!"

The janissaries leapt from the trenches. They stormed across the bridge and ditch with ladders, with arquebus, with scimitars, spears and standards. The pork-eaters did not yield.

Across the harbor, the Grand Crosses and Piliars on hand were gathered at the Magisterial Palace, as they'd been gathered without respite since the invasion's onset had erased the past. Moments before the Turkish assault got underway, de Cornet handed the Knights' petition to de Valette in his cabinet and watched a shadow of godly wrath cross the Monsignore's face. In the next breath the courier, stunned, saw a lioness bound after him as he stormed into the adjoining chamber. There Eminenza thrust the missive into a page's palm, ordering him to read it out before the Council. The page stammered helplessly; de Valette impatiently motioned for him to hand the letter back; only then did the boy gain the fortitude to read it through. With the final words a silence descended onto the chamber.

Heartbeats later, the Bailiff of Eagle ventured against the rumbling, "Who can gainsay such demands?" he declared. "The fort is lost, the lives of these valiant men are lost. Allow them to die honorably."

The Prior of St. Gil and the Bailiff of Caspe voiced the same opinion, followed by the representatives of the Grand Hospitaller and Grand Conservator. With an expression that seemed to go deeper than the matter at hand, Bishop Cubelles put it in that a revolt was underway in the castle. They had demanded too much of these men and were now reaping the whirlwind. "Anyone can see Fort St. Elmo is doomed. Withdraw these men and let us pray that the Vice Roy's relief arrives soon."

Only secretary Oliver Starkey objected in his imperfect Italian that progress on the defenses of St. Michel and the Borgo proceeded day and night, and that each hour St. Elmo granted them was a sacrifice well made. Moreover, the Vice Roy's relief must be at hand.

de Valette dismissed every one of them. "Those men," he told the Seigneurs, "have forgotten that it is not enough to die with swords in hand, as they seem so fond of, but to lose them in obedience to the Grand Master, as they have likewise sworn to do." He retired to his cabinet, ordering Starkey to pen a letter. "Tell them exactly what I have said, that they must lose their lives in obedience to us. Say as well that they must abandon their hopes in a relief from the Vice Roy, and that should they be withdrawn, the Turks will at the next moment besiege the Borgo, where they shall inevitably meet with the death they so vainly hope to escape. Tell them that St. Elmo is built on hard rock and that their fears of a mine are a result of their fatigued imaginations."

"That should shame them," said Starkey.

"Add that should they natheless decide desert the fort, I will be pleased to send boats to fetch them."

While Starkey made a fair copy of the missive, tho', the Monsignore walked back into the chamber, where the Crosses remained speechless at their dismissal. His Majesty has surely experienced like occasions, when he was forced to disregard the advice of his *Pashalar*. Long afterwards, people said that de Valette's harsh decision was the most fateful of the siege, of his life, for all instantly understood that he had pronounced a death sentence on Fort St. Elmo's defenders.

Yet it did not happen as rashly as people remembered. Seeing the expressions of umbrage on the faces of every Seigneur around him, de Valette yielded a step, and agreed to dispatch three commissioners to Fort St. Elmo to judge the true state of affairs.

They had been at it seven hours. Yakhshi's lungs heaved, burned with every breath; he had already received a gunshot wound in the arm, had retired to have it bandaged, and charged again with raised scimitar across the bridge. He could not comprehend how those diminishing numbers of infidel arquebusiers, hiding behind insignificant bundles of faggots upon the walls, had kept the *yenicheriler* at bay so long, but the ripple of the fire and the puffs of smoke hadn't ceased all day. Those metalled Knights swinging their immense swords upon the ramparts must be possessed by demons from another world—or they were demons from another world. Yakhshi saw more than one azab's spear or shield shiver at the approach of those devils. His men fought bravely. At each moment it seemed that only armslengths, palms, fingers needed to be gained to breach the fort, but each time stones rained down, ladders crashed and the ramparts held.

Of a sudden, Yakhshi was hit again and forced to retire to the trenches with a searing pain and arm dripping blood. He scrambled back from the bridge, over the leveled counterscarp and out of range of the guns, where he found someone to put another bandage on his arm.

Shahverdi, a *chorbaji*, was by him, also wounded with a hole in his cheek and gashes in his leg. "What iss going on there?" he said, spit and blood oozing from his injured mouth. "We have thrown eight thousssand balls againsst that fort. Why can we not take it?"

Yakhshi shook his head. "This is something beyond understanding," he said. "Their armor ... "

"No," Shahverdi answered, "thiss iss not armor."

At this moment, Mustafa, Piyale and Turgut picked their way over the rutted ground, approached the two officers. "Why does that fort yet stand?" Mustafa demanded. "Do not the *yenicheriler* call themselves the greatest warriors on earth?"

Both shrugged. "Perhapss it iss God'sss will, *Hazretleriniz*," Shahverdi ventured, his voice hardly greater than a mumble. "Our men give everything."

Enraged, Mustafa lit into Shahverdi about the shoulders with the stick in his hand. The *Chorbaji* said nothing and bore his punishment silently, with dignity. Turgut was saying to Piyale, whose ribs were yet swathed with bandages, that as they had been so foolish not to blockade the north of the island, infidel boats were passing easily between Gozo and Sicily. His ears in Sicily told him that the *kafirlar* expected reinforcements any day. "We cannot allow this to happen. Send one hundred galleys along the coast and you will prevent any succours from arriving."

"It shall be done," replied Piyale with a slight bow, making no attempt at argument.

Once the *Pashalar* moved off, *Chorbaji* Shahverdi spat to the ground. "Sshove your *firman* up your asss, Mussstafa," he cursed, "and fight the infidelss yourself."

The day's assault soon ended. As the defeated troops retired from the walls, a Spanish renegado called out over his shoulder, "Knights, you have done well today, and you will soon have the general assault you seem so much to desire."

Later, when the officers gathered together to reckon their losses, it seemed that another five hundred *yenicheriler* had fallen during the day, with several thousand wounded.

Again I helped ferry the injured to Birgu. By the time we set off, the bombardment had recommenced, but the Turks had made no attempt to replace the battery on Gallows' Point since Copier had cleared it the other day and we gained Fort St. Elmo with only the usual shooting from Alicate cave and Sciberras. The stars and three-quarters moon provided light enough to see the forlorn landscape, e'en for the drifting smoke. For what seemed hours I searched for Balthazar among the expressionless men who sat around the borders of the crumbling fortress, or who had thrown themselves atop powder kegs or grain sacks without thought of danger. At last I spied him asleep on a bench in the chapel.

He had a new gash in his leg. "Balthazar," I said, holding back tears as I shook him awake, "come. Let us get you to the Hospital."

He waved me off. "I say it makes no difference."

With wonder I regarded the Knight, unable to perceive whether his words were of heroic optimism or fatal resignation. "Pietru?"

"I believe he lives. Everyone behaved well today, Francisco, everyone. We lost only forty Knights." The wounded were five times that number.

"How many remain to defend the fort?"

He shrugged, groggily. "I believe four hundred, less. It cannot be long now."

In the warm candlelight of that little chapel, with its images still clinging to the sweating stones, I again sensed the presence of the immanent miraculous. Balthazar himself could not explain how these men at the extremities of exhaustion had summoned their last reserves and stood for seven hours on those ramparts, surrounded by thousands of screaming, bellowing janissaries who never ceased their attempts to deluge the walls. Balthazar remembered hurling stones, cleaving men, hurling burning fascines into the ditch. Mas, likewise, stood not far, swinging his two-hander, exhorting his men who again bore the brunt of the attack. la Cerda was hit in the arm, had it bandaged, returned.

I listened to the Abbé's account with unendurable agitation. "No tears," he said. "We die honorably."

Natheless tears came freely with the certainty that after this night I would never set eyes on Balthazar again. I turned from him, fairly running from the chapel, to attend to my duties. Both Pietru and la Cerda made their way to the grotto, asking to be taken to the town, la Cerda with his arm wound and Pietru with a arrow wound in his shoulder.

At Birgu the shafts of moonlight played on a confused procession of men carrying the wounded up to the Infermeria to be met by doctors guarding the door. It was no longer a matter of finding a bed for these hundreds; a spot on the floor would do, on a landing, on a windowsill. If not in the Infermeria, then in the auberges, if not in the auberges ... That presumed—the Italian Knights on duty passed their lamps over each man as he arrived, deciding in their feeble glow whether a wound was serious enough to warrant a place or treatment.

la Cerda presented his arm. "A mere scratch," the Knights said, turning him away altogether, tho' the puncture had gone clean through.

"The Devil! I fought all day! Let me in I say!"

Pietru, nearby, averred that la Cerda had fought with great bravery, but the guards persisted in denying him entry. To la Cerda's misfortune the dispute went on as the Grand Master himself descended from his nightly rounds. de Valette demanded to know what the commotion was about.

"The man's wound is hardly serious enough to warrant treatment," the Knights replied.

de Valette himself grabbed la Cerda's arm and a lamp, and without any hesitation ordered him arrested. For his part, Pietru was admitted, his wound being judged serious enow. The Serving Brothers rinsed the puncture with salt water and vinegar. After they bandaged it, Ix-Xabaw made his way down to Kalkara Creek and returned to the fort.

We carried some of the worst to the Auberge of Italy, where screams of the treated and dying filled the small hospital there. As we put down our cargo on the slippery, stained floors, I glanced up to see Vigo on his own rounds, and Isabella. Thro' her veil I hardly recognized her. She yet confined herself to feeding the patients from a silver tray and did not immediately notice me.

Isabella was uncertain of what to do when she came to a soldier whose broken jaw was bound together so tightly he couldn't eat; the doctors had failed even to force a tube into his stomach. "Dr. Jean," she said. Vigo ordered a clyster and his assistant soon brought a bladder filled with a preparation of eggs and broth.

"Help me turn him over," Vigo said to the Serving Brother and told Isabella to avert her gaze. She did not. With wild eyes the fellow shrieked his protests thro' his fixed jaw, but the physician, ignoring all, rolled him onto his side and forced a metal tube up his ass. Vigo squeezed the bladder. The patient shat up everything and they tried a second time.

Isabella had thought herself by now hardened to the daily injuries, but thereat she did avert her gaze, fairly staggering from the ward straight into my arms. "Francisco!" she exclaimed. "How is it ... over there?"

I could not find the words wherewith to describe the indescribable to she who had forbidden me from again setting foot in her house. I merely stared coldly at her. "Look about you," I said. "Imagine twenty men for each one here, the walls falling about you, the smell of bodies everywhere and sounds so enormous that they drown out your thoughts ... Forgive me, Signora, I must go."

Without another word I turned from her to ferry men back to the fort under the glowing sky and trembling stars.

The commissioners, carrying the Grand Master's letter, joined our convoy and arrived at Fort St. Elmo in the dead of night. As they passed thro' the sea gate the three Knights recoiled at the unearthly booming. "The Devil!" exclaimed de la Roche, a Frenchman, and clapped his hands to his ears, "how is it possible to live with such a hammering!"

The Spaniard among them, Don Francisco Ruyz de Medina, crossed himself, whispering "Madonna!" as they cast their eyes over the battered cavalier, the dirt and rubble all around, the breached walls and the shadow of the ravelin towering over everything. We led them to the keep, where the Bailiff of Negroponte, now recovered well enough from his arrow wound to walk, greeted the Knights and summoned all the men to the safer part of the piazza.

Don Constantino Castriota, the Albanian from the Langue of Italy, utterly failed to conceal his disbelief when Balthazar told him that much of the munitions had been destroyed in yesterday's chaos. But his surprise paled next to the garrison's own when, under the torch Miranda held, Colonel Mas, voice sometimes unheard, read out the Grand Master's letter.

"He wants us to die like pigs!" Medrano spat on the ground.

"No," rejoined Caravajal vehemently. "He wishes us to die like St. Elmo himself—our intestines unwound onto capstans."

Losing all patience, Medrano nodded desperately. "I say we make a sortie, this moment, and be done with it!"

Most of the other men moved for their weapons.

"Messers!" pleaded de la Roche with raised hands. "*Nous sommes arrivée pour juger la condition du fort et pour faire une décision raisonnable.*"

"Condition of the fort! By the Tears of Jeremiah, do you have eyes in your head?"

Don Constantino, surveying the castle, remained unconvinced. "I see no difficulty," he declared to the assembly. "All you need to do is build a second defense inside the outer ones and retire behind it."

An extraordinary laugh arose from the crowd of half-living men. "We are prepared to begin at once," mocked Colonel Mas, "if Don Constantino be so kind to show us how to do it. Does Señor see any material wherewith to build such a defense? Perhaps he thinks we should build those walls out of the iron the Turks send us each hour." A boom went off above and the men laughed again. "Does Señor expect us to labor while under a general assault, or in full view of that ravelin, from which the other day twenty-one of our sentries were shot down?"

"If you bring us mattresses from town," Caravajal put in, "we can both build such a defense and sleep on it."

Once more the men laughed, but Castriota insisted much could yet be done. de Medina, gazing about, demurred, saying the men were right and that a defense seemed to him impossible, at which Castriota took umbrage.

"Why don't you gentlemen stay until daylight," said Mas, "when you can better judge the condi—"

Mas never completed his words. An infernal roar consumed the piazza and all the men dove to the ground as a great stone from the Turkish basilisk buried itself thirty palms under the front wall, causing Fort St. Elmo to shake from top to bottom. "What was that!?" asked de Medina, getting to his feet, crossing himself with an expression of absolute terror.

"That is what we live with day and night," answered Negroponte.

"Messeri," said Castriota, brushing himself off, "I am afraid I must decline your kind invitation to remain for the day, as much as I might like; such was not our charge." With that he hurriedly made his way toward the sea gate.

Mas had no intention of letting a commissioner get away with it and bounded ahead, ordering the sentries there to close and bolt the gate. "You will remain our guest today, Don Constantino, so that you may make a proper assessment," the Colonel said. At his nod, the doors swung shut and the guards crossed their halberds across it.

For some time, as the sky lightened and the commissioners' eyes darted every more frantically from side to side, they remained house guests at Fort St. Elmo. At length, Negroponte, seeing that little was to be gained by this stalemate, sounded the tocsin. The entire garrison, distracted, gathered on the piazza and in the commotion Castriota and his fellow commissioners managed a swift departure. Shortly thereafter, I was also rowing toward Birgu with more wounded.

In the brightness of day, the commissioners made their report to the Council. While they stood in the chamber, a swimmer arrived at the Grand Master's Palace from Fort St. Elmo. They say it was Bajada. I didn't see him in the fort, but Toni was very fast and by now sometimes appeared in two places at once. The letter he delivered repeated the Knights' demand to be withdrawn from St. Elmo. Having been there, I knew their honor had been sullied by the commission. The commissioner de Medina understood and averred the situation to be hopeless. de la Roche was unsure but Castriota, out of spite I think, continued to insist that the place could be defended.

"Indeed," he said, "the fears of a Turkish mine are groundless. The enemy sappers were only making hollows in the wall wherein they might hide from our men." With a bow to de Valette he then startled everyone: "Eminenza, I am personally prepared to lead the defense of Fort St. Elmo, should you give me one hundred men."

Hearing the unexpected suggestion, Bishop Cubelles at once offered two thousand ducats to pay volunteers.

The Monsignore authorized Don Constantino to beat the drums. At the same time he had Starkey write to those in St. Elmo. "Tell them their services are no longer required, as Castriota will undertake the fort's defense."

Late at night, when the Knights had threatened to make their final sortie, Bajada appeared again at the Palace with yet another missive from St. Elmo. Toni, dripping wet as always, discerned a slight satisfaction crossing the Grand Master's face as he read the letter. "Eminenza, we have done nothing to abandon the fort and should Don Constantino arrive with a new garrison, we will be disgraced and dishonored. We are determined to perform our duties to God and the Religion and defend Fort St. Elmo unto death."

de Valette, tho', resolved to go through with his decision to reinforce the garrison. He stepped into his cabinet and burned all the letters.

Eighty-Seven

The drumbeat began at once. Within an hour, Castriota raised one hundred men who agreed to cross to Fort St. Elmo and die. Among them was Commander Monserrat, who offered to take charge of the fort should de Guaras be incapable. Another was a Capuchin monk. On the landing at Kalkara Creek whither the men rushed to assemble under torchlight, soldiers taunted two Jewish slaves.

"Why are you crossing over to certain death, Jew?" one Vespaziano demanded, hitting the slave on the shoulder with the flat of his sword. "There's no money in it."

"They want to die in the company of valorous Christians," put in Inigo, when the slaves remained silent, "and redeem the sins of those who killed Our Savior."

At last the two acknowledged that de Valette had offered them freedom if by some miracle they survived.

"Jews always drive a hard bargain," Vespaziano laughed.

Castriota would not go. Sometime before he reached the docks, he thought better of his offer and declined to take part in the expedition, but a private soldier, Captain Orazio Martelli, took his place. Martelli's lieutenants were carrying down colorful flags and standards from the auberges and Fort St. Angelo and handing them out to the men, for the Grand Master had ordered Martelli to deceive the enemy into thinking that a large force was crossing to St. Elmo.

Among those who boarded the boats at Kalkara Creek in the darkness was I. Esforzado, no; I could no longer stand by while Pietru and Balthazar ceaselessly risked life and limb in that fort. At de Valette's command, those of us from the mill loaded the boats with all the munitions we had made, the *granadas*, the fireworks, the fire hoops. I thought it best not to say farewell to Isabella.

So we crossed. E'en in the second week of June, the Turks hadn't attempted to establish again the battery on Gallows' Point and we had few casualties. We reached Fort St. Elmo as usual in the dark and unloaded the munitions. "What's that?" one of the Knights asked, seeing me carry a copper tube about a *braza* in length, a palm or two wide and wrapped around its middle with leather. "A *tromba de fuego*," I answered and took it thro' the sea gate.

Inside, we were greeted by the crackle of arquebus fire from the Marsamxett side. The enemy had been placing a great quantity of fascines and earth into the ditch near the bridge—preparation for an assault. Colonel Mas had gone out with his company and were making another attempt to burn the bridge. Before we had finished unloading the munitions, they returned and announced that they had succeeded in destroying some of it.

The men who were able cheered Colonel Mas and, as the sun came up, cheered Martelli's company. Miranda ordered all the standards placed on the ramparts, the drums beaten and trumpets sounded to convince the enemy Fort St. Elmo yet stood. The Turks responded by repairing the bridge and stepping up the bombardment. As dawn broke I gazed around the fort, as I did each time I had ferried succours to the place. I supposed with the reinforcements five hundred men lined the arms or walked about the piazza amid the supplies and rubble, attempting to buttress the walls with whatever they might. Hardly a man among them was not bandaged or bleeding. Somehow they not only remained alive, but fought. I watched a man shitting against a wall, another kneeling by the keep eating bread, a third removing boots from a dead companion. I watched the Capuchin step over the stones, calling the troops together for a sermon. When the men had gathered 'round on the piazza, he preached to them, reminding everyone that today was the Pentecost, that on this day tongues of fire had appeared in the sky, filling all the disciples of the Lord with the Holy Ghost. Hearing these words and taking the friar's blessing, the men went to their posts fortified with new strength. Afterwards I too sought out the Capuchin for his blessing but, having finished his sermon, he quickly departed for Birgu with the sick old Governor, Broglio.

A few hours later, as I was carrying fire hoops to the ramparts, a familiar voice barked at me amidst the ceaseless, infernal booming. "What are you doing here?"

I faced Balthazar. "In bringing you fire weapons I have missed the ferry back to town, so am forced to remain with you today."

"I forbade you to do this," he croaked, holding a piece of cooked meat in his bare hand.

"Look at you," I said, regarding the Knight, what was left of him. "You are wounded, limping, gashed from top to bottom, more dead than alive. You are in no position to forbid anything. *In qualsiasi caso,*" I put my arm around his shoulder, "I am now well past the age to decide when I may fight at the side of an old friend who has saved my life more times than I remember."

It was near midday then, the sun high, blackening skin. Of a sudden, the cannonading fell away and the deathly silence in its wake put an abrupt end to our conversation. An assault must be coming. Aye, at the next moment Miranda sounded the alarm and I rushed to the ramparts with my wheel-lock. As I yanked one of the twelve apostles from my bandoleer and charged my gun, I could see the enemy approaching Colonel Mas's Post. At first a mere reconnaissance seemed underway, with feather-topped scouts and janissaries prowling everywhere about the walls, but then they began to run forth with the ladders. By now the ditch had been largely filled with rock tumbled down from the walls, dirt, fascines, bodies, and not much of a height remained to be scaled.

But Mas, who had been without rest and was by now covered from head to toe with wounds and bandages, showed no weakness. With the fresh Knights and arquebusiers, he refused to take a step back. The Turks were no less obstinate and this reconnaissance went on for hours, balls whizzing this way and that, from the ravelin as well. Those Jews that had come over were fighting, tho' it seemed neither had ever fired a gun. One was hit at once, wounded in the arm. E'en the *buonavoglie,* the debtor-oarsmen, behaved well with bucket, gun or sword. At length the Turks retired, with many new bodies littering the ditch. Toward evening I walked down to the cistern, where Pietru found me drawing some water.

"You have been hit," he said. *Craa-aaack* from above.

I glanced at my arm. An arrow wound. "I hadn't noticed," I said. "You have been doing this every day?"

Ix-Xabaw nodded without humor. "Every day, Cikku. This was not a large assault."

"I know. I want you to help me." We had lost a dozen men in the reconnaissance, with many more wounded, but that no general assault had taken place made me guess the day was not done. Pietru and I began hauling barrels to the ramparts and filling them with seawater. Medrano stepped up to us.

"What is that for?" he wanted to know.

"Have the Turks begun using *granadas?*" I asked.

"Not many."

"I think they will," I said. "If the resin sticks to your armor, climb in."

That evening, balls ploughed into the ramparts as usual. Night had fallen, the moon was near full. Men sat scattered around the piazza, at their posts, in what was left of the canteen. Some cooking persisted around small fires haphazardly lit where it might be safe. After supper, the defenders attempted to sleep against Vulcan's pounding. I recollected Djerbé, thinking that nothing there had approached this and, failing to sleep more than a few winks at a time before being roused by the next crash, my entrails began to know what these men had been subjected to since the new moon. At about the third night watch, the enemy cannon abruptly fell silent. As the first enemy firework exploded above the fort, everyone was suddenly awake.

I ran up to Mas's Post under the glare of the fireworks that were already bursting everywhere overhead. My eyes beheld a vast sea of torches spread over the entire mount above us, tho' those flames were almost unnecessary, so far did the flares arcing thro' the sky dispel the darkness. Screaming "Allah!" and *"Allahu ekber!"* thousands of janissaries rushed towards us with such clamor and fury that my heart ceased to beat. As the fireworks lit their ferocious faces, the infidels sped their ladders to the walls and placed them.

"Here!" I shouted to Pietru next to me. "Light this!" With some tongs I grabbed one of the fire hoops we'd fashioned and Ix-Xabaw put a torch to it. As the hoop went up, I hurled it over the walls; with luck it fell about a janissary, instantly causing his robes to burst into flame. The other soldiers, seeing this success, picked up the hoops we had stacked at their posts and at once a cascade of burning circles was tumbling down the wall, a waterfall of fire that inundated the attackers below. A few steps from me, one of the men whirled one of our fire balls around his head and let fly the burning comet. Within moments, the air began to smell of flaming pitch and resin and was filled with the screams of those we burnt alive.

But the janissaries came without end. At each heartbeat fireworks from both sides flew into the sky, crackling and booming and falling from heaven, burning as they were lamps. Fire arrows, too, streaked thro' the night, crisscrossing it with blazing yellow tails. Cinders floated down everywhere like fading stars and covered us with soot.

"Aah!" Mas screamed as a Turkish pot hit his breastplate, bursting into flame.

"Into the barrel!" I cried and he jumped without hesitation, as the nearest men to him doused the flame. The Turks had learned well.

Our men too picked up the *granadas* we had stacked on the ramparts and began hurling them at the enemy in full fury. Explosions filled the ditch and the smell of shit began to mingle with the other scents, for we had added dung to many of the pots, hoping to make them more repellent to the foemen and cause sickness among them. We had searched in vain at the Infermeria for the flesh of one struck down by the plague, hoping to fill fire pots with that as well, but we did chop up some men who had died from the pox and put their pieces inside.

"Xabaw, come, it is time."

We ran down to the place I had left the *tromba de fuego* and brought it up. I had filled it with the usual mixture of gunpowder, liquid resin, alquitran and oil of juniper, yet I worried. Such instruments were hardly trustworthy and I had seen fit to make a few changes to that which my Venetian master, Vannoccio, had taught me. Shouldering the tube on the leather band I had wrapped about it, I nodded for Pietru to light the fore end, which I had closed to a narrow opening, having found this produces a longer flame. I had also attached some bellows to the rear to pump it.

Pietru put a torch to its mouth and the flames leapt forth with a ferocious whoosh. "*Alla!*" Xabaw exclaimed, jumping back.

"Work the bellows!" I answered and we ran to the rampart's edge where the bridge met the fort.

The battle around us paused as both comrades and foemen watched this two-headed beast breathing fire from its nostrils. We stood on the ruined wall, shooting flame onto the janissaries who raced across the bridge and up the steps they had emplaced. We shot flame onto them and roasted them alive. As they screamed their last, tumbling into the ditch, the smell of burning flesh overcame the other perfumes.

The light of the fireworks roused the Grand Master at Castle St. Angelo and soon all of Birgu had come to the walls of Kalkara Creek to gaze upon the infernal scene across the harbor. de Valette walked to the spur of St. Angelo, ordering his gunners to fire upon the Turkish platforms. "Why do you hesitate?" he demanded of Diego there.

That one shook his head. So bright were the fireworks exploding over Fort St. Elmo that night had changed into day. Diego and the other gunners could lay their pieces by the light of the enemy's fire weapons alone. "*Fuego!*" de Valette commanded and Diego fired.

Not far from them, Isabella found Dr. Jean with a crowd of others on the top story of the Sacra Infermeria. They stood silently listening to the explosions, watching the blazing streamers shoot everywhere into the air, as had Fort St. Elmo been transformed into a great fountain spitting forth flames. They watched the shimmering stars fall to earth and fade, before which vanishing other comets streaked heavenward and exploded into yet brighter suns.

"It is a volcano in eruption," said Vigo, not knowing whether human eyes had ever witnessed such a sight.

No words came to Isabella until, unbidden, a line from Virgil: "'*Facilis descensus Averni* ... It is easy to descend to Hell, the harder task is to climb out again' ... There are truly men in that place?" she whispered at last, hands pressed to her mouth.

"There are. Francisco went over last night."

She looked at the doctor in horror. Even her dreams had not prepared her.

Dawn was breaking and still the battle raged. Mustafa and Turgut watched from behind the Turkish trenches as wave after wave of janissaries stormed the fort, only to flee in terror as they were caught in these infernal hoops and burned alive. Furiously, the *Pashalar* walked forward and found some officers, every one of them wounded or burned. "Why cannot you take that fort?" Mustafa demanded for no less than the tenth time.

"It is the fire weapons, *Zat-i Aliniz*. They have made hundreds, thousands, and each of those circles catches one or two of our men within. There is no escape from them."

The other officers nearby agreed. Reluctantly Mustafa called off the attack and the *yenicheriler* retired. Enraged, Turgut ordered the bombardment to recommence at once. "I want every gun belching iron at those dogs without cease!" he barked and removed himself to his galley.

Yakhshi limped back to the camp at the Marsa with a severe burn on his left arm. He counted himself lucky. He knew that much of his *boluk* had been destroyed today. The count had not been made, but already there were whispers of more than one thousand *yenicheriler* killed. He would not have thought it possible.

When the light broke and we saw the hordes of janissaries retreating to their trenches, we who yet stood on the ramparts let out a cheer. But shots from the damned ravelin let us know that the danger hadn't vanished and the defenders retired to the safer parts of the piazza to find nourishment.

More dead than alive, I sat against a wall of terre-plein with Balthazar. For a long time neither of us said anything. At length, when he had gathered the strength, Balthazar said, "The men fought well."

I looked about the remains of this place I had helped build. "You had said all our questions of yore would be answered by this siege. 'What is valor?' you often asked. Do you at last have an answer?" Imperceptibly, Balthazar nodded. I went on: "Should Fort St. Elmo fall this day, I do not think Christendom will forget what has taken place here."

For a moment Balthazar pondered, as well as he could in his condition. "In the old days, Francisco, I oft' said that the Knights were a relic of a bygone age. What the world will remember is that last night their weapons also passed into times of yore."

"How many lost?" I asked.

"Miranda says sixty, of course many more wounded."

I crossed myself. "It is another miracle. Do you think, Balthazar, that God has come to Malta?"

"I think," he said, "that if the relief does not come to Malta forthwith, no miracle shall save us, e'en your fire weapons."

"Salvago left for Sicilia nearly a week ago," I said. "It must be soon."

Eighty-Eight

Before departing for Naples, Fra Rafael Salvago stood at the ancient harbor of Zaragoza as gulls circled above them and soldiers boarded the relief galleys, and gave final instructions to Commanders St. Aubin and Cornisson. "Be careful. Dragut has arrived on Malta and has increased the galleys prowling about the islands. We left Gozo with Turkish dogs on our tail. I'd advise you to pass around Gozo to the west, and make land on the southwest side of Malta. The road may be clearer."

Salvago's warning only served to augment the unease Vergã sensed this morning among the soldiers and crew. Each man knew the danger facing them, and before they boarded the boats more than a few began muttering that the hastily arranged relief was ill-omened. Vergã himself wondered at the enormous black bird, the likes of which he had never seen, that settled briefly on the *S. Giacomo* and at once took wing. The sight of it sent a shudder thro' the troops and more than one adventurer took off then and there. En route, some of the men said they had seen the same bird in the sky and crossed themselves, but between Sicily and Malta they encountered no enemy galleys. Two nights later, tho', as the relief neared the islands, Vergã slowly perceived they were heading toward Gozo. At once he protested to the Captain, reminding him of Salvago's warning that the Turks had taken to guarding the channel.

But the Captain answered that if the Turks were everywhere, then one road was as good as the next, and he persisted on his course. Yet already in sight of the Gozo harbor called Mgarr, like the village on Malta, he suddenly gave the order to turn about.

"What do you think you're doing?" said Vergã with sensible anger.

"Don't you see, Señor, there are two Turkish galleys guarding the harbor."

Vergã peered across the dark expanse. "I see nothing."

"Are you blind, man? Look." The Captain pointed. To Vergã's eyes the channel remained empty.

"You'll land this boat, *picaro,*" he barked. "Put in on the Malta side if you so fear phantoms."

The Captain erupted. "Do not dare speak to me in such tones, bastard!"

"You're a gutless, sniveling coward! Land this boat, I tell you!" Vergã spat on deck and drew his dagger.

At once the *comiti* were on him, binding Vergã's arms behind him. The Captain raised his fist and would have struck him had not at that moment one of the *gente* shouted that St. Aubin's galley had also turned about. Instantly the entire crew was consumed with terror—they must get the Devil out of here. Vergã, forgotten in all the confusion, glanced larboard, uncertain himself. What was out there? Convinced he saw the black bird in the darkness above, he made no further protest as the relief turned about and hauled back to Sicily.

"Where is the relief?" de Valette asked Romegas in the candlelight of his cabinet in the Magisterial Palace.

Romegas shrugged, having no idea. He went on to say that the men in Fort St. Elmo had fought with extreme valor the previous night, but that the Turks in their fury at the loss, had been pounding the place all day with a greater ferocity than ever. de Valette could hear well enough for himself. Moreover, so many wounded had come over to the Infermeria that the number of able men remaining in the fort had again fallen well below four hundred. The Grand Master nodded, authorizing a new call for volunteers.

One hundred and fifty fresh men came over that night, bringing with them mattresses, baskets, fascines and tow wherewith we might construct interior defenses for the fort.

"You see, just as I told the damned commissioners!" growled Caravajal at seeing the mattresses being carried thro' the *porta del soccorso.* "We'll sleep on our defenses!"

We didn't sleep on them. We propped them up on barrels and planks, facing the accursed ravelin, so that they might afford us protection, and we filled the baskets with earth for the same reason. We slept behind those, such as we slept; some filled their ears with wax and muttered it made things worse. The pounding went on at all hours for several days, exceeding anything of the previous weeks and I could not imagine those pieces had time to cool between shots. No fort had ever suffered such punishment. One day a thousand balls smashed into the walls, the next day two, then three. One day we thought five. It was often as rain in a torrent, *boom-boom-boom, boom-boom*, no longer every moment, but every breath. I do not know how to describe the cave of thunder we lived in, or the effect it had on us, which would persist forever.

Sometimes the guns would fall silent in the middle of the night and the enemy officers would beat a call to arms just to rouse and disorient us. But to our surprise no assault came, only the iron fury of Turgut and the Pashas, enraged that this small castle, which should have fallen in three or four days, yet managed to defy them.

Each twilight I sat with the others behind mattresses or barrels and gazed about the spectral landscape in which we existed, neither alive nor dead. By now Fort St. Elmo resembled some ancient desert stronghold, walls eroded by the elements over the centuries until the sharp, original outlines had begun to melt into formlessness. This erosion had taken place in half a moon. From the midst of the rubble arose our makeshift defenses, and all about them were scattered cooking pots, spits and the remains of fires, as if the wind had uncovered long-buried relics. The remains of the ravelin, the curtain, the piazza were all covered with corpses; entrails were mixed with the earth; the stones were slippery with blood and everywhere the eye lit on heads, arms, legs separated from their bodies. Pairs of eyeballs leered from the debris and we leered back through blackened faces as groans ascended everywhere from the earth of this living cemetery. While the enemy dragged their dead away from the ditch, we burned ours outside near the cavalier and the smoke of human flesh mingled with the smell of gunpowder and the stench of corruption.

Tho' we spared no effort in attempting to repair the fort and maintain the defenses, the men ate and prayed. Between roars of the guns they continued to tell stories. One evening around a fire, Caravajal was speaking of a Frenchman and a Spaniard who had joined a sortie from a besieged fort to be taken prisoner by the Sultan. His Majesty said he would spare the Frenchman's life if he told him what quantity of provisions remained in the fort. The Frenchman replied, "Sufficient for a month."

The Sultan put the question to the Spaniard, who replied, "Sufficient for two months, if not three."

His Majesty declared the Frenchman should be bastinadoed for telling a lie.

But the Spaniard said, "Your Majesty, he tells you no lie. For there is no more than a month's provisions for eaters like the French, but there is twice as much, or more, for the Spaniards, who live sparingly and are satisfied with a small matter."

If e'en the French among us laughed, it was the laughter of men who no longer had the strength to quarrel amongst themselves, and at each sunset saw with greater clarity that they were doomed. During those days I came to feel closer to Balthazar than e'er before, because tho' neither of us would say it, we both knew we were taking our final leave of one another. One night in the middle of the month, I said a general assault must soon come.

"Yes, of course," he answered as we sat, as usual, against a wall.

"We cannot survive it," I said.

"I know." He picked up a hand by him, tossed it away.

"Balthazar ... " I faltered, "do you remember on Gelves, when we almost captured Turgut? Imagine if we had done it!" This was not at all what I had hoped to say.

"Almost captured him!" he repeated, smiling. "*Moy foy*, your memory is rosy. Now getting to Constantinople last year, that was something—and getting out!"

"Malvasia."

"*Mort de Dieu*, there was an exploit—unfortunately failed." He shrugged. "And what about that time when we tricked the Greek merchant into giving us a galley?"

"I don't remember that," I said.

"How could you forget, my friend?"

I gazed at this companion with whom I had lived thro' so much and from whom to my own misfortune I had learned so little, whose beard was now caked with blood as well as stippled with grey. My heart burned to tell him how much I was in his debt, but I could not find the words to utter for fear of appearing foolish, knowing as well that he would disapprove of such sentiments. "Do you regret your vow of obedience,

Balthazar? that you did not rise higher in the Order, or that you did not retire to write your memoirs?"

He shrugged, or made a motion more ambivalent. "Perhaps the last. As for the Order, you see Francisco, unlike most of my brethren, unlike Parisot or Romegas, I have slowly come to see the world as a question. To live in a kingdom where answers flee as quicksilver is hardly comfortable, but everyone knows the great battle we now fight is the last Crusade, and regardless of whether Grand Signor or Grand Master triumphs on Malta, the kingdom of certainty is vanished forever. Villegaignon understood this, I have said so before. We Knights have no place in such a landscape. Perhaps you do, my friend."

The conversation proceeded no further, for the cannon then fell silent. We expected another burst of Turkish music or perhaps the assault itself, but soon shouting from the walls told us that an emissary was approaching under a flag of truce. All the officers—Negroponte, Monserrat, Miranda, Mas, Medrano, la Motte, Vañon—gathered at Mas's Post to see a Turk picking his way toward them thro' the ditch. When he stood below the ruined wall, he surprised everyone by addressing them in excellent and lofty Italian: "Mustafa Pasha *Hazretleri* knows that the valiant Knights have resolved to abandon this fort, but that the Grand Master of your order, against all reason and practices of war, has forced you to remain in the ruined castle. For this reason Mustafa Pasha generously offers you liberty and safe conduct to whither you desire, that you shall have better treatment by the Sultan Soliman than by your own cruel Grand Master, if only you should lay down your arms and leave the fort."

The only answer the emissary received were several arquebus shots and *granadas*, which scared him off into the night.

"They must be getting desperate," sneered Medrano.

"Perhaps," answered Negroponte more seriously, "but they seem to know what goes on here. Who has told them?"

Someone muttered it must have been the Jews, but at least one of them was already dead. Each officer went to muster his company. After some hours, it was discovered that one of Medrano's fifers had disappeared.

In the grey dawn Yakhshi admitted to himself that all was not well,. Around the pot at camp, his *yenicheriler* were openly grumbling about the progress of the siege. "We expect losses," *Oda-bashi* Carullah was saying, "but more than two thousand of our men have fallen trying to take that fort. The *topchular* have not sufficiently leveled it."

"How level do you expect it to be?" barked Yakhshi. "If it were any more level you could walk across it like a desert. You will do your duty as a son of the Sultan or I'll call you a dog."

Carullah's face burned with shame and he got to his feet and left the pot.

Hiyer, Yakhshi didn't know what was taking place. As they watched the numbers of the dead mount, more and more soldiers had been behaving dishonorably and Piyale had already taken from some of them their *timarlar*. The field hospital overflowed with the wounded and dying and, though they had cleaned up the big spring, it seemed every fourth man yet had cramps in his stomach or the shits. *Peksimet* was low and the daily ration had been reduced until Uluj-Ali could bring back more supplies from Barbary. He had just sailed to Africa with four galleys laden with the sick and wounded, and was expected to return in a few days with stores of oil, raisins, honey and butter. If things got much worse ...

The army needed a success. *Evet*, one of the gunners had sunk an infidel galley in the harbor, but yesterday the *Beylerbeyi* of Rhodes had been killed by a shot from the big fortress while he was inspecting his guns. Yakhshi decided to tell Mustafa about the low spirits of the men and walked over to headquarters. The *Pashalar* were speaking about this infidel fifer who had crossed over, saying that he wanted to come to the True Faith and that he knew how to capture the Santarma fort. No one took him seriously about either matter, but Mustafa was well aware of the havoc discontented *yenicheriler* could wreak. He and Turgut agreed to personally lead the grand assault.

I need not speak of the two attacks on the fifteenth of June, which like the others were repulsed with heavy casualties, some four hundred Turks and sixty Christians. Afterwards, the Grand Master sent over more supplies and reinforcements. The bombardment hadn't let up. To be sure, its strength, and the many false alarms the enemy raised, foretold one thing: The grand assault was approaching.

Two hours before dawn on Saturday, the sixteenth of June, the guns again fell silent, leaving that unearthly quiet that no one any longer believed and that we all feared. For good reason. From that silence a single voice arose, drifting down Mt. Sciberras. The instant the foreign melody of that lone muezzin reached our ears, we were on our feet, grabbing breakfast, collecting weapons. The assault did not come at once. When the muezzin stopped, the entire enemy camp responded with a shout whose size alone told us what we were in for. The muezzin's singing and the response went on until the first rays of the sun, when the *iayalarlar* took up their accursed warbling and the musicians began pounding their drums and cymbals. With the rising light, I climbed to the walls where, standing by Pietru, I gazed upon the sea of men and banners he and Balthazar had first seen rise two weeks before. I could not count the numbers gathered above us for the attack; some said eight thousand. I do know that when the horns and trumpets added their voices to the shouting, the trilling and the beating, it produced a noise that no one had ever heard, and we thought the end of the world had come.

Pietru and I embraced and brought up the *tromba de fuego*.

They came from every side with ladders, screaming *"La ilah illa'llah!"* and all else. They attacked the front of the fort, battered by their guns for weeks now. They attacked the Post of Mas from the Marsamxett side. They attacked de Sengle's cavalier at the water's edge. The determination of the foe was a wonder to behold, but ours was no less; nay, it was greater. Juan de Guaras had ordered each Knight surrounded by two pikemen and an arquebusier, and in case the arquebusier had no time to reload, the pikemen could put a haft into his hand. We had again piled up fire weapons on the walls and for every scaling ladder placed against the wall, a hoop was lit and hurled by tongs into the ditch. Not a moment passed without a *granada* exploding, or when you did not see a soldier whirling a fire ball around his head, letting fly. As the Turks crowded into what remained of the ditch, three and four men together cast down upon them the gaming tables, which had been driven thro' with iron spikes. Troops threw down iron hooks on chains to yank weapons and standards from the arms of the climbing foe, and sometimes yank their heads.

With the fire tube in hand Pietru and I ran to the bridge, where Turks had made a breach in the wall and were once more attempting to storm the fort. The heat from the *trompe* was as an oven. The thing belched and sputtered, spitting forth its flames, and with the wind blowing against us we more than once nearly cooked ourselves. Somehow amidst its all its groans it held and we dispatched one infidel after another. Neither were the Turks sparing of their own *granadas*, and as the hours wore on, it became a common sight to see a Knight climbing into a barrel to douse himself before he roasted alive within his armor.

Again and again the enemy poured in fresh troops. Men too wounded to fight carried water and they refreshed us, but every one of us knew we could not keep this up forever. I quickly lost sight of Balthazar; old Miranda, not far from me, took an arrow in the thigh. He refused to retire. The Colonel ordered one of his men to bring a chair up to the battlements and he continued wielding a pike all day.

The west wind caused problems. Smoke from our own guns and the fires in the ditch were blowing into our eyes and at times no one could see anything. When the *tromba de fuego* was spent, Pietru and I ran down to recharge it. We had just done this from supplies that had been gathered together in one corner of the piazza and were making our way up the steps to the walls again when the wind carried a spark from somewhere, which lit the store. At once it went up in flames, sending the fireworks fizzling and crackling in every direction. Men afire hurled themselves screaming into the cistern. Comrades ran to cover them with blankets, but in the confusion of battle many burnt to death and we lost half the munitions. Seeing this, Ix-Xabaw and I turned to each other and swallowed, not believing we would live past sunset. Again we took each other's hands and returned to the bridge. Truly, the writhing sea of foemen that stretched up Sciberras had in no way diminished. This day even the dervishes were taking part.

Balthazar stood on the cavalier with Sagra. The Turks were making every effort to attain the tower, sending in their high-born and experienced men. For all the battering the cavalier had sustained, it was so massive that it yet retained some of its shape, and now thirty Turks had gained its spur, which jutted out toward the water. Seeing the foe climb the spur, placing their ladders to the gun platforms above, the Knights did not wait a heartbeat before employing fire hoops and *granadas* here as well. One of Balthazar's pikemen hurled a javelin to which a *granada* had been tied. It hit its mark; the pot and the janissary exploded over everyone around him. The numbers were great, tho'. Archers stood everywhere about the base of the tower. Having survived the bombardment of the tower for three weeks, Sagra now took a shaft in his thigh. For some moments he fought with his broadsword as the enemy gained the lower platform, then he and the other Knights retreated up the steps to the higher platform, where the big culverin had stood. There he took another arrow in his leg and an arquebus ball thro' his neck and collapsed. Balthazar and another carried him down across the bridge into the fort and returned to the battle. The janissaries yet crowded the lower tier, bringing forth ladders and Balthazar took up one of those weapons he loathed, a fire hoop.

As he had previously, the Grand Master watched the fighting from the walls of Fort St. Angelo. The midday sun illuminated the battle with sharp clarity. Across the brilliant ribbon of blue, metal glinted through the smoke; fireworks shimmered briefly in the daylight: blue, red, green; white standards surrounded the crumbled yellow limestone of St. Elmo. No one watching this assault could doubt it was the fiercest of the siege. The waves of barbarians crashing against that fort would soon inundate it. de Valette walked over to one of the gunners, Diego, who stood by his pieces at the fortress edge.

"Señor," said the Grand Master, pointing, "do you see the enemy scaling Colonel Mas's Post?"

"Yes, Eminenza, I think so."

"Can you assist the defenders?"

Diego glanced at the Grand Master. "Monsignore, Fort St. Elmo lies six hundred paces across the water. No one can aim so surely."

"It is a risk we must take. Open fire."

Diego did as he was told. He and his mates loaded a fifty-*libbre* piece, leveled it and touched the match; the gun roared. A few heartbeats later he saw a puff of smoke and dust arise from the fort and knew that he had laid his gun too far to the right. "I fear we have hit the defenders, Eminenza."

de Valette ordered him to try again.

This time Diego aimed a *dito* to the left and the shot fell true. The Grand Master left him.

Vigo and Isabella again watched the spectacle from the Hospital. "Were this nighttime, I do not doubt that we would witness a greater ... conflagration than we saw a week ago. We will see many wounded tonight, if any."

"What do you say, Dr. Jean?" asked Isabella.

"This battle has raged five hours and the Turks show no sign of breaking off their assault. If by a miracle Fort St. Elmo holds, we will receive many wounded; if it does not, we shall receive ... none. Signora, be prepared to open your house for the casualties."

"My house?"

Vigo nodded. "Yes, Noble Lady, God gave death to man, but he also gave him physicians whom He endowed with His mercy that they might help their fellow men delay death until the last possible moment."

Isabella acknowledged the mild reproach. Watching the battle, she felt yet another attack of panic but held it at bay, even as she understood that her fragile spirits were on the verge of deserting her. She would open her house, of course. "This can get much worse, can it not, Doctor?"

"Yes, Noble Lady, it can get much worse."

The first shot from Fort St. Angelo landed at Colonel Mas's Post. The flying rock splinters killed eight men instantly and wounded at least that many others. Seeing their chance, the Turks began to storm the breach. Pietru and I ran over, as did many others, but all of us knew this was the end. Within moments the Turks would overwhelm us. Truly, they were overwhelming us as they poured over the ruined parapets. The men fought bitterly, desperately. When swords and half-pikes failed, they went for their daggers. When daggers failed, bare hands. Yet so great were the janissaries' numbers and so fierce their determination we could not stop them. Then the second shot from Fort St. Angelo landed in their midst, sending twenty of them to Hades, and Fortune blew the other way. Not knowing what hit them, the barbarians retreated, but only for a moment.

The battle raged on.

For seven hours we knew nothing but exhaustion and will. It was not enough. Caravajal went down as befit him. A janissary on the wall took his sword arm with a blow from a scimitar. As the blood gushed forth from the stump, the Spaniard yet grappled as he could with this foeman with his remaining arm, declaring, "Do what you please, for tho' I have not an arm to defend me, I still have a heart and know how to die!" The Turk freed himself and ran the Spaniard thro' the gut with a knife.

Caravajal struggled to his feet and cried out, "Let my life die, for reputation lives!"

Those were his last words and in the next instant his head was taken.

Medrano was struggling with a magnificently dressed Turk who had gained the wall and planted one of Mustafa's standards atop a gabion. They fought hand to hand on the edge of the wall, neither yielding a step. Finally, with his hand around the Turk's throat, Medrano managed to push him over the wall onto the sea of his comrades. Crying that the infidels would never take this fort, he grabbed the standard, hurling it down upon the one he had overturned. In the next instant he fell over dead with a ball in the forehead.

Pietru and I ran down to recharge the *trompe*. Luckily, a barrel of the mixture remained and we were able to do so. But this time when we mounted it on my shoulder and lit it, the thing exploded.

Eighty-Nine

Yakhshi stood on the ravelin, stunned. With his wounds, he had not stormed the Santarma fortress, but he had fired all day on the infidels from this tower and had seen everything. The fort belonged to them. Why had the assault been broken off? Was it that shot from the big fortress that had killed so many? The *Boluk-bashi* intended to find out. God, he'd fuck the mother of the cur who again let Santarma slip through their fingers.

Yakhshi struggled angrily to Mustafa's headquarters at the main camp and with a bow requested to see the Pasha. Along the way he discovered he'd lost twenty men this day. By now more than half his *boluk* had been killed and he didn't like it. He would tell those *Pashalar* that unless they came up with a sensible plan for taking the fort, the *yenicheriler* would refuse to fight.

At headquarters he was told to wait, for the *Pashalar* were conferring. Yakhshi heard familiar voices shouting from within the marquee.

"This is a disgrace!" Turgut cursed. "What kind of women have your *yenicheriler* become, that with four thousand arquebusiers and archers in the trenches, they again failed to take a ruined castle?"

Mustafa replied sharply that Turgut's corsairs had fared no better, though the road had been cut by the *yenicheriler*. Unyielding, Turgut demanded to know why Mustafa hadn't sent in fresh troops for a final assault. Mustafa's anger at the shame of this day in no way ceded place to the corsair's, and his anger only deepened as Turgut attempted to fix the disgrace on him.

"You witnessed with your own eyes the bravery of the *yenicheriler*," Mustafa replied. "The day was long and to ready fresh troops would have taken much time. What are men? We have thousands in reserve. Do not fear, the fort and Malta shall be ours."

"Ours!" The famous contempt was easily heard without the tent and Yakhshi knew Turgut had scoffed. "We have thrown thirteen thousand balls against that fort in the past weeks and have lost four thousand troops. de Valette has been like a fox and is determined that it will live to the last. He must know that relief is coming. Why else would he cast away his few, as we do the many? We must heed the little fifer who says they have no more ovens for cooking in the fort and that all the bread comes from the town. I will put two more guns on my battery at Marsamshet and build a new one by the cave where your men are already firing on the boats that cross the harbor." Turgut added he would again send men across the harbor to the spur with the gallows. "We will put an end to Santarma once and for all."

Having heard all this, the *Boluk-bashi* thought better of confronting the *Pashalar* and sullenly retired to his tent. Turgut, at least, spoke boldly.

When Romegas brought word that Fort St. Elmo had held against the grand assault, de Valette repaired to the Chapel of St. Anne to give thanks to God. Nor did he fail to thank l'Isle Adam for his example lo those many years ago at Rhodes. Yet, while he prayed above the tomb of his predecessor, he could not but understand the peril of Fort St. Elmo and in the morning wrote to Don Garcia:

Illustrissimo e Reverendissimo Signore: Since I dispatched to you Salvago, I have twice written to you via Notabile and via Gozo, and I can only hope those letters have reached you. Not having received from you letters or messengers, I ordered a special envoy to leave immediately for Messina with a dispatch.

de Valette reported that the envoy never managed to get out of the harbor and ran his fregata into the ground in order to save himself from the Turks. He told the Vice Roy of the disposition of the enemy fleet, which had moved from Marsa Scirocco north to St. George's Bay because the infidels were short of water. They were now waiting to get into Marsamxett. Most of all, he made certain that the Vice Roy understood the barbarians were besieging Fort St. Elmo, "which God has until now preserved for us, and I trust will continue to do so."

This hope is based on yesterday's events, when an attack of four hours was successfully met by our valorous troops, fully trusting in God. The Turks had established a bridge on the western Marza Moxet side, and four desperate attacks were repulsed with great loss to the enemy, but not, however, without harm to us, as to my great grief Captain Medrano was slain. This success has so greatly encouraged our troops that I hope the castle may hold out until your arrival, especially as the enemy's battery is not so furious as before. If I could have a few companies of soldiers, or even what was available on our two galleys, I do not think that the enemy could ever take the castle from us. As it is, while awaiting help, I have sacrificed all I possessed, both of stores and men.

We, even if we must all perish, fully trust in your devotion and noble courage, knowing that you will not neglect us, and as you know in what a perilous position we will be in if your help is delayed, we hope you will send us immediately some companies of soldiers, especially as they can easily get through by landing at Pietra Nera, as the Turks have abandoned the eastern side of the island. Our salvation depends on you. In you, after God, we place all our hope. I warmly entreat you not to abandon us, and firmly trust in your faith and goodness. May you remain in health. Da Malta á 17 di Guigno 1565. Servitore di Vostra Eccellenza, Il Gran Maestro Fra Iehan de Valette.

Having satisfied himself with the tone of the letter, de Valette ordered Starkey to have two ciphered copies made. He then ordered a *fregata* be carried overland to a small bay in the area the enemy had abandoned, with instructions to carry the first copy to Sicilia. He gave like instructions for the other copy, offered a silent prayer to God, and repaired to the Hospital.

God had not wished me to die. I awoke late at night in a bed in a large, splendid house. Slowly, as my eyes became accustomed to the darkness, I perceived Isabella asleep in a chair at my side, the candle by her spent. For some time I regarded her, understanding neither my whereabouts nor, truly, why I lived at all. At length, Isabella, sensing that I had awoken, lifted up her head and discerned my gaze on her. She at once fell to her knees, clasping her hands together.

"Thank God," she said, "we have been praying since last night."

"What happened?" were the only words that came to my head.

"Your weapon burst," Isabella replied, lighting the candle, "knocking you and Pietru senseless. Another soldier was able to damp the flames with a blanket, but as no one knew whether you were alive or dead, they sent you back on the boats yesterday. The burns on your neck and back were not serious and we have salved them."

My hand at once went to my neck, where I felt the bandage covering a slippery ointment. "Pietru?"

"He was not so badly hurt and remained in the fort."

"Balthazar?"

Isabella offered only a faint smile. "He was wrestling with a Turk on the great tower and fell from a platform. His injuries are serious, but he lives and lies in the Auberge de France."

Only hearing this did the full import of Isabella's words strike me. "The fort has not been taken?"

She crossed herself. "It is a miracle, truly. So many have said that they could no longer stand for exhaustion, and had the Turks attacked but once again, St. Elmo would have fallen. God was with us. The damnèd barbarians lost above a thousand of their best men. Would that they had lost them all." Isabella pronounced those last words with a hardness I'd never before discerned in her voice, and for a moment I wondered at it.

It was of small consequence this day. The fort may not have fallen, but cannonading from Sciberras told me that its siege continued. "Mas, Miranda ... they all remain?"

Biting her lip, Isabella nodded again. "Medrano was killed. Tho' he was a private soldier, Parisot will have him buried with the Grand Crosses. Vañon is dead; la Motte died today of his wounds; Sagra is in the Infermeria. Methinks he will survive. Mas, Miranda, Monserrat and the Bailiff of Negroponte are all wounded, but fight on. Parisot has sent over three hundred more volunteers."

"I must go," I said, attempting to rise from the bed.

Isabella resolutely pushed me back. Such was my exhaustion and the pounding in my head that I lacked the strength to resist. "Dragut has again put men on Gallows' Point and is building a battery near the Alicate cave. Succours will no longer get thro'."

"Then Fort St. Elmo is doomed."

"Yes," she said with a fatal resignation, "Fort St. Elmo is doomed."

When Isabella returned at daybreak I had already slipped out of the house, determined to do something, anything. Making my way to Fort St. Angelo, I found Diego at his post. With an outstretched arm, he pointed to Turgut's gun battery being built at the cave, this side of St. Elmo, as well as to a trench Turgut had ordered dug—it led from the ditch of the fort down to the water's edge near the sea grotto. If a boat managed to get past the new battery, fire from the trench would stop it from reaching the *porta del soccorso*. Turgut's only mistake was that he had not done this weeks ago, for now, surely, Fort St. Elmo would be cut off.

To see better, I climbed to the top of the cavalier. Turgut's men had also overrun Gallows' Point. For a second time Mareschal Copier had led a company out to meet them and was now cutting them to ribbons. Again my eyes were drawn across the Great Port to the new trench. It seemed to me that I saw the bright robes of a nobleman glittering there. Stronger than e'er before, the terrifying sense welled up, overpowering me. With my hand to my brow, I staggered, knowing that at long last, my moment of grace and opportunity had arrived.

"Is that piece charged?" I shouted to the gunner nearest me.

He nodded.

"Fire at that trench!"

Following my outstretched finger, he laid the culverin and fired. Wide. "That's near six hundred paces," he protested. "It's only luck if you hit anything."

I answered: It is not luck; it is *kairos*.

We loaded the piece again. This time I took aim and touched the match. The gun roared. A heartbeat passed, two. A distant cloud of dust in the trench—and the bright robe was gone.

"Who was that?" the gunner asked.

"You have just witnessed the death of Dragut," I replied. With unfettered elation, I raised my arm into the air and roared.

The gunner's jaw dropped. For a moment he regarded me with an expression of awe, which slowly dissolved into a grim smile.

"You're jesting," he said.

By nightfall, whispers had raced thro' the Borgo that I had killed Dragut and everywhere I went people clasped my hands, naming me their deliverer. The hours did nothing to diminish my elation. After fifteen years, I had been released from an invisible chain.

I went to the Auberge de France to tell Balthazar the news and entered the refectory, which was being used as a hospital ward. There, amidst many in like condition, I spied Balthazar roaring at the top of his lungs as Vigo and a French Knight on duty manipulated his leg with the help of a long wooden lever-*ambe*. At length Vigo said, "I apologize that it took this long to get to you, Balthazar, but there have been ... so many, and we ... so few. We have put your thighbone back in its socket. I am afraid that it may be some months before the pain disappears ... if ever."

"Months!" shouted Balthazar. "I say, who here has months! Just be certain I can walk, my friend."

"You will walk, my friend—wait a few days." Vigo fed the patient a vial of laudanum and, as he departed, turned to me and said in a weary voice, "I am pleased to see you alive, Francisco." He laid his hand on my shoulder; I clasped it for a moment in my own and he moved to the Auberge de Provence.

"I have fulfilled my destiny," I announced to Balthazar, sitting on the edge of his bed.

"Then you may die a happy man," he replied drowsily as the laudanum took effect. "This is why you were not meant to perish in Fort St. Elmo. As for me, I am also happy. The fall was long, but luckily the Turk was beneath me. I expect a full recovery ... "

We talked for a time, exchanging what news we had. As Balthazar fell asleep, I promised to visit him on the morrow, and departed.

Despite the death of Turgut, the Turks kept up the bombardment of Fort St. Elmo as if nothing had transpired; nay, with ever more fury. After vespers I found Isabella at her home. She had already heard the news. "Parisot wishes to speak to you," she said, "at the Palace."

I apologized for intruding; I know she had forbidden me from setting foot in her house again, but as I had awoken here ...

"We must put that behind us, Francisco," she answered with a somewhat distant air. "Understand, though: I no longer have the strength to save your soul. You must save it yourself."

The old nurse on the divan was moving her head slowly from side to side, muttering—shrieking—something in turns; an ancient Cassandra prophesying to herself alone. She seemed far frailer than the last time I had set eyes on her.

"Oh, how I hate the old witch!" Isabella fairly shouted, tearing at her hair. "Why does she not die already!"

"She is merely an old, frightened woman, Signora, with whom you enjoyed reciting verses." Without waiting for a response, I took my leave.

At the Magisterial Palace a page announced me to de Valette. The Grand Master looked upon me with more than his usual severity. "People are saying you killed our great enemy Dragut. Is this true, Señor?"

I nodded.

"How do you know?" he asked.

"I know," I replied. "For this purpose God kept me on Malta."

While we thus stood face to face, the same page announced a renegado from Lombardy. Bowing profusely, the fellow said he had this very morning seen Dragut laid low in a trench, his brains oozing from his mouth, nose and ears. He had lost the power of speech and Mustafa ordered his body covered to prevent the troops from learning about it.

"If you're lying," answered de Valette, "I'll have you hanged."

The Lombard swore on his mother's grave that he was telling the truth. Dragut had been inspecting trenches when a shot from one of the Turkish guns hit the scarp and sent a splinter into the corsair's head, behind the right ear.

"You say it was an accident?"

Fervently the Lombard nodded.

de Valette dismissed the renegado, scarcely able to conceal his joy. With hands clasped before him he lifted his eyes to Heaven and sank to his knees. At length he rose, regarded me with a mixture of wonder and disbelief, and dropped into my hand two priceless diamonds.

Vincenzo Anastagi had just returned to Lady Gausconi's home in Notabile from the daily sortie. It had not been much different from the others: Turks foraging, hunting for slaves and booty; a skirmish, some killed. The infidels do not know how to fight on land. Anastagi put his helmet on the table, thinking to write a dispatch, when the door opened and Lady Emilia presented his lieutenant, Vincenzo Ventura.

"Sir, we have captured a renegado. You'd best come with me."

Anastagi followed Ventura to the cathedral square. There a crowd surrounded two young men, one dressed in Christian garb, the other in Turkish. "I found this one in the countryside," said Ventura, pointing to the one in Turkish clothing, "and brought him back. This one," he pointed to the other, "claims to know him."

"Who are you?" Anastagi said to the one dressed as a Christian.

"I am Stefano from Modon," that one replied. "I was captured by the Turks five years ago but wish to return to my mother church."

"And you know this man?"

Stefano nodded hurriedly. "Yes, I saw him in Mustafa's tent the other day. He is a fifer for Captain Medrano and was telling the Pashas how to capture the fort."

At once, furious cries arose from the crowd of people on the square. Unsheathing his rapier, Anastagi silenced them. "Strange, one day you are in Mustafa's tent, the next you are here," he said to this Stefano, then turned to the fifer. "Is it true?"

"I just wanted to find a boat to Sicily!" that one cried. "Nothing more!"

"Were you in that tent?"

The renegado remained silent.

Anastagi nodded to his lieutenant and had the fifer tied to the tail of the nearest horse. With terror in his eyes, he immediately confessed to everything. Anastagi turned, letting the mob at him. They cut him up with pointed bamboo and knives. The last words Anastagi heard were, "O great goodness and mercy of God!" He had not decided what to do about this Stefano but told Ventura to find Bajada or another courier to take an urgent message to the Grand Master. It was probably too late.

Turgut might have been dead, but Mustafa had no intention of leaving off the siege. He continued building the new platform and the trench to the sea grotto to prevent succours from reaching Fort St. Elmo. He had put boats in the water too. For a few nights after the general assault on the sixteenth, the Grand Master attempted to send over more food, mattresses and sails to the defenders, tho' it become ever more hazardous. E'en before the Turks emplaced guns on the new platform, arquebusiers and musketeers in the trench could prevent the defenders from using the sea gate for any purpose. Fort St. Elmo had been cut off.

Everyone in Birgu sensed the desperation descending from the Grand Master's Palace. There was scarce hope now for the fort; yet de Valette refused to abandon it, to no purpose dispatching boats and swimmers. Our desperation was no less. We the gunners atop Castle St. Angelo kept up fire on the new trench with little effect as it was so distant and well covered. Only Turgut's foolishness had allowed me to kill him.

The evening before the Feast of Corpus Christi we were bombarding the now-completed platform. At once a great explosion, not one of our guns. The mill had gone up. I sped over. The place was in flames, a cloud of black smoke belching forth thro' the ruined roof into the sky. Barrels of seawater stood nearby for such an emergency and we brought buckets. Of a sudden I thought, "Flaminia!" I couldn't find her inside. Eight men who'd been working or sleeping there were dead. Next to it was another store, going up also. I emptied my buckets, charged within. Flaminia was staggering to her feet, not knowing what had taken place. "I didn't do it," she said. "Don't be angry, *mio cuore*. Don't beat me."

I thought her words strange under the circumstance, and I brought her forth saying, "I know you didn't do it."

We managed to put out the fire but had lost two quintals of powder, a loss we could ill afford. The Turks saw the flames and cloud and you could hear them rejoicing full across the Port. They e'en launched fireworks. de Valette would have none of it and ordered us to fire ten or eleven shots into their lines. We did this with our heaviest pieces and they shut their traps.

Thenceforth, Eminenza forbade any common people from entering the fortress.

The mood at Fort St. Angelo was grim, and for this very reason the Grand Master decided to celebrate Corpus Christi as always. de Valette himself carried one of the poles to the canopy, along with the Grand Crosses, and Cubelles carried the Monstrance. But it was not as always. Soldiers ringed the town with muskets and arquebuses. With the interior defenses rising and the threat of enemy fire, the customary route to the Conventual Church was blocked. The men, women and children who joined the winding procession would drop to their knees, imploring Christ to deliver us. Isabella knelt near me in the crowd; each time a Turkish gun went off she shuddered, crossed herself and with a fierce determination written on her face, continued her prayers. de Valette, carrying his baton and with a napkin on his shoulder, served food to thirteen poor men at San Lorenzo, and the Grand Crosses also handed out food from silver services to the begging poor. His Majesty will surmise that the Monsignore's bearing did much to bring fortitude to the people on that dark day, but no miracle plays were performed and no miracles were granted.

Ninety

Pietru no longer slept at his post behind the parapets of Fort St. Elmo, for there were no longer parapets. There was no longer much of anything but a great heap of rubble. For some reason the Turks kept up their bombardment day and night, now with thirty-six pieces, but most of the balls glanced off the stones, just shoving them around. Only the great tower standing outside the walls resembled much its original shape, because it was so heavy. Early in the week the Grand Master had sent over hundreds more mattresses and sails. The men had used the mattresses to improve the shelters on the piazza. They'd stretched the canvases over their refuges and posts, dousing them with seawater to protect them from Turkish fireworks. It worked well enough, but with the enemy trench now only a stone's throw from the grotto, it was too dangerous to go out to collect water. Drinking water was running out too, and bread.

Why the Turks hadn't made another assault Pietru didn't know, except he'd heard that Dragut had been killed—May his carcass be stuffed with sand and nailed to the Doors of Hell for all eternity! They'd also been busy laying the new trench and battery, and after the general assault spent a few days collecting and burning their dead. Smoke from the fires sometimes drifted into the fort and burned the eyes.

Some of the men were convinced the assault would come yesterday, the Feast of Corpus Christi. They'd celebrated, without much happiness. Only thirty or forty men could squeeze inside the chapel and anyone who stood in the open was shot. Pietru remembered how he'd helped build Fort St. Elmo nearly fifteen years ago. He was proud of it then and now. They had defied this great army for a month, far longer than the defenders themselves had believed possible. With the last reinforcements there were again five hundred here, not a man among them who wasn't drenched in his own blood. Each one of them understood he was soon to die and the hours not spent in improving the defense were devoted to prayer and bidding farewell to one's comrades. Most of Pietru's comrades had already

died. The birds had fled weeks ago. The only thing left was the ceaseless
boom-boom-boom and the ringing in his head, and the only one to say good-
bye to was the fort, a good man. Ix-Xabaw knew he hadn't led much of a
life but was saddened he would never again see his wife and friends. He
only hoped someone would remember him.

The bombardment stopped at dawn. Again the infidel prayers, the
music, the unearthly trilling, the scent of *afione* wafting over the stones.
The attack, when it finally came in late morning, came from all sides.
Janissaries, azabs, corsairs. As far as Pietru could see, the numbers were
no less than during the last assault. The only thing less was their own
strength. He ran to the bridge opposite Colonel Mas's Post. They'd
repaired the breach with stones, but Pietru knew the Turks would be back.
That bridge was causing no end of trouble. Last night, an Italian lowered
himself down on a rope to burn it. He managed to get back without being
killed, but he couldn't set the bridge alight, so well had the Turks covered
it with damp soil.

Sure enough, the Turks stormed across the bridge. Pietru was loading,
cleaning the touch hole and firing as fast as he could, but could see no
end to them. Men near him hurled down rocks, fire hoops and *granadas*.
While he was ramming the scouring rod into his gun, a Turk appeared
on the wall above him. Pietru clubbed his shins with the arquebus, then
ran him thro' with his knife. As he stood up, a ball caught him in the
arm. Ix-Xabaw fell, saw that he was bleeding badly, rolled over to see
where the shot had come from. He thought the cavalier; janissaries covered
it. Janissaries were everywhere. At the front of the fort, they were pulling
down gabions with ropes and hooks as the defenders threw spears. With
arquebus balls bouncing about everywhere, Pietru stumbled down to the
piazza to be bandaged. Glancing over his shoulder, he glimpsed Colonel
Mas, never ceasing to wield his two-hander as the Turks tried to bring
down the repaired wall before the bridge. The accursed ringing never
stopped.

Yakhshi and some of his men had gained the big tower outside the fort.
The advice of the fifer was good. He'd said Turgut's battery had put so
many holes in the tower that they could find some to hide in. They'd sent
in some *azablar* with picks to make these places a little deeper, and it
worked. The infidels were yet above them on the top of the tower, but

they couldn't see the *yenicheriler* who had moved into these cuts below. Yakhshi and what was left of his *boluk* commanded the entire curtain. He began to pick off the knights in their splendid armor, one after another.

During the week, the besieged had found means to block up some of their dismounted pieces with wood and rope. Pietru had helped with this but knew the makeshift carriages would be difficult to point and he didn't think they would hold for long. As he climbed back toward the bridge, he saw Commander Monserrat at the wall opposite the big tower aiming two of these pieces at the janissaries perched there. The guns went off. One of them flew up into the air, nearly killing its gunner. The other held and killed some of the janissaries. Pietru sped over, joining the arquebusade now being directed against the cheer, but Monserrat had already been killed.

For a time the Turks retreated, frustrated at the resistance the shattered remains of this fort yet put up. Pietru did not for a breath believe they had gone for good, but he emptied his lungs and went to find some water. The cistern was dry. The Bailiff of Negroponte, old and wounded in three places, limped among the men, encouraging them, consoling them. Miranda on his stool near the bridge and Mas, both no less wounded than de Guaras, also shouted out encouragement to the men, but Pietru already understood this day was different than the others. Too many had fallen.

Within a few hours, the Turks were back, again gaining the big tower. For a second time they were chased away and for a third time they returned, once they had dismounted the remaining guns with shots from their own pieces on the ravelin. As the day wore on, Pietru scampered from one powder barrel to another, finding them empty. He crawled with parched lips from one dead arquebusier to the next, snatching apostles from their bandoleers or powder from their horns to fill his own gun. Everyone who remained alive was doing the same. Pietru did not know why he lived, but kissed the wheel-lock and crossed himself on the cuirass he wore. He fired, glanced at the sun baking them all and realized he was so dry he no longer sweated.

Toward evening the powder ran out and Ix-Xabaw took up fire hoops and *granadas*, but these had become scarce too. By sunset they'd tossed the last of them and he snatched up a pike from the hand of a dead man. Now the Turks had again breached the wall at the bridge and were charging thro'. The defenders gathered around Mas, who continued to swing his *montante* as Miranda behind him slashed with a halberd. Pietru ran thro' a corsair coming over the top, noticing from the corner of his eye how few defenders remained. Most were throwing rocks.

Twilight fell and the Turks retired. It seemed they'd waited too long this morning before launching their final assault. Pietru felt no elation. Not one of the men let out a cheer. As the enemy walked back to their trenches, Ix-Xabaw looked around. The fort was breached everywhere, most of the men dead. He counted. But for Mas, Miranda and de Guaras, none of the officers remained. Of the five hundred who lived this morning, only sixty now stood, every one of them dripping blood.

They retreated behind the barrels and mattresses, spiking all the guns and making a last attempt to repair the breach at the bridge. Thro' the ringing in his head, Pietru heard with clarity the groaning of the wounded that filled the air everywhere. Those able to walk dressed each other's wounds, but few went out to tend to the dying for fear of the arquebus fire from the ravelin and cavalier. All night, Juan de Guaras, the Bailiff of Negroponte, came to comfort the survivors and knelt with his men in the chapel. The few Knights, knowing this was to be their final night on earth, buried the holy relics and chalices beneath the floor of the crumbling chapel, and all the soldiers confessed to each other their sins. Pietru had lost his cross and talismans. The key to his wheel-lock alone remained to him. Clasping it tightly in his fist, he begged his wife and lost children to forgive him, and he prayed to the Lord to have mercy on his soul for the sake of the blood He shed for their redemption.

The waning moon was still up when de Valette's page announced a swimmer at the Magisterial Palace, mayhap Bajada. Negroponte had sent the swimmer to tell Eminenza what had taken place at St. Elmo.

"The men request further reinforcement and succours if you wish them to continue fighting," the messenger said. "Otherwise the fort is lost. They have killed two thousand Turks this day, but only sixty men remain."

de Valette did not turn from the window at which he stood. "The men of Fort St. Elmo have taught the Grand Signor a great lesson, that we will never yield to his tyranny. I pray to God that the fort not be taken."

"E—Eminenza, how?" asked the swimmer.

Romegas, at hand, said he would take some boats over to the fort. de Valette reluctantly nodded his assent.

Lescaut knew well the desperation of this act, but lost no time in summoning a handful of trusted men. They loaded the barque that usually brought water from the Marsa with drinking water and provisions; they loaded a dismantled galley and some other boats with weapons, and the small fleet set off.

"What can we hope to gain from such a hopeless gesture?" Captain Fanton pressed Romegas, who answered only that they could die with brave men as they swore to do. But they had hardly gotten into the Port when Turgut's new battery and musketeers from the new trench opened up on them. Under the rain of balls, Fanton dropped behind a wale and shouted to Romegas, who knelt by him, that they couldn't reach the fort. The Commander wouldn't hear him, got up and ordered the crew to row on. In vain; after a few more breaths a dozen Turkish boats met them. Romegas peered into the farther darkness. Piyale's fleet was already moving into Marsamxett. Lescaut steadied his shaking hands and ordered the relief to turn back.

As dawn broke, Yakhshi, with a fresh wound in his leg, was once again perched on the big tower, surveying the fort. He spat on what had taken place yesterday. Well over one thousand brave men killed and still they had not succeeded in capturing this heap of rubble. Yet as he gazed down onto the ruins and saw only a handful of defenders within, he knew that Santarma was at long last theirs.

The assault came again by the bridge. Yakhshi watched that knight at the repaired breach swing his great sword like the son of Shaitan, and the other one on the chair behind him waiting his chance with a spear, and once again he could not help but admire their desperate valor. The breach was opened again in short order and Yakhshi expected the storming to be over quickly, but those sixty defenders who had no weapons but swords, pikes and stones yielded not a step. Finally, after hours, one of them came forth beating a drum. Yakhshi lowered his arquebus, seeing that a parlay was going on, but he knew what the end would be. A messenger was sent to the Pasha and soon the answer came back: No mercy.

At once the men on the other tower began shooting and hurling rocks, and soon the *yenicheriler* were through the breach. They quickly surrounded the knight with the two-handed sword and cut him into little pieces. One of his comrades, seeing this, ran screaming with his spear at the attackers, but was killed and hurled into the ditch. The old knight in the chair with his pike soon had his head cut off and another old one with a two-handed sword fell from a ball from Yakhshi's own gun, he thought. The *Boluk-bashi* climbed down from his position and, stepping over the corpses, entered the fort by the bridge. The remaining defenders were crammed amidst their barrels and mattresses in the square below, selling their lives at a high price. One knight was desperately trying to send smoke signals from a fire, probably to tell the infidel master that defeat had come. Leaving off that stupid attempt, he ran with some others around the wall into the little church. The *yenicheriler* and *azablar* were killing anyone who groaned. Mustafa had offered an *altun* for each knight's head.

When Yakhshi made his way down to the square, he saw that the some of Turgut's men had beaten them by coming thro' the sea gate. They'd captured nine of the knights in the church and twenty or thirty of the Maltese.

"Give them over," the *Boluk-bashi* ordered.

The nearest of the corsairs spat to the ground. "Stick your prick up your ass. These are ours for ransom."

Yakhshi angered and named him the stone that had been bled upon by a two-cunted cow. These corsairs were mere rabble, undisciplined rabble. Weapons were suddenly drawn and a scuffle broke out, but everyone was exhausted and Yakhshi did not see that it made much difference. Let the infidels be sold into slavery. The fort was ours.

When he and the others were surrounded on the piazza and the corsairs came pouring thro' the sea gate, Pietru knew the end had come. The sword in his hand clattered to the ground, as did all the lances and halberds by him. E'en as the infidels shoved him toward the chapel, Pietru understood he would sooner die than be sold into slavery again. At that instant, Fra Balthazar's words came to him: Save yourself. The chance came moments later when a fight broke out between the janissaries and the corsairs. Without a heartbeat's hesitation, Pietru bolted toward the sea gate, several other Maltese on his heels. The corsairs didn't lose any time. Ix-Xabaw gained the grotto only paces ahead of his pursuers and, not caring whether the enemy waited in the trench nearby, or whether he lived or died, dove into the water. His wounds ached and his cuirass weighed him down, but he heaved harder than ever before in his life. He heard nothing but the sound of his own desperate breathing. After an eternity, he gained de Guiral's Post on the far side of the Port, dragged himself ashore and collapsed.

As Piyale's fleet sailed into Marsamshet harbor to the sounds of trumpets, the *Chorbajiler* tore down the banner of the infidels and hoisted the Turkish flag over the smoldering ruins of the Santarma fort. Yakhshi watched the ensign go up, but felt little joy at the sight. They had hurled nearly twenty thousand balls against this place to take it. They had lost nearly six thousand men, their best men. The *Boluk-bashi* took one last look around the heap of stones, covered everywhere with corpses and buzzing flies, and walked up the hill.

That day pyres sent their smoke over the sea and campfires burned all around the Marsa. Piyale had already been drawing up decrees for the transfer of *timarlar*; there would be dozens upon dozens. Towards evening Mustafa called all the men out and now they gathered in a big circle not far from headquarters. Yakhshi stood with the others, watching first Uluj-Ali's men carry Turgut's body to a waiting galley. Many whispered that Turgut had remained alive until this very day, only to send his soul to God the moment he knew Santarma fort was taken. Yakhshi wrinkled his nose, certain only that Turgut was dead and Uluj-Ali, who had just returned with supplies, was now himself appointed *Beylerbeyi* of Trablus. He would take Turgut to Trablus for burial, ferrying the sick as well, and was to carry grain to be made into bread. When they would see Uluj-Ali again, Yakhshi didn't know, but his bones told him that Turgut's death was the worst omen.

Once Uluj-Ali departed, some of the corsairs brought the Maltese *kafirlar* they had taken to the center of the circle. They had hidden the nine captured Knights and refused to turn them over, but Mustafa paid the corsairs for the Maltese and at once ordered them beheaded in the presence of the army.

Piyale stood outraged. "We have taken the fort. What is the reason for such senseless cruelty?"

"I remind you, Piyale," Mustafa answered, "that the Sultan has ordered us to leave no grown person alive." He then spoke of what the fort had cost them and that the infidels must know the Turks were not finished.

Piyale continued to protest, but Mustafa paid no heed and the order was swiftly carried out. Mustafa next commanded the heads of the last knights who had fallen brought to him and put on spears overlooking the big fortress. As the Pasha walked back to his tent, Yakhshi thought he heard him muttering, "If the son has cost us so dear, what shall be the price of the father?"

When that evening Toni Bajada reported to de Valette that the heads of the Bailiff of Negroponte, Colonel Mas, Colonel Miranda and Commander Monserrat were those adorning the lances on the battery opposite Senglea, he thought he had never seen such wrath cross a man's face.

But it was the next morning, the Feast of St. John Baptist, that no one ever forgot. Maugre the loss of Fort St. Elmo, the Grand Master had commanded that the feast of the Order's patron saint would be observed and he led a procession of Knights and soldiers to San Lorenzo. On the church's steps, whispers swirled that the Religion had lost thirteen hundred men during the siege of the fort, including one hundred and thirty Knights. As if overhearing and taking these currents to heart, de Valette drew himself up before the portal, tears in his eyes, yet proud.

"Yes," he said, "it is true. By the Will of God we have lost many of our best men and brave Knights, but in the course of war first the one is successful, then the other. I fear nothing from an enemy who has suffered such great losses, who might well be said to have been conquered by his victory. Our disaster is recompensed by the immortal glory won by those who defended the castle, and which must inspire all of us who yet live. For this reason I do not grieve. I order all the women to cease bewailing the loss of their husbands or sons, for such tears only bring succour to the enemy, and they are not worthy of those who died so nobly."

At this speech the crowd raised a cheer, reinvigorated with courage, but after celebrating a solemn Mass within the church, de Valette reappeared, only to be met on the same steps by a runner, begging the Grand Master to come quickly to Kalkara Creek. He hurried over. A crowd had already gathered at the banks there, but at once made way for

the Monsignore. Floating in the water before them were upon thirty
bodies tied to boards, yardarms, crosses. The red and white tunics left no
doubt these bodies were of Knights—most headless, some without
stomachs, all with deep, bloody crosses gouged into the middle of their
chests and their hearts ripped out. Mustafa had had them thrown into the
water, thinking the current would carry them across to Birgu, as it did.

Many witnessing this revolting spectacle sank to their knees, wailing,
covering their mouths in horror. Within moments, it seemed, news of
Mustafa's unsurpassed barbarity swept the Borgo. On every lips were cries
for vengeance, e'en while the cries were choked with the knowledge of
what we could expect from the Turks. At the sight of those mutilated
bodies, the Grand Master lost all restraint, every one.

I did not see de Valette at Kalkara; I saw him several hours later, when
followed by two servants carrying a barrel, he strode toward me and Diego
at the gun platforms atop Fort St. Angelo. From across the entire plaza
we sensed his terrible fury.

"Fire these into the Turkish camp!" he ordered abruptly.

Diego and I glanced into the barrel. Freshly decapitated heads. Turkish
heads.

"E—Eminenza ... ?" I sputtered.

"Are you deaf, Señor?" he roared. "Carry out my orders, or I'll have your
head as well!"

For an instant only did I dare gaze onto de Valette's face. This was no
longer the countenance of a man; a beast raged before me. Under that fury,
which exceeded anything of nature, Diego and I did as he ordered. We
rammed the heads of those prisoners into the barrels of our pieces and
fired them one by one across the Great Port.

I staggered to Isabella's house, where a servant nervously showed me
in. I found Isabella standing before the couch in her sitting room. "Die! I
want you to die, no barbarian shall live!" she screamed at the nurse,
beating her with every strength. "Die! Die! I curse you!" Isabella cried
again, now garroting the old woman, but I could see that Giansevere had
some time earlier passed from this life.

When Isabella heard me, she turned, face red and wet, and hurled
herself into my arms. "Have you ever heard of such cruelty!" she shouted,
wracked with sobs. "Is there no mercy on this earth?"

I told her what Parisot had done and she backed away from me in equal horror, hardly crossing herself before she was again convulsed by tears.

"God Almighty, we are all to lose our souls! Every one of us!"

I fervently hope His Majesty will forgive me for speaking plainly of these matters. Many told of how Piyale Pasha himself recoiled at Mustafa's barbarity, and I pray Soliman the Lawgiver had not countenanced it, for it was that moment, when the bodies of those valiant Knights washed up on Kalkara Creek, that every person on Malta understood surrender was impossible. At the same moment I, who had become hard, felt deep within me a small sense that the cruelty was devouring us. Beholding Isabella in a condition I had never seen caused something within me to break. She had attempted to save my soul. I would attempt to save hers.

Ninety-One

Candles again burned late at the Vice Roy's residence in Messina, and Don Garcia de Toledo must have wondered why messengers always arrived in the dead of night. By the time Don Garcia had deciphered the latest dispatch from the Grand Master, placed in his hands by a Maltese named Orlando, the sun had risen. He did not require the morning's bright light to perceive the desperation underlying the brave mask de Valette had worn while penning this letter, and without delay he sent for Rafael Salvago, who had just returned from the mainland. The moment Salvago stepped thro' the door, Don Garcia handed him the message.

"Then Fort St. Elmo yet holds?" the Knight said, wonder evident.

"Three days ago it held," corrected Toledo and ordered his servant to bring breakfast.

"We must send reinforcements at once," Fra Rafael went on, accepting the proffered chair as his voice changed from wonder to urgency.

It was with a severe puzzlement that Don Garcia regarded the emissary before him. "What do you believe I have been doing, Señor? Twiddling my thumbs? Your two galleys departed again for Malta yesterday with two of mine under my Captain General, Don Juan de Cardona. The six hundred troops available to me are on those vessels, including His Eminence's nephew Henri Parisot, recently arrived, and Maestro de Campo Melchor de Robles."

"It seems insufficient," the Knight replied sullenly, despite his knowledge of Robles's brilliant reputation.

At this the Vice Roy simply erupted. "You will address me as Eccellenza, Señor. And what, I may ask, is your proposal? Are Doria's ships arrived from Genoa? The Papal troops?"

Salvago conceded no to Illustrissimo Eccellenza; Gian Andrea had sent his galleys north to collect the soldiers Chiappino Vitelli was raising in Tuscana, while Alvaro de Sande was rummaging about Napoli. His

Holiness had pledged troops and those were also en route. "Spain, Eccellenza?"

With lessened heat the Vice Roy moved his shoulders. "I know galleys are coming but have heard nothing of late. It is yet early to have received word from Philip's cell in Escorial, but now that dispatches from Malta are reaching the capitals, believe me, every Christian in Europe will be rushing to the Grand Master's aid."

"Let us pray that is so," Salvago said, rising and taking his leave without having eaten, while Don Garcia glanced about the room, pensively considering the portraits of his forerunners in this office.

The weak glow of the lamps hardly brightened the expressions of old Fra Pedro de Mezquita and Vincenzo di Anastagi while they sat at the latter's desk in Lady Emilia's house. The past days had been especially difficult. News from the harbor was scarce, couriers often being taken en route to Notabile. Five nights ago, four galleys—the long-awaited relief—appeared off the island. Its chief Juan de Cardona sent out a skiff with a Knight aboard who gained the Old City. The fellow, Juan Martinez de Oliventia, reported with disgust that the Vice Roy had instructed Cardona not to land had St. Elmo fallen. It yet stood, so far as Mezquita and Anastagi knew. Mezquita sent Oliventia back with Esprit de Brunesay - Quincy to plead with Cardona to land the troops, but strong winds prevented them from getting anywhere and, shaking their fists into the air, the two Knights watched Cardona set off to Sicily again without them.

Mezquita could hardly control his despair at the turn of events, Anastagi his anger, both of which this hour deepened as they deciphered a letter Toni Bajada had just brought. Before vanishing into the night, the messenger himself had revealed its contents and the news could not be worse: "Fort St. Elmo fell yesterday." Bajada also told of the bodies at Kalkara Creek this morning and the edict the Grand Master issued after: All Turkish prisoners are to be executed, henceforth no quarter given. The two Knights breathed heavily; it was the first time either remembered any such order in the endless struggle between Christian and Infidel. No mercy.

Once Anastagi had deciphered the text before them, he read aloud the Grand Master's words about the taking of the fort:

... we are reconciled to the disaster, knowing that it must be due to the Will of God, who thus may have wished to give us a warning, without ruining us altogether, as it is not possible to doubt his goodness and omnipotence. I do feel we have the right to complain justly of those who have left us without help, and that during thirty-seven days our most gallant troops have withstood the full brunt of the enemy's attack (and this more by divine help than by human effort), while not the least succour or relief came from those from whom we had the right to expect it, and though they might have helped us more than once.

But I will put up with anything, knowing that such suffering is sent from God from who we have received all good, and from whom we hope to receive good in the future. I have understood from what has happened that we can place no hope in human help, since no letter, prayer, entreaty, or warning has brought assistance, nor even our orders moved those who ought to have obeyed.

Want of time prevents me writing on this matter to Don Garcia de Toledo. We leave it to you to inform him and our other friends, and had they listened to our demands, or sent us even slight help, we would not have lost Castle St. Elmo, in the defense of which we have sacrificed most of our troops. If Don Garcia does not hurry to free us from this siege, I fear he may not be in time ... However, we fully trust in God's love and providence, and God may at last move Don Garcia to hasten to our help, as our salvation now depends on how soon he may come.

The Grand Master requested that Mezquita immediately dispatch to Birgu the four companies of parish troops that had been held at Notabile, and he closed saying, "I pray to God to send us help from elsewhere."

Having finished the letter, Anastagi and Mezquita looked long at one another. "I have never heard in Eminenza's voice such anguish," the older man said.

Anastagi sat back, but before he could answer, Emilia knocked on the door with a service of food, requesting to enter. The two men admitted her, allowed her to read Anastagi's copy. Her face paled at once. "If Parisot has lost hope, we must all die," she said, her hand going to her mouth as tears betrayed her.

Hereat Anastagi did speak. "Eminenza's has every reason to despair at this dark moment, but we are not defeated. We shall send another courier to the Vice Roy tonight."

Mezquita himself was hardly encouraged. "Of the last two we sent out, one was captured; fortunately the Turks do not seem to have deciphered his letter. I fear we are lacking small boats."

"Then have the men build one!" Anastagi said forcefully, and at once set pen to paper, informing the Vice Roy of the destruction of Fort St. Elmo.

Blaij Vergã sat twiddling his thumbs on a barrel on the dockside of Pozzallo at the southern tip of Sicily. Since the first blighted attempt to gain Malta over two weeks ago, he felt like a pigeon flying in circles. They'd made a second attempt, only to be forced back to Pozzallo by contrary winds. They'd made a third attempt. Five, six days ago they reached Malta with four galleys, but word came down that the Vice Roy had ordered Captain General Cardona not to disembark troops if Fort St. Elmo had fallen. Cardona sent out a boat to discover whether the fort stood, but the crew never came back and Cardona returned to Sicily.

Here they were, stranded at this God-forsaken Pozzallo again. Vergã glanced at the men playing the forbidden *zecchinetta* nearby. These adventurers who'd come to win fame and glory couldn't even find enough whores to fuck and played that idiotic card game instead. Anger was increasing by the hour; tempers flared. Maestro de Campo Robles, on whom everyone put their hopes, was cursing ceaselessly and only the puny jester he'd brought along attempted to humor him. The usual ill will between the Spaniards and French, not to mention the Germans and Italians, wasn't helping. Two Englishmen had shown up too—God knows from where—but they could hardly speak a word to anybody. If this kept up, half the contingent probably would disappear—no, all of it.

As Vergã sat on the docks wondering what next, a commotion arose nearby at the Order's *patrona*. He went over. It seemed that within the last watch a bedraggled Juan Martinez de Oliventia, who Cardona had put ashore at Malta, had stumbled onto the dock from a small boat with another Knight, de Quincy. Now Rafael Salvago, having galloped down from Messina, was at this moment also rushing onto the embankment. Vergã followed Salvago aboard. No one present knew with certainty whether St. Elmo had fallen. Seeing the state of things, Salvago lost no time in giving St. Aubin and Cornisson new instructions: Leave immediately. Again. de Cardona was hardly pleased, but Salvago showed him a dispatch from Don Garcia and the Captain General acceded. The muscular Robles, keenest to be underway, lifted his eyes to Heaven and the strange, thin jester he had by him, said, "Luck comes with the Trinity."

"This is the fourth attempt," replied Robles and his jester smiled toothily, counting on his fingers.

Thereat Salvago took Maestro de Robles aside for a brief *teste-à-teste*. Only when de Robles nodded to Salvago, who made at once for the gangway, was Vergã able to grab the emissary's arm.

"Did His Holiness speak of my dispensation?" he asked.

"Yes he did," Salvago breathed with evident distraction. "It ... hangs in the balance. Your long service to the Religion and Romegas's petition work in your favor, but the circumstances of your birth do not. The Order's statutes are difficult to circumvent—even for a pope." For an instant, Salvago paused to cast a glance at the white kerchief yet adorning Vergã's arm. "Your case may have to wait for a Chapter General, and not all the testimony has been favorable—"

"No?"

"*Vertu de Dieu*, no. Violating Christian women can be overlooked, but pillaging Christian ships ... Some say you couldn't even name the three vows of the Order and that to admit you would be a disgrace."

"Fifteen years of devotion for such an answer!" Vergã cursed inadvertently at hearing this. "The bastard!"

"No, you are the bastard," returned Salvago. "That is the long and short of it."

"Who spoke against me?" Vergã suddenly erupted. "No, *Vertu de Dieu*, that can only be one man."

Salvago knew he had slipped and said no more, e'en as Vergã was consumed with indignation and mounting rage. Seeing him fume impotently, Salvago washed his hands of the affair and merely disembarked. That evening, after all the troops had once again been boarded, he watched the small relief set sail and returned to Messina.

It was daylight when Don Garcia and Rafael Salvago greeted the next courier from Malta, one Chevalier Tomas Coronel. As the weary messenger staggered into the Vice Roy's residence, Salvago examined him at arm's length with some alarm. "You have had a difficult crossing, Tomas?"

Coronel nodded as a servant thrust a glass of wine into his hand. "Mezquita and Anastagi sent me. The Maltese carried a boat from the Old City to the Gozo channel. *Mon Dieu*, at Gozo they didn't have anything but a barque strung together with rope for lack of nails and covered with ox hides. Torrellas from the garrison there let me have it, and we bailed it out every league of the way. Since Pozzallo, I have run six horses into the ground, myself as well."

Don Garcia was not much interested in the messenger's tale of woe. "What can you tell us?" he said, with undisguised irritation.

With the greatest reluctance, Coronel put the dispatch from Notabile into the Vice Roy's hands, and breathed. "Fort St. Elmo fell five days ago, Eccellenza."

Salvago thought the Vice Roy turned white as a sepulchre as he cast about for aqua vita. "A relief of four galleys sailed from Pozzallo two days ago," put in Fra Rafael. "You have no news of them?"

Coronel shook his head and Salvago knew that only the Grace of God had allowed the *piccolo soccorso* to sail before this news arrived—otherwise Toledo would have forbidden its departure. Salvago, now with Coronel's added voice, begged, pleaded with the Vice Roy for a larger relief. Papal troops were beginning to mill about Zaragoza's harbor under Pompeo Colonna and more soldiers were arriving each day. They reminded Illustrissimo again what the Knights of St. John had done for all Christendom and the expenses they incurred only last year ago at Peñon de Velez. Don Garcia showed little gratitude, especially when his guests told him for the hundredth time what the fall of Malta would mean for Sicilia and Europe. "If Fort St. Elmo lies in smoldering ruins," Salvago pressed on heedless, "we cannot afford another moment's delay. I beg you for four thousand foot. You will soon have them and it will suffice. I am certain."

"Are you?" asked the Vice Roy.

Hours later, while they were yet engaged in this animated discussion, another messenger arrived at the residence, handing the Vice Roy a dispatch. Don Garcia excused himself as he lumbered over to his desk and broke the royal seal.

For some time Salvago and Cornel stood watching, agitated, perplexed.

At length, the Vice Roy addressed them. "Messeri, this letter is from King Philip himself. I am not at liberty to reveal its contents. I can only say I am unable to satisfy your request at this time." With that, he begged forgiveness of the two Knights and escorted them to the door.

It was again the dead of night, between the twenty-eighth and twenty-ninth of the month, Vergã believed, when the relief force, having skirted Gozo to the west and encountering no enemy vessels, came to anchor off a place on the south of Malta called Petra Nigra, Black Rock. Maestro Robles, wasting no time, waved Vergã behind him and the two of them put to shore in a caique with a second oarsman and the Knight Quincy. No sooner had they gained the shore with its steep cliffs than voices called out to them from the darkness above. Maltese, hiding in caves.

The landing party climbed up the path to be met by some of these peasants, holding torches, clothed in little more than rags. In their pitiful Italian they informed de Robles that Fort St. Elmo had fallen.

Vergã sucked in his breath, knowing that this was the worst possible news, and not only because Captain General Cardona would refuse to disembark the troops under such circumstances. But as he pondered the future of Malta and Christendom, the Maestro de Campo turned to him and Quincy. "You are not to reveal a word to Cardona, do you understand me? This relief *must* land." Robles's countenance brooked no dissent. "Quincy, you know the Governor of the Old City?"

"Distantly. He will be surprised to see me," that one smiled.

"Go to him with Vergã. Have the cavalry brought at once to aid with the succours. I will return to the *patrona* to inform Cardona all is well."

Quincy and Vergã saluted, making off with some of the Maltese to Notabile. Robles returned to the galleys, told de Cardona that Fort St. Elmo yet held. Well satisfied, the Commander ordered all the troops disembarked with supplies, which was accomplished in short order. As de Robles and over six hundred men stood atop the cliffs, surrounded by barrels and munitions, they watched de Cardona with the four galleys set sail for Sicily. The Maestro de Campo breathed deeply. At last the *piccolo soccorso* had landed on Malta.

Ninety-Two

When the same night after I had fired Turkish heads across the Great Port, Pietru Galea staggered into my room in the Borgo, I broke into tears. I never expected to see anyone emerge alive from the smoldering ruins of St. Elmo, and the sight of the stocky Gozitan before me was as great a miracle as I had witnessed in my life. He did not immediately speak of the fort's final hours. I perceived only that he had been wandering about Birgu in a sort of stupor, half deaf, exhausted after his ordeal, wounds to be tended.

My room was already crowded, but I gave Ix-Xabaw a place on the bed and went to fetch a doctor. With the cries of the wounded everywhere, persuading a physician to see a lowly farmer was no small task, but I prevailed upon Vigo himself, who followed me to the room. As he salved and bandaged Pietru, we both listened to his story with an astonishment neither of us forgot. Once Vigo put him to sleep with laudanum, I turned to the doctor.

"How is he, Dr. Jean?"

"Better than most. In a few days he will fight again." The doctor's words carried a certainty that this siege was far from over.

"Doctor," I said, "you and I have been acquainted over many seasons. I have watched you use your art to heal the sick of body and the wounded. I have never heard you speak of the soul."

There was puzzlement in Vigo's eyes. "What do you mean, Francisco?"

"How is one to cure the soul in the midst of this ... this ... ?" I waved my hand.

"Ah," he said, glancing at the flickering lamp on my windowsill. Both of us were keenly aware that for the first night in a month most of the Turkish guns had fallen silent. "Mayhap you should consult a priest—or God. I think to save the soul is a more difficult ... *task* than to fix an arm. As Isabella fights off panic, she becomes ... hard, like—"

"—a soldier. *Captivo*. Hours ago she made to strangle the old nurse, but that one had already died. I threw her body over the walls."

"Ah," Vigo repeated. "No consecrated ground for the infidel woman."

"As we are shown no mercy, no mercy to the enemy." I thrust a copy of de Valette's edict under the doctor's nose.

The physician had seen it. "I believe God has breathed his mercy into the cures by which physicians treat their patients. The wise man who recognizes God's mercy will not scorn it, Francisco."

"You have sworn an oath to help the sick, is that not true?"

Vigo nodded.

"Knowing the Grand Master's decree, would you treat an infidel prisoner should one fall into your hands?" Mournfully Vigo glanced out the window and lowered his head, but he made no answer. "You have not told me how to cure the soul, my friend," I went on.

"If I but knew. I do not know where the soul resides; I do not believe it is to be found in an ... incorruptible bone lying in the breast, and if Christ alone is the soul's salvation, then I fear no mortal doctor shall ever be able to treat it. Perhaps in some far distant day, men may know better. I, like Isabella, like you, would give thanks to know that we shall retain our souls by the time this is over."

"Like me?" I asked.

"Yes, Francisco, like you. Your questions assure me your soul lives. Always remember, God is merciful."

The morning hardly assured me. From Castle St. Angelo we watched the Turks loading the guns they had captured at Fort St. Elmo onto a ship that later took them to Constantinople, where they'd lie in that same field by the Gun Foundry with its century of other trophies I'd seen daily. At the same time, the Turks had begun to drag their siege guns from Sciberras back towards the Marsa, e'en while they kept up bombardment on the Post of Sanoguera at Senglea's spur. One did not have to be a seer to guess that Fort St. Michel would be their next target, and when we spied infidel engineers crawling over the Corradino heights, which overlook that fort from across the Poret de Senglea, we became certain. If there was ought to rejoice at, it was that during the entire siege of Fort St. Elmo de Valette had been rushing to strengthen Senglea's defenses, specially the wall facing Corradino, which neared completion.

Once Pietru roused himself, we limped off to find Grezz on l'Isola, whither I'd taken her a month ago. Yet unable to recall much about his escape from St. Elmo or after, Pietru asked if others had lived. Aye, five or six Maltese had in a last desperation flung themselves into the harbor, either at Pietru's heels or after nightfall, having hidden among the rocks. I told Ix-Xabaw I had killed Dragut. At first he didn't hear me, so dulled were his ears after a month of cannon fire, and when he heard me, he didn't believe me.

No wall protected the stretch called Bormla that joined Birgu and Senglea at Galley Creek's landward end, and the Turkish guns made it dangerous to walk there. So we jumped into a *fregatina* and joined the other boats crisscrossing the creek. As Ix-Xabaw caught sight of all the houses in Bormla yet standing, he shook his head angrily. "This is bad. The Turks will take those houses, Cikku, and use them against us." He was surely right.

Fort St. Michel loomed over the inner end of Senglea. As we walked past, the shadows of its heavy guns fell across us. Enclosed by the vaulted wall de Sengle had built, the original tower became the fort's cavalier and the whole now distantly resembled the star of Fort St. Elmo, but larger and taller.

Glancing toward the Turkish engineers marking out their platforms atop Corradino, we knew it was not tall enough. A deep, wide ditch surrounded St. Michel and I was glad to see the ravelin had been repaired, but Ix-Xabaw shuddered at the sight of it. Facing Corradino stood the gun battery Pietru had helped build, not far above the water. Tho' it wasn't on the Bormla side, they called it the Post of Bormla because the Maltese would man it. Pietru intended to fight there.

We came across Grezz in the Grand Master's garden, the same garden where d'Homedes strolled lo those many years ago. On de Valette's orders, the people were cutting down the plentiful mulberries, orange trees and palms, for brushwood to make gabions had run out. When Grezz caught sight of her husband, she first regarded the man bandaged from top to bottom and with his arm in a sling as were he a spirit risen from the grave. Of a sudden she ran to him and embraced him. Then she slapped him. I could not understand a word of the torrent issuing from her mouth, but when she began sobbing, I guessed she warned him to ne'er be such a fool again as to leave her for a besieged castle.

Flaminia also helped clear the garden. Approaching her, I said I was sorry that Grand Master had forbidden her to work in the arsenal. She nodded, understanding his edict, then addressed me with a little of her old haughtiness: "Some people say you did not kill Dragut, Francisco, that you are a liar. It this true?"

"Of course I killed him," I replied with heat. "Anyone who says otherwise is a scurrilous *picaro*."

It was apparent that the *quiraca* wished to speak of something else. Absently touching the bandage on my arm, she said, "I do not think I will be made a concubine of the Sultan, Francisco."

I nodded. "No mercy is to be granted us, Flaminia, none." She was too old, *in qualsiasi caso*.

For a moment Flaminia glanced down at her dirty feet, then at the Turks pacing on Corradino. One of the guns from Fort St. Michel boomed. The *quiraca* shuddered against her will. "People say l'Isola will be next, then Birgu. I am worried about my little one, Francisco. Mama and Papa are terrified."

I knew not how to reply. Flaminia should have taken them to Sicily. "We must pray to God for His protection, Flaminia."

"Will you look after Francesca if I perish, *mio cuore?*" she said unexpectedly.

Again no answer came to my lips. "You shall not perish, Flaminia, *mio cuore*," I said, laying my hands on her. "I won't allow it." I left her then and walked farther along the peninsula.

Senglea's land was no smaller than Birgu's, but because the place had been nigh uninhabited until fifteen years ago, fewer houses and churches filled it. Near the tip of the promontory the big windmills stood alone, rising from empty hillocks, and beyond them, on the spur, rose Sanoguera's Post, where his men were risking their lives drawing water for the earthworks and constant repairs. The bombardment had scared all other souls away. And truly, the windmills were proving too tempting to the enemy—while I stood there, a ball crashed thro' one of the vanes.

I crept toward the post, by now a bastion itself, one being constantly hit by gunners atop Sciberras. Looking onto it, my confidence was none too strong and, hailing one of the arquebusiers working on the walls, I asked what was needed.

The fellow, who called himself Francesco Balbi, laughed. "What we all need—time and a miracle." I could offer fire weapons, I said, to which he replied that a bridge across Galley Creek to Birgu would be helpful. "An assault must come against this post, how I do not know. I do know we will need to escape, and the only way to cross now is by boat." By way of afterthought, the arquebusier said that should I happen across some ink, he would be grateful to receive it, for he fancied himself a wandering poet—indeed he 'd taken up the gun only to feed himself—and he was keeping an account of these events.

"I am sixty years old," Balbi remarked, "and I have never witnessed the like. I think no one alive has either."

Had we known what we were yet to witness. I carried dirt for a time, but as I was of little use with my left arm bandaged, I took a skiff back to the Borgo, promising to find the poet some ink.

Especially after the explosion at our mill, work at the St. Angelo and Birgu arsenals continued day and night, preparing for what we knew must come. I stayed at the castle well past *l'hora della ruffiana*, when I went to Isabella's house and discovered her writing. All the sleeping rooms were occupied by the wounded. Isabella had put the servants in the cellar and had also given their quarters over to the wounded.

"Are you penning dispatches?" I asked, seeing her at her table.

"Yes."

"Good. Europe must know." As before Flaminia earlier, I had no ready words to utter in these circumstances.

Isabella regarded me with the same pale, hard countenance she wore of late. No, it was worse: Her skin, drawn tight over the bones of her face, made her look hungry and older than her years. We were all becoming hungry. At length she said, no longer angry with me but distantly, as if we were not well acquainted, "I prayed with Parisot last night, in the chapel again. l'Isle Adam gives him strength. I ... hardly recognized him my Godfather. This was a man transformed into an avenging angel."

"You have always known him for a fearless warrior," I reminded her.

"This was something beyond. He stared without seeing me. His eyes shone like glowing embers, the wrath of God—No, I did not find God in that face." She shook her head in a terrible awe. "We shall all die, or the Turks will, before he yields a step."

"Mustafa gives him no choice. No surrender, no mercy."

As if unable to contemplate her guardian in such a light, Isabella, staring fixedly at her clasped hands before her, moved to another matter. "What does the silence of the guns portend, Francisco?"

I could only tell her what mine eyes told me. "The Turks are moving their cannon and must erect new platforms. I believe they intend to surround us on every side. They have sixty-five pieces, or a few more."

Isabella swallowed hard. "What a price to pay for a few days of silence!" she suddenly cried, as if to her own portrait. "What possessed me to leave Florence!" She went on, her voice utterly exhausted of spirit, saying that a spring they'd found recently in the Borgo had dried up and that the water in her cistern was going down faster than she'd expected. "*Haqq it-Torok*," she croaked in Maltese and lowered her head to her desk, as were she a pile of bones and dust waiting to be scattered by the wind.

I put my arms around her and said, "Mayhap you should write verses, Noble Lady."

At length she looked up, first at her paintings, then at me, smiling so faintly I hardly convinced myself. Her voice did not smile. "How will verses help against sixty-five guns, Francisco?"

"It will give you strength, and so it will help everyone."

Again she offered the faintest smile, touching her scarf, still bound over my wounds, but shook her head. "Should I be so sinful as to write them," she went on in that gleaning, expressionless voice, "no one, I fear, will ever read them."

"Isabella," I said, "on that executioner's galley a year and more ago, I gave up all hope. Despite your ministrations, some of the stripes you have seen will never heal, but I would not have your soul fall into the same abyss."

"How is one not to?" she shouted suddenly, sharply.

I gave her the only advice I had. "When we were slaves, Pietru and I pledged not to let each other die and we kept each other alive for four years. Let you and I take the same vow and the rest will follow."

Slowly Isabella rose from her place and we swore, embracing each other, not as a young master and mistress who might once have become lovers, but as two souls, what remained of them, who desperately sought a path up from Purgatory.

During the next days, while the sun baked the island with African heat, the Turks moved their main camp across the league from the Marsa to the heights overlooking Birgu and Senglea. Tho' they had lost upon six thousand men taking St. Elmo, the sight of the yet overwhelming force dragging their artillery in great chains across the hills instilled every one of us with a terrible dread; this foe surely meant to strangle us in his grasp.

Or pulverize us. Their engineers lost no time and, as I had forewarned Isabella, it soon became certain that every hill around Birgu and Senglea would be adorned by siege cannon. Day by day we watched the sappers constructing stone breastworks atop the Corradino heights, breastworks that stretched the entire length of Senglea, and we knew again the attack there would come first.

Four days after the Feast of St. John Baptist, I stood with the gunners at the Post of France, having brought there some powder, when Balthazar, helped by a crutch, limped up behind me.

"It is good to see you walking so soon," I said, sweat running down our cheeks, as we watched Mustafa erect his pavilion above with its red, white and green banners. Balthazar replied that I well knew what Knights were made of, to which I agreed e'en as I recollected a remark he had made years ago in a tavern. "'A stewpot for Turkish guns,' you once called this place. We are about to be cooked."

Nodding, Balthazar added, "The Grand Master should follow Niccolò's advice, to allow the men to watch enemy activity and skirmish with them in order to breed contempt."

Comforted and not that Balthazar had regained his wits so soon after being wounded, I asked whether the barbarity at Kalkara Creek four days ago was not sufficient to breed all contempt.

"Fear, hatred, yes—contempt, no. Niccolò speaks of inflaming your men against an enemy, but methinks that to inflame them with blind hatred serves only to incinerate one's soul." Balthazar spoke as if peering into my depths. "One must convince oneself that one can win, that the enemy is not invincible. Aye, the Turks have not lost in a century, yet we see the blunders they have made here, on Malta. We are whittling down their multitudes. de Valette knows in his soul we can somehow win. We must believe with him. Let us spit on the enemy."

There under the bright sun, we spat off the ramparts.

At that moment the skirmish began. de Valette, having climbed to the Post of Provence, sent out through the gate a large company of arquebusiers to occupy the abandoned houses of Bormla, then ordered a thousand Maltese to go out with picks and axes and demolish those nearest the Post of Aragon. Soon enough, the Turks atop Corradino caught sight of what was underway and without any orders they dashed down the hills to put a stop to it.

The spectacle below was altogether strange, Maltese knocking down houses while our arquebusiers traded fire with the Turks, who retired into the empty houses for powder and refreshment, all while we the gunners played havoc with the enemy. More and more Turks joined the fray, until by morning's end it seemed a general assault was erupting. Thereat de Valette quickly ordered a retreat behind the walls. We lost one Knight.

"You see," smiled Balthazar, taking the match from me and firing the last shot, "the Grand Master has been reading Niccolò."

I thought it unlikely. Hardly had this action run its course when a Turkish spahi leading some men down from Mustafa's pavilion approached under a white flag. de Valette, still at the Post of Provence with Romegas at his side, sent out some men to meet them. Balthazar and I watched from our position as the Turks sent forth a single old man, a slave. Blindfolding him, our men led him in thro' the gate. Now everyone hurried over to Provence, where Romegas was saying, "No, Eminenza, I have no news of the relief. Let us face facts: The damned Vice Roy has abandoned us."

As the Grand Master shot a burning glance of despair and anger at Lescaut, the old slave was brought into his presence. It was a Spaniard of mayhap seventy years who, quivering under the blindfold, told His Eminence that Mustafa wished to send the spahi an emissary to him.

"An emissary!" de Valette roared. "Why? Tell me yourself what he is ordered to say! It is your duty as a Christian!"

Now the old man was truly quaking. "The e—emissary comes from M—M—Mustafa and P—P— Piyale," he croaked, only slowly gaining mastery over himself. "M—Mustafa demands that you sur—render the island to the Sultan. He will grant you the same terms he granted the Knights at Rhodes—your people, your property, your artillery and safe passage to Sicily. All he w—wants is the barren island. He suggests that you do not display the same stubbornness that you have at Fort St. Elmo. Accept his terms or he will be forced to mete out the same punishment he did there."

Romegas spat onto the ground. "Hah! They're getting scared."

"Hang him," said de Valette.

Now, as His Eminence's men grabbed him, the old Spaniard did befoul his trousers. "For the love of God, mercy!" he pleaded, dropping to his knees. "I am only a slave who has been forced to bring you this message."

de Valette ordered the guards to remove his blindfold. "Tell your Pashas this: If any other emissary dares come here, I will cut out his heart and hang him from these walls. Say to Mustafa: Do your worst; I do not care. My faith reposes in Jesus Christ, who shall deliver us from your hands. Nay, he shall grant us victory over you. Tell that to Mustafa, do you understand?"

So saying, de Valette had his men carry the slave to the edge of the ramparts and show him the height of the walls and the depth of the ditch below. There, the Grand Master added, as by afterthought, that the ditch was the only ground they could afford Mustafa—to bury him in it with all his janissaries. The Spaniard managed to stutter he understood. Thereat de Valette had him blindfolded and led out thro' the gates.

Having witnessed the scene, I turned to Balthazar and asked, "Is that what you would call contempt?"

Balthazar smiled wanly, saying it would suffice. Then he sighed, confessing that there was a fine line between contempt and bravado.

Isabella saw a different Grand Master. The next night she brought him food at his home. Having, she thought, steeled herself against her own panic, she regarded with a certain detachment the pitiless visage his had become. In the past she might have expected a warm embrace, to sit at his side while clasping his hand. No longer. They sat apart, he eating, she watching. At length she said she did not believe they could survive the looming onslaught, and hoped only find the strength within to meet death. Parisot cast down the chicken leg in his hand and stood.

"No!" he shouted, clenching his fist as if to persuade both himself and l'Isle Adam, "not when the walls had been undermined and breached, not when all but two cannon were destroyed, and not when the Jews and

D'Amaral treasonously plotted to turn over the fortress. We have not come close to that place."

While Isabella once again shrank at the force of his will, two sentries from Fort St. Angelo ran into the house, requesting that the Grand Master follow them. Together all four dashed to the cavalier atop the castle, whence they saw the distant fire signals from Notabile.

"They started not long ago, Eminenza," one of the sentries offered.

"What can Mezquita or Anastagi be telling us?" de Valette asked without expecting an answer.

He got none.

While the Grand Master railed helplessly, not daring to send a man thro' the Turkish lines, Francesco Balbi, who sat at Sanoguera's Post with the ink I had given him, lifted his head at the sound of a distant voice calling from across the water. First Balbi glanced across Galley Creek to St. Angelo. No. He brought his gaze around directly before him, across the Great Port. Yes, hailing Sanoguera's men from the base of Sciberras was a Turk.

"What do you want?" Balbi called back, first in Spanish, then in the lingua franca, then in Italian.

The answer, in Italian, was a boat. Was this another envoy? No, the fellow wanted to desert. Rightly suspicious, Balbi quickly conferred with Commander Sanoguera's nephew Don Jaime, then with Eminenza himself. de Valette told them to send out a boat, but they didn't have one outside the great chain.

"You must swim!" Balbi called across the harbor.

Nothing loathe, the fellow stripped off his clothes and dove into the Port, but at once everyone saw that he was no fish. Halfway across, he began sputtering and flailing. Without losing a heartbeat, three of the best swimmers from the post dashed into the water and hauled out to meet him, but at this moment the Turks atop Sciberras and Corradino descried the commotion and opened up with arquebus and musket. Balbi and the rest of Sanoguera's men returned fire and all at once the spur of Senglea was engulfed in crackling and smoke. By some miracle the swimmers dragged the Turk ashore, waterlogged and coughing his lungs out but otherwise unharmed.

"Thank you," he said. "My name is Mehmed ben Davud."

Balbi and Don Jaime took him to the small house nearby where the Grand Master once kept his animals. While they found ben Davud some trousers, he told them he was high-ranking spahi of noble Greek ancestry, who had been raised since boyhood as a Turk after the infidels took his town of Patras. ben Davud, who appeared to be about fifty-five, refused any refreshment but water, for it was a Saturday and he was fasting, but he said he was resolved to return to the faith of his forbears and asked to be conducted to the Grand Master most urgently.

Balbi rowed him in a skiff across to the Palace, where de Valette regarded him with great suspicion, only at long last convincing himself of ben Davud's noble birth and sincere intentions.

This was well, for ben Davud said forthwith, "Eminenza, I am the envoy Mustafa sent two days ago. Would that you had received me then, for I have much to tell you. First is that there will be a determined assault by both land and sea on the whole of the island with the windmills, and you must be well prepared for it."

"*By sea?*" whispered a startled de Valette. "Impossible."

"I fear it is possible," ben Davud answered. "By sea. The other thing you must know is that last night a relief landed at the Old City. I was scouting toward the south and killed the only other person who might know of it."

Some there swore that Jean de Valette threatened to behead ben Davud should the information prove untrue, but others said that the Grand Master could not stand for the tears of joy streaming down his face.

Ninety-Three

Four days after they'd sent Tomas Coronel to Sicily, and having had no word from either the Grand Master or the Vice Roy, Fra Vincenzo returned from the morning sortie, dismounted at the water trough and sought out Pedro Mezquita to report his failure to approach the Borgo. He knocked at the door of the house the Governor had commandeered, Fra Pedro appeared, but before either man could say a word an agitated sentry ran up to them.

"Señors, if you would come at once. A Turkish envoy waits below the walls."

With a glance at each other and no less agitation than the sentry's, Mezquita and Anastagi sped after him to the ramparts. Far beneath them a Turkish officer sat on horseback, bearing a white flag.

"What do you want?" called out Mezquita.

"I bring a letter from Mustafa Pasha to the people of the City."

Mezquita ordered the same guard to go out thro' a sally port and meet the envoy. Not long afterwards, a large crowd gathered before the cathedral as the Governor and Anastagi poured over Mustafa's letter.

"In the name of Soliman the Lawgiver, Father of the World, Deputy of Allah on Earth and so forth," Anastagi read aloud, "Mustafa Pasha tells the people of Malta that the Lord of Lords offers them true friendship, freedom to keep their religion, their laws and ancient privileges, and good treatment of all the inhabitants who have been nothing but slaves to the Grand Master. You may have all this if you surrender yourselves to the Great Sultan. Otherwise you will be put to the sword as the men in the fort."

Anastagi finished reading and looked up, puzzled. For a horrible moment, Mezquita thought de Valette must have surrendered. "We know nothing!" the old man cursed with the unease that had infused him, everyone in the past week. Truly, the only news they had was what the cavalry their eyes brought them daily—the Borgo was now surrounded by an infinite Turkish host.

But Anastagi scoffed. "Hah! Pedro, you know Parisot would sooner die than yield. This is a trick."

Anastagi was right. Parisot would sooner see them all die than yield. "What do you say to this?" Mezquita asked the people gathered around, Knights and peasants, men and women.

"Tell him we fuck his mother—!" someone shouted.

"—on the way to the Kaaba!" a former slave put in.

Instantly, the crowd burst into laughter and cheers and Mezquita penned a brief reply on the back of Mustafa's own letter: "All of us in the Old City, Knights and Maltese, are sworn to defend our Religion unto death." He gave it to the sentry and told him to tell the envoy that we fuck Mustafa's mother on her way to the Kaaba.

The crowd dispersed. Lady Emilia, who had run thither to the square when she heard the commotion, now hurried back toward her house. Weeks ago she had finally understood that she was a prisoner entirely at the mercy of the Turks. Cows, sheep, wheat for food and good water to drink were yet abundant in Notabile, but she could not avoid noticing that oil, wine and vinegar had already sensibly diminished. Despair rapidly growing, Mezquita's defiant response to Mustafa now fully unnerved Emilia and she hardly noticed when she accidentally brushed Matteo Falzon. Rarely did she catch sight of Falzon on the streets of tiny Mdina. E'en so, Emilia had said no more to him than *"buongiorno"* since the year of the Tribunal.

For the first time in a decade, they paused, he bowing slightly, she slightly nodding her head. "How are you faring, Master Falzon?" she asked, apologizing, glancing over her shoulder as if afraid Cubelles stood within earshot.

"Like you, Signora, I am alive, tho' after the Governor's rash action of moments ago, I fear it shall not be for long."

"Do you truly believe he should surrender the City, Signore?" she asked, aware she was being drawn into a conversation she would do well to avoid.

Falzon invited her towards his door. "Mezquita does not speak for everyone trapped within these walls. It is not enough that the Knights have stolen our land and liberties; now they demand we die for their faith—"

"—our faith, Signore," Emilia cut him off.

Falzon bowed imperceptibly, managed to say, "Pardon, Signora," before Emilia cut him off in a shrill voice. "Master Falzon, would you refuse even now to fight for your vast holdings? During the dark night of the *razzia*, did you not speak of killing your wife and children before allowing them to be taken by the infidels?" The very memory sent a shudder through her.

"I did, Signora," Falzon replied, "but age brings wisdom, to some. You will forgive me for saying that under the Turks I would not be suffering my present misfortunes, and I hardly need tell you that most of the landowners have come to curse the tyranny of the Knights. Why you do not share our feelings, I have never known." He breathed, chuckled somberly. "My vast holdings? The Grand Master and the Inquisition have threatened to confiscate them. Be assured, gentle lady, someday when all this is ended, the threat will be carried out."

"If you are speaking of insurrection, Master Falzon," Emilia answered, not being able to collect her wits in the least, "or if you are threatening to betray this city through your black arts, I will report you to Mezquita at once!"

Falzon managed to laugh, softly. "Calm yourself, Signora. I have offered to provide marriage dowries for four orphaned girls, should this siege be lifted, and if my vast holdings remain in my possession, I fully intend to carry out the promise. Sorcery? Ah..." He sighed ruefully. "A most interesting subject. I am told I possess the power to vanish in a barrel, that I have signed a pact with the Devil in order that my bones will reunite after death and I shall rise as the Antichrist." Falzon paused bemusedly. "Would that I could vanish; I have tried ... Now, Lady Emilia, may I offer you some wine? My cellar has not yet run dry and we may speak of more pleasant matters."

Much to her own surprise, Emilia accepted the invitation. Shortly thereafter she, Falzon and his wife sat in his courtyard, shielded from the sun on this hot day, sipping wine and speaking of pleasanter times while Anastagi hanged an Italian who on the cathedral square declared that the city should surrender.

That night, at the witching hour, the dreams of a soundly snoring Pedro Mezquita were abruptly shattered by the hand of a lieutenant fiercely shaking his shoulder. With a grunt Mezquita sat up on the bed, rubbed his eyes in disbelief. Was not standing before him the same Esprit de Brunesay-Quincy who had gotten stranded with Oliventia ten days ago? Indeed it was. And this other fellow. He also looked familiar. Blaij Vergã.

"We bring good news," said de Quincy. "A relief has landed at Petra Nigra, not two leagues from here."

"The relief has landed?" Mezquita replied dully, believing his ears no more than his eyes.

"Above six hundred men under Maestro de Campo Robles. We must speed them hither at once."

Instantly Mezquita was on his feet, fumbling with his breeches. "Rouse Anastagi!" he ordered his lieutenant. "Rouse every foot and horse. Let's go!" A swig of wine and—

Well before dawn the *piccolo soccorso* was safely ensconced in the Old City, having encountered not a single Turk the entire night. Mezquita and Anastagi at once lit signal fires atop the towers to inform the Grand Master.

"Will he understand the meaning of these pyres?" asked Robles, sitting on a barrel on St. Paul's Square surrounded in the dark by his hundreds of men.

Anastagi shrugged. "This is not the greatest difficulty. In the last days the Turks have completely surrounded Il Borgo, and at this moment I confess not to see a path to get you and your men in."

"Drinking always, never thirsty; mailed in armor, never clanking," said the peculiar jester Robles kept by him.

"Swim like fish?" Anastagi said as he shot a harsh glance at the little man, thin like a reed. "You may have to. We must get a courier to the Grand Master and discover a solution—any solution."

While they stood on the square, one of the children Mezquita had posted on the walls cried out in a shrill voice: "The Turks!" Anastagi's men were off, returning some time later with a young Greek of the city whom they hurled to the ground. "No Turks," Anastagi's lieutenant Ventura reported, "just this spy, tempted by the Devil for a drink at Mustafa's fountain."

After the Greek confessed and they'd quartered him, Anastagi turned to Robles. "So you see, Maestro, not only must we get you in, we must get you in before the Turks find you out."

While Anastagi and Colonel Robles urgently contemplated how to move the relief to Birgu, the Grand Master was having a like discussion with Romegas and the Turk ben Davud in the Magisterial Palace. Quickly they decided only Bajada could be trusted for the task and sent for him immediately.

When the swimmer arrived they explained the situation. Toni agreed that to pass between Birgu and Mdina would no longer be simple. "Can you swim out the Port and around the coast?" de Valette wanted to know.

"It is possible, Eminenza, but the Turks have men on both sides of the mouth. And," Bajada shrugged, "I can swim but the relief must walk. I should find a clear road. Allow me."

ben Davud offered that south of the Kalkara hill few Turks were to be found. Before de Valette could warn him to be careful, Toni was gone.

That night Bajada dressed himself as an infidel, crept out of Bormla, walked up the hill past a vineyard there and straight into the Turkish camp. So many thousands were about that no one even asked him what he was doing there. Later I asked Toni whether he was worried that someone would recognize him and suspect he was a spy. He said yes, but no one did. With ironclad calm he walked thro' the camp, talking with the *azablar* and *yenicheriler*. He learned half of them by now were sick with fever and the stomach illness, and the rest grumbling that nothing had gone as planned. Here it was the first of July, Turgut dead, half the *yenicheriler* killed, the *Pashalar* arguing, the summer heat upon them, flies and mosquitoes buzzing everywhere.

The news cheered Bajada so much he needed to force himself not to whistle. His cheer diminished when he heard the Turkish music and singing and sensed, thro' everything, that the enemy intended to prevail. A *yenicheri*, catching sight of him, ordered the fellow with the nicked ear to bring bread. Bajada did as he was told. The officer looked at him, grunted thanks and went back to the fire, where an imam was reminding them that anyone who fell in battle or died of illness would cross the Sirat bridge over Hell to Paradise without having to give an account of himself. Others were throwing shells and making tattoos.

Having reached the southern end of the camp, near Kalkara hill, Bajada saw that, truly, few soldiers were about and began walking toward the coast. A sentry challenged him.

"Where are you going?" that one demanded in Turkish.

"To catch some fish," answered Bajada, stroking his moustaches. "Do you want one?"

The sentry said yes. Bajada came back later with some fish and the fellow was contented. Again he slipped away, this time gained the coast without meeting anyone. He took off his Turkish clothing, hid them under a rock, and went on dressed only in his Maltese trousers. A few hours later, he reached Mdina.

"The coast road is clear, until Mt. Kalkara," Bajada reported to the Governor as the sun rose. "There are Turkish troops near there. It may be possible to get the relief behind the hill, down to Kalkara Creek, then cross."

"You do mean swim like fish?" asked the jester, puzzled.

"We'll become mermaids if necessary," put in Robles harshly.

"I will go back tonight to see if it is possible to reach the creek," Bajada went on. "I warn you, it's within sight of the Turkish camp and the path will be dangerous. I'll ask that boats be made waiting."

Robles wanted to move immediately but, tugging at his beard, conceded the risk was too great. Anastagi took the cavalry out to confirm Bajada's report. When they returned, Anastagi said the coast was indeed clear until the environs of Kalkara. That night, humming to himself, Bajada walked back along the sea cliffs, skirting the Turkish campfires, which were so close he could even make out the words to the songs being sung and the curses. He tugged on his nicked ear. Luckily, the moon was new. Without encountering a soul, he walked to the Rinella promontory, then crossed over between the Kalkara and Salvatore hills. From there he crept down to Kalkara Creek and let himself quietly into the water. Not a glass after, he stood before the Grand Master at the Magisterial Palace, as usual dripping wet.

"Can you have boats waiting in the creek tomorrow night?" he asked de Valette.

"Of course," that one replied.

Bajada said they would make the attempt. "I am not confident, Monsignore. One sound from a horse or soldier could doom us."

"We have no choice," said de Valette; again Toni was gone.

The next evening in Mdina all the forces of the relief stood ready. Robles ordered every man to silence. They'd greased the wheels of the baggage carts, made certain every horse was freshly shod. An hour before sunset, Robles mounted his horse, prepared to set off. At the gate, Mezquita caught up with him, thanked him for the seventy soldiers he was leaving behind, then raised his voice: "It is too dangerous to depart now. Wait until dark, Señor."

"We have leagues to march and each one of us knows the peril." With that Robles ordered his men out of the city. Aye, the sky was yet light, but luckily no Turks were here at the center of the island. The column hugged the coast for hours, marching in utter silence. About half a league from Birgu, Toni went ahead to scout the road. Near the place he had been the first night, Turkish sentries stood at the edge of camp, truly but fifty paces from him. He crept back to Robles, uneasy, disquieted, doubtful.

"We cannot pass without being discovered, Señor. It is impossible."

Robles wanted to press on, but Bajada would not permit it. "Let a few of your men come with me. They will see for themselves."

The Maestro de Campo sent a few of his men ahead with Bajada and soon enough their own eyes told them—the sentries were too close, the fires bright; other soldiers roamed nearby. To pass was hopeless. While Bajada and the other scouts despaired of what to do, a great miracle took place. The Scirocco had been blowing, rare at this time of year, and on its back it now swiftly carried in a thick fog. Seeing this, Bajada offered a thanks to God and whispered, "After me—our great chance has arrived."

They ran silently up the path to the impatient Robles. "Now! This is the moment! The Lord has parted the Red Sea!"

The Maestro sent the horses and the baggage carts back to Mdina with a few soldiers and a corpulent old Knight who found it too difficult to walk. Once more he commanded his adventurers to absolute silence and threatened to kill anyone who carried a lit fuse. "Life is a mist of error and tears, lifted only by a sometimes fog," said the jester and the men trod softly on, dripping with wet and hardly able to see beyond their own noses.

Thus cloaked, the *piccolo soccorso* passed a stone's throw from the Turkish camp and crossed behind Mt. Kalkara, invisible to enemy eyes. Bajada told me he was certain the Turks must have heard the footsteps or the occasional clank of armor, but because of the fog they mayhap thought a sea monster was near and took fright. Thus cloaked, they reached the hills; Toni and a few others crept down to Kalkara Creek and found—no boats anywhere.

"We'll have to fight our way in, by Castille," decided Robles without hesitation.

Bajada again urged patience upon the Maestro. With dawn dangerously near, he swam the inlet, and was met by Romegas's men guarding the other side.

"The relief has arrived! Where are the boats, you fools? It will soon be light!"

"We were afraid the Turks would see them. We'll bring them at once."

Thus at last, Robles and his tired men ferried themselves across Kalkara Creek and entered the Borgo thro' a gate near the Post of Germany. They found de Valette in the Magisterial Palace on a bed in his cabinet, fully dressed, listening to a report from one of the guards. When the Grand Master caught sight of de Quincy and Robles at the door, he sank to his knees and raised his hands to Heaven, thanking God for their deliverance. With tears in his eyes he ran down to the gate, embracing all the officers and, as the sun rose, ordered every bell in Birgu to be sounded. His command was joyfully obeyed.

Ninety-Four

I can truthfully say, Your Majesty, that had the Turk ben Davud not come over to our side, and had God not sent that mist to give safe passage to the relief, Malta would have fallen, with unfathomable consequences for Christendom. His design, tho', was certainly not apparent that day.

Isabella was repeating her morning Paternoster before setting off to the Auberge of Italy when she heard the bells. For an instant, she continued the drone of words whose meaning had become lost to her. Only when the clanging insisted did she break off and glance up, startled that anything could penetrate the hollow fatality that of late surrounded her. Before another instant passed, she realized those bells were sounding no alarm but celebration, and at once she was speeding to the square with everyone else in the Borgo. Only as the parade of soldiers clanked by accompanied by all the cheers and gunfire did Isabella begin to understand what had transpired, and as she watched the women everywhere flinging their arms about the men, falling to their knees, she too felt herself growing lighter.

At the Grand Master's order, standards of the relief were being planted on the bastions of Fort St. Michel and the arquebusiers were firing one after the other. Each measure was designed to convince the enemy that many more had arrived than a mere five hundred.

Aye, five hundred some, forty-seven Knights and a jester among them, bystanders told Isabella. Not a large number to stand against the tens of thousands of foemen who remained, less than half the number who had fallen at St. Elmo. Yet no words could describe the joy that was filling the streets, that was raising spirits like a spring rain after winter. For the first time since the onslaught began, Isabella felt a light creeping in, a small thought that victory might be possible.

Before long Blaij Vergã marched past with arquebus resting on his breastplate. Such was Isabella's elation that the sight of her kerchief adorning his arm drew forth only an unforeseen and delighted laugh. Without thought she gratefully extended her hand and invited him to her house for lunch. As his *quiraca* appeared from around the corner and threw herself upon him, Vergã promised to appear at the appointed hour.

Lunch was hardly worthy of the name. Isabella apologized for the meagre fare, a cup of wine for each, barely drinkable water, some bread her servants had baked from the grain stores, some pressed olives and figs, cheese.

"No apologies are necessary, Señora. Seeing you safe before me is reward enough."

Isabella flushed, raising her cup in a toast. "To Maestro de Campo Robles and his brave men of the *soccorso*, who shall be our salvation," she said as if wings had been given her. "You must tell me all about it for my dispatches, Señor. Europe will be hungry for every word."

Even as she said it, Isabella grimly realized that perhaps no one at all would read her missives, yet alone all Europe. But Blaij readily returned the salute and, as the wounded in the house gathered 'round, he didn't hesitate to recount every detail of his adventures. On the first attempt to land, the Turks chased them clear back to Sicily. On the second attempt, a storm nearly sank both ships. The third attempt was very near. They sent Martinez de Oliventia ashore, but he disappeared and no one knew what became of him.

The men were so eager to land, Blaij said, they almost swam, "but despite my protests and Robles's, Cardona turned back. The worst of it, Señora, was sitting with nothing to do in Sicily, not knowing the fate of the brave men in Fort St. Elmo, or your own."

"Señor," replied Isabella playfully, "I should think you would have more important matters weighing on you, but every soul among us is truly grateful for your endeavors and, God willing, we shall see the island saved."

Those around the table applauded Vergã loudly.

"I should inform you," he went on with a perceptible irony now coloring his voice, "His Holiness has granted plenary indulgence to anyone who dies defending Malta. All sins are to be forgiven, a place in Heaven in exchange for your life."

At this juncture, I arrived. The sight alone of this rogue would have been enough to inflame me, but to see him sitting in Isabella's dining room with her kerchief tied around his arm was simply too much to bear. Yet, as always, greater affairs stood between us. Francisco de Aguilar from de Guiral's post, who Isabella had invited as a friend of de Valette, could not fail to observe the twin scarves tied onto our arms.

"*Siempre alcanza lo que quiere ...* " Aguilar chuckled, singing the popular tune, "He who is brave and bold, wins the lady that he would ... "

At once everyone around the table, including Isabella, who grasped her lute, took up the refrain, "But the courageless and cold, ne'er have conquered and never could."

I raised the cup Isabella handed me, glaring at her. "And never could," I whispered icily on this warm day, then, turning to Vergã said, "The Maestro Robles, true to his character, has asked to be posted at once to Fort St. Michel, the most dangerous position. Why have you not joined him?"

"I shall with great pleasure, should Romegas send me," he answered. "As you well know." Thereat, glancing at the bandages on my arm, Blaij asked pleasantly, "And how have you come by your wounds, Francisco?"

"Like everyone here, at Fort St. Elmo, while the brave and bold were taking the sun in Sicily."

What answer Vergã expected, I do not know, but even his rapier understood that to challenge a man who'd fought at St. Elmo wouldn't go down well. Truly, one of the guests chuckled, "Careful, Señor, this is the man who killed Dragut."

"Some say," another laughed, as he was able thro' his broken jaw.

Afterwards, I took Isabella to the cellar, where we could be alone for a moment. "What is the meaning of this?" I demanded. "You invite into your house the man who denounced me to Cubelles!"

"He denies it," she said, returning to her recent coldness. "Señor, I did not know you had a claim on me ... Ah," she sighed, now placing her hand on her brow in confusion. "Of course he lied. He is a villain, but he is at least alive ... Francisco, you have sworn to keep me from falling into the Abyss. Why then do you gainsay me the first song that has found my lips since this Hell began?"

"Forgive me, Isabella. It shall not happen again."

She laid her hand on my chest. "Francisco, I swear to you on my life, I merely bound his wound that night on the road to Mdina. If in his foolishness he has taken a bandage for a lady's token, think naught of it ... Truly, I should not have invited him who has done you such harm, but I have done all to prevent war between the two of you...Ah, I am so weary."

I embraced her. E'en as I promised to Isabella uphold my vow to her, I saw plainly why Vergã had cast aside his own oath to me. Consumed with jealousy, I stepped from her door but at that instant my intents were cut off by a furious bombardment from the Turkish guns on the hills.

"My God!" Isabella exclaimed, throwing herself again on me at the deafening cannonade that was causing the ground to tremble.

The festa had ended. When Mustafa caught sight of the standards of the relief planted so insolently before his eyes atop Fort St. Michel and the Post of Provence, his fury knew no bounds. His gunners had already finished some of the platforms on Corradino and on a hill called the Mandra, which stood landward above Fort St. Michel. With twenty-four heavy pieces, including one that hurled shot of one hundred sixty *libbre*, they lit into St. Michel, Bormla and Provence all at the same moment. The greatest bombardment in the history of the world had commenced.

That did not immediately prevent Blaij Vergã from calling on Isabella the same evening.

"Señor?" she said, startled to see him standing on her threshold.

"Forgive me, Señora," he replied, "I merely wanted to be certain you were safe."

After all that came before, Isabella was disarmed by the simplicity and sincerity in his voice. "Señor Vergã, it is not well for you to appear at this house," she natheless replied with strength. "You are an evil man."

To Isabella's surprise, Vergã only smiled sadly. "His Holiness has seen fit to deny me a dispensation at present to join the Religion. He grants a place in Heaven for all those who die on Malta, but at a word from my enemies not a place in the Order for a man who has risked his life in the service of God for fifteen years."

"I should think Heaven would be the higher honor," Isabella responded, puzzled. The confrater stood taller on the street than she on the step, and over the years she had sensed the man's power, the same sort of strength she felt in Parisot. But Vergã's was without faith, *captivo*. At this moment, tho', she perceived in his tone a different emptiness, the same hopeless solitude that had followed her throughout her life, everywhere.

Thereat Vergã cocked his ear to the *boom-boom boom* that accompanied the balls already slamming into the town's bastions. "To stay on Malta means certain death. I have had the honor to save your life more than once before. Allow me, please—"

Abruptly forgetting herself, Isabella reached out her hand, even touching Vergã's arm, but the touch awakened her to the lasciviousness of the act, and she swiftly withdrew. "You have won my scarf, Blaij Vergã," she answered, "and that shall suffice. But be certain there shall be a place in my heart for those who fight bravely and save all of us. Now, to your duties. Good night, Señor." Without a word more, Isabella stepped into her house and bolted the door.

Musket shot from the Corradino heights across the Poret was tearing up the water—and not only. It was slamming into the spars Pietru and his comrades were attempting to drive between the rocks a boat length off the bank of Senglea; it was slamming into the boats themselves that swarmed around the spars. Now with the dawn, balls came raining down more heavily on them, and men were being hit. They couldn't risk it any longer.

At last, Martino, not far down the *stoccado*, yelled, "Let's get the Devil out of here!" and everyone swam the few strokes to shore, then dashed incontinently for cover through the nearest gate.

For a short time, Pietru sat with Martino on one of the ship's masts that had been brought down, panting. He didn't know how they'd get this palisade built. When a few days ago the Turk ben Davud foretold to the Grand Master that there would be an attack on Senglea by sea, His Eminence at once ordered a big fence built along the whole length of the Isola facing Corradino.

"The Grand Master is clever," Ix-Xabaw said to Martino. His plan was to raise the *stoccado* far enough off the bank so the Turks would have to jump from their boats into the water and get their robes soaked, weighing them down in an assault.

"Yes, very clever," agreed Martino, "but how are we to get it built?"

"Eh?" Pietru grunted.

"How are we to get it built?" Martino repeated more loudly.

Hereat Pietru nodded and vainly tried to clean out his ear with his finger. With the constant Turkish fire, they had to work mostly at night, in the water with torches—and that made it all the more difficult.

"There is another thing I don't understand," Martino said. "How can the Turks attack by sea? They would not be so foolish to come thro' the mouth of the Port. The guns from Castle St. Angelo would take care of them like that." He snapped his fingers.

This had troubled Pietru as well. No one was sure what Mustafa was planning, and if the Grand Master knew, he wasn't telling. While Martino and Pietru thus sat on the ship's mast, wondering at the Grand Master's design, none other than His Eminence himself appeared with ben Davud, Robles's jester and some carts behind. Pietru had never been so close to de Valette and he got to his feet, speechless, then fell to his knees as the Monsignore drew near. The Grand Master motioned the workers to rise and asked about progress on the *stoccado*.

"E—Eminenza," said Pietru, nearly shouting against the roar of the enemy cannon hitting St. Michel at the other end of l'Isola, "we are doing everything, but the Turks have muskets eleven palms long and if we go outside the walls during the day they slaughter us. We must work at night when it is difficult to see. The moon is still thin. The water is deep and the rocks are hard. Where we can't drive in stakes we have been hammering and binding the ships' spars together like crosses ... But we try."

de Valette smiled faintly; he wanted to know only one thing: "Will it hold if a galley hits it?"

Pietru and Martino glanced at each other, then rocked their heads. "We do our best, Eminenza. Who can say?"

Pietru expected at the next moment to be thrown into prison, but the Grand Master merely nodded. He pointed to the carts they had brought, which Pietru well saw were filled with chains for galley slaves. "You'll pass them through the heads of the spars for more strength. When will the palisade be finished?"

Again the workers glanced at each other, and toward St. Michel, under bombardment. "l'Isola is long, Eminenza," said Pietru. "Another week."

As the words fell, the Monsignore crossed himself and moved on without speaking further. Pietru knew e'en then that he would tell his children of this moment, if he ever sired another brood, how the Grand Master had asked him questions and how he had answered without faltering—overly much—and how he had not been arrested.

Flaminia had not in her entire life felt such terror, not during Dragut's *razzia* or the first time she thought she had been stricken by the pox. Overnight the Turks had added twelve pieces to their batteries, and thirty-six guns were now bombarding Fort St. Michel, Birgu and Senglea, not only from Sciberras across the Port but from most of the hills on the landward side. Only Kalkara and Salvatore were free of cannon, but she'd heard all day how Mustafa, learning that the *soccorso* had come by way of those hills, was certain to build platforms there as well. Within a few days, guns would be pointed at them from every side. Madonna.

Sitting beneath the walls of Fort St. Michel amidst a pile of old rope, Flaminia could hardly think for the thunder of the artillery. The brushwood for repairs they'd cut in the Grand Master's garden had already finished. They were reduced to rope. Flaminia finished tying up the bundles of the pieces she had cut with cords, hoisted a few on her shoulder and climbed them up to the parapets overlooking Bormla. There she mixed the bundles with the soil others had brought up and stuffed everything into the holes that had already been made by the enemy guns.

Of a sudden, Flaminia was thrown from her knees, hitting her head on the ground. When she came to her senses, she saw that several other women not far from her had been killed. She felt blood dripping from her arm and brow and climbed down the steps, to a place behind the walls, where she ripped a piece from her dress. She did not believe they would treat her at the Hospital. While the *quiraca* sat, bandaging her arm, the Grand Master appeared with the noble Turk who had come over and a jester in bright colors who looked like he was starved. Flaminia got slowly to her feet, curtsying as she could, embarrassed that she was so covered with filth.

To her amazement, the Grand Master addressed her, asking if she was the woman who had helped pay the soldiers trapped at Fort St. Elmo. She nodded, eyes cast to the ground, at which the Monsignore held out his ring for her to kiss. She did so, quickly, kneeling, never having believed she would touch the person of the Grand Master in her life, still not believing it.

He said nothing more to her, but turned to one of the men by him and ordered him to put Turkish slaves on the walls instead of Christians—in that way the enemy would not fire at them.

"It shall be done at once, Eminenza," the Knight said, and the party moved off.

Ninety-Five

The brazen clanging of the bells from the infidel churches had already reached everyone's ear, and scores of men were standing on the ridge wondering what the new banners flying from the fort of the windmills could mean, when a scouting party of *spahiler* rode in, bringing with them eight soldiers, a fat Knight who could hardly walk and the horses they were taking to the old city.

Moments later everyone was shouting that something serious had taken place. Mustafa Pasha stormed out of his pavilion at the camp's center, knocking over more than one flag, shoving aside anyone who dared be in his way. Seeing the Christians on their knees before him, he ordered that they be bastinadoed at once. Yakhshi was near enough to hear their shrieks, but this was nothing next to the silence that came after, and Mustafa's rage that erupted like a volcano from the silence.

"Bring me the men who were on watch at the southeast before I draw another breath!"

"It shall be done, *Zat-i Aliniz!*"

Before the sun had moved, the *yenicheriler* threw the quivering sentries to the same blood-drenched grass where Mustafa had just beheaded the infidels. The *yenicheriler* bastinadoed them and when the curs confessed, Mustafa took the stick in his own hand and beat them senseless. Once they were half-dead, he decreed before the officers that any sentry in possession of a *timar* would be dispossessed of it, and the others would have their pay reduced. Then he ordered the bombardment from the finished platforms to commence instantly.

As the cannon erupted, Yakhshi's *Oda-bashi* Carullah ran up to him, worried, confused at all the rumors swirling about. "What's happened?"

The *Boluk-bashi* pointed down the hill. "Last night five hundred infidel soldiers crept into the city under our noses."

"In the big fog?"

Yakhshi nodded.

Carullah began to wail, wringing his hands. "Five hundred felled five thousand of us at the Santarma fort! How can we defeat such demons, spawn of Shaitan! Allah does not will us to leave this accursed island!"

"*Herze merze soyleme!*" Yakhshi struck his underling across the face with his good hand. "They are men behind rocks. They can be defeated." He was beginning to wonder whether he believed his own words.

The next night the *yenicheri*, stroking his moustaches, looked down on the fires here and there lighting the small cities and managed not to frown for the first time in weeks. The five hundred fresh men worried him enough that he was smoking *afione*. His *Oda-bashi* was right—five or six hundred of those fanatics had turned what was to have been a wedding into a bloodbath. Discipline was bad. With grain beginning to run low, the irregular *akinjiler* and *azablar* were spending as much time foraging as fighting. The quiet of camp in the old days was no more. But they yet had thirty-five thousand men; some knew how to fight. When his arm got better they would triumph and he would go home to his new *timar*.

Yakhshi smiled at the thought. Each day his arm did move more freely and the arquebus balls left no more red and pus than he expected. Better was that Mustafa Pasha had awarded him gold, silks and—an honor a *yenicheri* rarely received—a small *timar* for his valor at the Santarma fortress. Yakhshi was eager to see his new land, and the two dozen cannon now stirring the ground beneath his feet only increased his longing for the quiet of home. The noise would get worse. He did not think anyone had ever faced such a merciless bombardment as was building, but he was glad of it. When all sixty-five pieces were mounted, that would be the end of the infidels.

He hoped it would be the end of the mosquitoes. These Hell-sent demons were far the worst part of the undertaking. Surely they caused the sickness around him and with each sting on his hands Yakhshi prayed to Allah for their utter destruction.

At that moment his horse neighed behind him, reminding the *Boluk-bashi* it was time to move. Yakhshi got up from where he'd been crouching and, swatting as he was able, cursing the heat and the flies too, walked with the reins in his hand to meet *Chorbaji* Shahverdi. Together they rode out from the new camp in the direction of the old one, with what was left of their men guarding a line of slaves. Once they passed beyond the campfires, all was darkness but for the brilliance of the stars above and a few pinpricks of light in the distance.

The gashes Shahverdi got in his cheek at Santarma yet prevented from talking much above a mumble, but he seemed to be in good humor. "It iss an excccellent plan," the *Chorbaji* said, spit seeping out through the hole that wasn't knitted. "All honor to Musstafa. Allah has blesssed him with wissdom and clevernesss."

"Indeed, it is an excellent plan," Yakhshi replied. "Let us put it into action and go back to Constantinople."

They passed the place of the old camp, where the hospital tents remained full of sick and wounded, and the house of the infidel master. It looked much as it had on the day they'd arrived, seven infernal weeks ago, except that the trees in the garden had been cut down for wood. Once the company reached the Santarma island, the *Chorbaji* sent the slaves down to Marsamshet harbor. Lines of torches were everywhere. Yakhshi couldn't help but glance in the direction of the ruined fort; while he breathed he would never forget that place.

They waited only a short span under the stars; soon the ropes were stretched while grunting filled the air. Heaving for all they were worth, the slaves began hauling the boats up from the water along the path they'd cut during the past days. As the *yenicheriler* watched, some of the infidels let the rope slip from their grasp and one of the boats slid down the hill, scraping loudly.

"Insolent dogs!" Yakhshi shouted, ordering the *gumi* to flog them. Then he turned to Shahverdi: "How many boats will go over?"

Shahverdi didn't know, but he had heard talk—Mustafa and Piyale wanted anything that could be dragged or carried.

Yakhshi remained mounted much of the night, hitting the fucking mosquitoes. Late, one of the Jewish merchants who'd followed the fleet offered him a potion he vowed would protect anyone from all insects. He also complained that the army had captured too few slaves, though he'd heard that Maltese lived in many caves around the island. Yakhshi bought the potion and told the merchant that because there was little for the *yenicheriler* to do before the next assault, he would take some slaves if he could.

Next morning the main camp was all commotion. At last, *Beylerbeyi* Hasan had arrived from Cezayir-i Garb with twenty-eight vessels, including seven galleys, twenty-five hundred men and grain. Everyone cheered as Mustafa and his officers received Hasan at the pavilion. The *Beylerbeyi* wasn't as renowned as Turgut, but he was the son of the great Khair-ad-Din himself, not to mention married to Turgut's daughter. Yakhshi could see everyone's spirits lifting as they had when Turgut first came, more so when Hasan paraded in his bright robes and gold, declaring before one and all, "No more fearsome warriors are to be found in all Barbary than my braves."

Yakhshi suspected that Hasan was eager to perform some heroic act, because he'd arrived so late on the island, and he became certain of it when Mustafa and Piyale escorted him to the ruins of Santarma. Many *azablar* and sappers were about digging up the cannon balls that had been shot against the tower so they could be used again. They'd found one gun that was still good, and they'd mounted it farther up the hill with eight or ten other pieces, which now fired across the harbor at the big castle and against the island with the windmills.

When Hasan saw the charred remains of the pyres all around and heard about the cost of the siege of Santarma, he exclaimed, "If I had been here with my braves, Mustafa, you would not have had to reduce this fort. We would have taken it the first week!"

Yakhshi watched Mustafa's face twist up in anger at such boasting, but the Pasha replied in the way of a crafty old soldier: "I shall be happy to allow you, Hasan, to lead the assault on the island with the windmills, so you and your braves can show us your valor."

Hasan, for his part, was very pleased with the offer. "Give me eight thousand men and we will begin today, by land and by sea."

"You shall have your eight thousand men, Hasan," replied Mustafa, "once we have weakened the defenses with our bombardment and all the boats are in the water."

Ninety-Six

No one slept. For two nights at least twenty heavy pieces sent their iron crashing into Fort St. Michel and Senglea. Birgu remained safer, but the air shook to the thud of the guns and everywhere the ground quaked. On the third morning, well before the Angelus, I abandoned thoughts of slumber and set off to St. Angelo. I was making my way thro' the crowds huddled on the streets when the Grand Master himself, walking with his lioness from his home to the fortress, hailed me and asked to what use should we put injured slaves.

The Turks, after all, had not ceased firing on their own.

"Let them make matches for arquebuses," I said. "We have tow. The forges are going day and night, and they can also make shot or nails in the Birgu arsenal."

"Whither are you bound this moment?" de Valette asked me.

"To the castle—after the explosion the stock of fire weapons is yet low." It had been building. In our fury we had been piling up every sort of combustible we imagined on the castle plaza. "Eminenza might inquire of the doctors and alchemists whether they are able to distill quantities of water for drink. Isabella says her stores are falling faster than she expected." I recalled Djerbé, thinking enough distilling apparatus might have saved more lives to be taken into slavery.

Thereat the Grand Master asked after my arm and I replied I hadn't been too seriously wounded. We walked together across the moat and into the fortress, where to my surprise Balthazar was waiting above. Still able to walk only with a crutch, he requested a task at the mill.

Before I could answer, sentries ran up, begging de Valette to come quickly. We rushed over to the tip of the castle on the side of the Great Port, Balthazar limping from behind. Francisco Balbi was there, pointing to the very extremity of the Port, the Marsa. We couldn't see much, truthfully, but as the maws of Turkish cannon flashed above Senglea, followed an instant later by their roars, he and the sentries assured us that swimmers had confirmed their fears: The faint noises they'd heard during the night at Don Sanoguera's Post were of nightmares, not of dreams.

"There are six enemy boats in the Marsa," Balbi said. "Slaves carried them from Marsamxett harbor over the neck of Sciberras last night."

Balthazar and I glanced at each other, at once reliving that unforgettable night on Djerbé so long ago, a night we now recollected with a fondness of more exuberant days. "Mustafa seems to have learned something from Turgut," Balthazar said.

"Turgut," I answered, "learned something from Mehmed the Conqueror." That one had carried boats from the Bosporus to the Golden Horn in order to seize Constantinople one hundred and twelve years ago.

"Mehmed remembered how Hannibal took boats over the Alps to Lake Trasimene," quipped Robles's jester, who by now was constantly at the Grand Master's side, ceaselessly attempting and mostly failing to cheer him.

"A long tradition then," Balthazar smiled grimly, but the gravity of his expression could not equal the darkness chiseled onto the Grand Master's face. All of us surrounding him now knew precisely how the Turks intended to attack Senglea by sea.

Early next morning de Valette walked to the spur of St. Angelo and again watched the cannon flashes above Senglea. As a ball sailed full across Senglea, Galley Creek and crashed into Birgu, the sentries told him there were now twelve enemy boats in the Marsa. That afternoon we learned of Hasan's arrival from Argier. The Grand Master took the news heavily, because the thousands of fresh men Hasan had brought were five-fold the number that had arrived with Robles three days ago. Worse was the news Romegas gave him at the Palace:

"Piyale is building a large platform on San Salvatore."

de Valette rushed to the castle wall overlooking Kalkara. Along the creek, below Germany, England and the Infermeria itself, men were filling boats with rocks and sinking them to erect a second palisade. Directly across the creek—barbarians dragging Turkish guns up Mt. Salvatore and Piyale's colorful marquee standing behind them.

"Gargantua is angered that mice crept in between his legs," offered the jester, making a walking motion of his fingers.

The Monsignore merely glared at him. "I would not presume to have read such profane literature, Signore, but I am more concerned that Gargantua will soon be pounding his fist on this town."

Late that night Isabella found de Valette in his home near the Post of Castille, with his servants and slaves clearing out his papers and belongings. "Parisot, what are you doing?"

The Grand Master glanced over his shoulder, then as the booming suddenly became louder, turned fully on her with alarm. "This house stands exposed to the battery the enemy is raising on San Salvatore. Tomorrow I shall order it demolished. Isabella, your house is only a street away. Be prepared to abandon it."

The elation that accompanied the *soccorso* three days ago had passed; bewilderment alone flickered across Isabella's face. "Where are we to go?"

Parisot, fully engaged in the task of emptying his house, did not much consider her question. "I don't know," he said.

As cannon fire raised the sun, de Valette learned that there were thirty enemy boats in the Marsa and thereon did exactly as he had threatened: He ordered his house first among all demolished and the stones be used for the inner defenses. Halberdiers herded out the slaves from the bagno and marched them to the house, where they began taking it down block by block. They had not been long at the work, also demolishing some other homes by it, when the common folk of Birgu began to gather and look on. Having seen the great gun platform being built across Kalkara Creek, their curiosity that the Monsignore should order the destruction of his own home quickly turned to fury.

A woman shouted they were all going to die because of the godless animals.

The halberdiers ordered the Maltese to move on or lend a hand, but a merchant picked up a rock and hurled it. At once all was chaos. People were stoning the slaves, leaping on them with screams, tearing them to pieces with the knives and swords in their hands. The slaves, chained together in pairs, could do little to defend themselves and the halberdiers stood by motionless.

All the noise brought Isabella running from her house, and Vigo, who was on his way to the Hospital. Seeing the battle before her eyes, Isabella unthinkingly grabbed a stone herself. "Signora," Vigo said firmly, stepping up to her, "what demon has possessed you?"

She halted, glanced at the rock in her hand, dropped it in horror, understanding in that moment she had not triumphed over fear. Then, with no more hesitation, she ran to the nearest guard. "I beg you, Señor, put a end to this before all those creatures are killed!"

Thunder in his ear defeated by the importunacy of the lady's eyes, the guard roused his fellows. With halberds and threats they slowly restored order and forced the townspeople away.

"My gratitude, Doctor," Isabella said to him, offering her hand and lowering her head in shame. "I have repeatedly sworn, repeatedly ... but ... "

Vigo, shaking his own head, emptied his chest. "I have already seen slaves cut off their ears rather than continue this never-ending, hopeless toil. The Turkish cannon are cutting the poor creatures down by the dozens in Senglea, as they will here. The Monsignore was quite mistaken that the barbarians would not fire on their own ... *quite*."

Isabella looked at him sadly as they approached the Sacra Infermeria. For a moment Vigo halted, gazing at the great structure that rose above Kalkara Creek. Again he breathed. "We cannot move the Hospital."

Dawn next the Turks opened up from Salvatore on Castille and Germany with six heavy pieces. They were firing on houses too. Luckily, the most exposed had been demolished and walls built from their stone to protect the others nearby. More than forty guns were in action now. Thenceforward our lives were played out against a seamless canvas of booms, rumbling and crashes, as this tiny Borgo became an anvil for the Sultan's wrath.

In the Magisterial Palace a window shattered to the floor. A page rushed to clean up the broken glass while de Valette opened the remaining windows in his cabinet. "We can do nothing to strike at them!" he said with a resignation heard by all. "How many boats in the Marsa now?"

"The numbers increase each hour ... " said Romegas. " ... fifty. There is no doubt the infidels will attack by both land and sea. Uluj-Ali has also returned from Tripoli with bread."

de Valette pounded the table with his fist as the Palace shook under the guns striking the castle from Sciberras and our guns atop the fortress booming their reply.

"There is other news," Romegas continued, stepping aside to announce a wet Bajada. It were as if he did not wish to put himself at risk by divulging the courier's report, as, truly, de Valette's expression told him he might.

"Tomas Coronel has gained Notabile," the swimmer offered, pulling a sheep's bladder from a greased wine skin slung across his shoulder. Toni had just come from Mdina, skirting the enemy lines by going north, whence at great risk he crossed Sciberras and swam the harbor. "Pompeo Colonna, Cornisson and St. Aubin are sailing with three galleys and twelve hundred men, five hundred from the Pope himself." Bajada unwrapped the dispatch and handed it to the Grand Master. "They want smoke signals from St. Angelo to know whether to make land or not."

"And ... ?" The Grand Master, both Romegas and Bajada saw and heard, well divined that the courier hadn't revealed everything.

"Eminenza," the swimmer answered, quite slowly, "this message may be too late. The signals were to be set last night."

"Last night!" A distant thud rattled the glasses on the table. "Have you seen any galleys?"

Toni shook his head.

"Why only twelve hundred troops?" The Monsignore was pacing now, clenching his fist. "I have asked for ten thousand."

"Ten thousand, hah!" Romegas scoffed. de Valette ceased in mid-stride, glaring at him. "Coronel," the Commander went on, "says the Vice Roy has received secret instructions from King Philip, but that he refuses to divulge what they are. Tomas thinks Philip is farting on the pot because he doesn't trust us the Knights. Damn king in a monk's cell. But Don Garcia isn't blind to the danger threatening Sicily. He has released the ships."

"How do you know this?" de Valette asked.

Lescaut merely threw a glance at Bajada.

All words ceased as a ball crashed nearby and shouts arose from the plaza. de Valette patted the head of his lioness and walked into the Council chamber, following some Seigneurs outside. A small shot had hit the protecting wall on the Sciberras side that he'd ordered built from the demolished store houses. "How can a relief enter with the Port surrounded?" de Valette asked aloud as they returned to his study.

"We can have them go to Città Vecchia again," Romegas suggested.

"I do not believe God will send a second fog ... Bajada, return to Notabile. Tell them we shall continue to send signals, as Mezquita will from Città Vecchia. Perhaps they can land to the west ... I shall give you a letter tonight."

Hereon the famous swimmer hesitated, tugged at his ear. "Eminenza, I came by Sciberras because one of Commander Romegas's slaves escaped. He knows me well. I could be recognized in the Turkish camp."

"One of your slaves *escaped*!" de Valette roared at Lescaut.

"He refused to work on the walls. I think the dog let himself over with a rope two nights ago. I'll go myself."

de Valette stared hard at his deputy. "Mathurin, we well know you would have preferred to have died in Fort St. Elmo inflicting every harm on the enemy, or be this moment with Robles on the bastions of St. Michel. As I have said before, I say again: We cannot spare you. You are my lieutenant, and should I perish, you must step into my place ... Have no fear, your hour shall come ... soon enough."

Romegas protested no further, but Bajada remained disquieted. "Governor Mezquita sent out four couriers," he asked. "Have any others arrived?"

de Valette slowly shook his head. "Still, you must go. We shall send others with you."

The Grand Master himself escorted Bajada out of the Palace and mayhap for that reason only, events unfolded as they did. Catching sight of me at the mill, he asked whether I would accompany the courier to Notabile.

"E—Eminenza," I answered, "I do not know the countryside so well as Toni, nor can I match him in the water. I'd be but a hindrance."

"No matter," Toni put in with as much cheer as he was able, "we both have nicked ears. They'll bring us luck."

After dark Toni and I betook ourselves first to Isabella's home, accompanied by a limping Balthazar, who yet helped at the mill. Houses only a street away were shuddering and every so often a scream cut through the night air, causing the soul to tremble. My companions waited outside. "The Monsignore has asked me to accompany Bajada to Mdina," I said to Isabella alone. "We'll leave shortly. Do you have any dispatches?"

Isabella nodded and fetched them. To say farewell to friends and loved ones each day had become so difficult that no one did anymore. "You shall take care," she said, tightening the kerchief about my arm.

"Of course. I'll return tomorrow night ... Isabella, are you certain it is safe here? The houses ... "

"Parisot has moved into his steward's house, but for the moment this quarter is as safe as another."

"Promise me that if this street comes under the guns, you will take shelter in my room or elsewhere."

Isabella nodded, whereat I noticed blood on her palms. Aye, she answered, she had been praying so fervently just now that she'd injured herself. She then confessed that had Dr. Vigo not stayed her hand this morning, she would have cast stones against the slaves, such was her blind rage. "Each hour is a struggle," she admitted heavily.

"Once," I replied, kissing her bloodied hands, "Balthazar revealed to me how, tho' a Knight, he swore to himself not to step beyond his vows. Let us learn from him. We have vowed to survive; God willing we will survive with honor."

After the two of us embraced, I stepped onto the street, only to find Vergã approaching the threshold. Before I drew a breath he said to Balthazar, "Knight, do not be so vain to think I am ignorant of who interceded with the Pope against me."

"Do you threaten me?" Balthazar asked with a disdainful laugh, and without waiting for an answer turned to Bajada and me, wishing us a safe journey.

Overhearing this, Blaij abruptly said, "You are going to Mdina?"

"Yes," I answered, perplexed by his sudden interest, "Coronel has brought word that another relief is en route. We must make arrangements."

To my greatest surprise, Blaij immediately insisted he accompany us. With our enmity again laid bare, I well perceived that only a single combat could come of this, but why Mdina? Ensconced in my first astonishment, Balthazar added an equal one by seconding the plan. Unable to fathom either design, I said it was up to Toni. "We may have to swim." At that Blaij flinched, but in no way backed off. Toni himself reluctantly agreed; yet ill at ease about being recognized in the Turkish camp, he had, aye, decided to swim; natheless he'd be grateful for the company and protection.

Before we set off, Balthazar took me aside to piss and said simply, "I was mistaken not to have disposed of that one long ago. Should he cause the slightest trouble, kill him. You have my leave."

At de Guiral's Post, we stripped down to nothing, stuffed our clothes in bags and threw them over our shoulders. I tied my rapier onto the strap and we covered ourselves with dirt, for the moon was approaching fullness and its light would throw a further hazard upon us. We waded into the summer water and swam in the channel's center clear out the mouth of the Port. At once our road was barred by enemy galleys sailing back and forth from Marsamxett down past Gallows' Point, blockading, patrolling.

There was nothing for it. We treaded water like dogs until Blaij was gasping for breath; for all his years at sea, he detested the thought of water and only his natural strength prevented him from finding Neptune. "What we do for the Order, eh?" he panted, but Toni had already perceived his mistake.

"We must rest," I groaned.

Halfheartedly, Bajada nodded and we made for Gallows' Point. There, at the base of the rocks, we heard Turkish soldiers joking above us. Since the enemy had begun work on the gun battery atop nearby San Salvatore, plenty of men were camped here, and for glass after glass we were completely baffled as to how to go farther. We remained motionless until the moon had nearly set, when Toni decided we must swim directly out into the sea. We followed, keeping below water as much as we could. Of a sudden, the dark shadow of a galley was bearing down. Toni motioned us under, and under we went, holding our breaths as the oars splashed not an armslength above our heads. As the galley passed we dared put only our lips above water, and waited again until it was at a distance.

We swam further out, well past the patrols, then south along Rinella, now dotted everywhere by campfires of those who worked on the platform or guarded the promontory against further Christian reliefs. Toni shuddered at the sight of the place, but we were mere specks in dark, and God gave us strength to swim beyond the fire light and track of the galleys. At long last we crept ashore at one of the cliffs where Toni kept extra clothes hidden. For a time we sat, two of us panting and utterly exhausted; then we dried ourselves and our weapons, dressed and pressed onward to Mdina.

Because of our slowness, the sun had risen by the time we reached the city and we came upon Anastagi at the gate preparing for a sortie. By him stood one Fra Aleran Parpaglia Piemontois, nephew of the same Vañon who'd perished at Fort St. Elmo; he had also just gained Mdina—from Sicily.

"Do you have news of the relief?" Bajada urgently asked Piemontois.

None, other than what we already knew but, sweet succour, all Europe was in a colossal panic, troops from every land rushing to Sicilia.

Bajada interrupted his account, saying we'd brought a dispatch to be taken to the Vice Roy. "The Grand Master will continue sending signals from St. Angelo for the next days—"

"It may be too late," Anastagi replied needlessly. "God knows where Colonna is." Before his next breath, tho', the Captain handed the letter over to Lieutenant Ventura, ordering him to dispatch a boat to Sicily from Gozo that night.

I offered that signals might be set at Mdina, thinking Colonna could land nearby, but Anastagi countered that even should the signals be discerned, there was no longer any path to St. Angelo. "However, come with us," he said. "We'll think on't."

So Vergã and I, running with some bread and eggs in our hands, got mounts and joined the cavalry. Only then did we learn the reason for Fra Aleran's presence. Such was the present extremity and the Knights' desperate resolve, that Piemontois had come on a small barque with a plan none of us could wholly believe: He intended to capture a Turkish slave, have the slave lead him straight into Mustafa's tent, then assassinate the Pasha before giving up his own life.

"Let us find a slave," said Anastagi and we rode out of the City.

Nothing unfolded as foreseen. Toward the south, near some caves where we'd heard a whole village of Maltese were living, we encountered a company of Turks. At once Anastagi and Piemontois charged the enemy horse and a fierce skirmish erupted. Some of the foe incontinently sped into the caves; Anastagi and a group of his men followed, Vergã and I amongst them, while Piemontois confronted the spahis and janissaries who remained outside. Rushing into that tremendous labyrinth, we could hardly believe our eyes—a hundred Maltese in the meanest condition living beneath the rocks in darkness, their shelter lit only by fires and filled with smoke.

It seems the Turks had been there for some hours and we caught them with their pants down. Aye. Their leader had taken a beautiful fourteen-year-old girl aside and was violating her on a bed of sheepskins when we ran in after the fleeing soldiers, weapons unsheathed. At the sight of us, the janissaries sped thro' the caves to another way out, while we grabbed torches from the Maltese and followed in hot pursuit. The leader fled with the girl, but seeing he could not escape with her in hand and refusing to yield her to anyone, he lopped off her head with a single blow of his scimitar. By the time we found our way after them, the janissaries were climbing down the seaside cliffs. Our arquebusiers fired and the chief was killed.

We returned to the skirmish still boiling on the other side of the caves. Piemontois, carried away by the fever of battle, was charging and recharging the foe, heedless of the spahis' skill with the bow, and as we came on to the fight, he went down with an arrow thro' his throat. At almost the same moment, tho', the Maltese Luca who was so deft with the sword, executed the *botta* for which men offered him gold and disarmed one of the janissaries, taking him unharmed. The other Turks scattered. All told, Anastagi's cavalry had killed about thirty of them.

When we approached the captured barbarian, he looked up sullenly at those about him. After some moments, I recognized my old acquaintance Yakhshi from Constantinople.

At Mdina the *Boluk-bashi* had scarce been tied up in a room above the gate when an argument erupted about what to do with him. As Piemontois had foolishly gotten himself killed, Anastagi was in favor of interrogating the Turk, then quartering him. "He is of no use to us now," the Captain said in disgust, "unless one of you is willing to carry out Piemontois's plan."

Vergã glanced at me as if hurling a challenge, but no one stepped forward. I did offer to question the prisoner.

As I entered his cell, Yakhshi looked up at me and said in Turkish, "Pork-eater, I knew I'd see you again someday."

I handed him a cup of water and crouched opposite. Full of cuts and deprived of his headdress as he was, the janissary remained formidable, his moustaches no less fearsome than of old, his forelock proudly declaring his rank. "What were you doing at the caves?" I asked.

"We went to take slaves, but I heard that the caves were the dwelling of the *basilisco* and we went off to find one when your *spahiler* came upon us."

"I do not think basilisks live on this island, but for the ones I have cast and you have brought. And those do not kill by their very gaze." Mayhap they did. "I tell you the Grand Master has ordered all Turkish prisoners to be executed. The chief spahi here will see you quartered."

Yakhshi did not even ask to be ransomed.

"You once took me to a *tekke*," I said after a long silence, leaning against the wall. "I regret there are none here. Do you have my wheel-lock?"

"Until today. If my wounds had been fully healed, that Maltese *kopek* would never have disarmed me."

As I gazed on this my enemy, I tried with no success to summon the youthful ignorance that once led me to save a frightened *chavush* on Lampedusa. Here before me sat a deadly foeman, an officer in an army intent on killing every Christian of this island and inflicting every barbarity on them besides. The Knights, the Maltese—I—would see him quartered without pity. Yet the *chavush* had saved me in Constantinople and this one had taken me to a *tekke*. "Do you know the *chavush* Abdallah-al-Waryagli?"

"I met him the day you tested your big gun at the Foundry. I would not be surprised if the Sultan sends him here with the reinforcements."

"*Reinforcements?*"

"Mustafa has requested them."

Truly that was a useful intelligence. Yakhshi, tho', clammed up at once, seeing he had already divulged too much. "Tell me of the Turkish camp and I'll get your wheel-lock," I said.

"Of what use is a wheel-lock if I am to be quartered?"

"You may find it yet of use. Otherwise I will bastinado you myself."

Yakhshi decided it was a fine weapon and slowly began to recount his part in the siege, those events I have already narrated. I sought out Luca and bought back from him my wheel-lock, then told Anastagi on the

square that I would take the prisoner into the Turkish camp, to fulfill
Piemontois's design.

"You have lost your mind!" Anastagi replied with disdain. "This is no
simple slave you can lead by the nose; this is a colonel of the janissaries.
He'll kill you at the first opportunity."

"I think not, but I'll keep him bound."

Blaij, sitting unnoticed nearby, overheard this conversation and insisted
he come. "Never," I said. "You don't speak Turkish and will expose us in
the enemy camp."

"Half the Turkish camp doesn't speak Turkish," he growled.
"Piemontois didn't either. He intended to tell the enemy he was deserting.
We'll do the same."

Anastagi declared both of us mad, but the Knights' desperation was
extreme. That night, Blaij and I rode out of Mdina with an escort and a
bound janissary. After near two leagues, the company turned back with
the horses and the three of us were alone.

As we walked on with Yakhshi before us, I fully perceived that the
kairos was upon me; there would never be a better moment to do away
with Vergã. But what of Yakhshi? I said a few words to him in Turkish,
at which Blaij warned me to silence. "I know what you plan and I won't
allow you to get away with it," he threatened.

"I must tell him something if we are to get into Mustafa's tent," I said.

"You'll tell him exactly what Piemontois intended: That we know the
situation is hopeless, that we want to desert and we can tell Mustafa details
about the defenses. When we get to Mustafa's tent, we'll throw ourselves
on him with our knives, kill him and be killed. If you attempt to turn
Turk again, I'll kill you and die in the service of Christ."

Vergã pronounced those words with a conviction that Romegas would
have envied, yet I could not but feel something unseen, unfelt lurked
behind this. Steeling myself, I ignored his accusations.

We walked on. As the enemy camp grew near, shots suddenly *thpped*
through the air and we dove for cover behind an old stone wall. Yakhshi
and I ended up on one side and Vergã on the other. We could not say
whether the fire was in our direction and waited in silence for approaching
footsteps. We heard nothing but our own breathing.

"Getting into the Turkish camp isn't proving so easy, Esforzado," Blaij
whispered. "Do you have the stomach for it?"

Strangely, I heard a slight falter in his voice; I made no reply.

"You have always undertaken hopeless endeavors, Barai," he went on, baiting me, yet as if speaking to himself. "What is more hopeless? This war or conquering Isabella? She is worthy of the effort ... In peaceful times she'd choose me, you know. Hah, I have already had her." Thus he lost control and brazenly raised his arm above the wall, flaunting Isabella's kerchief.

Fury blinded me. Instantly I was on my feet, as was Vergã, weapons drawn. At last. No one would know, here in enemy territory, how Vergã died. But Yakhshi had meanwhile managed to cut his bonds with my knife and was also up. E'en as Blaij lunged, the janissary grabbed his wheel-lock from my saddle holster, aimed and shot Blaij's rapier from his hand. The noise brought us to our senses; we dashed off in one direction, Yakhshi in the other.

Exhausted after a full day without sleep, we collapsed on the ground near the coast. Cold sober now, both of us realized that any hope in our mad designs—whatever they may have been—had been dashed. I told Vergã that if he didn't want to drown alone or be captured, the only thing for it was to swim back to Birgu.

Luckily, we were much less than a league from the town. Creeping along the rocks, we got into the water and retraced our path of the previous night. The peril hadn't lessened, but as we approached the line of enemy boats, their attention was drawn by three galleys on the horizon. Our heads scarcely above water, we watched the white signals from Castle St. Angelo rising against the dark sky, warning the approaching vessels to turn about. Turn about they did and disappeared into the darkness. In my mind's eye, I saw de Valette pounding on his table, despairing that he had no choice in refusing the relief: The Great Port was completely surrounded.

For the two of us, tho', the commotion saved our lives. The Turkish galleys had drawn away from the harbor's mouth, firing uselessly after Pompeo Colonna's vessels, and we swam in unmolested. How bitterly I regret not having killed Blaij while the *kairos* was mine.

Ninety-Seven

Once again Pietru scrambled behind the wall of l'Isola as the sun rose and Turkish arquebusiers on the opposite shore opened fire on those building the palisade. The *stoccado* was nearly finished now, running all the way from Fort St. Michel to the spur of l'Isola, but each day work on it became more perilous. The Turks were pounding the wall with thirteen heavy pieces and the Post of Bormla above them with six, sending rock crashing into the water from primes to complines. So furious was the bombardment that the infidel gunners weren't letting their cannon cool between shots; the thunder became almost continuous and smoke enshrouded the heights of Corradino. Neither did the janissaries intend to let the palisade be finished and their muskets of eleven palms didn't cease sending shot the size of eggs across the channel that would blow a man's head off.

Ix-Xabaw sat once more with Martino in a sort of stupor. The ringing in his head had never stopped after Fort St. Elmo, and he felt as a ghost walking among those who lived. Martino was saying something he couldn't make out very well, that they must finish the fence. Yes, they must, at all costs. Mustafa had by now put above seventy boats in the Marsa and an assault on l'Isola must come soon, any day.

"God, I'd fuck the Tur—"

Pietru's exhausted words were cut short by a huge explosion, an explosion so powerful that it instantly cut thro' the wall that now surrounded him. So powerful he felt it more than he heard it. The blast surely came from across the water and at once he and Martino ran up to the Post of Bormla to see what had happened. Aye, atop Corradino, a great black cloud was billowing into the sky above the Turkish platform, flames beneath.

"By Jesus, what's that!" exclaimed Martino.

No one could say, except that the whole Turkish battery had fallen silent—and was remaining silent as Turks there scrambled frantically with blankets and buckets to put out the fire. "Come on," waved Pietru, "we can work on the fence."

They risked going out. Sure enough, no one was shooting. Well into the night, Pietru and his comrades drove piles amongst the rocks and bound crossbeams, strengthening the whole palisade with ropes stretched to stakes driven into the shore. Only late did they learn their guesses were right—one of the big Turkish pieces had exploded, sending the nearby powder stores up with it and killing forty men.

"Do you think it was one of yours?" Pietru asked me when I saw him.

"My guns don't explode," I answered. "If you let them cool."

The Turks understood what the explosion had cost them and decided to make up for it. Early next morning, the sun was sparkling off the blue of the creek when the alarmed voice of a sentry suddenly cried out, "They're attacking the palisade!"

Rousing himself from his fitful sleep at the post, Pietru glanced over the walls. A small group of Turkish swimmers had already gained the *stoccado* and were hacking at the ropes with axes.

"*Ghaggel! Haffef!*" Martino shouted. "*Tahlix hin!*"

About five of the Maltese, all swimmers, dashed out thro' the sally port below, fully dressed in cuirass and morion, fully armed with short swords and bucklers, and ploughed into the water.

The Spaniards and Italians gathered on the ramparts of St. Michel to watch the spectacle unfolding beneath them—five men in armor swimming against a like number of Turks dressed in loincloths who sat wielding axes atop a palisade.

"By my Mistress's bright eyes, I would not credit what I see," said one.

"May I be buried in Neptune's grave," answered the other. "Those peasants aren't sinking."

No, they weren't. Ix-Xabaw felt only rage at the barbarians who were destroying his island, and he struck at the nearest one, who sat astride a crossbeam, trying to cut the ropes with his hatchet. That one returned the blow with the weapon in his hand. Pietru blocked it with his buckler and threw himself against his enemy, dismounting him from his perch.

Crashing into the water, the Turk swam for his life into the creek; Pietru climbed over the fence and was after him. The same picture was unfolding everywhere nearby. Martino caught up with his foeman, climbed onto his back and slit his neck with a knife as he would a kid. As the blood colored the water, the others got away.

Before long the Turkish swimmers returned, more of them, and this time with long ropes that stretched clear across the Poret to big capstans mounted below Corradino. They had already gained the fence and tied the ropes to the heads of the stakes. With a wave from the swimmers, those on the shore opposite bent their backs to their engines and the whole length of the palisade began to creak. Now the Turkish swimmers, having secured the ropes, took off.

"*Ara ma nhalluhomx!*" Martino, seeing this from above, shouted.

Again the Maltese ran down and out the sally port, this time to be met by hot musket fire. At once a ball grazed Martino's leg, but he paid no heed and was on the fence, cutting the ropes with a hatchet. As Pietru sliced a rope with an axe in one hand, shielding himself with his buckler in his other, he thought only that he was tired of being wounded. The work done, he and his comrades dashed back behind the wall.

All day the Turks returned, attempting to overturn the palisade, and all day the same Maltese swam out after them, cutting the ropes and fighting them off in the water. By sunset, the infidels seemed to have become waterlogged and ceased their efforts.

"The Turks don't swim very well," Martino said, wringing himself off as night fell.

"They should stay on land," agreed Pietru.

The next morning I went to St. Angelo to take my place at the mill and crossed to the tip of the castle, where the Grand Master stood among the sentries, gazing toward the Marsa. He had no need to explain what the sight before our eyes portended.

More than one hundred vessels—every *fusta, fregata* and brigantine the Turks had, and several galiots besides—crowded the inner reaches of the Great Port. Mustafa had learned well from Turgut, from Mehmed.

Were that the last of our worries. From Sciberras opposite the Turks continued to hit Sanoguera's Post as his men constantly attempted to build it back up, e'en while they also constructed a gun platform under the windmills. In the other direction, fifty galleys crowded around Gallows' Point and Rinella, disembarking thousands of troops or sappers there, we did not know which. Each of us swallowed hard, but we were granted no time to ponder the matter, for at that moment the Turks sent two balls at us from Sciberras, which smashed into the castle wall nearby and sent us sprawling to the ground.

"Eminenza?" every voice asked at once.

de Valette rose, brushing himself off, dismissing our concern. "You shall take all the fire weapons across to Robles in St. Michel," he said as we walked to the other side of the castle, as if nothing had transpired. "The Turks there have already attempted to seize the ditch, and yesterday saw some fierce fighting." Hereat the Monsignore paused with a glance toward smoke-enshrouded Corradino. "Those bagpipes and cymbals and the infernal singers disturbing the night with their barbaric sounds are the worst of it." After we had taken across the fire weapons, I was to return to Galley Creek embankment to aid with the deployment of the floating bridge that would join Birgu to Senglea and to provide the men at Sanoguera's Post a road wherewith to escape.

The Grand Master's expression told me he was angered at having to refuse Pompeo Colonna's assistance. "At least we know all Europe is rushing hither," I offered.

"Is Venice?" he asked, a grim jest unexpectedly from his lips.

I had heard nothing of Venice and made no answer.

We took the fire weapons to St. Michel's by boat. A second chain had already been laid across the inner extremity of Galley Creek, tho' the Turks had not yet attempted to bring any boats thither and the iron links surely provided no protection from cannon fire. After a week of bombardment, Fort St. Michel's walls were beginning to show the same signs as St. Elmo's had—and the Turks hadn't yet emplaced more than half their guns. Inside the fort, men and women were everywhere running about, making repairs as well as they could. I guessed Flaminia was here but did not see her. Pausing to cover my ears, I did catch sight of Captain Juan de la Cerda. It seems de Valette had released him from prison to fight at St. Michel but the soldiers didn't speak to him. Truly, more than one spat at his feet and others mocked him as he carried stones with the rest.

"Your arm looks perfect now, Captain," they taunted under the booming.

I could see the fire in la Cerda's eyes, but said nothing.

The task done with Robles's thanks, we returned to Birgu, where on the embankment I found Balthazar tarring some large barrels. Dozens upon dozens sat upon the docks, strung together with rope. Nearby lay a bed of planks, also strung together by rope, ready to go atop the barrels.

"Fine work for a Knight of St. John," I said, sitting by him and taking up a brush.

Balthazar did not directly reply. Rather he told me that Blaij Vergã had already informed Romegas I had freed a janissary. I looked him in the eye and said it was true.

The Knight sighed. "Francisco, I tell you the matter is grave. Be certain the Grand Master will call it treason and hang you—if you are lucky."

"Balthazar," I said, still regarding him in the eye, "I have never had your capacity for knowledge and wisdom, your ability to stand outside the world and view it entire. God knows, I'll ne'er be the philosopher you are, and mayhap a man does not know what he has learned until he is ready. Forgive me, I speak clumsily, but I have of late tried to remember your many words to me. You once said you would not go beyond your vows. That janissary did me a good turn in Constantinople and was unarmed. Fifteen years ago on Lampedusa, when I was young and knew more than I do now, I saved an unarmed man and you sided with me in the matter. If I have condemned myself by doing what I did then, at least I have regained myself."

Balthazar nodded at my speech, perhaps the longest I'd e'er made, and slapped me on the shoulder. "I had hoped you would correct my error and dispatch that rogue—or at least discover what he was up to. Now that I have brought to ruin his scheme to become a Knight, his fury becomes wilder, but Francisco, you have handed him the ten of swords and he has played it. Let me think. For the next days, I fear, you will be safe unless you are killed in the greater threat that looms imminently."

By nightfall all the barrels were tarred and dried, and the Maltese began to pull them out one by one into Galley Creek, swimming with them across the inlet. Once that was done, they faced them with the bed of planks, binding it atop the barrels with rope. The Grand Master had waited until the last possible moment to construct the bridge for fear that

the Turks would fire on it, but now Birgu and Senglea were joined, and
Balbi the poet had his means of escape.

Late I went to Isabella's house. It stood only two or three streets from
the Post of Castille, and each shot of the guns was so powerful that it
robbed us of speech and breath. She'd already heard from Vergã's lips
about Yakhshi and, my words punctuated by the concussion of the
artillery, I told her what I had said to Balthazar. She gazed on me first
with a puzzled expression, then it changed to a softer one and she rested
her hand on my chest. "You do make me brave, Francisco," she said at
length. "Try not to fear Parisot. I promise not allow him to harm you.
Put aside your jealousy of Vergã as well. I have only wanted to make peace
between you and swear again he means nothing to me. Truly, after what
he has now done ... "

As people do, Isabella was coloring the matter to protect herself as well,
but a new eruption of the Turkish cannon on Salvatore spared me a reply.
A painting fell from the wall while a not-distant shriek split the
nighttime, and I grew alarmed. "It is too dangerous now in this quarter,"
I said. "We must find you another place to live without delay."

Isabella smiled faintly, but shook her head resolutely. "There is no place
any longer, Francisco."

Returning to my room, I passed Flaminia's house, which was e'en more
exposed than Isabella's, sitting on higher ground. I saw a light burning
in her room above and called out. She came to the window with a candle.

"Flaminia, I would not have you living here. It is too perilous."

The bandaged whore replied that with her parents, her daughter and a
few others besides, there was nothing for it; she had no place to go. She
said something I didn't hear, because of a cannon shot, then came down
to the door as the street trembled beneath my feet.

Flaminia had also heard rumors that I had freed a Turk. "Is it true,
Francisco?"

"I shall not deny it," I replied.

She lowered her head. "I do not understand these things, *mio cuore*, but
I know Blaij Vergã is a bad man." Thereat she suggested poison, which
she could easily get me. For the present I demurred and spent the night

with her in my arms, she afraid for me and I afraid for her, as the earth shook around us.

Ninety-Eight

If there are days that change the course of the world, Your Majesty, then surely the fifteenth of July, *anno* 1565, was one of them. The bombardment kept up relentlessly all thro' the previous day, so much so that de Valette ordered the floating bridge moved closer to Castle St. Angelo to protect it from the enemy guns on the Margarita hills. All night, the infidels pounded their cymbals, blew on their horns and bagpipes and sang, the sounds of which drifted across the water. So much did it vex the Grand Master that he went to sleep in the Borgo, preferring the danger of the Turkish guns to their music.

Two hours before dawn, a deathly silence fell over the entire harbor, a sure sign that the assault would come today. The tocsin sounded and the drummers beat the skins, but the sudden hush had already wakened everybody. In the darkness, those of us atop St. Angelo could not make out much, except that a large commotion was taking place in the Marsa and another on Rinella. As the sky lightened, we gradually discerned Turks clambering into the fleet of boats that occupied the inner end of the Great Port, while in the other direction we watched thousands more troops landing at its mouth. At length a cannon sounded from the Mandra and was answered by another on Sciberras. The assault on Senglea had begun, by land and sea.

The Grand Master had ordered me to man one of the guns at St. Angelo. Balthazar stood nearby too, this day full armored despite his injury, for de Valette intended to hold ready a large *soccorso*, while Robles and his men bore the brunt of the attack on Fort St. Michel. Pietru was down at the Post of Bormla, and Balbi had managed to remain alive at Sanoguera's Post; I could see it plainly from my position—if not Balbi himself—the place by now looking little better than St. Elmo had at the end. The plaza near the mill behind me was empty. If I had not been told to fight this day, I knew I had been among those who supplied Senglea with upon thirty thousands of fire weapons, which Robles would hurl against the eight thousand men preparing to storm St. Michel.

As the infidel boats sped toward them, Balbi and his comrades at the spur of Senglea could not at first comprehend what was transpiring. The small vessels seemed so much larger than they should. Only as the swarm neared and the light brightened did the defenders perceive that the Turks had lined their boats with bales of straw and woolen sacks filled with cotton to protect them against gunfire.

For a time Balbi, even Don Francisco Sanoguera himself, stood atop the battered post, marveling at the fleet spreading out across the Great Port and rowing so furiously in their direction. They must be the flower of Dragut's men and Hasan's Algerians. A rich turban adorned every head, not a brave among them but wore a robe of crimson damask; the gold and silver cloth many boasted shone splendidly in the morning sun. With cries of *"halla, halla!"* they waved scimitars from Alexandria and Damascus that glinted blindingly, their bows and arrows as well, while each vessel bristled like a hedgehog with fine muskets from Fez.

"What a magnificent spectacle ... " remarked the stout Sanoguera, dressed in his resplendent armor and tunic of the Order.

" ... were it not so fraught with danger," replied Balbi, lighting his match.

As the fleet neared Senglea, we on St. Angelo above let loose with every piece at hand. *"Fuego!"* I cried, Diego cried as our guns boomed, and our shots raised fountains of white from the water. The distance was long enough. Powder, straw, balls—a hit! The boat was smashed into pieces and went under. In the same heartbeat Sanoguera's pieces and those below the windmills went off, *boom-boom, boom-boom.* Three more boats plunged to the bottom of the Port and fifty more souls sped to Paradise.

"Por estas Barbas que nascieron à la Fumada de los Canones!" cried Diego. "We have them!"

The situation appeared otherwise to Balbi. The cannon fire from above his head had put a few holes into that swarm of midges, but did nothing to halt its advance. Moment by moment the sound of the infidel horns and tambourines grew louder. Balbi guessed two thousand men sat in the approaching boats. A large barque led the others, full of dervishes with long hair and tall hats who were reading prayers, auguries for the day, every one without doubt favorable. Near it, dashing back and forth, was a lighter caique, well armed, in which stood a resplendently dressed corsair waving a green banderole, directing the others. Balbi took aim at him but missed. "Ah, lady, I love you, why do you scorn me?"

"*Allahu Ekber! Allahu Ekber!*" With each cry the speed of the vessels increased and the oars, it seemed, danced to the gay jangle of the tambourines. The arquebusier looked about him. Sanoguera's men numbered sixty.

As the boats entered the Poret de Senglea, they fanned out all along l'Isola—from Sanoguera's Post past the Sicilians' to the Post of Bormla—and Balbi crossed himself. Jesus, Joseph, Maria—half were surely heading directly toward him. "They intend to ram the palisade," said Sanoguera.

Don Francisco was exactly correct. Those hundred boats, stretched along the entire curtain, rowed at top speed straight into the *stoccado*. Amidst all the shouts and war cries, Pietru, from his place at Bormla, heard the groan of an underground giant as the fence shuddered and creaked—and held. He sighed, crossed himself with eyes raised to Heaven, fired.

Under heavy arquebusades from the wall, Turks were jumping from the boats, taking to the water everywhere and, just as the Grand Master had hoped, getting soaked thro' to their bones. It wasn't enough. Balbi watched Sanoguera's nephew, Jaime, run toward the Post of the Sicilians to fire the two mortars they'd brought thither from the galleys, but he had no time to load them. Turks and Algerians were already everywhere, some climbing the palisade, others swimming the few strokes to shore, still others hoisting ladders over the *stoccado* and carrying them to the curtain. The fence ended here at the spur of l'Isola and numbers of the braves merely waded around it.

For his part, Balbi was anything but confident. The walls around him were low from the bombardment and the ladders easily reached the top. He again fixed his match in the dog leg and discharged his arquebus; the ball pinged off the blue scorpion painted on the yellow shield below. Cursing, Balbi made to reload, but the enemy was advancing so rapidly he had no time. He cast down his gun and with two hands picked up a big stone. Others were doing the same; they would fight with pikes, swords, shields—rocks.

Things rapidly got worse. One of the soldiers, Ciano, was lighting a fire ball at the post. He didn't know how to handle it and the fool swung it into the others nearby. Instantly they all went up, and the *granadas* we had sent down there. Amidst the explosions, one after another, Ciano himself caught afire. Some others came to rescue him and they caught fire too. The men finally smothered the flames, but Ciano and four or five others were severely burnt, and most of the fire weapons destroyed. Balbi glanced at the thick pillar of smoke rising behind him and knew there was nothing for it. He picked up another rock and hurled it down upon a foeman's head. Rocks were more certain than fire weapons in any case.

Seeing that many of the Turks had landed at the front of the spur, Don Francisco himself mounted what was left of the parapet with his sword and shield to rally his men. Balbi followed, not entirely believing the scene below him. Turks churned up the water everywhere, clambering toward the walls with great determination, setting ladders at the foot of the post, which they saw as the easiest place in the world to enter. The poet stole another glimpse at the sixty who defended this place and thought the Turks were right. Nor could the enemy fail to recognize a nobleman by his armor; soon enough a shot glanced off Sanoguera's breastplate.

"Hah!" he exclaimed, thumping it. "German armor!"

In the next moment, a janissary wearing a large black headdress with gold ornaments and who knelt at the foot of the battery aimed upward and hit Sanoguera in the left groin. The shot went through steel, and Don Francisco fell over dead at the very edge of the parapet. The Turks shouted for joy and instantly sped up their ladders, intent on claiming their prize.

Balbi himself lost not a heartbeat. He bent to grab the Knight's body, but Sanoguera was stout and his armor heavy, and the old arquebusier could not by himself lift it. His fellows rushed over and there at the very edge of the wall they struggled for Sanoguera's remains. The Turks were so close that they were pulling down on the legs, as Balbi and his comrades pulled up by the arms. Finally Balbi kicked one of the leering corsairs in the teeth and they wrested the body from the foe, but not before the enemy had gotten Sanoguera's boots. I saw all this from St. Angelo.

Balbi did not know what was to become of them. After they'd dragged Sanoguera's body away from the wall, he looked up to see the corsair leader in the caique waving his banderole for the boats to pass to the other side of the spur, where the wall was largely ruined, where no palisade protected them and where only the great chain guarded the entrance to Galley Creek.

"Is that King Hasan?" the arquebusier asked aloud as he ran again toward the wall.

"No, his lieutenant, Candelissa, the meat-eater," said a voice next to him. Alfonso, the Spanish renegado from Algiers, introduced himself.

Balbi replied that he was happy to make Alfonso's acquaintance, tho' he feared it would not last long. As they picked up more stones, Candelissa sent ten of the largest boats, each carrying one hundred or one hundred fifty men, around the promontory in order to land.

Balthazar and I watched everything from above. It was a sight my eyes could not credit then and that I have never believed since: Those boats were rounding the spur of Senglea into Galley Creek, toward the chain. But in their fervor the Algerians had forgotten that the whole creek was commanded by de Guiral's Post at water level. The battery sat almost directly below me at the foot of St. Angelo and I could see perfectly the astonishment written across de Guiral's moustaches when he realized that the boats had come directly into the maw of his guns. At once the Commander ordered his pieces loaded with bags of stone, pieces of chain and iron thistles. Then he waited.

"*Fuego!*" de Guiral cried so forcefully that those of us above could hear him without difficulty.

Five of his guns roared. It was a complete massacre. The chain and thistles tore into those boats, sinking four of them at once. Screaming, the Algerian braves—those who hadn't been cut in two—struggled to make land, but hardly a one of them could swim, and most drowned as the water everywhere about them turned red.

de Guiral didn't rest. He recharged his pieces and ordered a second salvo. "*Fuego!*"

This time a *fregata* and four other boats went down. We on the ramparts of St. Angelo let out a cheer, embracing one another, while Balbi and his recent acquaintance Alfonso did the same on Senglea. The jester was speechless and the Grand Master himself smiled.

Balthazar and I sped down to de Guiral's Post with extra kegs of powder, should he require them. The Abbé yet limped perceptibly, but he refused to show pain and I could scarce keep up.

"Señor," I bowed to the smoke-encrusted Commander, taking his hand, "if I may say so, you have almost certainly saved the island today."

"Señor," said Balthazar, bowing as well, "today you may have saved Europe."

At the moment the boats were ramming the palisade, King Hasan of Argier gave the signal for the remainder of his troops to advance from the hills against Fort St. Michel. Hasan marched with his braves himself, exhorting them toward the great breaches the Turkish guns had made, instilling them with his own courage. Atop St. Michel's gun battery, Robles watched the colorful banners approaching above the vast sea, accompanied by the gayest music and infernal cries. For well over a week his men had endured nothing but a constant pounding and the Maestro verily welcomed the sight of Hasan's braves with the Turks close on their heels.

He told his men that this was the moment for which they had come to Malta and that they should commend their souls to God.

Kissing the hilt of his sword as the infidels ran, screamed, poured themselves into the ditch before St. Michel, Robles ordered the gunners atop the battery to fire. Between them, the fort and the Post of Bormla boasted ten pieces, sacras, demi-cannons, full cannons and culverins. The men filled them with stone and iron scrap and the cries of "*Fuoco!*" never ended. With the fire from Bormla at the side, the corsairs were caught in the middle and cut down in waves. Hardly a one of them reached the top of the wall alive, so furiously did Robles let into them.

Hasan was not to be so easily frightened and he sent fresh men across the ditch again and again. Hour after hour they came. During that morning, Robles's men did not think to spare our fire weapons, hoops, *granadas, trombas de fuego.* They loaded their cannon with fire tubes we had made—roulades of heavy paper filled with powder that burst into flame when shot forth from a gun. Those tubes got under the feet of the enemy and, I tell you, turned more than one into a candle. The soldiers defended the walls with pots bound to the ends of pikes and with Greek fire that could not be extinguished but by vinegar.

Neither, tho', did the Turks withhold their own fireworks and soon the air was filled with devices flying in every direction. Robles's men had dug out a great ditch behind the breaches to trap the enemy, but the dirt they had piled up by the wall was so high that they'd been forced to build a wooden gallery across it, and under the fireworks the enemy was hurling at them it went up in flames, destroying many soldiers. Other Knights were jumping into the water barrels to douse the flames from the Turkish fire pots.

We watched all this from the castle, but the morning was not half gone before Fort St. Michel disappeared in a great cloud of smoke and fire, and no one outside could discern what was taking place within. To those inside the cloud, there was nothing but the ceaseless crackle of arquebuses and roar of cannon, dismembered corpses, an evil stench that infused everything and from moment to moment strange music drifting down from the hills. Robles, scarred everywhere, was everywhere, encouraging his men; de Quincy as well, at the breaches, wading always into the thick of battle.

It was thick, for sure. Pietru, firing on the enemy from Bormla, below St. Michel's battery, thought he had never seen so many men. He couldn't count them, but he believed they outnumbered those who had come against St. Elmo in the grand assaults. This morning they'd been lucky at Bormla. The corsairs had been so intent on storming the front of St. Michel itself, they'd all but neglected his post. Of a sudden, everything changed. King Hasan, seeing that his braves were not getting anywhere against Robles, directed that they attack the Post of Bormla.

The assault came, those waves and waves of shrieking men. Pietru cast down his gun and with Martino by him, lit a fire hoop, casting it over the walls. They had no time to pray.

Our celebration at de Guiral's Post was rash. With their first boats sunk and bodies floating everywhere in the scarlet water, many of the outlying vessels turned around and directed their fury against Senglea's curtain, where Don Constantino Castriota, that commissioner who'd declined to fight at Fort St. Elmo, now had his hands full at the Post of Sicily.

For a short time we guessed, Balbi guessed, the Turks had abandoned the assault on Sanoguera's Post. The arquebusier allowed himself a sigh, thinking to pen an epic verse about this day. He had no time. Maugre the slaughter de Guiral had inflicted, Candelissa, showing the utmost contempt of danger, himself disembarked on the spur of Senglea, waving his surviving soldiers on, truly ordering the empty boats away so that his braves would have no choice but to fight or die.

Fight they did. As the smoke from the still-burning fires covered him, Balbi could only admire the foe's tenacity. Not only had they come ashore after the carnage he had just witnessed, but already they were joining their fellows to scale the walls. More boats filled with janissaries, the arquebusier perceived, were waiting out in the harbor, not knowing what to do as the guns from the spur, from the windmills and from St. Angelo prevented them from making land. Balbi and Alfonso grabbed more rocks and hurled them upon the attacking braves. Don Jaime and Don Federico, the Vice Roy's son, were helping man the windmill guns. Friar Roberto walked amongst the defenders with a crucifix in one hand and a sword in the other, exhorting them to fight for the Faith of Jesus Christ and to die well. The enemy took this as an invitation and came, amidst all the smoke and fire, and before long the Turks had gained the walls, planting no fewer than six standards on the ramparts. Without looking about him, the poet knew little time remained. They simply did not have enough men.

Romegas had waited two months for this moment. His men, Captain General de Giou's, the Bailiff of Eagle's and others had already gathered on the embankment at Il Borgo, whence the fighting across Galley Creek was plainly visible to all. Not long before, Balthazar himself had picked up his *montante* and bid me farewell, saying he expected to see me this evening.

"Eminenza," Romegas said to the Grand Master, who'd also come down to the embankment, "our men are putting up a brave resistance, but if you do not allow us to cross now, all will be lost."

With evident reluctance, de Valette nodded and gave his consent. Balthazar put on his helmet and, fire in his joints, hurtled across the floating bridge with the others.

They'd been fighting off King Hasan's men at St. Michel and Bormla for three hours. Each time he hurled a fire hoop or pot, Pietru could see Hasan in the distance, darting back and forth behind his men, vainly attempting to grasp the fury wherewith their attacks had been met. Pietru had not much time to smile, but he guessed Hasan was not happy. Truly, without any warning the King ordered his men to retire and the Algerians were suddenly running from the walls as fast as they could. Cheers went up all along the curtain, but those shouting and brandishing their weapons had hardly taken a breath when the Agha of the janissaries resumed the attack, and Mustafa himself, advancing with his spahis. The sight of those horsemen, mail and helmets glistening, spiked bucklers in one hand, bows or axes in the other, instilled in Ix-Xabaw more dread than the bravest of Hasan's braves, and sure enough the rain of arrows began.

When Balthazar arrived at St. Michel with Romegas and his men, he could hardly see for the smoke and fire consuming the place. Romegas at once headed to the most dangerous of the breaches, where de Quincy fought atop a mountain of corpses and amidst a company who, after nearly six hours of one assault by fresh men after another, were exhausting their last strength. Everyone was here. Juan de la Cerda stood at a second breach wielding his sword with purposeful fury, and near him that rogue Fuster. Balthazar caught sight of Vergã. For an instant, he considered killing both, but as one villain sped with his arquebus up to the parapets and the other swung his sword, Balthazar took his place at the breach by de Quincy.

Balthazar intended to thank the Chevalier for his role in getting the *soccorso* to Malta, but no sooner had he raised his two-hander then de Quincy went down with a ball to his head and afterwards did not stir. The arrows rained all around and Balthazar swung.

Yakhshi and what remained of his *boluk* had been ordered into the boats to follow Candelissa's braves. They had spent some time in the harbor not knowing what to do with cannon fire coming at them from three directions. At length they decided to make for the tip of the island, but hadn't advanced two strokes when a ball crashed thro' the hull of his boat, killing half those on board and hurling him into the water. The spur wasn't distant and somehow Yakhshi flailed to it amidst all the bodies floating about him, nay, using them to keep afloat, but his arquebus was useless and he flung it to the ground as he climbed onto the rocks. Wet from head to toe, he drew his bow and when he had loosed all his arrows at the foe above, he cast that down too and unsheathed his scimitar. At last, with the others who had survived the carnage, the *Boluk-bashi* readied to scale the walls of this place. He glanced up to the ruined parapets and saw—

—children.

Tearing down the Turkish standards above were hundreds of dirty-faced urchins armed with slings, who lost no time in launching a rain of stones on the corsairs and the *yenicheriler* below. Yakhshi snatched up a shield from one of the fallen. He'd rather collect pork-eating children than kill them, but he would kill them. Watching Candelissa, who disdained every danger, he waved the men to the ladders; before they got to the top of the walls, the Knights had arrived.

When those high-voiced boys, loosed across the bridge by the Grand Master, ran to Sanoguera's Post with the Knights at their heels, cries of "succours and victory!" on their lips, Balbi offered a word of thanks to the Lord. Once more he glanced about him. The friar was wounded, clasping his arm. Don Jaime and Don Federico were dead. They'd been at the windmills when the enemy gunners on Corradino, seeing the trouble the Sicilians were giving those assaulting the curtain of Senglea, had opened fire. Don Federico was hit by a cannon ball and a shard from his cuirass struck Don Jaime in the face. Only a handful of Sanoguera's men remained, and in another few moments everything would have been lost. Now those children hurling their stones were crying out "St. Elmo's pay!" and with the Knights behind them, strength had returned.

"All is fair," thought Balbi.

It was becoming a complete rout, Yakhshi discerned. Candelissa had ordered the boats away, leaving everyone trapped. Worse, the battery across the channel had kept up its bombardment. With his men being slaughtered and the knights arriving above, Candelissa suddenly lost his invincible courage. Yakhshi watched speechless as the Algerian splashed thro' the shallows into his skiff and took off, his oarsmen hauling for their lives.

"Traitor!" Yakhshi cried, at once understanding they'd been abandoned.

Every warrior at this place took up shouting, "Traitor! Traitor!" but Candelissa did not send back the boats.

For a moment the *Boluk-bashi* didn't know what to do. He was no swimmer himself, but to stay on this ground meant death. A piece of iron from across the inlet grazed his leg, wounding him again. No longer did he have a choice. Yakhshi dove into the blood-red water, splashing, floundering, grabbing wood, bodies, anything. A large black bird had settled on a body nearby, picking at its eyes, and the *yenicheri* took this as an evil sign, but some of the boats in the harbor braved the cannon fire and at last a hand reached down to pull him from his misery. All around men were drowning while cheers went up from the spur of the island.

From Castle St. Angelo, it all seemed as in a dream, the Algerians retiring from the spur of Senglea, leaving the water clogged with dead, e'en as the guns fell silent at St. Michel. Such a victory would be sung about for ages, of that all of us who witnessed it were at once certain. Our rejoicing only increased when God gave one of the sentries to spy a magnificently clad figure, galloping furiously on horseback toward those galleys gathered about Rinella. We decided to take him down and fired several shots. We missed but were so close that the concussion knocked off his turban as he sped on. Later, renegados told us it was Piyale himself. Seeing the catastrophe unfolding in the harbor, he'd gone to warn the galleys not to enter as they had intended. When we learned this, we laughed, as well as we then could.

The cheers had not yet died down when the soldiers and Maltese set about gathering booty. Balbi himself collected a few trophies, including a gold amulet and a wheel-lock, but the swimmers were the most amply rewarded. Diving into the harbor, they made to the boats, sunk or abandoned, and collected bows, scimitars, gold, folded papers with writing, *afione* everywhere, not to mention every manner of foodstuff: honey, sugar, bisket, raisins butter, fresh water ... all of which showed the Turks had intended to occupy Senglea. To no one's surprise, these stores rapidly disappeared. Toni Bajada himself came back dressed like a spahi in a whole suit of mail.

Eager to discover what had become of Balthazar, I made my way down to the Borgo, intending to cross over to St. Michel. On the embankment I spied Isabella, who was walking from the Infermeria toward the castle with the same wonderment written over her face as everyone else. Catching sight of me, she ran headlong to my arms in joy. I lifted her from her feet into the air, neither of us being able to say a word for our tears of happiness.

"Whither are you bound, Francisco?" she asked.

I nodded toward St. Michel.

"Let me come. There will be wounded."

We crossed the floating bridge to Senglea and soon after entered the smoldering fortress, which smelled of naught but smoke and death. Barely alive men covered by cinders sat everywhere, and men dragged away fallen comrades from the breaches at the fore where the fighting had been heaviest. Making our way to one of gaps in the wall there, I stepped thro' and gazed down into the ditch. E'en having lived thro' a week at St. Elmo, I had not in my life seen such a mass of corpses. Below me, heaped everywhere in the ditch, upon the counterscarp, upon one another, lay thousands upon thousands of dead Turks and Argerians. I could not number them. I turned back to Isabella, intending to prevent her from gazing onto this sight, but she was by me, her hands at her mouth. As the groans of the half-buried wounded filled the air, Robles's men began repairs; one of them boasted three thousand foemen lay at our feet.

"How many have you lost?" I asked.

"Forty Knights, two hundred soldiers," he answered.

We came across Balthazar sitting atop a barrel with a cup of wine in his hand, speaking to Romegas. Neither had been seriously hurt. Romegas, to the contrary, was in the highest spirits, laughing, boasting. "The Grand Master may need my advice," he said jovially, moving his shoulders, "but my arm needs exercise from time to time."

Pietru walked into the fort them. He had only received one cut to his arm from an arrow.

"Commander Romegas," said Isabella, "you shall have the wounded brought to the Borgo as soon as possible."

"Yes, of course, Signora."

Draining his cup, Balthazar shouldered his *montante* and the four of us walked back to Birgu. "Do you truly believe, Balthazar," I asked, "it is possible for two salvos to change the course of a war?"

He smiled. "Of course the import of events unfolds only with the fullness of time, but I believe de Guiral performed a miracle today." Already people were saying he had killed nearly one thousand of the best enemy troops with those shots. They had surely saved Sanoguera's Post and Malta, that much I had said before, and of that I was certain.

"Only God performs miracles," Isabella said.

"Aye," rejoined Balthazar, "but two hundred years hence, when men look back to understand why we Europeans do not speak Turkish, I say they will remember de Guiral ... It is strange what changes the course of wars ... this bridge ... a Grand Master's foresight."

We crossed the bobbing bridge in those tired but raised spirits, spirits mayhap higher than they'd been since the outset of this great contest, spirits higher than they had a right to be. By the time we reached the Borgo's square, church bells had begun to sound and people had taken to dancing in the streets. There, amidst the rejoicing, the most unexpected sight greeted our eyes, which we fully understood only later.

Not long after the fighting had died down, some of the men from Sanoguera's Post brought four rich prisoners to de Valette, the only ones who had not been slaughtered or beheaded on Senglea by the Knights and Maltese. The Grand Master tortured them and now, the questioning done, was releasing them into the streets. We watched the Turks on their knees, begging for their lives according to the custom of good war. I was close enough to see de Valette's pitiless visage. I had only seen a face so hard on the day he ordered me to fire heads across the harbor.

With no hesitation now, Isabella ran to her guardian. "Parisot!" she cried, "do not do this thing, I beg you! It is senseless."

I made to follow Isabella, but Balthazar grasped me by the arm. "My friend, there is nothing for it, and mark my words, you should not at this moment put yourself in a more perilous position than you will shortly be."

Wresting myself free of the Knight, I stepped forward, but he was correct: there was nothing for it. The Grand Master handed the Turks over to the common people who, crying, "St. Elmo's pay!" tore them to pieces. Pietru himself joined the mob, and I could not find it within myself to gainsay him.

Isabella ran to me, croaking, "P—Parisot has not followed any advice."

The Grand Master shot a burning glance in our direction. He had yet to learn I'd freed a Turkish janissary.

That evening, while the bells continued to peal, the Grand Master ordered the captured Turkish standards to be placed in San Lorenzo. A solemn Mass was celebrated and a *Te Deum* sung. So many people had gathered about the church, rejoicing, that Isabella and I could not enter, but we stood in the streets amongst the crowds and with tears in our eyes listened to the angelic voices drift over us.

Ninety-Nine

The Turks were hardly finished. That very night they crawled into the ditch at St. Michel again, digging a trench toward the ravelin. Heavy fire from Captain Antonio Martelli's Post at the front of the fort caused them a lot of trouble, but the infidels persisted and captured the big barrels of earth Robles had ordered stood near the ravelin. They also succeeded in building stone shelters from the rocks that had fallen from the fort's walls, which protected them from Martelli's fire. After that, the barbarians wouldn't go away.

By morning, before they had buried their dead, the Turkish cannon roared again. All the guns on Corradino, all the guns on Sta. Margarita and the Mandra, the guns on Salvatore. No one doubted for a moment that the ferocity of this bombardment was ought but revenge for yesterday's failure. The pounding brought one solace alone: It showed that Mustafa had abandoned daring plans for a sea assault and had decided once and for all to grind us into dust.

Parting her veil, Isabella could hardly credit the numbers of wounded that lay in the Hospital's great courtyard. Soldiers lay everywhere, shoved against the fountain and every column, in the chapel and on the streets outside. In the name of God, how could five physicians and that number of surgeons possibly cope with this deluge? She followed Dr. Vigo to the surgery, where a soldier from St. Michel was having his head trepanned because a rock splinter had split his skull. A lifetime ago Isabella had grown accustomed to broken bones and bloodied tissue and, and e'en gazing onto a man's brains no longer made an impression on her. She could not, tho', avoid catching sight of a like operation nearby, which had a greater effect: A Serving Brother held a soldier's head down on a table. Vigo told her that the side of his skull had been smashed in. A surgeon placed a sort of drill over him and turned the crank; the bit entered into the side of his head; the surgeon twisted the screw the other way and pulled up the crushed bone. They had given the patient the sponge soaked with mandrake and belladona, but he screamed his lungs out anyway.

"Dr. Vigo," a Serving Brother said, running up, "the medicinal stores in the apothecary are falling quickly. In a few weeks ... "

Vigo could say nothing except that the Grand Master had requested medical supplies from Sicily.

As they carried food to the top story of the Hospital, Vigo paused at the landing. The huge gun platform across Kalkara Creek now held at least twenty-five pieces before Piyale's pavilion, and as they watched, chains of slaves were dragging an immense basilisk to the summit. The guns in action were already pummeling the Post of Castille and their ceaseless *boom, boom-boom, boom-boom-boom* made speech almost impossible. Vigo and Isabella crossed themselves at the sight and continued upstairs.

They did not take another step. As an enormous roar engulfed everything, the two were thrown from their feet and tumbled down the stairs, Isabella landing atop Dr. Vigo while dust and rock fragments fell over them. Some moments passed before they regained their senses and helped each other to their feet.

"Are you injured, Milady?" Vigo finally asked.

Isabella slowly brushed herself off and with some uncertainty shook her head. But she understood at once what must have just taken place. Without the least panic, she ran upstairs with Vigo, knowing that the Sacra Infermeria had come under bombardment.

On the third story, a hole had been blown through the wall. The floor and beds were strewn with rock, and one of the wounded men had been killed with a splinter thro' his eye. Vigo at once ordered anyone who could walk to leave the ward and go downstairs.

"Signora," he said to Isabella, "rush down to get help. We must clear these wards of patients."

Isabella was already gone. Luckily, the shot proved to be but a warning; at least the Turks were more interested in hitting the Post of Castille, and no more balls crashed into the Infermeria that day, while those who could carried the injured down to the courtyard. There, the Knights on duty and Serving Brothers frantically tried to make room.

"Ahh," sighed Vigo in despair, "what can we do?"

As he stood near the front door, an infidel slave approached with an arm broken while he had worked on the walls near Castille. In the most pitiful Italian he begged to have his arm fixed. Vigo gazed on the slave in disbelief, when as if thro' time he found himself in Jerusalem, at the first Hospital, the Blessed Gerard by him.

"Come," he said.

During the same hour the news I had freed a janissary reached de Valette's ears. He sought me out himself at the mill atop St. Angelo. "Did you free a Turk?" the Grand Master roared.

I merely looked up from my work, making powder, and said nothing.

"Against my decree? I'll hang you!"

He but motioned to the halberdiers; they seized me by the arms and, tho' I knew these men, they dragged me down to the dungeons, cast me into the cell and slammed the iron door shut behind me. Taking the small oil lamp from the shelf, I passed it over the scribblings on the wall and at length perceived that I sat in the same place I had thirteen years earlier. Truly the circle had closed. I hardly knew what to think of all this; indeed, my mind was in such a fog that I thought nothing. Some hours later I was on my knees in prayer when a guard admitted both Balthazar and Isabella, who bade me not abandon hope while they interceded on my behalf. Once his fury was spent, Parisot would see reason and could not wish my neck.

"Eminenza," Balthazar said to de Valette in the Magisterial Palace against the thunder of the guns, "you have threatened to hang a man who helped bring news of the descent in time for you to prepare. Time and again he attempted to kill our great foeman Dragut. Now he has freed a Turk he once knew as a slave. Do you truly believe he has betrayed the Religion with this small act?"

de Valette replied with little interest and much wrath: "No quarter to the enemy."

"In that case, you must hang me first, for Barai acted on my advice."

"Me as well," said Isabella, stepping up to him. "Parisot, Francisco has fought well for you against the Infidel. Mustafa's cruelty has blinded you."

In a speechless rage the Grand Master glared at both of them, and with naught but a furious wave of his hand, he banished his unwanted visitors from his sight.

It was Balthazar's passion, tho', that surpassed any Isabella had known. "If Vergã was so eager to enter the Turkish camp," he declared on the streets below, "I do not believe it was to foil Francisco's design or die a hero. Nay, I say it was not."

"Desist, good Balthazar," cried Isabella, "I beg you. Francisco has admitted his crime and you have no cause to think Vergã did ought but act as a true Knight in a hopeless attempt to kill Mustafa. Romegas affirms it."

Balthazar at first gazed on Isabella in sadness. "Crime, Isabella? How did his crime differ from yours of yesterday, when you pleaded with your Godfather to show mercy on four helpless Turks? I say Francisco's crime was that he seized his *kairos*, as at last you did your own." For a moment Isabella stood before him, shamed, but Balthazar did not release her. "And why do you yet make excuses for that scum Vergã, who has never ceased his efforts to destroy his rival? You cannot truly believe he cares for you; he cares for nothing."

Isabella shook her head in a defiant confusion. "I *am* indebted to him for my life and he *has* sought to protect me. He knows what it means to be treated with scorn by your—" She abruptly halted. "Ah, Balthazar, you are right, the Devil has tempted me. He intends that I be made deaf to evil by that man's songs."

"Methinks," said Balthazar, now with a more ironic humor, "that woman has often blamed the Devil for the jealousies she inspires."

"You cannot accuse me, Sir," Isabella replied, flushing sensibly, "of such immodesty—. Dear Balthazar, since those days when I rode carefree over the hills, I have learned I am but a small, weak person on this God's earth. Surrounding me are naught but warriors—one a stern, impassive monk who brooks no dissent; a second perhaps kinder commoner who struggles to find his heart; a third a wicked bastard who acts as he pleases." Her eyes seemed to be asking the Abbé for advice, but as he returned her gaze with an expression betwixt pity and censure, she silenced herself. "We would do well to not to prolong this conversation, Balthazar, at least until we have Francisco released, for by our own words if we do not succeed, we will hang with him."

I sat beneath Castle St. Angelo, not knowing what was taking place above, expecting to be executed at any time, spending my hours in prayer and meditation. I did not know that only two days after the grand assault on Senglea, Balbi, now at Fort St. Michel, watched as the Turks attempted to build a bridge across the ditch to Martelli's Post at the front of the fort. He and the other arquebusiers opened fire, but the Turkish janissaries had well concealed themselves in their shelters and picked off anybody who showed his head.

Balbi crept up to the tower while the Turkish battery on the Mandra continued hammering the fort, each crash sending stone high into the air. He found Robles directing the withdrawal of some cannon, which had been dismounted. Balbi informed him of the bridge and at once Robles climbed down to the curtain to look.

Balbi asked whether they could try to bombard the bridge.

"How?" the Maestro de Campo answered, ducking as a ball ploughed into the casemate atop which they stood. "The Turks are hitting the tower. We must move the guns. Breaches are appearing at every moment and must be filled. Worse, you see, the Turks have well chosen the place for that bridge." It was true. The bridge stood in a perfect position. The guns from Provence and Aragon in Birgu could not hit it because the angle was too narrow, and neither could St. Michel's own guns, which being atop the tower, couldn't be aimed low enough.

Somehow never losing heart, Robles ordered his men to begin constructing a second wall with firing loops behind one of the breaches and he moved off, having made no decision about the bridge. By the next morning, tho', five legs were in place. No one could forget the like bridge at St. Elmo, which so nearly caused the loss of the fort. Something needed to be done at once.

"I'll take my men out with some cables and we'll pull it down." It was Henri Parisot de Valette, the Grand Master's second nephew, who'd come with Robles's *soccorso*.

"With janissaries everywhere," the Maestro objected, "it is pure folly."

Parisot answered by putting on his helmet and gathering his men. "We cannot allow that bridge to be completed."

Balbi watched Parisot's company rush from the sally port, rope in hand. Rather than creeping out silently, they made a lot of noise. At once the enemy jumped from their trenches and shelters and opened fire. Parisot himself was dressed in the richest armor, inlaid with gold, which glinted like the sun itself. The janissaries couldn't miss and, truly, within a heartbeat the Commander fell under a rain of fire. His men were desperate to recover the body, but to expose themselves was fatal. Time and time again the soldiers crept out into the ditch, only to be forced back by the Turks. At last, someone brought a halberd or a glaive and, hiding in the corner of the gate, they hooked one of Parisot's legs with the weapon. With the greatest pain and effort, they pulled the corpse toward them while the arquebus shot glanced off the stone and earth. After an eternity, they grasped the body with their hands and carried it inside, having achieved nothing at all.

That night Isabella approached de Valette in the Chapel of St. Anne, where Henri's remains lay upon the altar, surrounded by candles. The Grand Master, kneeling in prayer before the body of his nephew, rose to his feet when he heard footsteps behind him, and turned to his ward with little expression on his face.

"I am sorry, Parisot," Isabella said, walking toward the altar. She lit a candle, placed it on the stand and gazed for a moment at the young man she had known only distantly.

Parisot took her in his arms. "I am grateful to God that he was granted a glorious death, as befits a warrior, and I shall not mourn for him more than I would for any other Knight. We shall see that he receives a fitting burial."

"And François, your other nephew?" she said, glancing once more at the body of the dead Chevalier.

"He lives, at the Post of Provence."

Abruptly, Isabella freed herself from her guardian's embrace and dropped to her knees before him, clasping his legs with her arms. "Parisot, with St. Michel in such desperate straits and Birgu surrounded, you cannot afford to needlessly lose those near you, in whom you can place your trust. I beg you," she said, refusing to withhold her tears, "release Francisco. He has served you well and you need him to make weapons. At the very least allow him to die honorably with the others."

The Monsignore, unable to bear his goddaughter at his feet, lifted her with his own hands and the two walked out of the chapel into the night sky throbbing with the flashes of cannon fire. Isabella thought her words had reached the Grand Master, in his present disposition. As she waited for a reply a runner came up to them and informed His Eminence that the Turks had begun to mine Fort St. Michel. Before a glass had turned I was led forth from the dungeons.

When I faced de Valette and Isabella, I too dropped to my knees before them, kissing the Grand Master's ring and Isabella's hand.

Tho' it was late, de Valette wasted not a breath. "Do you know of Tadini's invention at Rhodes?" he asked me.

"Yes, I have heard of it," I nodded. Eminenza himself had spoken of the device, long ago.

"Make one up, quickly, and take it to St. Michel. It may prove valuable."

de Valette neither smiled, nor gave any explanation for my release, nor did I ask for one. I bowed, nodded faintly to Isabella and ran to the Borgo.

Many say that Gabriele Tadini was a spirit who lived in a future age and, had it not been for him, Rhodes would have fallen months before it did. Of his miracles, the most miraculous was this: He stretched a fine parchment over a frame and hung some delicate bells across the face. The tympanum proved more acute than a man's ear and with his device, the great engineer discovered and destroyed many enemy mines. For my own version, Flaminia had shown off a Turkish tambourine she'd picked up after the assault on Senglea. I took it from her, fitted it with a finer parchment and hung small bits of amber across the face. Before crossing to St. Michel, I rushed to the Post of France to tell Balthazar of my release. The noise there was terrific. The Post of Castille stood hardly a *braccio* away and the Turks on Salvatore were letting them have it with everything.

"How many guns?" I shouted to Balthazar, hoping he would hear me over the thunder.

The Knight turned to me with astonishment at my presence, but after a heartbeat he said simply, "At least thirty now."

While we stood there, a huge explosion went up at Castille, followed at an instant by shrieks and cries. I knew perfectly that my basilisk had gone into action. No one could now doubt that Mustafa had chosen Castille for an assault, and the Grand Master was powerless to prevent it. When we recovered from the earthquake my gun had caused, I held up the rattling tympanum and said to Balthazar, "I am to St. Michel. The Turks have begun to undermine it."

Balthazar, getting leave from François Buçera, came with me.

Fort St. Michel was all commotion. Men ran about carrying stones and building inner defenses under the bombardment from the Mandra and Corradino; a bridge stood outside in the ditch, and a mine was being dug somewhere.

"How do you know there is a mine?" I asked Robles.

He pointed across the ditch to a dim hole in the ground. Enough Turkish sappers were crawling in and out and dragging dirt-filled baskets behind them that I could ought but believe it. "The only question is, what is the direction?"

"They will have to go deep, under the ditch."

Robles nodded. He'd already begun the countermine. I had learnt of mining and countermining from Vannoccio but had no experience in battle. The only truth in mining, my master always said, was that a man would be buried alive or blown to Heaven. Before I could nod to Balthazar, he asked Robles for a short sword. la Cerda volunteered at once to come; since his arrest the Captain's every action was to wash away the stain of cowardice. Having just emerged from the shadows of Fort St. Angelo myself, I voiced no objection. Robles nodded. Balthazar then caught sight of Blaij Vergã and Antonio Fuster, both posted here by Romegas. Fuster stepped forward, but Balthazar said, "Let that one come," and pointed his chin to Blaij.

Fuster glared at Balthazar, but Robles said, "Vergada, go."

For an instant Vergã, casting no less a glare at the Abbé, hesitated, then grabbed a sword.

I removed my shirt and the four of us descended by ladder into the shaft.

At the same moment Captain Martelli ordered some men to make a second attempt to destroy the bridge. Balbi joined the small company as they rushed out the sally port by the front ditch. At once dirt was flying into the air around their feet, as the janissaries lit into them, and they incontinently fled back into the fort. Quickly they resolved to dig a trench from the port to the bridge and fetched shovels and picks.

While Balbi attacked the earth, a Maltese engineer, Girolamo Cassar, was also desperately casting about for a means to destroy the bridge. He ordered some of the soldiers to begin hollowing out a big cavity in the inner wall of the fort at about the place where the bridge would meet it.

As some of the Maltese took up their picks and commenced swinging, Cassar retired to a room under the tower, where he hammered together a sort of half-shell from a barrel, strengthening it with heavy planks and earth in between. That done, the engineer drilled some holes in one end and called for men to carry it. Pietru, having just run down from the Post of Bormla because the bombardment there was too hot, hoisted one side onto his good shoulder.

They carried the contrivance to the walls, where the men hacking at the stones put down their tools. "Signore," one said, "if you intend to poke a cannon out this hole, we need to know the exact height of the bridge. We cannot guess."

"We won't guess," Cassar replied. Taking a pick from one of them, he told Pietru and three others to follow. "Have a gun ready here."

On the ramparts above, they attached ropes to the shell and Pietru and his comrades lowered the engineer over the wall, encased in his own invention. "He's become a turtle," grunted Pietru, shaking his head.

When Cassar reached the level of the bridge, he himself took the pick he had brought down and began chopping at the wall from the outside. Whether the Turks understood the portent of the strange sight dangling before their eyes in the hot, starry night, no one could say, but this did not stop them from firing on it. More than once the shell was hit, but Cassar's armor held, and he hacked.

The tunnel was not two *braccia* high, filled with half-naked men on their knees passing baskets of dirt from fore to aft, lit by oil lamps and torches. The air was hot, foul—nay, hardly could it be breathed, and I told the men to get some bellows with leather tubes down here or dig some vertical shafts.

"There's no time for that," coughed Balthazar.

"There is time enough to suffocate," I answered.

A few men scampered up the ladder and brought back shields, which they waved like fans. Whatever Balthazar's intent in summoning Vergã, neither man took his eyes off the other, each of them kneeling in this dim place, and I could only wonder whether infidel or Christian bodies would litter this shaft by the time we were done.

We crawled forward, over the dirt and stones. I could hear Vergã's heavy breathing behind me, quickening. Aye, the space was close; I

perceived it was too close for him. After thirty or forty *braccia* we reached
the end of the tunnel, where the sappers were frantically digging with
picks and shovels, filling the baskets.

"Do you know where the enemy mine is?" I asked.

"Shh," said one of the men, putting his finger to his lips. Everyone
broke off digging.

"Ah, it is stifling in here," said Vergã, tearing off his shirt.

"Shhh!" hissed the soldier again and put his ear to the ground.

We all listened. The sound of Turkish digging could be heard, not so
far distant—but how far and in what direction? A few *braccia* and we could
miss.

Despite the waving of the shields, it was truly stifling in here. "Try
this," I said and held up Tadini's device. As I turned the tambourine, all
eyes were on the bits of amber hanging by their threads across the drum.
In one direction the fragments of Flaminia's talismans began a barely
perceptible dance. "*Desgraciadamente*," I said, "one must not only have a
device, one must know what it tells us." I continued turning it, then back,
being unable to confidently divine the tambourine's message. "I think
that way."

The others nodded and we dug for dear life. Inside of an hour we struck
the infidel mine.

Balthazar and la Cerda crashed in thro' the hole we had made,
practically on their knees, followed by me and then Vergã. There was
hardly room in the Turkish shaft to stand, yet alone to fight, but we had
surprised the infidel sappers who defended themselves with shovels and
picks. We grappled with them, two of us in armor, two of us in breeches.
For a heartbeat, I thought, Vergã hesitated, not knowing which direction
to turn, and in that instant he got the point of a pick in his shoulder,
dropped his blade and grabbed a torch from the wall.

"You fool!" I cried. "There'll be powder—!"

la Cerda managed to snatch the torch before Blaij did anything mad.
Vergã kicked the infidel in the balls, then picked up his sword and off'd
him. Before long more of ours were pouring thro' the hole. The enemy
sappers who could flee got out of the tunnel and Robles beheaded those
we captured. After we cleared the shaft, we sealed it with a keg and the
Maestro de Campo posted a guard.

At almost the same moment, Cassar had finished his work and called for the Maltese above to raise him. Pietru and his mates pulled and the engineer climbed back over the parapets, not having received the least harm. They ran down to the lower level, where the other workers were already rolling a cannon thro' the hole they had made.

"*Fuoco!*" The first blast got one leg of the bridge. The second blast another, and shook the remainder of the legs until the whole structure tottered. The men raised a cheer.

When the splinters of the bridge rained down upon him, Balbi was crouched in a trench almost directly beneath it. Despite the enemy fire, during the night they had managed to dig their trench all the way to it. Now, with its legs loosened from their moorings, the bridge would go down easily. As arquebus fire continued, the men crept over the edge. Balbi helped bind the legs with tow and paint them with tar. Soon, Alfonso scrambled forth with a torch. As the flames leapt up, others rushed out from the sally port with more tow, tar, wood. At last, by sunup, the bridge was destroyed and only one charred post was left standing.

"*¡O llama de amor viva que tiernamenta hieres a mia alma en el más profundo centro!* " remarked Balbi.

"I think they were aiming elsewhere," replied Alfonso.

One Hundred

I do not know how to describe what happened next. In the before-dawn of July 22, everyone in Birgu and Senglea awoke to a sound no human ears had ever heard. The Turks had begun bombarding us from every one of their sixty-five pieces. Forty guns on Salvatore hit the Posts of Castille, Germany, Auvergne, Fort St. Angelo and Birgu. Another twelve hit Birgu and Fort St. Michel from Santa Margarita and the Mandra, thirteen more on Corradino pummeled St. Michel and the Post of Bormla, three or four others on Sciberras continued to pound what had been Sanoguera's Post at the spur of Senglea.

Amongst these pieces were the ten eighty-*libbre* guns, two sixty-*libbre* culverins, a great gun of one hundred sixty *libbre* and two terrible basilisks which cast stones of six quintals.

The ground shook without pause. Within hours every remaining glass window in Birgu had been shattered. Houses not hit directly began to crack. The men and slaves repairing the walls of Castille were struck down dozen by dozen. We didn't know that the Turks would keep this up for six days and six nights, in the summer heat and under the spattering of stars. We only knew that it was as if the enemy intended to undo Creation itself. Aye, when those guns were fired together, the sound was so great that people heard it distinctly at Zaragoza and even Catania, forty leagues away, and all of us were certain that the end of the world had arrived.

The first night after leaving the mill, I crept along the streets of Birgu to Isabella's house. At each moment I turned, pressing myself to the walls to guard myself from falling stones. The houses about me trembled and shook, cracks appeared before my eyes, and the sky above constantly changed from black to green to a ghostly white. I truly wondered whether the souls of the damned were soaring above, released for the Last Judgment. The square was already filled with people who had no place to sleep, and the nearer I got to Isabella's home the bleaker the landscape became. Townsfolk were running with their few belongings toward the other end of the Borgo, but there was no place to shelter. As I made my way toward Castille, the concussion of the guns was so great I thought I'd be knocked over. With my hands covering my ears, I reached Isabella's house.

It had been hit.

Isabella flew into my arms. "Francisco!" she cried, tho' in possession of herself, "a ball crashed into the roof. One of the men there was killed."

She might have been a mime for the thunder. "Will you heed sense now?" I shouted in return. Furniture was rattling, skipping along the floor. Plaster, dust fell onto our heads, onto one of her portraits, which lay unnoticed on the floor. "You must abandon this house."

"Whither will we flee?"

I had no answer. My own room was full and unlikely safer. "Let us move everyone into the cellar," I shouted again.

We dragged the wounded from above to below and laid them by the servants, but the flicker of the lamps showed there was not enough room for all.

"The cistern," Isabella and I said together. Water stood at the bottom of the big reservoir. As the house above us quaked, we filled every jug and urn and succeeded in lowering the water enough to put some stones on the cistern's floor. We chopped Isabella's dining table in half with an axe and lowered the pieces thro' the narrow mouth, laying them across the stones.

"Stay with me tonight," she said, at the last seizing her prized lute.

I nodded. The servants handed us candles as we descended by a ladder into the cistern and put the metal bars across the mouth. There, on our makeshift bed, a few *dita* above the water, we lay in each other's arms.

It was a night of terror. The house shuddered, was hit again. One of the servants climbed down and huddled amongst the urns in the corner of the cistern, in the wet. *Boom boom boom boom boom.*

"The Day of Wrath has come," Isabella said with absolute conviction, clutching my chest. "God has abandoned us."

Yes. The vibration continued relentlessly. With each crash, Isabella flinched and hugged me closer. Sleep was impossible. We spoke little against the noise and when we did it was necessary to put our lips to the other's ear.

I thanked her for her intercession with the Grand Master, which had surely saved my life. For her part she doubted it. I conceded that mayhap she had used her scarf merely to bind Vergã's wound after all. She confessed to having given the brute on occasion more attention than was proper. The house continued to shudder and we renewed our pledge to keep each other alive, and if only one remained, to give the other a proper burial, and to hold that one's memory sacred forever.

We could not believe our ears when we heard drummers beating the morning Angelus, and we climbed from our tomb to see that the house above yet stood, tho' small debris and dust lay on the chairs, divan, everywhere. We ate some bread and water in the cellar, and I went to the mill, Isabella to the Hospital, where she expected worse.

From St. Angelo, the Post of Castille appeared to be Vesuvius and St. Michel might have been Mt. Etna, and as we continued to produce fire weapons of all sorts, we could only gaze onto those places with a horrified awe. Shortly after I arrived, de Valette himself appeared. As always now, he was accompanied by two pages, one who carried his shield and helmet, the other who carried a pike, and that infernal jester. This morning not Romegas but Commander Maimon of the Arsenal was at his side. For an instant de Valette's eyes locked with mine, but he said nothing. I knew from his gaze, tho', that he would have preferred to hang me and that, if I ever enjoyed his favor—no longer. Indeed, most of the men threw hard glances in my direction. Once His Eminence had departed, Diego spoke to me, under pretense of asking about ingredients for fire pots, and he did not fail to reveal his mind: "You freed a janissary," he said.

"Yes, I did," I replied as I tied a rope to the neck of a sack I had stuffed with tow and powder and dipped it into a barrel of tar. "I once knew him."

"Some say you are a Turk in your heart."

"People say anything." I shoved the fire ball into his hands and went to check the saltpetre cauldrons. People did say anything. When we took our meals, some who had formerly jested that I hadn't killed Dragut now declared outright that I was a liar. I perceived then the matter would never rest but did my best to turn a deaf ear, which today was the only sort any of us had.

de Valette and Maimon had gone down to the wall along Kalkara Creek. It was now wholly dangerous there with the Turkish guns and musketeers only one hundred fifty paces across the water, pounding the wall, picking off any target. The Grand Master had already ordered the slaves to build up the walls so the janissaries could not see anyone walking near Germany. But supplies for repairs were now perceptibly dwindling.

"We have run out of wood," shouted one of the engineers there.

"I can break up the smaller boats," suggested Maimon after the engineer repeated himself twice more against the roaring, as some of the nearby parapets crashed to the street.

The Grand Master ordered him to go ahead, to which the jester remarked, "Not alive, I live longer than any man. Not able to stand, no one stands without me. Not of earth, the earth is full of me."

"Bones?" said de Valette. "I shall bear them in mind."

As they inspected the works, one of the slaves, near dead with fatigue, at last decided death was the only escape and climbed atop the wall, hoping the Turks would shoot him; at once they obliged. The Grand Master ordered his and any other cloaks of dead slaves to be collected and made into sacks, which could be filled with earth. Looking about as the smoke from Castille passed over him, de Valette ordered more houses demolished and their stones to be broken into pieces small enough to hurl by hand.

At Fort St. Michel, within this bombardment beyond comprehension, soldiers, women, children, slaves struggled to repair the breaches the enemy guns now opened at every moment. The wall facing Corradino had been broken thro' in so many places that the houses behind it had come under fire. Never faltering, Robles ordered grass from the awnings of houses be made into sacks and filled with wet earth for repairs.

Balbi watched Juan de la Cerda, who refusing to show fatigue, carried earth-filled sacks and stones like everyone else. Of a sudden, an explosion at the breach they were attempting to block caused Cerda to reel, to fall. As he got up, another struggling to his feet faced him—Blaij Vergã. They stood on the verge of toppling on each other for a moment, regarding one another. To Balbi it was as if Cerda was challenging, daring Vergã to say something.

At length la Cerda himself spoke. "It was a little hot down there for you, wasn't it, Vergada? How many days did my company defend Fort St. Elmo? Because I told His Eminence the fort could not be defended, people call me a coward. You begin to know what it was like."

"I've called you nothing," said Vergã angrily just as another ball hit nearby. He flinched and threw himself to the ground as dirt flew into the air, covering them both.

E'en as he staggered la Cerda laughed. "*Picaro.* The feared Vergada sees the face of defeat looming. May you receive your dispensation from the Pope!" Vergã took a faint-hearted swipe at la Cerda, but that one was already stumbling off through the smoke, laughing.

Late that night I again made my way to Isabella's house, thinking first to go the Post of France to see whether Balthazar remained alive on that most dangerous side of town. The bombardment was more terrible than the previous night. No place in Birgu was safe. As I climbed toward France, now steadying myself against the walls, now brushing off the dirt that fell from the roofs, now picking my way over dead horses and crushed townsfolk, I came to the Bishop's Palace. Between the Satanic belching of the Turkish guns, a faint cry reached my ears.

"*Aiuto!*"

At first I thought my ears had deceived me, and I paused on the pile of rubble where I found myself. I looked about me. The palace itself had been hit and partly destroyed. Again I heard the cry.

"*Aiuto!*"

I walked through the door into what was left of the palace, coughing amidst all the dust coming from Castille, and found the roofs surrounding the courtyard mostly collapsed. Someone was trapped beneath. I pulled away a few stones to see the dim form of a richly dressed man caught under a fallen beam.

"Ahh, bless you, my son," he breathed.

The deep, parched voice was of Bishop Cubelles himself. For a moment I stood motionless, as motionless as I might, buffeted by the concussion of the guns. Then I sat down on the beam above him. *Boom boom-boom-boom-boom.*

"I beg you to help me, Signore. What are you waiting for?"

The crescent moon had set, and the stars were so faint for the dust that I could scarce make out the figure who lay beneath me. When the guns relented, I spoke: "My name is Francisco de Barai."

"If you were the Grand Turk, it would make no difference! In the name of God, give me your hand! You speak to the Bishop of Malta!"

"Are you hurt, Eccellenza?" I asked, having to repeat myself.

"Of course I am hurt!"

The tremendous noise forced him to repeat himself as well. "Perhaps it would be best if you rest where you are until morning," I replied.

"You dare!" the Bishop shouted; he was evidently not so wounded as I had thought. "Who are you?"

I picked up a rock, tossed it in my hand. "I have said: I am Francisco de Barai. Truly, you do not know me, Eccellenza?"

Once more the guns drowned out everything and I put my hands to my ears. Not twenty paces off, the wall of another house crumbled to the ground. "No, I do not know you," Cubelles finally answered.

"Hmm," I grunted, brushing off the dust settling on my hair. "That is strange. Only two months ago you summoned Fra Balthazar for not denouncing me as a renegado."

"Ah yes," groaned Cubelles. "What of it? Renegados must be punished."

"Precisely. Tortured, arrested, made slaves again." I stood above him, loosed my trousers and pissed nearby. "As you see, I am not cut."

"You loathsome snake. That is not the only proof."

I sat down again. "No, of course not. The word of a liar carries greater weight ... I could agree to release you on your word that from this moment forward you will not pursue me."

"Agreed, you scoundrel! I have not pursued you!"

"No. I require more. Thirteen years ago, when you first began your Tribunal in Malta, Eccellenza questioned me."

"How do you expect me to remember?" the Bishop shouted, as he could. "This is mad! The Tribunal questions many."

"Of course, Eccellenza," I said. By now I perceived that the Bishop's face was itself blanched, also covered with dust. "You had threatened Isabella Guasconi with something terrible enough that she denounced me to you. Tell me what it was and I will release you."

"*Vellaco!*" Cubelles now cried with all his might. "The *Dies Irae* is upon us and you sit above me prattling about trifles! You shall burn in Hell for this blasphemy! The proceedings of the Tribunal are secret!"

I got to my feet. "My soul died some time ago," I replied. "And as a better man than you once told me, we live in a vindictive age. I gave Isabella my vow that I would never speak about it again, but I have not made that promise to you. Tell me with what you threatened her and I will save you."

Cubelles spoke. He revealed to me the knowledge wherewith he had threatened Isabella, no, threatened Isabella in order to destroy his enemy de Valette. The prospect was too terrible, and I was sacrificed. This night I was satisfied. I pulled the stones away, lifted the beam and helped him to his feet. He did not thank me. He warned me vengeance would be his, to which I said, "You had best go to the castle, Eccellenza," but he knew that already.

That night I again stayed with Isabella in the cistern. It was completely dark, for we wished to spare the candles. We only knew of each other's presence by our breath and touch. As the earth all around seemed to prepare itself to swallow us, she told of how the Sacra Infermeria had been hit again several times and that they'd cleared the top floor. "O Francisco, there is no place whither to move the injured. And hundreds more flee thither each day to have the doctors treat the wounds they receive at the walls. Vigo and the others toil incessantly. Sometimes I think he sleeps on his feet. He is a saint."

"I think so," I said.

A loud crash from above silenced us; surely part of the roof had caved in.

"The Infermeria is running out of herbs and drugs."

"Has he received news of the medical ship he requested?"

Isabella shook her head against my shoulder. "All the couriers to Notabile are being captured. We know nothing; no word has come from Don Garcia ... I saw Parisot at the Hospital today. He hopes the relief will arrive tomorrow, for it is the Feast of St. James." I nodded. St. James, Spaniards knew, was the patron saint of Spain and Don Garcia the Vice Roy a member of his order.

During this night the enemy sometimes broke off the bombardment to sound the attack. This was most often a false alarm, intended merely to further the bewilderment of those on guard and make certain the troops never got any rest. In that it succeeded. Throughout the daylight, the bombardment continued with unabated fury. Hardened soldiers who had lived through Rhodes or Vienna could not credit their senses. At the Post of France, virtually within the mouth of Vesuvius, I discovered Balthazar kneeling with his sword in hand, reciting, *"Terra tremuit et quievit dum resurgeret in iudicio Deus."* In their extremity, the common people spoke of hearing trumpets, or seeing smoke from the pit, or of beasts with ten horns and seven heads rising from the sea, or another speaking like a dragon as it rose from the earth.

Toward evening the platforms on San Salvatore and Sta. Margarita suddenly quieted as a party of Turks leading a Maltese in chains hailed the sentries at Provence. When the envoys got close enough, the sentries saw that that prisoner was the same Orlando who'd been a courier between the Old City and Sicily. In the last days he'd been sent by the Vice Roy with ciphered dispatches for the Grand Master but had been caught by the Turks in the Gozo channel. Orlando asked to speak to the Grand Master.

de Valette came but concealed himself behind a parapet and the Bailiff of Eagle spoke instead, asking what they wanted. With a spear to each side of him, Orlando mocked the forces of the Grand Master, reminding him that the Sultan's troops still numbered thirty thousand, and that no relief would come. The ship carrying medical supplies had been captured, the Vice Roy had but fifty galleys and these were so badly equipped that he would never allow them to confront the might of Piyale Pasha's fleet. Thus, Mustafa was once again offering them the most favourable terms for surrender, hoping to avoid what had taken place after St. Elmo, which would undoubtedly be repeated if stubbornness rather than reason acted as a guide.

de Valette answered through an interpreter that Orlando was to be congratulated, for he had risen from the position of a humble mariner to that of ambassador. "Will you ransom him?" he called out to the Turks.

The Turks replied that the Pashas would not part with him for any price.

"Not even for a mule?" the interpreter asked at the jester's behest.

As the Turks understood they had been insulted, His Eminence scared them off with musket fire and the bombardment commenced anew.

Maugre his bravado, the news Orlando brought weighed heavily on the Grand Master and weighed more heavily as the next day, the Feast of St. James, came and went without any sign of the relief. By evening de Valette decided he must tell the people the truth. He walked to the clock tower in Birgu with his suite, ordering the drummers to summon the people. When a crowd had assembled on the square, he glanced at the piles of dirt and wagons of supplies about him, the ever more shattered houses, not a few with arms and legs protruding from the rubble. The red sun, rats. The guns were firing and people pressed up close in order to be able to hear. Even so de Valette waited for the artillery to quiet.

"I am at a loss for what to say," he confessed. "The time for the fulfilment of Don Garcia's promises has gone and we can no longer expect a relief from Sicilia. I expect no aid save from God, who is our true succour and who has preserved us until now. It is in God alone that I put my trust. I ask you to remember you are Christians, that you are fighting for the faith of Our Lord Jesus Christ, for your lives and liberties, and that you cannot expect more mercy from the Turks than was shown to those who defended Fort St. Elmo. I can only promise you that I will be the first to face all dangers."

Those around him cheered the Grand Master, and soon word of his speech spread throughout Birgu and Senglea, renewing everyone's courage. Isabella, who stood near, again thought she had seen the ghost of l'Isle Adam at Parisot's shoulder, but it mattered little: As the houses crumbled around, soldiers and townspeople pledged once more to die sooner than fall into the hands of the Turks.

One Hundred One

The cistern became our home. Each night we climbed down into that dark vessel with the household servants and wounded about us and made our bed on its stone floor, which was now dry. Everyone in Birgu did the same if they could, but despite such measures, dozens, hundreds were crushed each day under collapsing walls. The Grand Master himself moved again from his steward's home to a merchant's shop on the square, which became headquarters. Flaminia's family also took refuge in her own cistern. I passed the house one night to see that it had been partly ruined. I entered, finding the house mostly empty of furniture, which had been taken for the defenses. Below in the cellar, Flaminia was weeping over the body of her mother, who had been hit in the head by a falling stone. Her father, sitting below in the cistern, rocked slowly back and forth with his head in his hands, as his granddaughter Francesca sat at his side in the glow of a single candle, vainly trying to comfort him. Flaminia and I dragged her mother's corpse out into the street and left it there among the others.

Inside, I helped her make a small shelter over the mouth of the cistern with some of the remaining shelves. "She never hurt anyone," Flaminia moaned softly. "She said her prayers every day and went to the village church on Sundays."

I had no words of consolation and stood there as dully as Flaminia herself. She asked again that I bury her and her daughter in consecrated ground, and again I told her I would not, for she would live. The once-rich *quiraca* cast her eyes about the cellar, saying only that water was low and that she expected to die of thirst if not of the bombardment. She had no customer this day and begged me to spend the night with her.

"I know you have never loved me, *mio cuore*," she said, "but perhaps mistress Isabella would take pity on me this night."

With Isabella's leave, I climbed down the ladder into Flaminia's cistern and stayed with her family. Isabella, herself too frightened to stay alone, went to Parisot's headquarters to spend the night there. Everything happens in war.

In such a way life went on. The Grand Master, knowing that an assault on Castille and another on St. Michel must come soon, ordered the morning Angelus to be rung two hours before daybreak instead of one, and for drummers to beat the call as well, in case the bell should not be heard. The measure would have been needless, for no one slept at night, but so dark were the cisterns one could not tell when morning came either, and so loud were the guns that the bell's voice was often lost.

During those endless nights, enclosed in our hollow cave that echoed with our own whispers and groaned as the earth outside bent and warped, Isabella finally revealed that Vergã swore to be my half brother. I answered that, as always, he was a lying *picaro*, but Isabella said that in his own mind it was as true as stone is hard and served to give cause for everything since our childhood. Mayhap it also explained my stupidity in trusting him. I did admit to Isabella that I had at times suspected my father, like most men, was imperfect, but I'd ne'er heard a whisper of a half brother. Someday I would seek out my father and, if he lived, learn what was to be learned.

During those nights, as Isabella and I lay in each other's arms fully expecting to die, we at last became reconciled to one another. Gone in the darkness was my jealousy. Gone was the distance that had for years stood between a noble woman and a merchant's son. It was as if we, along with the world about us, had been leveled. The Turkish guns had defeated pride and forced us to come to a small peace within the great reckoning. As the water fell, we gazed on the urns with dispassion, finding strength in each other to face what might come. We did not sing, but we kissed each other tenderly and traced each other's lips with our fingers and discovered brave smiles. All was forgiven.

Three or four days after the bombardment began, Flaminia climbed out of her cistern to make her way to Senglea for work on the repairs. She'd gone only a few streets, picking her way over the rubble and bodies, where directly in her path one of Birgu's doctors, a man called Cadamosto, stood feverishly waving his arms. Flaminia couldn't understand what he wanted; he'd never been one of her customers. She took her hands from her ears and looked behind her, but no one was there.

"Come!" he shouted. *Boom boom-boom.* "Come!"

Flaminia ran after him into the house and down into his cellar. Holding a lamp, he directed her gaze into the cistern. She peered down. Between the roars she heard before she saw—the sound of water, gushing. Then she did see—a fountain, right at the bottom of the cistern!

"Do you understand, Mistress Flaminia?" shouted the doctor with joy. "The tremors have opened it! I must tell His Eminence at once!"

Before a glass had turned, the Monsignore himself and a multitude of townspeople were squeezed into Cadamosto's cellar, regarding the spring, which now almost overflowed the cistern. Everyone was pushing and shoving each other aside with cups in their hands.

"'Tis a bit salty," said the jester, making a face as he tasted it.

The Grand Master put a goblet to his lips. "'Twill serve," he rejoined, and everyone knew they would not die of thirst.

Within moments word of the miraculous spring had spread throughout the town and people were running from all quarters with jugs, urns, pots. The Grand Master himself went to the Church of San Lorenzo to give thanks, while Flaminia went to her own church and lit a candle to God.

"Why haven't they stormed this place?" Vergã wanted to know.

No one around him had an answer, neither Balbi nor Alfonso nor Fuster, nor any of Romegas's other men who'd been sent there. A blind beggar could see that the condition of Fort St. Michel grew more perilous by the hour, an assault ever nearer. But the Turks hadn't made it easy for themselves.

"Look there," said Fuster. The works had already been so leveled that the ditch was mostly filled with stones, and enemy arquebusiers were carrying dirt-filled sacks for protection and planks to help them climb over the rubble. Taking up positions all around the front of the fort, the janissaries in their shelters got down to their daily practice. Almost nothing separated the Turks from the defenders except some gabions and big barrels of earth. "At Tripoli the walls were in better shape."

Before anyone could ask Fuster what he meant, Maestro de Campo Robles appeared on the ramparts with some Maltese behind him carrying rolled up galley sails. "Put these up over there," he ordered, pointing to one of the leveled walls.

"Do you expect the fort to fly away under sail?" one of the men joked grimly.

"No," rejoined Fuster with equal gloom, "he thinks to armor us in canvas against Turkish muskets."

"Precisely," said Robles and ordered the two jesters to lend a hand.

To be sure, the sails protected them. After they got them up, the janissaries could no longer see the men working behind and were able to shoot only by guessing. Mostly they missed.

Behind the sails, hoping that a lucky shot would not find them, the men struggled with the repairs. At midday they sat behind the walls for a meal, most of them staring down into their cups in which they could see the beating of the air in the rings of wine or water. As merchants came by selling bread and cheese, a messenger ran in also, saying Romegas wanted his men at the Towers. Not displeased to leave the doomed fort, Vergã and Fuster got to their feet and made their way out the back gate to Birgu.

They did not notice the urchin running well ahead of them who Balthazar had paid to tell him if either left Fort St. Michel. By the time Blaij and Fuster arrived at the Towers, they found Romegas speaking to Navarre. At the sight of him, Vergã sensibly flinched, while Balthazar afforded him hardly a glance.

"Parisot is anguished that we have no news of late from Sicily," Romegas said to the men gathering around him. "We are cut off, and that's the truth of it. He offers fifty *scudi* to anyone who captures a Turk alive for information."

"Now he wants them alive," muttered Balthazar.

Romegas's *soccorso* had been reduced to fewer than a hundred men, and the Commander was casting his net wide. "I'm adding fifty *scudi* from my own purse. I need men brave enough to go to Rinella tonight and capture a Turk. Not a word of this to the Grand Master. Vergada?"

Before Blaij could answer, Balthazar did. "Of course he is going. So am I." He glanced at Fuster. "So is he."

By evening, Romegas had gathered a dozen desperate men at the Towers. But as they readied to depart, the Grand Master himself appeared

with Toni Bajada, and Romegas instantly broke off their preparations.
Those standing about the Monsignore were thankful to learn that another
courier had by some miracle gotten through from Sicily. de Valette, tho',
was unable to disguise the irony in his voice as he told them the news:
"We may take solace that the nameless heretic who sits on the throne of
England has declared, 'If the Turks prevail against Malta, it is uncertain
what further peril might follow to the rest of Christendom.'"

"Apostates having turned, return with relief from the Infidel!" the jester
quipped. "Any day now!"

de Valette nodded heavily. "*Si*, the Protestants shall rescue Malta, if
Spain shall not."

Maugre Parisot's distemper, Balthazar saw a small light in the news: If
England herself had made such a declaration, then all Europe must truly
be shuddering. Surely relief would arrive ... sometime.

"From the messages I have received," de Valette continued, "I discern
that King Philip has bound Don Garcia's hands; he has no intent of
exposing the Spanish fleet to undue danger. Natheless, the Vice Roy has
once more released the two galleys of the Order with St. Aubin and
Cornisson, and he promises a relief of twelve thousand men by the end of
August, if we can only hold out until then." Everyone voiced the same
thought: A day was infinitely long, a month unimaginable "In the past
hours Governor Mezquita has begun sending smoke signals. The galleys
may again be attempting to make land, or ... " The Grand Master faced
Toni. "Signore, I need you to go once more to Città Vecchia."

Bajada turned as white as the smoke from Turkish muskets.
"Eminenza, we are surrounded on every side. Candelissa is blocking the
harbor with Hasan's ships. Since Commander Romegas's slave escaped,
the Turks are surely looking for me."

"Yes, the danger is extreme, and I plan to send four couriers. But we
must learn the meaning of these signals, and you, Toni, must go."

With a nervous tug on his ear, Bajada agreed. "I'll come for the
dispatches after dark, Eminenza."

Romegas offered to buy Toni supper and the company made its way to
a tavern that hadn't been hit, where they feasted in the cellar on bread,
eggs and cheese with some Spaniards from de Guiral's Post. After speaking
of the salvos that saved Malta, one of them turned to another and said,

"Francisco, that was quite a scene at lunch with Commander Guiral. What did you think you were doing?"

That one, the officer Francisco de Aguilar, remained silent with an annoyed expression on his face, refusing to answer.

The first explained: "Francisco took his meals with the Commander, but when the servant said they'd no more capon to serve, Francisco here fell into a rage, even beating the poor fellow. de Guiral told him never to appear at his post again."

"You'll have to tell your pretty wife to cook for you," put in Fuster. Aguilar snapped angrily at the suggestion, spitting out that Fuster could cook for him because his wife was, like the other women, too busy on the walls, while Fuster, true to his old ways, had managed to avoid danger.

At once Fuster threw down his bread, challenging Aguilar to prove his valor, but Romegas stayed the latter's hand, while casting a fierce glare at the other. "Think nothing of these slights, Francisco," he said. "We've all become short-tempered. Everyone knows your prowess and the Grand Master counts you as a friend. Robles shall be pleased to welcome you at St. Michel."

Strange, thought Balthazar, Romegas making peace, but de Aguilar agreed to change his post. Wishing to say no more about the day's unpleasantness, he sought another topic, asking, "How will you get to Notabile, Toni?"

"Yes, a good question," Fuster and Vergã put in at once.

"Messeri," the swimmer demurred, "you are esteemed and valiant soldiers, but you know very well I am not to speak of such matters." He tore the bread in his hand and took a bite. "I'll tell you, tho', I am very afraid."

Romegas slapped Bajada on his shoulder by way of encouragement, then said, "Ten *scudi* says Toni will make it."

Among those gathered, only Romegas seemed unable to perceive Bajada's discomfort at being the subject of this bet, nor understand the consequences of losing it, and was puzzled when no one took him up. Balthazar, tho', who had remained silent throughout, now said, "I'll propose another wager, Mathurin. I say that in our extremity someone at this table will lose heart and cross to the enemy."

At once everyone seated spat up their drink or choked on their food.

"You dare suggest such a thing, Sir!" shouted Fuster. "We'll have your head on a plate!"

"Very well," replied Balthazar evenly, staring Fuster in the eye, "I stake my head against that of he who goes over."

Already everyone present decided this was some distasteful jest on the Knight's part. "Whatever gave you such a thought, Navarre?" said Romegas with an uneasy laugh. "We're all here sworn to die for the Faith."

"Sworn?" replied Balthazar, snorting with a glance at Fuster. "As we were sworn at Tripoli ... ? Tell me, Mathurin, do you recall that time after Turgut's *razzia*, when you met Leone Strozzi off Calabria and nearly blew him—and me—to Heaven?"

"Yes, what of it, Balthazar? One-Eye had defrocked him."

"Aye, and within a few days he was frocked again, and once more your good friend."

Romegas had become visibly angry. "I don't understand what you're getting at, Navarre."

"Precisely," replied Balthazar, rising as an eighty-*libbre* ball crashed into the building next door, sending dust and stone bits onto everyone. "Gentlemen, I bid you good evening and trust I shall see one of your heads on a lance—or you will see mine."

After nightfall, having gotten the dispatches from de Valette at his headquarters in the Borgo, Toni put them in his sealed wine skin and waded into Galley Creek. From there he swam towards the Marsa. Luckily there was no moon, but tho' he'd waxed his ears, the sound of the bombardment seemed hardly to diminish with his strokes. Nay, the Port itself channeled the thunder and, e'en more than during the battery of St. Elmo, the booming echoed all around, as had every stone and grotto opened its maw. The stars themselves shivered.

Bajada spoke little about that night, which was his most harrowing. I know that after an hour he climbed ashore at one of the places where he kept hidden Turkish clothes. Many boats abandoned after the assault on Senglea rocked gently nearby, and beyond them a few men waded into a cove with fishing nets. Bajada hid himself in the deep shadows and silently dressed himself. When he was done, he climbed behind some rocks to the top of the rise and poked his head up. A multitude of tents stretched before him. Yes, a month ago the Turks had moved their main camp east to the Margarita heights, but in all that time the hospital remained here. As was his custom, Toni prepared to walk through the camp while speaking Turkish, and stood up.

He said later it was because of the wax in his ears, or the cannons pounding, but he heard nothing even as he was seized from behind by three fishermen. They stripped off the turban he'd wound and marched him in the direction of the tents. When they got to the campfires they tied him up against one of the few trees they hadn't chopped down. For a moment, Bajada listened to the groans of the wounded and dying when they were not drowned out. Then Romegas's slave walked up to him.

"Hey, this is Bajada," said that one to his captors. "You'll get a big reward."

Of the rest, Bajada revealed only that his courage began to fail him, and he wondered whether he would by mischance be the one to lose Fra Balthazar's wager. It was late at night, probably, when a Maltese slave crept silently up, concealing himself behind the tree and offering to free Toni if he would take him with him. Surely Bajada had nothing to lose. A moment later the two were on horseback, galloping like the wind out of the camp with the Turks on their heels. A league went by as the sky brightened, but they could not lose the enemy. A spahi killed the nameless slave with an arrow even as Mdina loomed on the rise, but Bajada himself had abandoned all hope of gaining it. Sometimes Toni said his horse tripped, broke a leg and that he scrambled through the gates. At other times his mount was shot out from under him, his shoulder was bruised and a spahi was about to kill him with a mace when Anastagi's cavalry charged out of the gates for their morning raid, swords raised and screaming. The spahi took one swing, missed Toni and was off.

One way or another, a panting Bajada entered the Old City after sunrise and handed Governor Mezquita the dispatches. "Signore, the Grand Master wants to know what your signals mean. Have the Order's galleys come?"

Mezquita shook his head sadly and offered the courier some food and drink. "To my sadness, no. Once more we are left entirely in God's hands and to pray for his mercy. The news is otherwise. Yesterday we captured some Turks and questioned them. Mustafa is making a determined attempt to get into Fort St. Michel by a tunnel."

"A tunnel?" repeated Bajada dumbly. "Does Señor wish to say another mine?"

The Governor replied only with a forlorn shrug. "We don't know."

For a moment Bajada was silent as he washed down some bread with water and picked up a handful of raisins. "The Monsignore sent four couriers. Have the others gotten through?"

"No," replied Mezquita. "You are alone, which means I also do not know how to get you back."

At St. Michel, Maestro de Campo Robles was surrounded by men at the base of the gun tower, Pietru among them.

"What did you say?" Robles asked, for the noise was so fearsome that the Gozitan farmer appeared to be moving his lips without speaking.

Ix-Xabaw repeated himself. "We think the Turks are digging a mine!" he shouted. "Near the ravelin!"

"Are you certain?"

The others nodded. "We hear picks in the distance, but we cannot say where. The noise is too great." *Boom boom.*

"Does that tambourine help?" the Maestro de Campo asked, stepping aside as a stone from above crashed down.

Everyone shook his head. Robles was unsure as to the best course of action. He told them to countermine in any direction they thought best, and to pray. Moments later, the guns fell silent.

In the merciful quiet, Yakhshi, accompanying the Agha of the *yenicheriler*, picked his way across the rubble under a white flag to the place in front of the fort where the bridge had been built. The Spanish convert they'd brought along called out to the men across the ditch saying they wished to parlay, and a few moments later the chief Robles appeared on the ramparts. As some of the *azablar* threw raisins, cucumbers, melons and other fruits to the infidels in the fort, the Agha extolled the virtues of this Robles through the Spaniard: "Mustafa Pasha *Hazretleri* well knows the reputation of the Maestro de Campo, who has fought with great valor in the wars of Hungary and Transylvania and now on Malta. The Agha would be greatly pleased and honored to speak with him."

"What do you want?" Robles answered severely. "I have nothing to say to you, so tell me quickly."

"What I have to say will take several hours. Why hurry?"

It was a good plan, thought Yakhshi. While the two chiefs were talking over tea, the sappers would quietly finish the mine. An assault would bring all the defenders to the place just above it, the engineers would ignite the powder and blow the infidels all to Hell. Afterwards, men in a second tunnel, which was being dug up through all the rubble by the ravelin, would break through and storm the fort from that place, killing the few survivors. A bold plan indeed. But many of their bold plans had come to naught and the men were tired. That is why they had been letting the guns do the hard work.

At hearing the Agha's proposal to talk for two hours, this infidel chief grew red in the face and he told the Agha to be gone. Indeed, he had his men hurl several fire balls in their direction and they were forced to scurry away.

"What are they up to?" asked Robles, scratching at one of the many new scars that adorned him. No one could answer the question. "This cannot portend good. I think they are readying an assault. Be on your guard."

Word went around. Some hours later, one of the sentries was sitting on his heels, eating one of the Turkish melons and swearing to his mate that if he ever got off Malta alive, he's never leave his mistress's bed again. "By the Sacred Kerchief of Veronica—Eh, what's this?" The sentry, Robert de Gamor he was called, put aside his melon, got onto his knees and crawled over the immense pile of rubble that had once been the wall this side of the ravelin. "*Si, o reniego la que me parió!*" Before his disbelieving eyes the tip of a lance poked through the rock. Robert scratched his head only for an instant before he was running to Robles, who sent Lieutenant Andreas de Muñatones to investigate.

Muñatones saw the lance tip. "Picks and axes, hither! At once!" he shouted, hardly believing his own eyes.

Heartbeats later his men were hacking away near the lance and within moments they struck the tunnel. Muñatones instantly hurled down three or four *granadas*. Not being able to see anything below for the smoke, he grabbed a pike with a fire pot tied to the end, cried, "In the name of Christ the Savior!" and leapt down into the tunnel himself. His men were on his heels, with swords, bucklers and arquebuses.

They could hardly see a thing, tho' the tunnel was lit with torches. Coughing with every breath and expecting to be blown into eight pieces at the next, Muñatones and his men pursued the fleeing Turks. They caught up with them near the entrance to the tunnel, and downed three with arquebus fire. Two others turned and put up a fight with their picks, but Muñatones's men wounded them and they ran off.

Wasting no further time, they searched the shaft, finding a side tunnel that led off to the mine, and which held five caskets of powder. But the Turks, having heard all the noise, were nowhere to be found. "Take the powder and seal it!" Muñatones told his men and the order was carried out.

The mine having been thus rendered powerless, Robles escorted Muñatones to the Grand Master. As the lieutenant stood in the merchant's shop, de Valette placed around his neck a gold chain worth three hundred *scudi*. After the soldiers departed, Eminenza went alone to the Church of San Lorenzo and thanked God for this deliverance, for truly, as the bombardment resumed in all its fury, he understood that God alone could now save Malta.

One Hundred Two

August was upon us. Neither the Turkish bombardment nor the summer heat relented. Those of us who'd survived Djerbé ran our tongues over our lips, discerning that the spring uncovered in Dr. Cadamosto's cellar would, if ought, merely prolong the agony. In those dog days, smoke hung constantly over the creeks, choking us, and when it didn't, the stench of corpses rotting under the harsh sun did. Many wore scarves across their mouths and noses.

Early on August second, fifty enemy galleys that had been blocking the mouth of the Great Port suddenly turned and made to enter harbor itself. At almost the same moment, Mt. Salvatore vanished in a cloud of smoke as Piyale's great battery lit into the Post of Castille. Commander Sagra had miraculously recovered from his wounds in St. Elmo and took charge of the batteries atop St. Angelo, but neither he nor the rest of us watching those vessels approach the fortress could understand what was taking place before our eyes.

"Candelissa cannot think to enter the Port!" Diego shouted, wheeling his gun into position.

"If they get past the chain … " I answered, as we touched our matches and fired on the approaching vessels. The thought of the Turkish armada in Galley Creek was too terrible to contemplate, but as the guns on Sciberras and Piyale's own opened fire on us, the unimaginable suddenly became manifest.

Just as we did, Romegas also opened from the Towers and was ordering his crew to the *S. Gabriele* in Kalkara Creek, where the *ciurma* was as always already in place. Musketeers from France, Provence and Auvergne hurtled toward this end of the town, taking up positions at the Post of England and atop St. Angelo itself, and the walls soon bristled with guns, even as Piyale hit them.

But hardly had Romegas declared to his men that he would go down fighting in the name of Christ than the enemy fleet halted its advance, coming only a little farther than Gallows' Point. All of us stood frozen at our posts. It was then that the Margarita and Corradino batteries opened up onto Fort St. Michel.

Balthazar was nearby at France, whence he'd been watching Piyale's sappers bring the trenches closer to the Post of Castille. He saw no hope for that place. At the southeast corner of Birgu, its massive bastions and horn works were all but crushed by the relentless hammering. To be posted there with those great stones rupturing the earth—against his nature Balthazar shuddered. But posts no longer meant much; the numbers of soldiers had been so reduced that Romegas now regularly sent men whither they were needed most urgently. Balthazar guessed that of the eight or nine thousand defenders who began this fight, one in four was now dead and only half the remainder were capable of bearing arms. Of the rude folk trapped in Birgu and Senglea, he reckoned four thousand had thus far been killed. Balthazar felt a fly crawling on his nose and wondered how much longer they could possibly hold out. Two and a half months was already beyond what anyone would have called a miracle.

A runner from Lescaut arrived at the wall and told the Knights to hurry across to Fort St. Michel.

Pietru and everyone else at St. Michel could do little but keep their heads down during this morning's bombardment, which he thought was the heaviest yet. Last night the Grand Master, somehow learning that an assault would take place today, had sent down more weapons and ordered everyone to be on the alert. Alert! Pietru glanced at the soldiers near him. These men were no more than walking corpses who refused to believe they'd died. Robles alone thought they could withstand a grand assault.

As the galley sails, now riddled with holes, fluttered in the wind above them, Balbi and Alfonso also wondered. Were it not for the Maestro de Campo, who seemed to be possessed by the fervor of ten, everyone at St. Michel would have lost heart. Scarcely four hundred men remained.

"Do you regret having come over?" Balbi, fastening his quill onto his helmet and closing his smudged diary, put the question to Alfonso. "The Turks will certainly kill us all."

The renegado let the rock dust fall between his fingers, admitted that at times he'd thought better of it. "I would have seen Spain again before dying. But dying in the company of brave men is better than dying an outcast in Algiers, tho' I confess that not every Moor I met was despicable."

The men said little, could say little. As always la Cerda sat apart; he held his helmet in his hand, morosely tracing the scrollwork with his finger. Antonio Fuster, searching for amusement, walked up to him and tugged at his arm, sneering with the tired jest that he wouldn't have admitted la Cerda to the Hospital either.

la Cerda appeared too exhausted to respond, but before he could, Francisco de Aguilar—who at the Grand Master's personal behest had come down to St. Michel—put in that the real reason de Valette had arrested him was of course because la Cerda told him Fort St. Elmo couldn't be defended.

"Aye, no one is despised so much as a man who speaks the truth," said Balthazar, walking into this company with his *montante* thrown over his shoulder. "Tell me, Señors," he then said to the company gathered about, "do you think St. Michel can be defended?"

la Cerda, deciding he'd best keep his mouth shut, merely cast a sullen gaze at the Abbé, who himself regarded these cutthroats and mutineers, daring each with his eyes alone to flee to the enemy and win him his wager. No one answered by word or deed. "Ah," he said, "and so the question before each one of us remains: Shall valor triumph over fear?"

Aguilar himself nodded at the tableau of half-dead men, chuckled. "Anyone would admit things don't look good at the moment, right, Vergada?"

Blaij at his side also nodded. Aye, things didn't look good.

The assault began. Azabs and janissaries, spahis were screaming under all the artillery fire, which kept up without cease. Even as the infidel troops began to scale the rubble filling the ditch, none of the defenders dared poke his head above the walls.

"How can they keep up the cannon fire while their own troops are climbing towards us?" Alfonso asked Balbi.

Balthazar, crouched behind the ruined parapets, was asking himself the same question. A few moments later he had the answer—no balls were crashing into the walls.

"They're firing blank charges!" everyone yelled at once.

The instant they understood the ruse, the men pulled back the sails and poked their heads above the rocks to see a multitude of Turks already upon the works with ladders and ensigns. It was not a grand assault. There were only five Turks to each Christian.

But the infidels' trick had given them an advantage and many janissaries and spahis by now neared the summit, intending to plant their standards on the parapets. Robles and Muñatones, both enraged, grabbed fire spears and went out to meet them, three arquebusiers at their heels. At the sight of these devils, with their smoking lances and flashing swords, the Turks retreated, only to pour wave after wave of fresh troops into the assault. Balthazar had no rest, finding a footing on the rubble that was once a fort, and he lost count of the number of heads he took. Fewer janissaries by far confronted them here than at St. Elmo, for that he was grateful, but balls enough grazed his cuirass and the issue of the day was far from certain. Intending to claim his wager, he never let Vergã, or Fuster, from his sight.

Perceiving Robles's perilous position, captains from nearby posts sent their men over. Pietru ran over from Bormla, but saw that this played into the Turks' hands, because with the Christians out in the open, the infidel gunners were now charging their guns with real shot. He dove for cover as the Grand Master's aide-de-camp went down before his eyes.

For five hours they went at it. Vergã watched la Cerda, not three paces from him, wade into the foe, refusing to yield a step. At last Vergã, losing his own strength, rushed to the water barrel, followed after a moment by la Cerda. "You're a man searching for death, aren't you?" Vergã said with burning lungs before they again threw themselves into the fray. Balthazar watched Fuster and Vergã closely. He'd insulted them into fighting well. Good. Natheless, the wager would surely be his soon. Pietru, firing endlessly, stopped feeling. By mid-afternoon, men on both sides were staggering. In the end, it was the heat more than arquebus or sword, but towards evening the Turks gave it up, leaving five or six hundred more dead on the slopes.

Robles gazed about him. Forty of his best men had died, including his own nephew. Yet, he was content and fell on his knees to offer thanks for the issue, promising the three arquebusiers who had followed him after the Turks an extra ten *scudi* in pay for the month, if not from the Vice Roy's hand, then from his own, should he live.

Three hours later, a messenger appeared, summoning men to Romegas. Vergã and Fuster departed at once and Balthazar, throwing down his cup, was after them with intent. At the Towers, the Commander addressed all those who had gathered without prologue:

"As mulberries are black, we are in a fix. No one is getting in or out of this Borgo. Bajada hasn't returned from the City and Eminenza is at wit's end. Today's attack wasn't the general assault. We must try again to capture a Turk and learn Mustafa's intentions. The plan is the same—I need men to take a boat to Gallows' Point and get one of the dogs. I offer fifty *scudi* above the Grand Master's reward."

The men gazed at the Commander with dulled eyes. "Are you coming?" one put it to him.

"I'd be first, and if I came back with my head on, Parisot would take it." Romegas turned to the others. "Fuster, Vergada? You fought today."

Both breathed deeply, nodded, then Balthazar as well.

"No armor," said Romegas. Unadorned by steel, they set out into the Great Port as silently as mice, but a glass hadn't passed when a larger Turkish boat caught sight of them. A breath later, swivel guns and muskets belching at them, every last man was screaming and flailing in the water. Balthazar hauled for life, shoving aside a rotted, fish-eaten corpse and, assaulted by memories of that catastrophic morning at Djerbé, thanked Romegas for his warning to remove armor. They managed to reach de Guiral's Post and crawled ashore—wet, panting, alive.

Romegas was unhappy at the abysmal failure, and more grieved at Parisot's increasing desperation. "One hundred *scudi* above the Grand Master's reward," he told his men the night after. "We have failed by water. Try land."

Fuster threw up his hands and returned to Fort St. Michel, but Vergã accepted the challenge. At once Navarre stepped forward and himself led the company of volunteers out into the ditch by the Post of Provence. As they waited at the sally port, Vergã turned to the Chevalier. "You do intend to kill me, Señor. Let us end it now, right here."

Balthazar eyes went to the broadsword by him. "The Grand Master would hardly approve, but please, Blaij Vergã, allow your desperation full flight; I intend to collect on my wager."

Vergã shot a scorpion's glance at the Knight. "At least one of us will surely not live through this siege," he said, and they sallied forth into the ditch. But they succeeded only in alarming the enemy, who scampered away to shelter and Balthazar was forced to order a retreat, having accomplished nothing but to put the infidels on guard.

They next night they fared no better when, having gone out with fifty men, the Knight Vazquez suddenly sprang ahead with a small party of seven or eight. Thereafter the only sound to be heard was the striking of swords, silence. On both occasions Balthazar kept a close watch on Vergã, but that one behaved in no suspicious fashion and Balthazar began to wonder whether he had mistaken the confrater's intentions. After all, his only proof was his nose and Blaij Vergã was held in high esteem.

At sunrise, below the clock tower, sentries reported that eight heads sat atop lances on San Salvatore. The Grand Master struck the tower hard with his fist as the bells rang, but was grateful that Vazquez and his men had upheld their vow to die rather than yield. In the evening, the Turks fired against Provence, Aragon and Auvergne to discourage any sorties, and none were attempted.

It was vespers; Vergã again sat under bombardment at Fort St. Michel, eating his supper. From time to time, when the guns quieted, he could hear the Turks taunting the defenders, reminding them that they had few men and no hope. While Blaij sat leaning against a wall, one of his bravi found him, handed him a paper. "Someone has posted these," that one said.

E'en as he read the sheet, Vergã's face turned red. It was a *libello famoso*, on which were scrawled several ink-written lines:

I know Blaij Vergã. I have heard him say on some occasions that on one of his caravans to the East he would go over to the Turks and renege his Christian faith and become Turk.

At once Vergã crushed the paper in his hand. Clasping his broadsword, he went out thro' the back gate of St. Michel and crossed to Birgu with one aim, but Fate decreed he cross paths with Isabella as she made her way to the Auberge of Italy on her evening rounds.

His rage was as terrible as the artillery, so terrible that unlike the guns he could barely speak, and he only thrust the crumbled paper into her hand. "Ah, Señora, you see the libels your lover Francisco and his protector have resorted to!" he sputtered at last. "Why did not God permit me to kill them both when I had the chance!"

Reading the few lines, Isabella knew that nothing could now stand in the way of a murder. "Señor," she said instantly. "I wrote this."

Vergã retreated as had he been struck in the face. Thro' his veil of fury he well discerned she was lying, but he could not oppose her. "Señora, think better of foolish words! Have I not shown you the greatest esteem? Have I not trusted you with my deepest confidences—?"

"Desist, Blaij Vergã!" Isabella commanded. As on previous occasions, Isabella felt the man's gaze attempting to transfix her, but she no longer allowed it. "I do confess your prowess at arms and your songs have intrigued me, even blinded me," she said with all force. "I much regret it, for Balthazar more than once sought to open my eyes. Yet despite every kindness I have shown, Señor, you have brazenly lied to me. It is not enough that you denounced to the Inquisition one you have sworn on the Holy Book is your own brother, destroying the reputation you Spaniards hold above life; no, you have turned over the same man to the Monsignore in an attempt to see him hanged!"

"He is a traitor who destroyed his own honor!" answered Blaij, not perceptibly calmer. "You know it to be true."

"I am done with you, Blaij Vergã! Never dare speak to me again. I no longer have words to utter that you will hear."

Isabella recognized, as a nearby house crashed to the ground behind them, the profanity of this intercourse, but she discerned no other means of frustrating Vergã's design. Vergã, too, seemed belatedly to sense that any hope of winning this lady were dashed. "You call me a beast, Señora," he said with a groan of a mortally wounded creature, "yet you desire me. You see in me a free man and your eyes and your hands have betrayed you. For my part, Señora, I have loved in return. There, your scarf still adorns my arm."

Hereat Isabella's voice, no less than her countenance, turned to stone. "And now I'll have it back." She held forth her hand. "Señor."

Isabella's demand, tho', miscarried. Enraged yet further, Vergã cast a dark, evil look at her and ran off into the streets.

After the next morning's Angelus, one of Romegas's slaves came to fetch Balthazar to the Towers. He arrived while it would have been quite dark but for the hellish light of the Turkish cannon. The Commander turned from his inspection of the guns and addressed Balthazar with impatience. "Navarre, those *libelli* muddy the reputation of a man who has fought by me for fifteen years. For those papers Vergada will kill you, and in the midst of this siege who will notice? I won't, do you understand me?"

"I ask only that you stand aside, Mathurin. And remember, as you and he are so fond of saying: He who doesn't believe in death never dies."

The conversation went no further, for the Grand Master approached then with his retinue and bade the two Knights accompany him to Castille. To their remonstrances that it was unsafe, he replied that the men must see him. The small party soon passed out thro' Birgu's inner defense walls and stepped onto the Post of Castille.

The sight before them was hardly to be believed. As the earth trembled under Salvatore's fist, soldiers, slaves rushed to repair breaches wide enough for horses to climb through. For naught. The curtain between Castille and Germany—what remained of it—was less stone than earth, and what was not earth was a rude tangle of dirt-filled sacks, galley sails and wood from the boats. My basilisk roared and a heartbeat later a fountain of dirt erupted twenty *brazas* into the air, covering everybody as the ball ploughed itself to Hades. To approach the curtain was simply too dangerous and Romegas insisted that de Valette talk to the men in the big, dry cistern where they took meals. They climbed down a ladder into the well and His Eminence asked the filthy Knights about him whether Castille could be held against an attack. Many of them had tears in their eyes and said that the place was such a ruin that God himself could not hold it. de Valette, rather than anger at the blasphemy, replied, "God will hold it, with our help."

Balthazar stayed for several hours, helping as he could with the repairs. At midday he retired to France for lunch, but his servant was nowhere to be found. Another ran up to him, saying Balthazar's man had told him to bring these eggs. Balthazar paid the fellow and sent him on his way. He put the eggs aside for a moment while he stopped his ears with wax. In that moment one of the Borgo's orphans grabbed the eggs and wolfed them down. Balthazar lurched for the rascal, but the little one got away. The Knight shrugged, found something else to eat and at the end of a watch went again to Castille. Against the inner wall he spied the same urchin convulsed by spasms on the ground, clutching his stomach. At once Balthazar lifted him to his shoulder and sped to the Infermeria, where he discovered Vigo.

"Doctor, this child has been poisoned. Can you help?"

Vigo, standing amidst the wounded and dying in the courtyard whose upper walls toward Kalkara were by now partly collapsed, raised a pair of helpless, shiny hands. "Balthazar, my old friend, we have run out of almost every drug. You see, I am using swine fat for wounds. If this is arsenic or *la cantarella*, there is surely no hope. I can try an emetic, perhaps tartar ... " Vigo fetched some preparation and got the child vomiting, but as he foretold it was hopeless. Balthazar stood vigil over the boy for some hours. When the child died, Balthazar silently grasped his broadsword and crossed to Senglea.

"Where is he?" he shouted, storming into Fort St. Michel. "Where is Blaij Vergã? Tell the coward that the Knight of Justice Balthazar de Marans des Homes-Saint-Martin awaits, and that his hour of reckoning is upon him!" The Knight stood beneath the cavalier with sword unsheathed, shouting against the guns. Of Vergã there was no sign. Balthazar ran from one post to another, casemate to casemate, stalking his prey, without success. At length la Cerda said Vergã had gone with Aguilar up to Provence. Again Balthazar crossed Galley Creek.

"Where is Blaij Vergã?" he shouted at Provence, standing beneath the bastion.

The men there were already eating supper. One of them shrugged. "He went with Aguilar down to Aragon to shoot at some Turks. They said they couldn't see the dogs thro' the loop holes."

Balthazar climbed the ramparts, crouching. Raising his head over the parapet, for a moment he saw nothing. Then, beyond the Post of Aragon, which stood across the ditch, he descried Aguilar, his helmet adorned with bright feathers, waving his arms as he ran toward the Turkish trenches. Blaij Vergã was nowhere in sight.

"You, arquebusiers, up here!" Balthazar shouted at once. The men below threw down their suppers and rushed up. Within moments an arquebusade had erupted from Provence, France and Aragon, but though the fire was heavy and the smoke thick, Francisco de Aguilar, in a mad dash, escaped to the Turks.

That evening, as the gayest music drifted down from the their camp, the enemy made a great display of gunfire and fireworks. The Grand Master ordered all the remaining arquebuses from the armories given out and fired thrice in return. "Well, Navarre," cursed Romegas with all fury when Balthazar found him at the Towers, "you've won your wager. Aguilar will burn in Hell for eternity. We may too, for Aguilar knows everything."

"Where was Vergã? The men said he was with Aguilar."

"He came up here, that's all. You'd better find him and grovel at his feet before he finds you." Romegas then told Navarre to help carry bread and watered wine down to St. Michel. He did this, refusing to declare the wager won, for Aguilar's head remained attached. As he watched the Turkish celebration, Juan de la Cerda came up behind him. "It only takes one moment," la Cerda said.

"Yes," Balthazar nodded.

One Hundred Three

The main camp was full of music and fireworks this evening, and spirits had not been higher for weeks. The *Pashalar* had summoned the officers to Mustafa's pavilion after meeting for several hours with the infidel who had come over, but already servants who'd been inside the tent were spreading the news that this Aghalar was an important officer who knew the master and had even heard council meetings. While they feasted, Aghalar was telling Mustafa and Piyale many things: that the infidels' powder and balls would soon be finished; that material for making fire weapons was running out; that their medicine already had; that most of their hafted weapons were broken and that soldiers were now taking oars from galleys, but most of these were twisted and useless for weapons and the dogs were reduced to using them for repairs. Most of all, he assured the *Pashalar* that in this Borgo remained only five hundred men fit for combat. Mustafa need do nothing more than continue the bombardment and enlarge the breaches and he would prevail, tho' yes, the defenders had sworn to die rather than yield and he would have to kill them all.

Yakhshi, hearing this while he stood waiting outside Mustafa's pavilion, shared some *afione* with *Chorbaji* Shahverdi. "What do you think?" he said quietly to his companion.

"The newss is good," Shahverdi replied, "but I am hot."

Yakhshi nodded. The ninth day of Muharrem was upon them. The heat had gotten steadily worse for weeks and the air was now everywhere befouled by the stench of rotting corpses. Shahverdi tried to swat a mosquito but was unable to move his arm much and Yakhshi watched the pain flash across his face. Since the assault on the island with the mills, the *Chorbaji* had another wound in his thigh and walked with a crutch.

"The doctorsss ssaid it is good we weahhr ssilk," Shahverdi mumbled. Since the battle for the Santarma tower, the hole in his cheek hadn't healed properly; Shahverdi probably never would be able to talk right.

"Why?" answered Yakhshi without any humor, "the heat?"

"Ssilk catchesss infidel arquebusss balls asss they go in and they can eassily be pulled out. See?" He pointed to his bandaged leg.

Yakhshi scowled at his companion. What had silks done for them? The fireworks and singing all around couldn't hide the truth: What was to have been a pleasant week's work had turned into a nearly three-month fight to the death on this accursed rock. The infidels had thwarted each plan, every assault. Of the *yenicheriler* hardly above two thousand remained, many looking worse than Shahverdi. Fish was plentiful, but the countryside wasn't yielding enough fruit or grain. If that weren't bad enough, after Turgut's death a rebellion had broken out in Trablus, and two weeks ago Uluj-Ali had gone back again with four galleys to put it down. Nobody knew when he'd return with provisions. If it wasn't soon, the men would raid the ships' stores—or worse. *Hiyer*, this undertaking hadn't turned out as any of the auguries foretold. Allah must grant them a victory.

Mustafa, Piyale, *Beylerbeyi* Hasan and Candelissa emerged from the pavilion with the infidel.

"They look happy," spat Shahverdi through the hole in his cheek.

The *Pashalar* were indeed in an excellent humor. Mustafa announced that after receiving the news the hero brought, he was ordering a grand assault tomorrow. He wanted at least four thousand men against Castille and another eight thousand against the fort.

"After so many were martyred during the last assault?" someone cried out above a bed of grumbling.

For a moment Mustafa was taken aback. Why were the *yenicheriler* officers not greeting his announcement with their customary fervor? With a somber smile Mustafa ordered everyone silent. The Pasha well knew he must treat this turbulent group with a light stick, in this accursed heat more than ever. "Do not fear, we have given the *kafilar* a beating that no one under Heaven has ever taken, and our honored guest assures us only hundreds of men remain in the town who can bear arms. We yet have tens of thousands—"

"Tens of thousands of rabbits," Yakhshi muttered.

"—who are eager to be martyred. Tomorrow will be the final assault. The enemy shall be destroyed."

"It'sss Mussstafa and Piyale who don't want to be martyred," whispered Shahverdi, dragging his finger across his neck.

Yakhshi nodded faintly. Mustafa would surely sacrifice another ten thousand men before putting his own head under the Padishah's blade.

"What about the infidel relief?" someone shouted. "Is it coming?"

Piyale answered that he wasn't worried. Yes, captured couriers said a relief was coming in the next days, but Piyale's own spies in Sicily assured him the Vice Roy had only fifty galleys. "We can easily defeat it," the *Kapudan* said.

Yakhshi shook his head, grateful at least that the *Pashalar* weren't arguing as much as two months ago. Perhaps that was because, since Piyale'd moved his tent to the hill with the big gun platform, the two rarely spoke to each other.

"What about the weather?" someone else asked. "In a month it will turn."

"Then we'd better be finished before then—" answered Piyale, cheerfully.

"—or we will stay for the winter," finished Mustafa, and Piyale hurled a glance at him.

The men groaned again, deciding they'd better make a good assault tomorrow. Dismissed with the others, Yakhshi would have returned to his *boluk*, if he'd had one any longer.

When Romegas entered the Grand Master's cabinet in the Magisterial Palace, he found His Eminence sitting at the table with his head buried in his hands. At once de Valette looked up, angry, yes, stricken more. "How could Aguilar betray us? He was a confident, a valiant soldier."

"The weak have given up hope, Parisot. We have almost nothing to sustain us—"

"We have rocks!" He waved Romegas silent and said they must go to the square and organize measures against the general assault that must come at any time against Castille and St. Michel, very likely in the morning. En route, he passed the mill where I'd been working late with others. de Valette told me to be sure Castille and St. Michel were supplied with powder and fire weapons.

I nodded, saying little remained wherewith to make combustibles; after tomorrow ... The man facing me was no friend, but he was too occupied to bother with recriminations. "Go to the posts," he said. "Be certain fires are burning for pitch. Have you made the boards studded with nails?" I nodded. "Have them taken to Castille. When the alarm sounds, go thither with your gun."

So few defenders remained that the Grand Master withdrew them from the posts he viewed as least threatened and, on Birgu's square, organized them into companies that would be sent at the alarm whither most needed. That night on my rounds I discovered Balthazar at St. Michel with la Cerda, told him that Romegas wanted him on the square. He'd be posted at Castille. "Have you seen Vergã?" I said as we set off across the creek. "He will kill you for those *libelli*."

Balthazar shook his head, smiling gravely. "He will kill me, but how could you think I wrote them? The style was terrible. Nay, someone else intervened. Unfortunately the good intentions misfired, badly; a boy is dead and you and I must be constantly on our guard. How could I have so mistaken that rogue? Aguilar, tho', is a tragedy. When such a brave officer runs, others cannot be far behind."

By the time we arrived at the square, it was very late and we told each other to get a few hours rest, hoping as always we would survive the next day. With the Turkish celebrations the enemy guns were quiet, but I climbed down into Isabella's cistern and put my arm around her.

The Angelus sounded into a clear darkness. Men lit the pitch cauldrons at St. Michel and Castille, tho' there was no sign of enemy movement. But an hour before daylight everything commenced to unfold as the Grand Master had foreseen. The Turks on Corradino began to move around to the Mandra, positioning themselves for a direct assault on Fort St. Michel. At the same time, boats were ferrying Candelissa's corsairs from Marsamxett to Rinella, where they disembarked. Whether you were de Valette atop the clock tower, or posted at Castille or St. Michel, the sight appeared the same—shadows of troops everywhere, infinite numbers, surrounding us. Today's battle would surely be no smaller than the great assault on Senglea of three weeks ago, likely larger. Without waiting for the alarm, I took my gun and ran to Castille. Balthazar was there. With only a few hundred men at Castille, Balbi and Alfonso had been sent over from St. Michel, tho' the situation there held by hardly a stronger thread.

The breaches at Castille were so wide that no one believed we could defend them for long. The arquebusiers placed themselves on either side, thinking that the attacks must come here, and we were not deceived. By sunrise, the Turks were at us, shrieking and yelling, clambering over the rubble that near filled the ditch. Only that the post was located at the corner of Birgu, against Kalkara Creek, prevented them from inundating it at once. The enemy, running across that strip of land toward the breaches, found themselves pressed every more tightly against the water. The casemates of Castille—what was left of them—were also full of traverses and angles, which trapped the foe between. Not for long.

"They are determined this day," Balbi shouted, running up to my side. "Aguilar has given them new courage."

"Aye," I replied as we overturned the pitch cauldrons, sending those janissaries screaming to Hell.

We did not pause to watch the multitudes crowding beneath the walls. We poured the pitch and flung fire hoops. Before long it was mostly up to us the arquebusiers. All the cannon had by now been dismounted. Knights amongst us were few. In the siege two hundred had already been killed and the Grand Master had posted some to guard places where no attack was expected. As the Turks mounted the ramparts, I saw Balthazar swinging his *montante* with some final desperation, and not far from him men in threes wielding galley oars.

At the same moment, the Turks made an assault on the Posts of Germany and England, along Kalkara Creek. With the fortifications there in the same state as Castille, they thought they could rush along the narrow embankment to Germany and overrun it. At England they were disembarking on small boats at the palisade below the walls, certain they'd gain that weak place, defended by old Starkey alone and some mercenaries. But cannon fire from the Towers and a cannon at England shooting fire balls made them think better of it and our foes left off, turning all their efforts to Castille.

Candelissa himself stood below, brandishing his scimitar, urging his Argerian braves on. We soon ran out of pitch; arrows were flying in all directions. Smoke and screams filled the air and sparks flew as broadsword struck scimitar. But the enemy's numbers were too great, and maugre every one of our exertions, the Turks were planting standards on the ramparts.

Thus it took place, in almost a single moment. With a great cry and a supreme effort, the enemy was over the walls and inside Birgu. I drew my rapier, felled one corsair as he ran through a breach, but another was behind him and suddenly blood gushed from a long gash down my arm. I prepared to die, but Balbi clubbed my attacker with his gun and finished him off with his sword. It was hopeless; we could not resist and fell back across the post to the inner defenses. There we continued firing as the Turks approached. I glimpsed Balthazar swinging, turning, running.

At Birgu's square, two terrified soldiers ran up to the Grand Master. One of them gave the news. "Eminenza, you must come at once to the Post of Castille. It has been breached and the Turks are within the Borgo."

Without hesitation de Valette, already wearing his cuirass, grasped his morion from one page and his half-pike from the other.

"Eminenza, no," protested Romegas. "You must not. The danger is too great. Take refuge in the castle instead."

The jester nodded, for one of the few times failing to find words.

The Grand Master, tho', was at no loss for them. "*Fratelli et figlioli mei, nel nome di Dio* ... My brothers, my children, in the name of God let us go and die together with our weapons in hand, for today is our day."

The aged Master wasted not a breath more and, with his retinue and Romegas's *soccorso* behind him, rushed to Castille to fulfill his pledge to die with his men. I cannot describe what the Grand Master's presence did in that most desperate fray. Indeed, it was one of those moments that was seared forever in the memory of everyone who saw it. Nay, it was a moment so talked about for years after that even those who had not witnessed it believed they had. I myself no longer know whether I saw the Grand Master on that fateful day, but I remember him with every clarity.

I remember that as the townspeople saw him rushing toward Castille, whence the Turks were streaming thro' the smoke into Birgu, they too—merchants, women, children—began running in the same direction. I remember of a sudden Flaminia appearing at my side. "What are you doing here!" I cried from my place behind the second wall. "Get away or you will die!"

"Yes, *mio cuore*, today is the day we will all die. Kiss me a last time!" We fleetingly touched our lips together. Flaminia picked up a stone and rushed ahead beyond the barrier.

I was out behind her. All around the Maltese were flinging stones, hurling rocks, shooting bows, bringing food and drink, dying. I turned around to face Isabella.

"My God, Isabella!" I cried, but she put her finger to my lips, kissed my crucifix that she wore about her and also picked up a rock.

de Valette made his way through the thick of it to the highest tower of the post. Men were rushing toward him to protect his person, and before long, twenty dead lay about him. Knowing that the Turks must have discerned the Grand Master in their midst, the Knight Sacquenville of his retinue sank fully to his knees, pleading desperately. "Eminenza! Do you want our enemies to kill you when everything would be lost?"

Thereat the Grand Master halted, but, grabbing an arquebus from a solider nearby, he pointed to one of the breaches where the Turks were pouring through. "This way, *figlioli mei*, this way!"

Everyone near, gaining strength from the Grand Master's person, rushed toward of the breach. Romegas, Balbi, Balthazar, Alfonso, Flaminia, Isabella, myself. At that moment, a Turkish arquebus ball grazed Eminenza's leg, drawing blood. Only then did he agree to retire, but no further than the gate to the inner wall, where watched the battle rage on as the jester bandaged his calf.

Human eyes had rarely beheld such a sight. Smoke rising everywhere. Men, women beside them, children atop ruined ramparts, pelting the foe with stone, cries of "from the hand, rabble!" on every lip. Soldiers above casting down fire hoops, fire balls, arquebusiers below aiming up at Turks as they scramble over the summit. Knights, armor ablaze, leaping into the salt-water barrels. Infidels, screaming their last as they are impaled on the studded boards. Balthazar with a Heaven-sent strength lifting a janissary fully above his head and tossing him into the ditch. A red standard with horse tails flowing from it poking its golden head over the rubble. The standard of the Sultan! Balbi and Alfonso hurtle towards it, throwing at it ropes with hooks. It's snagged by the golden ball and they yank. They pull one way, the Turks another, all the while others trying to set it alight. The ball falls off and the Turks reclaim their ensign, but the tassels are all burnt.

It went on and on. The Turks sent in twelve waves of fresh troops, but there was no one to relieve us. The Grand Master sent bread and bottles upon bottles of watered wine. We ran to eat behind a wall, charged forth again.

"You're bleeding!" I shouted to Flaminia, who wiped her forehead with her hand and nodded. Every man or woman fighting was wounded or burnt. Still we went back with our guns, our rocks, our clubs. Of a sudden, someone shouted that Candelissa had been killed. A cheer went up from ours, but still the Turks came without end. Five, six, seven, eight ... nine hours. Both Isabella and Balthazar staggered up to me while I gulped down water. She was panting, lungs aflame, both arms bloodied.

"I fear we need a miracle greater than that which the Grand Master can provide," I said, hoarsely, bent over on one knee, propped up only by my rapier.

Balthazar nodded grimly. Isabella nodded. We all embraced and, preparing to die, joined the fray again.

At St. Michel it was worse. Eight thousand Turkish troops, most of the janissaries, storming the fortress. Mustafa himself led them. The old warrior, first on horseback, then on foot, urged his men against the breaches their artillery had opened at Robles's Post and Bormla. Those places had been so leveled that the Turks knew they'd easily gain them. Luckily, Pietru thought as he commenced firing, Robles had foreseen this. The Maestro de Campo's Post and Bormla, at the side of the fort, almost faced each other and the janissaries advanced between them. The arquebusiers had been positioned behind the traverses atop the posts and caught the Turks as were they expected guests.

There were too many guests. No amount of boiling oil or scalding water halted their advance and each janissary seemed to fight with a new determination, as if the whole outcome fell on his shoulders alone. Soon enough, the Turks launched their fireworks and, as during the July assault, Fort St. Michel erupted into a hell, where nothing could be seen from the outside, and little more from within except the constant flames from the cannon, muskets, arquebuses, flame hoops and Greek fire. As janissaries stormed the breaches, men ran this way and that, thro' the thick smoke and the foul smell of putrid human entrails, across scattered limbs from mangled corpses. Apart from the gunfire, Pietru could hear nothing except

the groans and screams from the wounded and dying. He felt in his bones
that today was the last day.

A Turkish fire pot exploded nearby, covering Martino with a flame that
water wouldn't extinguish. They poured on it jugs of vinegar. Later, when
it happened to another and the vinegar was gone, they pissed on him as
I'd advised, but they held not enough and the fellow burned to death. At
Robles's Post the janissaries were at the breaches; la Cerda was there too,
pushing them back with boot and sword as they entered. Mustafa,
standing directly below, himself ran thro' two of the *yenicheri*ler who fell,
to be certain they were not killed by this mad dog.

An arrow caught Ix-Xabaw in his upper arm. He yanked it out as a
janissary poked his head over Bormla's summit. Pietru drew his sword
with his bad hand, preparing to rush the foeman, but he could hardly see
for the salt in his eyes. He turned to wipe his brow, tripped over a body
and looked up into the face of his wife. She grabbed his sword and with a
scream ran the janissary thro' the stomach. All around the women and
children of Senglea were rushing into the fort, crying, "Succours and
victory!" Some picked up stones and hurled them; others brought slings,
still others bows and arrows. At least, Pietru thought, he and his wife
would die together. After Grezz hurled a fire hoop, they stumbled for a
moment below, where she fed him some bread and cheese she had brought.
They returned to the post.

The river never ceased its flood against them. Hour after hour, Robles
strode amongst the men, fighting, encouraging, but even he, the Maestro
de Campo, could not deny his eyes. Muñatones was down; one of his own
men had shot him in the right hand. Fuster, displaying a courage born of
hopelessness or desperation, went down with a ball to his leg. Vergã was
hit in the arm. The Turks had no intention of retiring this day. By the
middle of the afternoon, anyone who was not dead was wounded and not
a man could stand on his feet. Robles staggered up behind la Cerda, who
stepped away from the breach as another replaced him, and fair collapsed
with his back against the wall.

He gasped for breath and also said, "Maestro, we require a miracle."

We were all gathered at the Post of Castille watching the Turks swarm
over the walls. Each person crossed himself, commending his soul to God,
and took a final glimpse at his nearest comrade. Of a sudden, the waves

of the enemy as if froze on the ramparts, and a moment later the Turks, for no reason anyone could discern, turned and fled headlong from their trenches, without any command from their leaders. Every one of us raised our eyes up for some sign in the heavens that had put terror into the enemy, but heard only distant trumpets from St. Michel sounding a retreat.

Isabella and I collapsed into each other's arms, desperately kissing each other with no understanding of what had taken place. As the enemy fled, Balthazar stumbled over, covered with blood from head to foot. We also collapsed against each other, sinking to the ground, turning our eyes to the sky.

"They'd won," he said, getting the words out with effort. "The town was theirs. The siege was ended ... "

Sometime before dawn, Governor Pedro Mezquita awoke with a start at his headquarters in Notabile. He glanced about the room, attempting to discern the cause of his fright, finding nothing except at length that the staggering thunder which had made sleep nearly impossible for the past weeks had ... ceased. Dressing instantly, he blew out the candle and rushed to Lady Emilia's house, where Fra Vincenzo, having also taken note of the silence, breakfasted.

"It must be an assault," Anastagi said, cracking an egg.

They took no immediate action, being unsure of what transpired. An hour later, Mezquita and Anastagi stood on St. Paul's Square next to a Calabrian spy they'd just strung up by one foot on the gallows. The renegado had come over from the Turks a few days ago. They'd put him in jail for safe-keeping, but a guard caught him passing a letter to a Moor addressed to Mustafa Pasha, detailing the weaknesses of Notabile and advising the Pasha to attack.

While children went at him with sharpened canes, stones and torches, Toni Bajada ran up to the Governor, reporting that St. Michel castle was in flames. At once Mezquita and Anastagi rushed after Toni to the towers. The smoke from the harbor only grew as they watched, and before too long the Knights were convinced a general assault must be underway.

"With your permission," said Anastagi, and hardly waiting for the Governor's nod, he descended to prepare the cavalry and infantry. Horses had been dying. Of the three hundred at the cavalry's disposal at the start of the siege, only sixty remained, most killed in the daily sorties, worked to exhaustion or felled by arrows. The City yet could field about the same number of infantry, most from Robles's *soccorso*. Anastagi would take everyone today.

He rode out the city gates at the head of the column directly toward the Port. Not knowing what lay ahead, the company proceeded with caution, but to everyone's surprise, encountered no resistance.

"They must all be at the fight," said one of the infantry.

It appeared true. They pressed on as the sun rose ever higher, until each man was drenched in sweat and caked in the dust clinging to it. When they came to a rise not half a league from the Marsa, Anastagi ordered the column to halt and the men watched the assault on Fort St. Michel. The smoke and flames were so thick the castle itself could not be seen, and the cries and screams were loud enough to be heard even here. No Turks were anywhere nearby.

"What can we do against that force with so few of us?" asked the Chevalier de Lugny, bringing his horse up next to the Captain.

Fra Vincenzo surveyed the landscape before them. The old Turkish camp lay not far below, deserted but for the hospital tents. Anastagi unsheathed his sword, raised it above his head. "For Christ and the Religion!" he shouted, and they charged.

The horsemen, followed by the foot, rushed thro' the camp. "St. Elmo!" "Succours and Victory!" The cries were on every pair of lips as they tore down tents, put them to the torch. A janissary with a broken leg struggled to his feet, attempted to grab his scimitar, which lay by his mat, and had his head lopped off. One of the spahis lying on the grass with his stomach in flames, groaned; the Knight above him reared on his horse and trampled him to death. Anastagi rode up to the big fountain, where three men were filling water jugs. Catching sight of him, they fled; Anastagi was after and struck them down with his own sword. For a watch, for two, his men rampaged thro' the camp and when they were done, no barbarian remained alive. Each horseman mounted a foot soldier on the saddle behind him, and in good order they quickly retired to the Old City, having lost not a single man.

"Mustafa Pasha *Hazretleri*!" one of the troops from the Santarma island said, running up to the Commander, bowing to the ground. "The infidel relief from Sicily has come! Look!"

Mustafa turned from his place below the fortress of the mills and saw smoke rising from the direction of the old camp. Alarmed, he mounted his horse and rode up the hill for a closer look. Truly, it appeared that a force had arrived. At once Mustafa had the trumpet sounded and prepared to attack.

Yakhshi was firing from his place in one of the shelters below the fort of the mills when he heard the trumpets. It had been a long day. He had limped ahead, retreated, shot, limped again, been relieved. At last, the fortress was theirs! Was Mustafa retreating? Word spread like a fire. The infidel relief had arrived from Sicily! When Yakhshi heard this from the fellow next to him, he was immediately on his feet, rushing to join the Pasha.

"It must be the relief," croaked Pietru to Grezz as they watched the Turks retire from the walls, "it must be the relief from the Vice Roy." With everyone else in the smoldering fortress they slowly stood up, not being able to credit their eyes. It was true: The Turks, having gained the fort, were retiring. Robles from atop his post let out a cheer, which was taken up by every man and woman standing on the ruined ramparts; then, unable to restrain his tears, the Maestro de Campo fell to his knees, and everyone else did the same, knowing they had witnessed a miracle to surpass all others.

Yakhshi fell into the column behind Mustafa and marched towards the old camp and hospital, preparing himself for another battle, a greater battle. The place was empty. For a time everyone walked around amongst the slaughtered dead, wondering what had happened. When a few frightened *azablar* returned from the hills where they had been hiding and told the Pasha what had just taken place, Mustafa went into a rage the likes of which Yakhshi had never seen. He blamed everything on Piyale, who had retired to his ships at Rinella. "If you had taken your troops at once to the old camp, this never would have happened!" Mustafa screamed at the top of his lungs, when they met at the pavilion.

Piyale replied with disdain, "I was informed that a great Christian relief had landed and, as always, saw to the safety of the fleet. Remember, beloved father, if my fleet is destroyed, your army has no way to leave this accursed island." With that he strode off. Mustafa wanted to return to the assault of the fortress, but the officers groaned. They were too tired and darkness at last was falling.

One Hundred Four

For a long while, as smoke rose curling about him, Maestro de Campo Robles watched the Turks retire. When he at last convinced himself his eyes were not deceiving him, and knowing that this great victory was due more to divine intervention than human prowess, he sent a messenger to de Valette, requesting that a *Te Deum* be sung at San Lorenzo.

The Grand Master, watching the Turks retreat from Castille, had also gotten to his knees, and by the time Robles's messenger reached him, he had already ordered the *Te Deum*. Everyone who was able gathered about the Conventual Church. Most of us were not able. We staggered to San Lorenzo, sat on the steps in a dull emptiness, lacking the strength to rise, hardly aware of the solemn voices singing within. Flaminia and Isabella sat near, tore strips from what remained of their dresses wherewith we bandaged each other's wounds. The *quiraca* approached Balthazar who also sat with us, his hands clasping his bloody *montante* and his head resting against it, and asked if she might tend his leg. Unable to utter a word, he nodded silently, placed his hand gently on her head.

At length Vigo came by and, gazing on all the injured surrounding the church, said in despair. "I am so sorry. I am so ... I can do noth ... " His voice failed him under the cascade of his own tears and I motioned for him to sit by me. After the *Te Deum*, the Grand Master led a procession from the church to celebrate this victory, but most of those who fought did not join it and instead helped each other down to Galley Creek, where we bathed our injuries.

Having tended to his cuts, Balbi took his quill from his morion and, leaning against a barrel on the dock, began to write. I asked what he would say in his book about today's battle. "That it was one of the greatest triumphs ever given to Christians," he answered.

"Given it was," I said and all of us wondered how many more such gifts we could sustain.

While we slowly returned to life, Pietru and Grezz limped over the floating bridge. "I do not think I can fight any more, Cikku," he said. "The new wound is deep." I implored Vigo, now standing helplessly again by me, to see to it. It was deep. The physician washed it with seawater, found some vinegar and bound Pietru's arm near where he had been wounded before.

"You are merciful, Doctor," I said as he hurried on to another.

As darkness fell, Ix-Xabaw began to sing. It was not a *Te Deum*; I doubt he knew the words. I think it was his song about the wind, about not hoping too much. At length Balthazar said, "Where is Vergã? The time has come for me to kill him."

None of us could believe the Knight had recovered sufficient strength, but he was right. "Yes," I said, "we can survive a great battle, but after those *libelli*, he will not allow us to live thro' the night."

At once Flaminia started.

"*Flaminia*," I said, casting the gaze of a wounded lion at the *quiraca*. "You know something about this?"

"W—we meant only to help," she peeped.

"*We?*"

The whore bowed her head, nodded. "Blaij's mistress was jealous over the attentions he was giving to the Señora." Hesitantly she glanced toward Isabella. "Men have no secrets in bed. Blaij told her he wanted to turn Turk and that he planned to escape with the Señora. We wrote the papers."

"You are unlettered," I objected.

"I can pay a scribe," Flaminia answered, the haughtiness she strove for defeated by exhaustion, fear.

"Isabella?" I asked, turning heavily to her.

Isabella shook her head with much exhaustion. "More than once he offered to save me, never clearly explaining his design. I refused."

Throughout this conversation, Balthazar failed to disguise his darkness. At length he addressed the *quiraca*. "Thank you for your good intentions, mistress Flaminia. Unfortunately, your meddling killed an innocent boy and very nearly killed me. At least—" with difficulty he let out a deep sigh—"I have won a wager, twice. *Vertu de Dieu*, I had better take Vergã's head with all haste." The Knight struggled to his feet, shrouded by weariness, and I knew I'd best accompany him, tho' my own legs were no steadier.

"But Fra Balthazar," said Ix-Xabaw, "he is gone."

"What do you say, Pietru?" Balthazar asked.

"After the battle, while the Turks were retreating and no one paying any attention, he ran down to them. I saw."

Balthazar grunted loudly. "I must talk to Romegas."

At the square, Romegas was having his own wounds seen to. When Balthazar told him what had transpired, the Commander took him aside. "Navarre, don't you understand, he is attempting to assassinate Mustafa."

"How would you know?"

"He told me about Piemontois, and that he intended to fulfill that one's plan."

Balthazar scoffed, such as he was able. "Aguilar flees because he cannot have capon for dinner. Vergã flees to kill Mustafa. *Certainement.*"

"I have known the man for fifteen years," Romegas shot back as the clock above chimed. "Since that night on Gelves when he proposed to kill Dragut, he has always attempted the impossible."

"I have also known him for fifteen years, but I'd sooner trust a whore who knew him for an hour."

Balthazar slowly walked to the Post of Castille, thinking Romegas was a bigger fool than he'd always believed, angry to have been deprived of taking the scoundrel Blaij Vergã's head, natheless thanking God to at long last be rid of him.

Afternoon next at Emilia's house in Notabile, Vincenzo Anastagi and Pedro Mezquita were marveling at the miraculous silence of the day, when a sentry surprised them by announcing a courier from Sicilia. The dirty, disheveled figure was no common courier, but a captain with many seasons to him, Andrea Salazar.

"Andrea!" exclaimed Mezquita, clasping the other old man by his shoulders. "What a pleasure to see you again ... An unexpected pleasure."

"Yes," put in Lady Emilia, bringing the tired visitor refreshment. "We had given up hope of receiving news from Sicily."

Salazar gladly accepted a glass from her hand, then his face darkened. "The infidels think nothing of cruising off Pozzallo itself, even Zaragoza, making the crossing ever more dangerous." The Captain seemed sufficiently astonished at his own presence that Anastagi was prompted to remark, "Natheless, Señor, you have arrived," at which Salazar nodded in perplexity, handing a letter bearing the Vice Roy's seal to Mezquita and a another missive to Anastagi. "His Most Illustrious Excellency did release Cornisson and St. Aubin again to ferry troops—"

"That was the last word we received," said Emilia, before Salazar could finish his thought.

"Yes," the Captain said as he gulped down the drink, "it was difficult. We agreed to rendezvous at Pozzallo, whither Don Garcia had dispatched me in a *fregata*—"

"Who agreed?" interrupted Anastagi.

"Cornisson and St. Aubin, as I have said. From Pozzallo they were to tow me to Malta, but arriving at Pozzallo they discovered that the Turks had put two galleys into the harbor and landed a party that killed some Sicilians and captured a Maltese. Realizing the Turks knew everything, they wrote to the Vice Roy for instructions. He ordered them to return to Zaragoza—"

"He did!" Anastagi erupted with a clenched fist. "Ah!"

"Yes, but they disobeyed and towed me to Malta as planned. Unfortunately, we sighted the Turkish galleys and, to make matters worse, the Scirocco was playing havoc with the seas. Cornisson and St. Aubin at last returned to Zaragoza, as Don Garcia had wished. For myself, I resolved to continue south. Fortunately, the weather calmed and I was able to cross in the *fregata* and make land."

This account left Salazar's listeners as much perplexed as enlightened. "What *is* your mission, Andrea?" Mezquita asked at once.

"To ascertain the condition of the Turkish forces—"

"Why did Don Garcia not release St. Aubin and Cornisson after the weather cleared?" Anastagi demanded at nearly the same instant, even more agitated than a moment before.

"You must petition him for an answer, Sir, but I know he wanted them to wait for the armada, which nears readiness."

At these words, Salazar's listeners abruptly fell silent and the profound quiet of the day returned. Trusting he might finally speak with impunity, Salazar continued. "When I have ascertained the condition of the Turkish forces I am to return to Messina and advise Don Garcia whether to release the armada."

Hereat Anastagi interrupted again, but with a voice now colored otherwise. "Hmm, this then is excellent news," he said, popping a date into his mouth, "for the Turks are already defeated."

"That I must see with my own eyes, tho' I trust you are correct, Señor. If you are, above ten thousand men will shortly arrive at Malta."

"Ten thousand!" exclaimed Emilia in disbelief and delight. "Then that charming young Salvago has succeeded!"

Captain Salazar permitted himself a faint smile. "To Fra Rafael is due great thanks and much sleep for the sacrifices he has made in the name of the Order. Largely as a result of his efforts, those of the Vice Roy, the dispatches received from Malta, troops from all Christendom have assembled at Zaragoza. Gian Andrea Doria has arrived. Pompeo Colonna remains. Don Alvaro de Sande, who will likely take charge of the land forces, is there. Don Juan de Cardona, the Vice Roy's Captain General, is ready to command the Sicilian galleys and Don Sancho de Levya those of Naples and Florence. Chiappino Vitelli has brought thousands of adventurers from Italy. France, Auvergne, Provence, Spain, Portugal, Burgundy have sent troops. The Knights of San Stefano, inspired by the example of the Knights of St. John ... all are waiting for the word."

Emilia threw her arms around the Captain, then clasped her hands together in supplication. "At last we are delivered!" She rushed into the big room, fell on her knees before the image of the Virgin to offer thanks.

"Let us hope her thanksgivings are not premature," said Salazar, glancing after her.

Anastagi but shrugged. "Nonsense. Please accompany me and I shall personally show you the condition of the Turkish army. As I said, they are defeated. After yesterday there can be no doubt." He turned to Mezquita. "With your permission," he said and escorted Salazar toward the square, where the cavalry awaited.

Night had fallen by the time the sixty horse rode out toward the Turkish camp. En route, Anastagi told Salazar of yesterday's grand assault. They'd had no word from the Grand Master since, but as the Turks had left off their efforts, he surmised that all had ended well, with several thousand more Turkish dead.

"You see," Anastagi declared, "the fight has gone out of the infidels. Don Garcia may believe me when I say they have no good men left. They came with hardly twenty thousand. All the janissaries were killed at St. Elmo and in the assaults on Senglea. The spahis are the worst riff-raff on earth. They can shoot a bow, but they fight for the Grand Signor only with reluctance, for they must equip themselves and would rather sit on their lands collecting taxes."

"What of the spahis and silahdars of the Porte?" asked Salazar. "They are said to be the best cavalry on earth."

Anastagi shrugged, continued on the same course. "The Greek spahis are better warriors, but they are so badly armed, with hardly more than lances or axes, they can't do anything. As for the azabs, well, they are hardly worth speaking of. Their spirits are so low that the Pashas have begun to cudgel them into battle. If Don Garcia but brings the relief hither, I can guarantee him an immediate victory, for as soon as the Turks see Christians they run away, as from the Devil, and they pray for nothing more than to leave Malta."

"I am glad to receive such an encouraging report," said Salazar. "What is the state of the defenders, may I ask?"

"They are mostly dead, but the Grand Master has resolved not to talk of anything that smacks of defeat."

Toward dawn they reached the village of Tarxien, southwest of the harbor. Leaving his company, Anastagi took seven men farther to a rise whence Salazar could observe the gun platforms on the Mandra and Margarita hills. "You see," Anastagi pointed out in the dim light, "they only build fortifications to protect them from our cannon, and do not even bother digging trenches behind them, and the fools sleep without sentinels." The horses' shoes were scraping loudly on the stones and so Anastagi led Salazar on alone to a wall quite close to Birgu. From there, Salazar was able to observe the enemy camp and all the works surrounding Birgu and Senglea. It seemed they could hear the Turks snoring.

"Let's go on by foot," suggested Anastagi. "We can get right up their asses." Salazar politely replied that he had seen enough and they headed back to Tarxien.

As they approached the village, several of Anastagi's men rode up leading two captured Turks. "Captain," said one of Anastagi's, "these dogs declare that Piyale has taken sixty galleys to land troops at Petra Nigra. He plans to attack Notabile in revenge for yesterday's raid."

"With your permission," Anastagi said to Salazar, "we must get back at once."

"Captain," the same soldier went on, "Piyale is bringing five thousand men."

Anastagi shrugged, turned again to Salazar with a flourish of his hand. "Do not be alarmed. Five thousand or twenty thousand cud-chewers makes no difference. We take care of them every day. Yah!" With that he spurred on his horse and his column wheeled toward the Old City.

To Mezquita, the situation did not look promising. From Notabile's towers he watched Piyale himself advancing from the direction of the coast at the head of twenty-five horse, surrounded by colorful standards and followed by what must have been five thousand foot. "Get everyone up here at once who can fire an arquebus," Fra Pedro said to his nearest lieutenant. Crossing himself, he added: "By Jesus, get the women up here too. Put them in armor if we have any to spare."

When the soldiers rushed thro' the streets, pounding on Lady Emilia's door and ordering her to the walls, she flinched, shuddered. She could not understand after the good news Captain Salazar had brought just yesterday what this could possibly be about. As always, memories of the earlier nightmare flooded back. In the years since the *razzia*, she'd never learned to fire a gun, nor had she any intention of donning armor. By now vinegar and oil were gone, tho' wheat and beef remained plentiful. But if she would not immediately starve, Emilia knew her heart could not withstand another siege. For moments she stood at her door, praying simply to die, but when the vicar ran past her with an arquebus in his hand and children at his heels, and when she saw some of the peasant women struggling to get a cuirass around them, she took herself in hand and followed. Not long after, Emilia stood with a thousand others on the ramparts bristling with arquebuses. The Turks had dragged along several pieces with them and opened fire. Notabile's gunners answered with their own and the blessed silence of the day ended.

Anastagi and Salazar advanced at the head of their cavalry through some olive groves owned by the Grand Master. They heard the cannon shots a long way out, and by the time Notabile loomed, they found it surrounded. "I intend to get into that city," said Salazar, "or die trying."

"I as well," replied Anastagi as the Chevalier Lugny and Lieutenant Vincenzo Ventura rode up, remarking that the only way in was through the gates on the other side. Anastagi nodded, as from below the City they watched a large number of Turks go after a herd of cattle grazing outside the walls. "We can't let them steal the cattle," said Anastagi. "We divide our company into four. I'll go after the animals. God willing, Gentlemen, we'll dine together tonight in Notabile."

That evening, the four officers gathered around Lady Emilia's table supping on beef, fowl and mutton, and receiving toasts from Governor Mezquita and Emilia herself, who'd opened her last bottle of wine for the occasion. "I hope you found seven or eight skirmishes not overly taxing, Captain Salazar," said Anastagi in a superior humor.

"Not at all, Captain," Salazar shrugged.

"It was difficult to believe our eyes." Emilia offered this with a raised glass and a certain wonder. Mezquita agreed. When he'd greeted the four men straggling through the gates not an hour earlier, his own eyes had blinked.

Swords aloft, the four Captains had charged Piyale's army. Anastagi went after the azabs stealing the cattle, but Mezquita above watched the Turks draw him in, surrounding the Captain at once by arquebusiers and soldiers carrying hafted weapons. "Ah!" Anastagi shouted, "rabble!" and plunged ahead into the foe's ambuscade.

"But how did you get away, Captain?" asked Emilia.

"The cows were no less startled than the Turks," Anastagi laughed. "As we charged into their midst, both cattle and enemy took to running in all directions. In the confusion, I ordered my men after the animals. They afforded us cover, even as we rounded them up and took them to that rocky grove you can see from the walls."

"But you lost men, did you not?" asked Emilia, offering him fresh bread from the oven.

Anastagi conceded it. "Yes, two or three, and a few horses."

Aye. The Turks tried time and again to steal back the cattle and Mezquita himself chased them away with artillery fire in order that Anastagi could slowly gain the city gates.

"But you, Captains," said Emilia, turning to Salazar and Lugny, "we lost sight of you in some of the olive groves and in the rocks. It appeared as if your horses were kicking up clouds of dust all over the plain."

"Indeed, Señora," replied Salazar. "The Turks blocked every road into the Città Vecchia and thus required us to circumnavigate." Salazar and Lugny each searched for a way in. They charged the enemy, found one road blocked, retreated, circled far and around, sought another path. All while losing pack horses as Notabile's walls loomed above them, coming nearer, receding.

Salazar had circled far around and found himself in the village next door, Rabat. The only thing separating him from his object was a garden with two fountains in it and a short road beyond. The garden was full of Turks, tho' luckily, most of them were drinking. His men charged with great ferocity and the fountain flowed red. They gained the road and Notabile's walls.

"That was well done," put in Mezquita, toasting him with a leg of mutton. "I am pleased my arquebusiers on the towers prevented the infidels from capturing you."

"But were not some of the Captain's men taken all the same?" Emilia wanted to know, emptying the bottle into Mezquita's glass.

The Governor had no choice but to concede, yes, several of Salazar's company failed to stagger thro' the main gate.

"From what I discerned," interrupted Anastagi, raising his goblet, "Lieutenant Ventura deserves our highest praise."

The young Ventura nodded appreciatively. "As the Devil is black, the Turks did give us a run." Piyale's own horsemen surprised Ventura and tore after his column, chasing him and his men thither and yon. From the ramparts all that was visible were small volcanoes erupting everywhere over the plain. Arrows flew about for hours, "and we couldn't break thro' the mass of barbarians surrounding Notabile. Of a sudden, the enemy briefly parted before us. I decided there was only one road open—"

"He charged," said Anastagi.

Ventura did. "Piyale's standard was taunting me and, letting out a shriek, I galloped straight for it." The Lieutenant snatched at it without success, but was so close that when he cursed the *Kapudan* to his face, Piyale's startled horse reared, throwing the Admiral onto a hedge of India figs.

"We saw Piyale's horse rear," Emilia agreed with curiosity. Ventura declined to tell a lady what he had shouted, but Emilia insisted that she was no longer a child.

"I cried, 'Infidel ass-fucker!'" Emilia blushed after all, for a moment excusing herself from the table. She returned with fruit to hear how the momentary diversion allowed Ventura to scramble up the ridge toward the gates. He dismounted, using his own horse for a shield against all the arrows whizzing about. His men followed his example and most of them gained the city as the people cheered.

Truly, Mezquita would not forget the sight of those men, who'd been battling their way into Notabile all day, staggering in at sunset, having had ten of their number killed, another ten captured by the Turks and at least twenty-five horses taken.

"I reckon we killed thirty of the enemy," said Anastagi, biting into an orange.

While the company thus ate dessert, a sentry arrived to report that Piyale, content with his prisoners and horses, was retiring to the coast. Lady Emilia sighed as Anastagi smiled, both with a rueful glance at the empty bottle.

Mezquita remained disquieted. "We can no longer doubt that the Turks have designs on Notabile. If they mount a serious attack, they could yet succeed in this siege—"

"Which means I should depart as soon as possible," said Salazar with a sweet in his hand. "Before sunrise."

Anastagi spit out a seed. "Are you certain you have seen enough? We can easily provide further entertainment."

"With thanks, no," replied Salazar, "but I will recommend to Don Garcia that he come as soon as possible, if he wishes to amuse himself.

One Hundred Five

What startled Captain Andrea Salazar most as he sat at the great table in the Vice Roy's residence at Messina was that not only he, but every other every other member of the grand council of war Don Garcia had convened, was present. Beside him in the mantle of the Order sat Rafael Salvago, who'd spent the past three months in constant motion, first between Malta and Messina, then amongst every capital in Italy pleading the Knights' cause and raising money. Opposite, the Vice Roy himself, appearing as he had for the last months as were he in need of sleep, one foot raised on the chair to his left to relieve an attack of gout. Facing His Excellency, none other than Colonel Alvaro de Sande, greyer after his years of captivity in Constantinople, but having regained much of his former corpulence. Salazar and Salvago could only wonder whether the hard stare de Sande threw at Gian Andrea Doria, sitting at the Vice Roy's right hand, was of absolute hatred or merely a disbelief that the twenty-five-year-old's burning, if sunken, eyes bespoke a resolve that he lacked half a decade ago at Gelves. To the Colonel's right sat the one-eyed Ascanio della Corgna, nephew of the previous Pope, who having been tossed into the papal dungeons by the present Pope for certain rapes, murders and extortions, had been released upon intercession of Cardinal Fulvio, his brother, along with payment of twenty-four thousand ducats; della Corgna would probably share command of the ground forces. To de Sande's left, Chiappino Vitelli, who having raised four thousand troops in Napoli, sat modestly erect with his helmet before him on the table. Pompeo Colonna and the Vice Roy's Captain General Don Juan de Cardona, both of whom had failed at least once to reach Malta, sat to Doria's right along with Pompeo's cousin Prospero, while the ever-channel-crossing and weary Cornisson and St. Aubin found places not far from Salvago.

"Your report, Captain Salazar," the Vice Roy invited him with an upturned palm.

Old Salazar rose dressed as a simple soldier, facing a ring of doublets, mantles, hats, feathers, gold chains and silver rings that would alone have put the Turkish army to flight. "Illustrissimo Eccellenza," he said with a bow, addressing himself also to the many potentates who stared down at him from their fearsome portraits on the wall, "there can be no doubt that the siege is won. Eccellenza must do nothing more than send the relief with utmost speed to Malta and the Turks will flee before you. Captain Anastagi has written a detailed report to Commander della Corgna. I have confirmed everything with my own eyes and you may trust it implicitly."

Don Garcia pressed Salazar for particulars, which he willingly gave, after which the Vice Roy said he would be pleased to hear opinions.

At once the scrawny Gian Andrea leaned forward, declared they should take the fleet and attack the Turks at sea, destroying Piyale's armada.

While three or four finely dressed servants carried in refreshment, Don Garcia pointed out to the esteemed Captain General that the Turkish fleet outnumbered their own by four ships to one, approximately.

"What would the Knights say to such odds?" Doria asked.

The young man put the question with a flourish of his hand and a glance at each of the Knights of St. John present, doubtlessly expecting their approbation, only to be answered by an uncomfortable silence. At length, wincing from his gout, the Vice Roy offered that he had no instructions from the King for a sea attack.

Fra Rafael, who'd been staring at the orange in his hand, put it down. "Would Eccellenza care to divulge this day what he is prepared to do?" he asked politely.

"Fra Rafael," said Pompeo Colonna, thinking to answer for the Vice Roy, "you above all know that the great force we have gathered here shows that the King and all of us regard this matter with the utmost gravity. If a sea attack is impossible, we can easily land the troops on Malta."

de Sande glanced up from the cake he was eating. "May I ask how many times have you attempted that simple matter already?"

While Colonna, a distant nephew of the famous Cardinal Pompeo, flushed, it was Don Juan de Cardona who replied: "*What* is Don Alvaro suggesting?"

"One might reflect on the Grand Master's own actions in sacrificing Fort St. Elmo in order to save Malta. It is Sicily and Europe that must be defended. Let us contemplate reserving the fleet for this larger purpose."

"Allow Malta to fall?" Don Juan's voice rang out.

The only sound was that of silverware falling onto porcelain, as half those around the table gazed at de Sande with every shade of perplexity, disdain and incredulity, for the Colonel's valor at Gelves had been lauded throughout Christendom. "Will Don Alvaro explain himself?"

This was Cardona again, but de Sande, hands folded, addressed Toledo alone. "Believe me, I well perceive de Valette's frustration, nay, desperation. Imagine for a moment—"

"Colonel, please address me as Eccellenza," interrupted the Vice Roy absently.

"My apologies, Illustrissimo Eccellenza. Imagine for a moment, if you will, being abandoned on an island with thousands of men, the summer heat upon you, food, water running out with no succours in sight, your men dying of thirst and sickness. Imagine thousands being taken captive by the Turks, to die in infidel lands or to languish for years in filthy dungeons. Imagine that this council launches a great invasion and it miscarries—"

"We have Anastagi's report," interrupted Corgna, poking at the letter as he peered at de Sande with his fiery eye. "The Turks have only ten thousand left, the 'worst riff-raff on earth.' Surely, Colonel, you of all people would never suggest that we cannot make short work of such a rabble."

"I would never suggest it," answered de Sande, gaze not having left Don Garcia's countenance. "I would like to know, Eccellenza, what will happen when ten thousand Christian troops have made land on Malta and Piyale turns and attacks our ships."

At this, both Gian Andrea and Cardona got to their feet. Gian Andrea turned to the window, gazing out onto the harbor with his finger on his protruding under-lip, while Don Garcia's Captain General simply walked out of the room.

de Sande took a bite out of his cake and shrugged: "I should also wish to know what Philip's intentions will be when he discovers that his Vice Roy is safe—" Before Don Garcia could respond, de Sande cut himself off with a raised fork. "Pardon, I do not wish to know. By any calculation the most prudent course for the King is to sacrifice Malta and strengthen his forces here in Sicilia."

Hereon della Corgna scoffed with outright disdain. "I could not have expected such a weak proposal from you, Sir," he returned. "Of course we must invade Malta. It would be the greatest sin in God's eyes not to dispatch succour with all speed to aid the Knights, who have ever fought bravely on the side of Carlos and Philip. Anastagi, whom I know well and trust, tells us precisely how and where to land for complete success."

"Colonel," asked the Vice Roy, wincing again, "are you or are you not willing to assume command of the land forces?"

de Sande remained silent for a moment, chewing, during which time Gian Andrea turned from the window. "The ground forces," Doria said, silhouetted against the light, "shall be assured of the fleet's complete and utter support. I swear this by the Holy Cross of Our Lord and Savior Jesus Christ." So saying, he walked awkwardly to the crucifix hanging on Don Garcia's wall, knelt before it and kissed its feet with his thick lips.

"Thus, we are resolved," said Toledo cheerfully, rubbing his hands together. "Don Alvaro de Sande, in the name of His Most Catholic Majesty, Philip II of Spain, I hereby commission you with supreme command of the ground forces. Ascanio della Corgna, I commission you as Quartermaster General. Pompeo Colonna is commissioned as Master General of the Artillery. Letters of appointment shall be drawn up immediately. I shall take direct command of the sea forces and in a week's time shall begin moving my galleys south to Zaragoza, where they will rendezvous with the Captain General Doria's and the others. At that time we shall proceed to Malta and lift this siege. Gentlemen, I thank you for your cooperation."

Fra Rafael and Captain Salazar turned to each other and both, with an almost imperceptible nod, sighed deeply.

One Hundred Six

On Malta we saw no end. Those who counted the bodies heaped before Castille and St. Michel reckoned we had killed two thousand more infidels during the great assault of August seventh and wounded twice that number, but if the flower of the Turkish troops had by now perished, Mustafa and Piyale turned to surer means. They launched headlong into a contest, Piyale determined to take Birgu by way of Castille before Mustafa took Senglea by St. Michel. The day after the grand assault Piyale's trenches were empty, for reasons we could not immediately discern, but we surely discerned the renewal of the bombardment the day following. Once again Isabella and I climbed down into the cistern with the household and fixed the bars over us.

"Will they never run out of ammunition?" Isabella said wearily as the ground quaked everywhere.

I shook my head in the lamplight. "No. They've collected their shot from St. Elmo and now do the same at Castille. They can cut stone balls for the basilisks here. They are also bringing powder from Barbary, for what they have on Malta no longer suffices."

Before sleep we washed each other's wounds. In the assault, Isabella had received a cut on one arm and had been grazed by an arquebus ball on the other. "What will you do when this is over?" I asked, wincing at the salt water she dripped onto to my shoulder with a rag.

Isabella stared at me in a hard bewilderment and gave her head a single, hollow shake. "What can you mean, Francisco? Do you expect us to live?" Isabella had long won her battle against panic, but her soul still struggled.

"Never forget our pledge," I reminded her and took her rigid form into my arms. Rock dust was falling on us, as always. "Isabella, we will survive. We have not died of thirst. We have not starved." That much could be said. Only the Devil would believe the price of food, two *scudi* for a chicken if you could find one, a *real* and a half for an egg. But thanks to the Grand

Master's foresight, we'd laid in sufficient stores of grain for bread, and because of the rationing it hadn't been exhausted. Water was short; the springs were holding. "Each day renegados tell us the Turks lose more of their spirit. In less than a month the weather will turn. They must either be gone or winter here."

"Winter here ... " Isabella repeated dumbly, leaning against my shoulder. "Francisco, each day at the Hospital I see men who will never walk again, never see again, never hear again. Tho' our soldiers perform miracle after miracle, the Turks can yet summon ten thousand, fifteen to battle. I do not believe Parisot can point to a thousand able to stand."

"A matter of weeks and the issue will be decided." Recollecting Balthazar's words I assured her, "We have seen no portents that presage our defeat ... But you haven't answered me, Isabella. What will you do?"

She could not fathom the question. "I would return to Firenze and write, but ... O Francisco, people today praise the ancients and claim that nowhere in the world does anyone approach the excellence of the Greeks. We far surpass their excellence in our ability to destroy each other. Malta is destroyed and I fear we shall spend years rebuilding her ... How, I do not know."

"Well," I said, as cheerfully as possible, handing her her lute, which we had saved, "let us sing. You know 'The Armed Man,' I think." At that, Isabella burst out laughing, but it was a laugh as if she—or I—were mad. Natheless, she gamely took up her instrument and the famous tune, only to falter after "fear the armed man." "Then," I said as I had before, "for the present you must write poetry." I handed her the book in which she sometimes penned verses, and her feather.

"I am so tired," she said.

"Try," I said.

Isabella wrote in her book for a short while, until she could no longer lift her pen, then fell atop me, dead to the world. *Boom. Boom.*

A few hours later we awoke with a start to an enormous crashing of rock and wood above us that refused to cease. For an endless heartbeat we could not comprehend what was taking place until bits of stone fell through the bars, and we suddenly realized that the entire house was collapsing onto us. As the rumbling stopped, I climbed the ladder but couldn't push aside the grate for all the debris that had fallen atop it.

"*Aiuto!*" I cried and received no answer; the wounded men and slaves who'd slept in the cellar had been crushed to death.

"*Aiuto!*" Isabella and I shouted together. "*Aiuto!*"

Again I put my shoulder to the bars and utterly failed to budge the weight of the stone. We cried and cried but not until dawn did Flaminia herself, walking nearby, hear our muffled shouts. Some townspeople pulled away the rocks and four or five of us climbed from the hole in the ground. We moved the bodies to a pile of such corpses nearby, then Isabella went to the Hospital to treat patients and I to the mill to lean whether any material remained wherewith to make weapons.

At St. Angelo I looked about me. Stores for everything were nearly gone: paper, powder, tow, pitch, liquid resin, juniper oil, alquitran, saltpetre, sulphur. "Another general assault and we'll be finished," I said to the Grand Master when he came by for his daily inspection. His suite followed, including the jester, who of late resembled a soldier, tho' with a red and green jack and a floppy plume fixed to his morion.

"Do not dare utter such words in my presence!" de Valette replied forcefully. "The powder will be finished, mayhap; we, never."

"When the rains begin, Eminenza," I said, "even the powder will be useless."

The jester interrupted. "Old and decrepit," he said with a crooked finger, "my sinews are of iron. Women cannot force me, my feathered offspring break the heart."

Shooting something not quite an evil sneer and not quite a smile at the little man, the Grand Master turned to me. "The armories are full of old crossbows. Have them ready."

Crossbows! Who remembered how to shoot a crossbow? Shaking my head e'en as I prepared to betake myself to the armory, I was forestalled by a runner from the town who approached the Grand Master. "Eminenza," the dirty fellow said, bowing, scratching his cheek, "Piyale has begun to mine Castille."

"A countermine," I said without leave and regretted it, for the Grand Master at once ordered me to Castille with my tambourine. "I am not Tadini," I answered, having once before demonstrated that hard fact.

"Go," de Valette repeated.

I told Diego to see to the crossbows and went.

En route I sought out Balthazar at the French Curtain and found him below, covered as much by bandages as armor, speaking with Francois de

Valette Parisot from Provence. Parisot, who'd commanded the ill-fated
expedition to Malvasia, was proposing to send men across to St. Michel,
for at this moment the place was under attack by a thousand Turks,
whereas Balthazar, seeing a greater number of infidels waiting in the
trenches opposite Castille, thought it unwise. "I believe this is what they
intend us to do and as soon as we go hither, they will attack Castille.
Malheureusement, we no longer have the men to strengthen both places at
once."

Of a sudden, the jester, running from the square, appeared and told the
Knights to stay put. Robles's men at St. Michel were holding. "They fight
as Samson with the jawbone of an ass." Parisot and Balthazar sighed, sat
down near a wine barrel. "The Turks continue their bombardment to no
purpose," the Abbé said, regarding me as I did the curtain above us, which
was in a better state than most of the works. "They merely move rock
from one place to another."

Aye. The only thing separating Robles's men at St. Michel from the
infidel trenches were the rocks the soldiers carried back into place after
the guns had moved them.

Hereat, seeing the Knight's gaze fall on the tambourine in my hand, I
said, "I'm to Castille to stop the Turkish mine. I would your help,
Balthazar. I am no mining engineer."

"You did well enow at St. Michel's," he answered with a certain
resignation. "Francisco, I can be of no assistance. You and the other
engineers know more of these matters than I."

Both of us knew that luck alone had guided our success at St. Michel,
but what struck me more was the leave-taking I heard in Balthazar's voice.
Not wishing to say farewell on such a note, I asked what he would do once
the siege ended.

"*Moy foy*," he smiled, "perhaps I should finally become a true Abbé.
Nay, that wouldn't sit well, would it, my friend? Mayhap it is at last time
to retire to write my memoirs. On the other hand, I have long wanted to
see the Newfound World and meet savages who don't know any better ...
" Balthazar laid his hand on my shoulder as of old, tho' the pain of that
simple act was written across his face. "Thank you for the question. I shall
have something to dream on tonight."

With that I left him and hurried to Castille.

The night next Francisco Balbi sat at St. Michel near Juan de la Cerda. As always, the Captain kept to himself, but no one at all was speaking much this evening. Two days ago the Turks had built a covered trench running from the barrels near the ravelin across to Robles's Post. It let them pass quickly to whichever place proved easier to enter, and yesterday a thousand infidels decided Robles's post was the weaker. The men fought for three hours, killing one or two hundred, finally repulsing the attack, but by now after each engagement every soldier felt in his bones that strength did not easily return. Thank God the same was true of the enemy, who rested for ever longer periods between assaults.

"May I say, Señor," Balbi ventured to la Cerda, "I do not know what took place at Fort St. Elmo, or why some men treat you with disdain when Aguilar and Vergã have betrayed us and Fuster enjoys the esteem of his comrades. I can only judge what I have seen with my own eyes, and no one has fought with greater bravery than you, Messer. You no longer need prove your valor, if that is what you have been attempting to do."

la Cerda returned a half-smile, saying the Grand Master alone assumed the right to bestow valor. Thereat he struggled up, preparing to move further away, when Maestro de Campo Robles himself appeared and waved the two men up to the ramparts behind him. After today's bombardment, Robles wanted to see the condition of the defenses.

"Maestro—" Balbi said, seeing that Robles carried his helmet in the crook of his arm.

It was too late. A crack from an arquebus and the Maestro de Campo fell over without uttering a sound. Balbi and la Cerda immediately called for help. Alfonso and some others helped them carried Robles down from the walls, but there was nothing for it. Before dawn he had died.

As news of the Maestro de Campo's death swept Birgu and Senglea, a great wail arose from the Christian forces. Robles had kept Fort St. Michel alive thro' the strength of his will alone, and no one could replace him. To make matters worse, a few hours later his Lieutenant, Muñatones, died from the wounds he'd received during the general assault. The Grand Master had Robles's body placed in San Lorenzo in a splendid coffin draped with black velvet, hoping to send his mortal remains to his relatives should God grant a favorable outcome. He ordered old Bailiff of Eagle to take charge of St. Michel, but everyone already knew what a terrible catastrophe we had sustained.

"There cannot be a worse omen," said Tiberio, one of the mining engineers, as we burrowed out from Castille. "It is the worst thing since the fall of St. Elmo itself. The Turks will now win this war and slaughter every one of us."

"Shut your trap," I answered. "Robles was a brave man. Other brave men shall take his place and we will survive. Let us dig."

The Turks were attempting to undermine Castille, but we could not at once determine where, for they'd rightly put the entrance to their shafts far up the hills. No one could doubt, tho', that Piyale would soon assault the breaches, we had so few men to defend them And so we decided: Before trying to discover their mine, we would put gunpowder in our own and when the Turks stormed the ruins of Castille, we'd fire it and destroy them.

We dug and dug, making certain the shaft twisted and turned to the agreed place. This time, we placed bellows and a leather hose in the tunnel, to little effect. Who knows why, but men need fresh air. The foulness and heat below exhausted us until, sweating and fainting, we decided to take turns at the work. Always a few had ears to the walls or ground.

"I hear them," one of the sappers said.

Instantly we fell silent and listened. With my head against the wall, I wiped the snot from my nose and nodded. Aye, Turkish picks and shovels were at work in the distance. How far? Which way? Above us? Below us? Most urgently, Would they blow us to bits? With my finger to my lips, I held up the tambourine, but as I'd warned the Grand Master, I was not blessed with Tadini's sixth sense. Neither were Tiberio or the other engineers. Tho' I believed I was mastering the black art of discerning the direction of a Turkish mine from the dance of amber, my comrades placed no stock in such witchcraft, and Tiberio proposed instead we examine the entrails of chickens.

"If we argue much longer," I said, "we will do so for eternity, for the Turks will blow us to Heaven. Do we go after them?"

We decided to halt and make the space for our powder here. Working frantically, we hollowed out a small room above the shaft and brought in eight casks of gunpowder from the post. We sprinkled powder on a long fuse, which we let all the way out of the shaft; we ran like the wind for fear of a spark, and we waited in the cistern for the Turkish assault.

We waited. Night fell and no attack came. Not knowing the cause, Tiberio and I thought to check the powder and crawled back into the mine. Halfway to the room, we discovered a hole in our shaft and realized at once that the Turks had tapped it. I drew my sword and we crept onward. Soon, we reached the space where we had placed the powder and our worst fears were confirmed. Every cask—gone. We got a few more men and torches and crept into their shaft, but they seemed to have left off the mine and no one was about. We sealed it with a few kegs of powder.

At last, returning to the post, we sat despondently in the cistern, trying to decide what to do next. We hardly had powder to waste on another mine, but we must discover the enemy's whereabouts. Our spirits sank lower. Someone climbed into the cistern to tell us that a white dove had come to roost for several hours in San Lorenzo on the most sacred image of Our Lady of Filermos. This portended a good outcome to the siege, most of us believed.

One Hundred Seven

When the *chavush* Abdallah al-Waryagli, just arrived with dispatches from Constantinople, put in at Marsamxett harbor, the soldiers guarding the fleet anchored there at once offered to escort him to Mustafa Pasha *Hazretleri*'s pavilion, which from where they stood would take the time for the sun to rise a palm. The emissary listened, agitated, confused. Yesterday, while yet far out to sea, he first felt the rumble of what with astonishment he took to be distant siege guns. By the time he reached the island the sound had become deafening and his first thought was to return to Constantinople. Having made land, he was assaulted by something more evil than the ceaseless thunder—the smell. He'd noticed it half a league out, the stench of corruption, decay, the presence of death. Throughout—and most keenly when he sighted the Sultan's great fleet at anchor—one question found its way again and again to his lips: Why is the Padishah's invincible army yet on this island?

Abdallah al-Waryagli followed his escort up the hill the Maltese called Sciberras, and watched oxen trudge past him pulling wagons loaded with ammunition toward the guns firing at the big fortress. One of the soldiers pointed down the long slope to the flag of the Sultan flying over the remains of the Santarma tower. *Evet*, Abdallah well remembered hauling stones for that place and was glad to see it destroyed, but he was not pleased when the guide told him what it had cost. "Nearly six thousand men, *Hazretleriniz*."

Abruptly the *chavush* halted, finally losing his disbelief at what had become evident: "The *kafilar* have not yielded, is that what you tell me?"

"By the Prophet's Beard," another answered, "they are beaten, *Hazretleriniz*. There are no more towers to take, just stones."

"But they have not yielded?"

The soldier shook his head. "No, *Hazretleriniz*, they have not yielded."

As they crossed the great harbor in a small boat to save walking around, the death smell became so overpowering that Abdallah al-Waryagli retched into the water. "We have lost more than ten thousand to the fighting and another ten thousand to sickness," the soldier said, paying little attention. "We cannot burn all the bodies. There are too many."

"How could this have happened?" al-Waryagli asked, erupting again.

"It is the Will of Allah, Master of the Day of Judgment," replied the soldier.

Long before the emissary reached Mustafa's pavilion, on the heights above the smoke-enshrouded town he remembered and hated so well, he'd covered his mouth and nose with the end of his turban and was shaking with rage. When he was presented to Mustafa, tho', he bowed deeply, asking that the Blessing of Allah and his Peace be upon the Commander.

Mustafa wanted to know whether the Sultan had received news of the fall of the Santarma tower.

"Yes, he received your letter with this good news, but not before in his impatience he wrote to the Doge of Venice to learn what had happened to you." al-Waryagli handed the Sultan's sealed letter directly to Mustafa. Whether Soliman had received a reply from the Doge he did not know, but en route to Malta the *chavush* had been pleased to learn that, when news of St. Elmo's fall reached Venice, the Venetians had danced in the streets.

"How has the Sultan greeted my request for reinforcements?" Mustafa asked.

al-Waryagli stared at him. "I know of no such request. And how is it possible that you should require reinforcements to reduce this small island, which was to take but a week?" The *chavush*'s anger was overtaking deference. "I tell you, Mustafa Pasha *Hazretleri*, if you return to Constantinople without having reduced this island, every one of the officers will be torn to pieces—after they are beheaded. If you return in triumph, every honor and riches beyond imagining shall be bestowed upon you and your men."

During this speech, Piyale Pasha entered the marquee and offered to take the fleet out some distance from the island and fire the guns in a splendid salute, as if to greet reinforcements, thus frightening the infidels. Mustafa accepted the plan, but it was clear to the lowliest servant in the tent that the emissary had put a great fear into both *Pashalar* and they at once renewed their determination to crush the enemy. Before discussing matters further with the *chavush*, tho', Mustafa pointed out that he must be weary after his long journey and suggested he rest before supper. A tent near the Pasha's own would be provided.

With a bow, Abdallah removed himself from Mustafa's presence and was guided through the camp. Not many steps away he halted, having caught sight of a wounded *yenicheri* sitting near a tall infidel, both of whom seemed familiar. He addressed the *yenicheri*. "You, do I know you?"

Yakhshi struggled to his feet. "*Hiyer*, we met at the Gun Foundry in Stamboul."

"Tell me," said the emissary, "what has happened here?"

For a moment the *Boluk-bashi* knitted his brows. "Much has happened here. I could spend all night telling you what has happened here, but you would not believe me. We did not expect to be confronted with so many fire weapons or such armor. More, we did not expect to meet a foe who would prefer to die to the last man than to yield. Most of all, we forgot that Allah does not love him who is boastful and that pride carries men off to Hell."

"You speak as if the battle is lost."

"A week ago another two thousand men fell in a mighty assault. The *Pashalar* have begun to beat men who refuse to fight. Hundreds of soldiers and oarsmen die each day of sickness in the stomach and supplies from Cezayir-i Garb and Trablus have been interrupted."

Abdallah, indeed, could scarcely believe he was hearing such words from a *yenicheri*, let alone a valorous *Boluk-bashi*. "Come with me to my tent and tell me more," he said.

Yakhshi shook his head, turning to the infidel by him. "I must watch this one."

"Who is he?" asked the *chavush*, certain he knew the man.

"Ah," said Yakhshi.

Such was the panic and disorder in the retreat from the fort of the mills a week ago, each soldier expecting to run straight into the Spanish relief, that no one actually paid much attention to the Spaniard who had come up shouting and waving at the rear of the column. He managed not to be shot and was instead swept along in the cascade of men moving up the hill. Only after the army understood the great debacle that had befallen it and was marching in wearied anger back to the main camp, did someone agree to take the new man to Mustafa, but by that time Yakhshi had caught sight of him.

The *yenicheri* immediately recognized him as Francisco's companion who had tried to take him to the camp a month ago. At once Yakhshi ordered the soldiers to halt and himself ran to the Pasha. Only after the *Boluk-bashi* repeatedly insisted the matter was urgent did Mustafa, whose humor was as terrible as it had been since the siege began, admit him. Yakhshi thought to bow deeply, asking that many blessings of Allah the All Wise and All Knowing be bestowed upon Mustafa, and said, "I believe he intends to kill you, *Zat-i Aliniz.*"

Mustafa thanked him for the warning, ordered the sullen Spaniard to be stripped of his weapons and brought before him under guard. Hearing out the newcomer through the *dragoman*, Mustafa appeared to greet his pleas favorably and ordered the infidel to be taken to Aghalar's tent, commanding Yakhshi to keep an eye on him. The *yenicheri* had no desire to play nursemaid to a *kafir*, but led him to Aghalar's pavilion, bringing a *dragoman* along.

That night Yakhshi sat in the tent with an *oda-bashi* as the two Spaniards talked. He didn't understand anything except for what the *dragoman* told him afterwards, but the two men appeared not to know each other well and guarded their speech.

"Do you find the food in the Turkish camp better?" the one called Verghond asked Aghalar, who was about the same age.

Aghalar nodded. "Much."

"You were right to go over," Verghond proposed. "The situation is hopeless. Malta must fall soon."

The remark brightened Aghalar's countenance. "I could not hope even to protect my wife," he said with a small frown. "I have heard you have wanted to turn Turk."

"You speak of those infamous *libelli*?"

Aghalar shook his head. "No, men who were with you on your enterprises say when you were losing at gambling you always renounced God and wanted to turn. They say you once went off to Greece, holing up in a village for weeks, saying that if the Order denied you, you would go to Turkey. I think you will now see Turkey."

Verghond shrugged. "It's all true, but what do I care? The Order has
denied me. I cannot gain the privileges rightfully mine. So, if the Turks
advance me, I'll fight for them. Maybe I'll become an Admiral."

"Mayhap we both will," said Aghalar with a smile. "You have no
regrets?"

Again this Verghond shrugged. "Only one. That a certain woman has
also denied me, and because of that foolishness she will surely lose her
head."

Having heard all this through the *dragoman*, Yakhshi decided that
Verghond did intend to come over, after all. At the same time he did not
think he would like this fellow very much.

Abdallah al-Waryagli could not follow every detail of the story the
yenicheri was telling him, but now looked more closely at the *kafir*. Slowly
the haze of time lifted. "You are Francisco's companion, who once tried
to kill me on Lampedusa, aren't you?"

Blaij returned only a sullen gaze, but Yakhshi now better recollected
the *chavush*. "*Evet*, you were Francisco's master in Stamboul. Yes. Francisco
and this one brought me into the camp a month ago when I was captured."

"Francisco alive?" asked Abdallah with some perplexity. "That is
pleasant to know." He told Yakhshi to bring their guest along to his tent.
Undoubtedly he would have interesting things to say.

Once Yakhshi had recounted to the *chavush* all that had taken place on
Malta over the past three months, Abdallah al-Waryagli turned his
attention back to Vergã, who had remained silent throughout. "So, Blaij
Vergã," he said in Spanish, "you intend to fight for us. Why?"

"The situation in the towns is hopeless," Vergã answered directly.
"Why be slaughtered by Mustafa? And everyone knows the Turks pay
better."

Despite the stench that pervaded the air, Abdallah was forced to laugh.
"There is a suspicion you intend to kill Mustafa Pasha. Why should we
trust you?"

Though the Spaniard sat captive in the Turkish camp, he yet displayed
a certain bravado, claiming that if he intended to kill Mustafa, the Pasha
would already be dead. "Aghalar," Yakhshi put in, "also said this
Verghond has long wanted to become a Knight but because of his birth
the infidel grand ayatollah refused to allow it."

"*Evet*," replied Abdallah, "the *kafilar* place great stock in matters of birth."

While the *chavush* fell into silence, pondering what he'd heard, Vergã surprised him by saying, "Tell me, Abdallah al-Waryagli, did Barai turn Turk while a slave in Constantinople?"

al-Waryagli stared at him with a grim amusement. "He never told you the story of the whore and the mad king?" Vergã returned a blank look. "No? During his time as my slave he told me much about you ... " For a moment Abdallah stroked his grey beard, regarding the soldier before him. "I think I shall buy you and take you to Constantinople. Then you may decide for yourself."

Vergã's eyes darted, like a cornered animal's. For a moment he seemed preparing to rise, to flee, but then he sank back, as if wholly, finally defeated.

Again Abdallah laughed. "On the other hand, I imagine the defenders have reached an unfathomable desperation by now. Perhaps you have indeed come to carry out a heroic act to prove yourself to the Grand Master—may his name be driven away by the sands of time! I shall propose to Mustafa that you fight in the next assault and we shall see where your loyalties lie."

Abdallah did not fully perceive the Turkish forces' discontent. The next day Mustafa and Piyale personally walked thro' the heat of the camp, calling the *yenicheriler* officers together. As they gathered about the *Pashalar* under the sun, in front of their tents and pots, Mustafa announced that another grand assault would be made on the fortress of the mills and the post called Castille. It would be the final, the supreme effort, and no retreat would be sounded until they had heroically taken the towers. Mustafa's astonishment could not have been etched more deeply in the wrinkles of his face: An absolute silence greeted him. Both he and Piyale glanced around, frowning, sensing the seething anger among the troops. The silence persisted, as oppressive as the sharp stink pervading the air, when of a sudden, without any warning even to himself, Yakhshi the *Boluk-bashi* did the unthinkable—he kicked over one of the breakfast cauldrons with his foot.

"We will not go," he said.

Mustafa Pasha regarded the warrior with horror and rage. That this *yenicheri* had won fame for his courage and had even been awarded a *timar* for his valor at Santarma did not long prevent Mustafa's fury from erupting. "Beat that man at once!" he screamed at the top of his lungs. "Beat him until death!"

Not a *yenicheri* or *spahi* moved.

"We will not fight," someone else shouted. "Too many brave warriors have died. Every man among us is wounded. We want to go back to Constantinople."

Mustafa saw he had a rebellion on his hands and that he must tread like a doe. If they returned to Constantinople without having taken the island, he told them, they would all lose their heads and the shame would be everlasting, in this life and the next. "The *chavush* who has arrived from the Sultan has said this exactly." Mustafa clapped his hands and had Abdallah al-Waryagli sent for at once, who confirmed everything.

But the *yenicheriler* weren't cowed and the sea of faces before Mustafa began to churn. For the first time since they'd set foot on this accursed isle, Yakhshi saw fear written across the countenance of Mustafa Pasha *Hazretleri*. Piyale, tho', for perhaps the first time since the siege began, refused to dispute the Commander. "Mustafa Pasha is right!" he shouted. "We cannot return to Constantinople in shame and dishonor, and I will not permit the Padishah's invincible armada to sail until the towers are taken. What are you afraid of, Sons of the Sultan? We must simply walk over the rubble."

"We have heard those empty words before!" a *chorbaji* shouted.

The men will not fight, Yakhshi saw, but the *Pashalar* will not yield. Somehow they must find a way out of this impasse, to save honor for everyone. "We will fight," he cried anew, "if Mustafa himself leads us!"

The men called the Pasha many names, but old as he was, "coward" was never one of them, and so Yakhshi wasn't surprised when Mustafa agreed. "I will lead you," he said, "as I have led you before." The Commander also announced that his engineers had devised light wooden helmets to wear under their turbans that would protect them from rocks and arquebus. These would be ready in a few days' time. The *azablar* should also dress in the clothing of *yenicheriler* and *spahiler*, and anyone who took part in the assault would receive extra pay of five *akcheler*. While these preparations were being made, the troops should rest and the gunners would inflict on the infidels such a bombardment that they would wish they had never been born.

One Hundred Eight

Over the next week our spirits sank to their lowest depths. For four days the Turks bombarded us without pause and with a fury equal to the most intense of their earlier batteries. Balthazar, as we huddled in the cistern at Castille, repeated that it was to no purpose, for the fortifications could hardly be more leveled than they already were. But without finding a jest, we watched the breaches there widen by the day and more houses in the Borgo and on Senglea crumble to the ground. Each morning in the dark townsfolk struggled with the wreckage above them and climbed from their holes, wondering that the sun rose.

Knowing another assault loomed, the engineers at Castille never ceased digging countermines in a desperate attempt to uncover Piyale's own before it uncovered us. We succeeded. We tapped into their mine and fired it; they dug another. The deadly game continued day and night. We knew that the moment they won, the curtain at Castille would come down and the next assault be upon us. We no longer had enough men to defend the breaches.

If ought prevented us from falling into complete and utter despair, it was the Grand Master, who never ceased to walk among us, sleeping at the most dangerous posts, always speaking of triumph and never of defeat. But even de Valette could not prevent the Turks from attacking and the assault came. The Turks themselves warned us. At St. Michel, many of the renegados in the trenches took pity on the perilous condition of the fort and often called out to the men:

"Hold on, you dogs, for you have not many oxen to kill. Only sheep are left and they are not fat!"

"There is not much flour and after the next banquet you may take a nap!"

Well, what they lacked in fat oxen they made up for in heavy iron, and tho' flour might have been running low, they had plenty enow for bread.

Thus, the nineteenth of August. The Pashas bombarded us without mercy and at dawn on the twentieth they gave the signal. For the Turkish soldiers, it was to be a last, supreme, heroic effort to take Birgu and Senglea. Once again they threw eight thousand troops against St. Michel and another four at Castille. This time they did not stop. For three days the fighting went on, with hardly a respite for either side. Those three days, of utter and complete desperation, surrounded the Borgo not only with a smoke that we would cough up from our lungs for weeks, but with a cloud of stories and confusion no one ever dispelled. Many are the tales and no fewer the versions of them.

Some swore that a great roar signaled the attack. "The mine!" people in Birgu were crying. "Piyale's mine!" The curtain came down and the Turks stormed in. I heard no mine explode, but by the fourth day of the bombardment, new breaches had opened up everywhere, huge breaches. What I remember on that day, what I saw, was Piyale's ensign rising above the walls. The women of Birgu saw it too, from their houses, and it struck them with terror.

Running through the streets, they shouted, *"It-Torok dahlu l-belt!* The Turks are in Birgu!"

Flaminia herself tripped over Romegas's feet, crying the same. Amidst this chaos, several Knights were also dashing toward the square, making signs to the Grand Master at the clock tower that the Turks were well advanced into the Borgo and that he must incontinently retire to Castle St. Angelo.

As on the earlier time, Eminenza would have none of it. He took his half-pike and his helmet from the pages, said that if today was their day to die, so be it. He ordered Romegas after him and his *soccorso*, of which but fifty men remained, and in a mass they advanced toward Castille against the stream of terrified townsfolk, not seeing a single enemy. While de Valette marched one way, the panic spread quickly in the other, as far as St. Angelo, where one of the gunners above opened fire on the town itself. Without doubt this gunner thought he was laying his piece against the Turks, but instead killed seven or eight of our soldiers.

The Grand Master pressed on to the walls and, seeing Piyale's standard and the other infidel ensigns brazenly confronting him, he shouted that he would have them removed from his sight and his men rushed forward to tear them down.

As the confusion unfolded, Piyale advanced his mine, but our engineers discovered it and we chased the enemy sappers away with fire, then closed the shaft. Piyale, raging, increased the fury of his bombardment for the rest of the day. The Grand Master's men, again, pleaded with him to retire to a safer place but still he refused, saying that an old man could wish for a no more glorious death than one met in fighting with his brethren in the name of God. With his pike in his hand, he fought as a simple soldier.

The general assault came the next day, on Castille and St. Michel at dawn. I crouched with Balthazar by one of the breaches, watching Piyale himself cudgel his soldiers towards us, watching azabs attempting without success to pass themselves off as janissaries as they charged. Arrows flew at our positions, but fewer than on previous engagements—the Turks were running out. We took little joy from this. Looking around, our defenders were spread so thinly, and our fire weapons and powder stores were insufficient to last beyond this battle. Women and children stood amongst the soldiers with rocks or pikes, Isabella and Flaminia both; no one gainsaid them. Had the enemy no weapons at all, he could yet crush us by sheer weight of numbers.

"Balthazar ... " I said wearily and we embraced each other as once more the Turks came upon us.

It was a day of visions. Mustafa, as he had sworn, led the assault against Fort St. Michel. Yakhshi saw an arquebusier above fire at the Pasha and knock his turban clean off, stunning him, and causing the old Commander to fall from his horse. Like a pig, Mustafa crawled to the ditch and hid there until dark.

Ix-Xabaw was again at the Post of Bormla. He had by now been too wounded to fight much, but he carried water and ammunition as he could. Some men called from the ravelin for more powder and balls. Pietru found a bucket of shot and struggled to carry it over. By the time he had lumbered across the ditch, the enemy was storming the work. He watched the janissaries and corsairs below suddenly part, making way for their engineers, who were rolling up a huge barrel encircled with iron hoops and filled with powder, chain, iron thistles, nails and arquebus balls. They lit the fuse and managed to heave it over the ravelin. Pietru covered himself, expecting to awake in Heaven, but he opened his eyes and saw that he remained in Hell.

"The match is long!" everyone cried at once. Together the men bent to the barrel, lifted it to their shoulders and hurled it back over the wall at the enemy. Only then did the infernal machine explode with a terrific blast, sending smoke, entrails and heads into the air. Such was the destruction caused by their own device that the Turks, screaming in agony and terror, fled headlong to their trenches, with the Christians after them. It was a massacre.

Later that day, the next, Balbi himself saw with his own eyes Cheder, the splendidly dressed Sanjak-Bey of Bosnia, go down. Cheder's men stormed the breaches of St. Michel with renewed fury, vowing to avenge their leader. In the next moments Balbi watched Juan de la Cerda, with a single, fiery glance toward him, rush out to be buried under the onslaught. The old arquebusier hesitated, crossed himself and resumed firing. He never forgot the glance la Cerda had thrown him and hoped his soul had at last found peace.

For myself, I saw the enemy advancing, in the morning, in the afternoon, hundreds wearing the new wooden morions for what protection they afforded. I saw our numbers and stores dwindle by the hour. We tried everything. We larded cannon balls so that when we fired them they might cause the robes of the attackers to go up in flame. Our success was slight. I saw Turkish fireworks launched into the sky and our own fire circles answer them. Hours passed. Without warning the wall near where I stood came down with a colossal roar and thro' the dust I saw a great breach. I raised my eyes and saw the black figure of Death, striding above us and the enemy.

"In the name of God, look!" I crossed myself and pointed, gathered Isabella to me. "Do you see it?" With a half-pike in her hand she nodded. The vision was as corporeal as had it been made flesh, if not flesh, then something infinitely more evil.

I lowered my gaze to the smoke and flames. There, advancing with the infidel troops, I saw Blaij Vergã. Loading my weapon, I made ready to fire, but Isabella, seeing the enemy streaming toward the gaps in the wall, had already run forward with her spear, prepared to die. Vergã, charging up the rubble, raised his eyes and halted. He drew himself up to his full height and for a heartbeat stood motionless, facing her, then turned as if to shield her from the oncoming enemy. Some saw in his expression an unfathomable perplexity, others an infinite remorse in a final realization of everything he had done, and still others genuine love. I think he was startled.

The moment was enough.

As Blaij stood frozen before Isabella, Balthazar strode up, shouted, "Those who do not fear death never die!" and with one blow of his *montante* took the traitor's head. The Knight picked it off the ground by the hair, spat on it and tossed it to Romegas's feet. As the Commander recoiled in amazement, one of his soldiers snatched it up and sat it on a pike. Balthazar watched, nodding gravely to Romegas, and declared the wager to be won. It was then that the arquebus ball caught Balthazar under the arm. He tottered.

"Balthazar!" I cried, running up, grabbing him. With my arquebus in one hand and my other arm under his shoulder, I led him from the post. "Is it bad?" I said.

"Sufficiently," he groaned, all the while refusing to release his sword.

With soldiers and common folk running every way and that, we staggered thro' the town to the Hospital. The place was, as it had been for weeks, overflowing, but I would not yield in my determination to get aid for the Knight at once. Moving aside two men lying on the street, I sat Balthazar between them, against the wall, and ran for Vigo. In my desperation I stumbled over wounded men in the courtyard, tripped over the steps to the upper stories, fell across rocks strewn along the corridors. At last I found the physician in a ward whose roof was open to the sky.

"Dr. Jean! Balthazar has been hit. Come instantly!"

As he had on other recent occasions, Vigo raised his hands, helplessly. "Francisco," he said, casting his gaze about him.

"In the name of friendship and all that is good, come at once, I beg you."

After a few eternal moments, Vigo freed himself and ran with me to the street. We removed the Knight's cuirass and pauldrons and operated where he lay. Vigo went at the ball with a long rod and forceps. With no drugs, the pain was so great that Balthazar was roaring his lungs out, and near fainted dead away, but at length Vigo found what he was searching for. "The wound is bad and I haven't any ... digestive to treat it. Fetch water, Francisco. The barrels are inside." I ran, carrying the water back in Balthazar's helmet and we did our best to wash the puncture. I ripped off my jack and we bandaged Balthazar with my own shirt, but he was bleeding badly.

"You must return to the walls now," said Vigo, laying his hand on my shoulder.

"I won't leave him," I said.

The doctor answered with a severe gaze. "Francisco, there is nothing more you can do. If Birgu falls today, all our work—his work—will have been in vain. Do not fear, I shall attend him."

"Go," whispered Balthazar himself in a voice barely heard. I slowly rose, not taking my eyes from the Abbé, who lay in a twilight between life and death. Seeing I was unable to move, the physician once more urged me to my post. While I stood rooted, the Grand Master himself, surrounded by his suite, hobbled up the street to the Sacra Infermeria. He had again been wounded in the leg and was using his lance as a crutch while Romegas aided him.

"Doctor!" Romegas shouted. "At once!"

But the Grand Master shook his head and ordered Romegas to aid him into the courtyard. I followed. There, in this half-ruined building, as Vigo himself knelt to attend the Monsignore's wounds, de Valette addressed the hundreds lying everywhere about him. "My children, the enemy is gaining the walls, our numbers are dwindling. Soon the Infidel will be within the Holy Convent itself. My own nephew, François Parisot, has just died before my eyes. I do not ask of you anything I do not ask of myself. I shall now return to the breach. I beg any of you who have one leg or one arm, who, if you cannot fight, can carry food or ammunition, to follow me now, for God, for your wives and children, for Christendom. Here we make our stand. Should Malta fall this day, I need not tell you what awaits civilization."

The Grand Master, gently freeing himself from Vigo's hands, limped out thro' the main door of the Sacra Infermeria. The physician rose. He, I watched many of these men, arms, heads and legs broken or burnt, some missing limbs altogether and others resembling the dead in burial shrouds, struggle to their feet. Some fell in the effort and a few died. With tears in my eyes I embraced Vigo and went out after the Grand Master to the street. To my astonishment, Balthazar was himself rising, more tottering, against the door of the Infermeria. "Balthazar," I said in alarm, "you cannot ... you must rest."

"Just help me. If I am to die, I would die with my sword."

I handed him his *montante*, which had all this time lain by him, and told him to wait here. Then I picked my way thro' the chaotic streets to the mill at St. Angelo.

I had made another *tromba de fuego* and carried it first back to the Infermeria. Balthazar had already moved ahead with the other soldiers as, arms under shoulders, they staggered to the Post of Castille. I could not comprehend what force gave these men the strength to make that journey, to throw themselves again into the fray. I watched a near-dead Abbé pick up a weapon with one hand that many would find too heavy to lift with two, and swing it as had St. Michel himself stood before me. I watched others equally injured perform prodigies of heroism, with lances or clubs or buckets or bread. I watched women and children fight with slings and rocks with a valor that ceded nothing to the men.

Amidst the swirling smoke, I walked along the walls with another fellow working the pump of my *tromba*, wreaking every havoc I could. No, this was the next day. The Turks attacked with the same fury. As their stores of arrows lessened, they made more deadly use of throwing spears. So few were we the defenders that only the Turks' own weariness prevented Castille from being taken. The battle was ferocious, but it was a ferocity after months of fighting, as were both besiegers and besieged struggling through a bog.

In an instant it changed. Towards the breach advanced a Turk carrying his own *tromba de fuego*. Worse, this fire tube he held on the end of a long pole was packed with shot the size of pigeons' eggs. This soldier, gaining the walls, began a massacre of our men with his weapon. I cannot say how many he killed, but this man alone with his *tromba* was putting terror into the hearts of the defenders, who began to panic. Seeing his success he mounted the ruined ramparts and turned it onto our fire weapons that had been stacked up nearby. At once they all went up, spitting forth smoke and sparks, whizzing into the sky with a great conflagration.

Witnessing this, I ran down to the breach and with my *tromba* set fire to all the powder sacks the Turks had brought up. Everywhere around me they ignited with an evil exhalation, shooting flames high into the air. The heat was unbearable and the smoke so thick I could hardly see a thing. I wheeled about to go after my foe and somewhere above the breach we met, turning our fire tubes on one another. I do not know exactly what happened next, a clunk, one of his balls hitting my morion. I staggered backwards as the longer flame from my *tromba* burnt him and he fled.

I awoke outside the Infermeria, next to Balthazar, who was propped up senseless against the wall. Isabella knelt by us, washing my right arm, which was alive with pain from the burns it had received. Watching her drift in and out of my sight, I slowly perceived that something was awry. "I think my left eye is blinded," I said.

She moved her hand from one side to the other and soon confirmed it. "You have been hit on the side of the head and there are burns," she said.

I struggled up on my arms. "Does the assault continue?"

Isabella shook her head. "The Turks have retired for the evening, but I fear that there is so little more we can do, we shall soon be at their mercy."

"Balthazar?" I glanced toward the Knight, seeing that he yet breathed, softly. "What happened?"

"God touched him with a divine strength," Isabella replied, this time shaking her head with wonder, "but he did not spare himself. The wound ... We must pray." Thereon she wiped a tear from her eye.

Tho' the Turks had retired from the walls at a great loss, fifteen hundred or more over those days of chaos, the defenses of Castille were utterly ruined. The same evening, I think, mayhap the next day or the one after, the Seigneurs of the Council assembled in the Magisterial Palace with His Eminence and trusted lieutenants to make the most desperate decision of their lives.

"We must abandon Birgu and move all the remaining Knights and soldiers into the castle." Romegas, seated at the Grand Master's right hand in the ring of chairs around the chamber wall, spoke the words, but every member of the Council present agreed, from Grand Mareschal Copier, to the Bailiff of Eagle, to the Bishop of Malta, to Oliver Starkey for the Turcopilier. With equal urgency they must carry the hand of the Baptist, the image of Our Lady of Filermos and all the most sacred relics of the Order from the town into St. Angelo. As Isabella had decided earlier, they must pray.

"Succour from Europe, if it ever comes, is too late," Romegas went on. "Now, here is the moment to remember the words of the Council at Rhodes to l'Isle Adam." Everyone present knew them.

One began: "When all human hope is gone, it is our duty to try to come to terms, so that we may vindicate our loss at another time and place ... ."

Another: "Wise men surrender to necessity. No matter how praiseworthy our death, let us consider whether it may not be more damaging to the Holy Religion than our surrender."

For a moment there was only the sound of the guns, a shaft of light from the setting sun, whereon Eagle or Copier added, "They will say of us as Carlos did of Rhodes, 'Nothing was so well lost.'"

When they had finished, de Valette hesitated, grasped the crutch by him and stepped down from the throne. Silently, he limped out of the Magisterial Palace and across to the Chapel of St. Anne, where he knelt above the crypt of l'Isle Adam.

"'When all human hope is gone ... ' That is what they have told you, isn't it?" de Valette turned to see his ward, who sat on a bench near him in the shadows of this dark, damp place.

The Grand Master asked why she was here.

"I caught sight of the Crosses and Bailiffs retiring to the castle amidst the panic," she said, "and foresaw what was to take place."

In the light of the tapers, Parisot nodded to Isabella. He regarded her dress, which was torn and covered with dirt and blood, and her bandaged arms. "I am now faced with the most difficult choice I have ever made. The Council to a man desires to retire to St. Angelo—"

"—and abandon the towns."

"*Si.* We have nothing any longer wherewith to defend them, but if we withdraw to the castle, the Turks will surely overrun the Borgo and Senglea, and we in St. Angelo shall find ourselves besieged by our own people as well as the barbarians."

"Parisot," his goddaughter knelt beside him with tears filling her eyes, "you cannot be contemplating this. We will fight with crossbows and rocks, but you cannot abandon your children who have laid down their lives for you by the thousands in this great trial."

de Valette reached out his hand toward her face and stroked her wet, bloodied cheek. "No, of course not, but I needed to gather my strength to confront them. The last days have been difficult. Thank you, Isabella. Help me to my feet."

The Grand Master returned to the hall and said to the Seigneurs the same words, that he would not abandon the rude people in the towns who

had fought so well, that the members of the Council had best be prepared
to die with them.

No one can doubt that, had de Valette heeded the Council's advice, the
siege would have been lost the next day—the next hour—and that the
Turks would have sat on Europe's threshold. When word spread that the
Council had abandoned them, Flaminia fell to her knees in despair, fairly
crawling into her church, asking the Blessed Mother why she had forsaken
her children. Her anger at the Seigneurs was shared by everyone, and from
then on they could hardly walk Birgu's streets in safety. Only the Grand
Master, appearing at the square, at the posts, was able to assure the people
he would die before letting them fall into the enemy's hands. Even in
those early moments, Your Majesty, we knew that for years to come the
people would sing the Grand Master's praise for his iron strength in
disregarding those who disregarded them.

Natheless, it seemed we were to die. Throughout the next day, baked
by the heat, arquebusiers arrayed themselves around the breaches and
waited. If the Turks had but attacked, victory would have been theirs.
Our powder and shot was as nearly finished as we were and, with few fire
weapons at hand, the Grand Master ordered the crossbows given out.

"We have been reduced to this," I said to Pietru in the Birgu armory
as we strung the weapons and put them in the hands of arquebusiers.

"They are more trustworthy than guns," answered Ix-Xabaw with a
faint shrug.

Truly. The Turks, tho', as emptied of strength as we, did not at once
attack. They rested. Somehow Mustafa and Piyale retained an adamantine
determination to take us by any means possible. The Admiral ordered his
sappers to construct a platform directly against the wall of Castille to
dominate the post, as the ravelin had at Fort St. Elmo, but in the dead of
night Commander Claremont of Aragon led forth a small group of men
to chase away the guards. With the platform, fortified by terre-plein,
mattresses and even felt padding turned against him, Piyale gave up plans
of an immediate assault. At the same time, he closed the mouth of the
Great Port with a chain of ship masts and planks, to what purpose none
of us could discern. We weren't about to escape. We surmised that their
spies had gotten word of the relief.

What the Turks failed to grasp during those few days is that we would have died without them. As I stumbled with Pietru to the Sacra Infermeria, unaccustomed to seeing with one eye, we witnessed something neither of us had ever seen. The few famished dogs that had escaped destruction were wandering about the streets, attempting to wrest free the bodies of people crushed beneath the rocks and eat them. Usually, the dogs could not pull them out and chewed off the arms and legs, scurrying away with their prizes. This is not what struck us. As we passed some ruined houses with the terrific heat and stench of putrefaction, one of the canines ran up to a corpse and a great black wing took to the air. At first Ix-Xabaw and I thought it a stupendous bat, mayhap Lucifer's wing, but we quickly realized it was a swarm of flies, an infinitude of flies. Many said whores carried the plague, while others knew it was flies. The Turks did not need to kill us; pestilence soon would.

At the Infermeria, Pietru and I found Balthazar yet lying by the wall where I had left him. "Is he dying, Dr. Jean?" I asked the physician.

At first Jean was only able to nod. "I believe so."

We had shed so many tears that my eyes were exhausted of them. But my soul felt a greater emptiness than I had known. With Vigo's permission, we got help and carried Balthazar to the Auberge de France, where another Knight had just died and bequeathed his bed.

As we departed the auberge, Pietru said, "Try not to feel sad, Cikku."

"What are you saying, Xabaw?" I cried with the roar of a wounded animal. "For that man I would sell Christendom to the Turks!"

"It is blasphemy to say such things, Cikku. He will always live for you ... for me too." For a moment Ix-Xabaw stood still with his head lifted to the sky. "And I think we are going to win," he said.

"Why do you think that, Xabaw?"

"Because I smell the wind coming, and the rain."

One Hundred Nine

Ix-Xabaw was right. Rain was on its way. Within a day the skies had begun to cloud over. "The winter season is approaching," I said to Balthazar as I sat at his bed in the Auberge de France.

For the first time since we had carried him hither, the Knight opened his eyes. I grasped his hand. "Then we have won?" he asked faintly. At length he seemed to hear the guns continuing their bombardment. "Ah, we have not yet won."

"We must hang on for another few weeks. You must hang on. Here, drink." I put a cup of water to his lips. He nearly choked.

"No, Francisco, from this wound I shall not recover—"

"I'll not hear such words from you!" I shouted. "You shouldn't have fought."

The Abbé was too weak to argue much. "What choice did we have?" he said, "What choice?" Thereat he nodded, sighing weakly. "Such is my reward for being too eager to collect a wager. Vengeance is mine, saith the Lord ... " For a moment Balthazar lapsed into a dream, then coming to himself his lips spread into the old reflective smile. "*Vertu de Dieu*, I suppose if I have saved Christendom from the likes of Blaij Vergã, my life shall not have passed entirely in vain. Do you think he was trying to protect Isabella? Mayhap there was a dram of good in him after all."

I cut the Knight short, admonishing him not to waste words on the villain and to sleep. It was, tho', strange to think that after so many years I had nothing more to fear from Vergã. Under the present circumstances this was scant consolation. Equally strange was that a small part of me would regret his death. The greater part already regretted that I hadn't killed him myself.

The next assault loomed. With both our forces reduced by half or more, the contest was now between the Pashas' will and the Monsignore's.

Having left Balthazar, I was picking my way to the Birgu armory to prepare crossbows when I passed Bishop Cubelles. He held his sleeve against his mouth and nose, but this did not prevent him from glaring at me as he stumbled over the rubble. "Do not be so foolish, Signore Barai," he said, "to think that this siege presents the greatest danger to you."

"Eccellenza is certainly correct," I answered. "When the Seigneurs of the Council vote to abandon those who have fought for them, what hope remains?" I continued on without a further glance, yet a shudder ran thro' me. The Inquisitor's power ceded no place to the Grand Master's, and Cubelles would surely make good his threat. Troubled, I continued on to the armory as the *boom boom-boom boom-boom* of the bombardment once again tore our world apart.

I'd not been long with the others, fixing old crossbows, when Flaminia appeared, asking to help. All bruised and bandaged, her hair unwashed and matted, she resembled more a savage from the Newfound World than a rich courtesan. Then, so did the rest of us.

"I just saw Eccellenza, Bishop Cubelles," I said, showing her how to fit the quarrels with feathers.

"So did I," she said, wrinkling her nose. "He looks unwell, *Ix-xitan jiehdu*. I know you fear him, Francisco. *Chiapar quista*." With that she removed a phial from her neck and handed it to me.

I smiled ruefully. "Flaminia, how many amulets or potions have you given me? Had I a trunk, it would be full of them."

"This one will protect you and your loved ones," she said, struggling with a feather and a bolt. "But do not open it until you are in true need. It is the most potent of them all."

Examining the painted phial, I saw nothing within, but to humor her I put it in my pouch. She then raised her eyes to the shuddering walls and asked me to tell her more about the Sultan's harem.

The same afternoon, as Alfonso ate bread and salted fish at St. Michel, he asked Balbi why he was keeping an account of the siege. "For the gold," Balbi answered, pausing in his writing.

"You intend to become rich from our sufferings!" Alfonso laughed. "Do you think anyone will want to know what has taken place here?"

The arquebusier shrugged. "Remember the old saying, *Hoc vere historiam belli contextere dextra, Si calamum arripiat qui tenuit gladium*. The true history of war is best written when he who wields the sword takes up the pen."

"You should be a poet," said Alfonso.

"I was," replied Balbi, glancing about the ruins. "You see the remuneration."

At that moment they felt the first drops on their hands and glanced at the darkening sky. "Thank God!" they shouted together, removing their helmets, crossing themselves. They caught the drops with their tongues, laughing and embracing one another. As the rain fell more heavily, they gathered up the grass mats they'd woven and fitted them over sticks. Knowing the guns would soon be useless, they cast down their arquebuses and took up the crossbows we'd sent.

The enemy cried out from their trenches, "You think the rain has saved you, dogs! Remember, our arrows fly farther than yours!" To prove it, the Turks loosed a cloud of shafts that fell into the fort.

As the arrows flew by, Pietru took up a crossbow and peered over the wall at Bormla. He no longer had the strength to wind the bow, but yet had strength to shoot it. The wind, the *tramontana*, was blowing and the rain becoming heavy enough that Pietru wiped his eyes in order to see his foe.

It was a strange battle that continued for two days: The infidels, wet to their bones, yet determined to take the fort at all costs, charging time and again with bows in their hands when their arquebuses misfired; the few Christians, no drier, drawing the weapons when they had two hands, firing them when they did not. Balbi observed that in the rain the crossbow's powerful bolts flew truer than the plain arrows of the Turks, piercing an enemy shield and often the man behind it. The advantage was theirs. And therefore ours.

"We have gone back to another age," said Alfonso.

"Perhaps we should have begun there," answered Balbi. "Or stayed there."

Ix-Xabaw experienced like sentiments when the next morning he peered over the wall and saw—"What is this!" he exclaimed, knowing only that he'd never seen such a thing as the one confronting him now. He scrambled down to warn Captain de Cabrera, in charge of Bormla, but by the time he found him with the Bailiff of Eagle and Captain Martelli, everyone knew.

"Crossbows and a tortoise!" Martelli was saying in bewilderment. "What do they think this is, Jerusalem? There is so much rubble before the fort, they'll never cross the ditch with it."

The *manta* the enemy'd built, or as the ancients called it, a *testudo*—a tortoise—was a squat machine covered all over with hides and shields. It didn't look much like a tortoise, Pietru thought, with those green and yellow birds, claws, wings and eyes painted on every one of its plates. The enemy seemed intent to roll it up to the barrels, stream out from under the shields and take the ravelin.

The matter was quickly growing urgent—they didn't have enough men left to go out and attack the machine, and Eagle knew it. While the Bailiff and his Captains cast about for some stratagem, the same engineer Girolamo Cassar who helped destroy the Turkish bridge, walked into their midst.

"Luck is with us," he said. "If they roll it close to the barrels, the *manta* will stand opposite one of the casemates angled from the front of the fort, where not too much rubble has fallen. We can make a gun port and wait."

Eagle ordered Cassar not to lose a moment. He and his Maltese once more began to hack away from the inside of the fortress. When they'd reached the outer wall, Cassar ordered them to cut through the mortar but not take out the stone. Then they dragged up a serpentine and waited.

Pietru prepared to give the signal from above. The *manta* was already creaking toward the barrels and ravelin, with forty or fifty men hiding beneath the shields, preparing to attack. Now the engine was but twenty paces opposite Cassar's casemate. Pietru dropped his arm. At once engineer's men pulled away the stone in front of the gun's mouth. The tortoise crawled directly before them, no farther than one could piss. Cassar instantly gave the order. The gun roared. The beast was blown to pieces and every one of the barbarians killed. Cassar's men embraced each other with cheers and the enemy abandoned the attack.

In the morning on the twenty-eighth of August, I went to the Auberge de France to visit Balthazar. The Knight was asleep and I sat by him for some time before he awoke. He was weaker than the previous day and could not speak much above a whisper. After some time he said, "The bombardment seems more feeble today."

"Last night the Turks began to embark some of their pieces," I answered. "Perhaps only those that no longer fire properly, for all the punishment."

At hearing these words, a radiant smile passed over Balthazar's face. "Then Europe shall not speak Turkish," he said.

Hesitantly I nodded. "I believe you are right. This siege has not ended, but God willing, we have won. The spirit has gone out of them."

"Then I die content," Balthazar answered.

At once I clasped his hands, tears flooding my eyes. "Balthazar, do not—"

"Francisco," he interrupted me in evident pain, "this wound will not be cured. The suppuration has not lessened and takes me with it. I say, my friend, no tears; I have told you more than once that the age of the Knights has passed. I have fulfilled my duty and there is nothing left for me on this earth. I go in peace—"

"Your memoirs—"

"You shall have to write them, if you ever learn how to write." With a long glance at his *montante*, which Pietru and I had stood by the bed, he said, "Keep my sword to remember me by, Francisco. I pray you never use it." Hereon he struggled to remove his crucifix from his neck. "I have for you three small requests. Go to Constantinople. Give my regards to Barelli, and thank him once more for all he did for Europe. Give this token to a certain lady I once knew ... " He told me her name and how to find her.

"The third request?" I asked, hardly able to control myself.

"Take the best ... "

"Balthazar—!" I cried.

"Shhh. We have said our farewells far too often to linger over them now. We shall meet again."

Those were the last words Balthazar uttered. As he did so, the Knight sank back onto the bed with the most peaceful expression I had ever seen on a man's face and sent his soul to Heaven.

For many hours I sat at the bedside, unable to move. At last I rose and staggered thro' the Borgo, seeking Isabella. I found her at the Auberge of Italy and told her what had taken place. She embraced me and for a long time we stood silently together, our tears flowing freely, mourning the finest man I had known.

One Hundred Ten

The northwest wind blew as had it been driven from the angered lips of Jupiter, lightning from his hand crisscrossed the black sky, the thunder resembled the cannonading of siege guns and the sea was run with white-topped waves that instant by instant broke over Rafael Salvago and the other four hundred soldiers aboard, threatening to drown every one of them and sink the *capitana* of Don Garcia de Toledo.

"To the Devil with Don Garcia," shouted one of the *sotto-comiti*. "I'd rather face the Turks than this sea!"

"You'll not curse the Vice Roy for the weather!" Salvago shouted in return.

"We must turn about!" one of the adventurers by him cried.

"I'll have Neptune swallow you before we do," answered Salvago and pushed his way toward the poop and the Vice Roy. "The men want to go back!" said Salvago to Toledo, as both of them held onto the rail for dear life.

"You don't think I know? We're not going anywhere, Fra Rafael, except where this damned storm takes us. Pray it's not to the bottom."

Aye, nodded Salvago, the eternal delays had put them into God's hands. After the great war council had finally decided to act, Don Garcia upheld his promise and departed from Messina for Zaragoza on the twenty-first of August. On the twenty-fifth, the entire fleet of fifty-eight heavily provisioned vessels set sail, south to Cape Passero and, at long last, to Malta.

Almost at once they had a stroke of good fortune off Cape Passero. A large Ragusan round ship out of Los Gelves and bound for Malta carrying powder, rice and biskets for the Turks was blown by a furious storm straight into the Vice Roy's welcoming hands. The crew surrendered without a fight and Don Garcia sent the prize north to Zaragoza.

But this moment, as a wave cast him to the deck and he struggled to his knees, Salvago understood they should have heeded the fate of that round ship. Midway between Sicily and Malta, the same winds caught the Christian fleet and the Council's entire design was blown from its course. Aye, design ...

Before the Vice Roy departed Zaragoza, Gian Andrea had set off on his *capitana* to ferry poor Juan Martinez de Oliventia to Gozo. Martinez—the same fellow who'd been stranded on Malta during one of the failed attempts to land the *piccolo soccorso*—was to carry dispatches to de Valette, informing him that a *gran soccorso* was on its way, and to give him instructions for the fire signals. Even then it was no certain thing that the *soccorso* would be able to make land. "That depends on God, Piyale and you, Martinez," said Don Garcia. Having taken Martinez to Gozo, Gian Andrea was to return to Linosa, a tiny isle but seven leagues north of Lampedusa, where he'd wait for Don Garcia and the main body of the fleet.

God alone knew what happened to Doria and Martinez. All Salvago knew was that the accursed gale had driven the armada clear to Pantellaria island, southwest of Sicily, halfway to Africa. Then this storm ... Gaining his feet, Salvago glanced at the pilot being lashed by the rain, fighting vainly against the tempest, which would sink them or carry them whither it would.

Only the next morning did the heavens dry their tears and the winds fall silent. Land was in sight—Favignana, west of Sicily.

"What shall we do now?" asked the drenched Salvago, regarding the battered *capitana*.

Caiques and feluccas had been passing back and forth amongst the galleys. By some miracle they hadn't lost a single ship, but every vessel was missing oars, a rudder or its ramming spur. "We make for Trapani for repairs," Don Garcia gave the order.

Trapani! Salvago cursed to himself. The westernmost tip of Sicilia—as far from Malta as possible! Fra Rafael turned, struck the rail with his fist, but he knew the Almighty had ordained this.

de Valette permitted himself a slight smile when Toni Bajada appeared at Birgu's square, having just managed to cross the Turkish lines from the Old City. "I had feared the worst, Signore," the Grand Master said. "We have not seen you for some time." Romegas slapped the courier, saying he'd now collect on his bet. Toni regarded the Commander and tugged nervously on his ear, admitting to the Monsignore he'd also feared the worst. Natheless, he brought good news from Mezquita: Gian Andrea Doria had personally left a Spanish soldier on Gozo, someone named Martinez, who was to arrange signals for the armada, should it appear.

"Should it appear?" de Valette asked.

Bajada said Mezquita had told him only that Don Garcia's fleet was to rendezvous at Linosa before proceeding to Malta, but no one knew where it was.

The jester opened his mouth, but the Grand Master waved him silent. This was, after all, the second piece of good news he had received today. From a Maltese who'd escaped the Turks, he learned that the numbers of enemy laborers dying from hunger and disease were greater than he'd known, and that some Turkish renegados had stolen a galiot and fled to Sicily. Thereupon, Piyale had blockaded Marsamxett harbor with a chain of masts and spurs for fear that other malcontents would attempt to follow.

de Valette dismissed Bajada. That the Turks had embarked some of their artillery was a further good sign, but he was far from convinced the siege was over. He knew only that tens of thousands of enemy troops remained encamped on the hills above them, continuing to mine Castille and Fort St. Michel, continuing to make assaults, while he had six hundred men who could walk. Truly, not all the news of the past few days had been good. Fra Balthazar de Marans des Homes-Saint-Martin had died of his wounds. He had served the Order well, in his singular fashion. His coffin now lay in San Lorenzo and de Valette would see it returned with honor to France.

"I would know what is taking place in the Turkish camp," said His Eminence aloud, not expecting Romegas or his jester to answer him.

Abdallah al-Waryagli could not but perceive a sharp desperation in the *Pashalar*'s demeanor. Each time Mustafa and Piyale deigned to speak to each other, claws were bared. So it was at this moment, in front of his eyes, e'en as the rain beat down on Mustafa's pavilion, drumming in everyone's ears.

"O Mustafa," said Piyale, "should we return to Constantinople without having reduced this island, the shame and disgrace will be so great that we shall beg the Sultan to take our heads." Which Soliman would do with pleasure, the *chavush* knew. "Yet, the winter season is upon us and great danger awaits if we tarry here much longer."

"My brave Piyale, renowned for his daring, we will take this accursed island," replied Mustafa, "if we must winter here to do it."

Mustafa's determination and insults did not go far to persuade the daring *Kapudan*, who paced before the older Pasha, waving his arms. "Your *yenicheriler* will revolt again before spending the winter on this rock, Mustafa. We have meal sufficient only for another twenty-five days and the ship from Djerbé, which was to bring us powder and grain, has not arrived. The thieves in Trablus have not sent all four thousand *kantarlar* of powder they promised and the only stores remaining to us are aboard the ships. Those we must save should the infidel relief appear."

Every moment since his arrival two weeks ago, Abdallah had been attempting, with slight success, to grasp how this great descent had so grievously miscarried. *Evet*, blunders had been made, but with such a force even the blunders should not have led experienced leaders into a swamp. Worst of all was the dishonor to the Padishah. Vienna itself had not been such a complete disaster. How could they ever return to Constantinople without destroying the knights?

"May Allah's Blessings and Wisdom be upon the *Pashalar*," the *chavush* said. "Neither of you wishes the ignominy of defeat to fall on your shoulders, or on your necks. I perceive all is not lost. The defenders are few; a single victory, just one, and Malta shall fall. You must tell the troops through me that the Sultan has ordered them to winter here. At the same time you should send galleys to Modon, where *caramusaliler* laden with *peksimet* are waiting to come here. It is beyond imagining that the greatest army on earth cannot destroy this island that has so brazenly affronted the Sultan and caused his subjects so much misery."

By the time Abdallah finished, he was also pacing with a clenched fist, but over Piyale's protests Mustafa accepted the advice. He decided to take the old city to winter there. If they failed, they would at least carry many slaves back to the Sultan to avoid his displeasure.

When the *Boluk-bashiler* and *Chorbajiler* heard the plan, a groan of lions and the hissing of snakes escaped their lips. Yakhshi himself shouted that if they wintered on this place, they'd starve, to which Mustafa answered that supplies were coming any day, and that the Sultan commanded it.

"Has the Sultan truly commanded this thing?" Yakhshi shouted out to Abdallah, standing by Mustafa.

"*Evet*," replied the *chavush*.

Mustafa cajoled and threatened, reminding them of the dishonor they faced, and once again offered them extra pay and rewards. The officers dispersed, grumbling, without giving consent. Yakhshi stepped up to Abdallah. "We have eaten in the same tent together. I think you are lying. Why did you not tell us when you first arrived that the Sultan commands us to stay the winter?"

"Two weeks ago we thought you *yenicheriler*, proud Sons of the Sultan, would take the towers, but you have behaved more like the baby elephant who, hearing a farmer call out, 'Look, there is a mouse!' grew up believing he was one. I remind you, Yakhshi *Boluk-bashi*, it is better to winter in the old town than on these naked hills."

Yakhshi clenched his teeth and threw a ferocious glance at the *chavush*. "By my forelock, *chavush* Abdallah, I swear if we winter here, you will too. I also tell you another thing I have learned on Malta, which you have not yet learned, or Piyale or Mustafa: Only Allah knows the course of war."

He spat on the ground and strode off.

When the tocsin sounded in Città Notabile on the last day of August, Lady Emilia already knew what it portended, for not many moments earlier Pedro Mezquita had run to the house to tell Anastagi: The Turkish army was marching on the Old City with four thousand men, janissaries among them. The mention of those troops no longer struck terror into the heart and, before the roaming pigs had been rounded up, Mezquita had ordered every man, woman and child to the walls, and made certain every ensign in the city was flying.

Once more Emilia stood with Mezquita on the ramparts. Around her were soldiers, women dressed in old armor, children, all the thousands of peasants who'd sought refuge here. She did not see Falzon. At the sight of the approaching forces, she caught her breath, feeling faint. Food stores were very low and not many more weeks would pass before the last cows and oxen were eaten. If the Turks wintered on the island, surely everyone in Notabile would starve.

Mezquita showed no fear; among cannon and culverins, the city boasted twelve pieces wherewith to defend itself and, as no serious assault had come, they yet retained plentiful stocks of ammunition and powder. Anastagi had already ridden out with the cavalry and a few hours later he returned with prisoners. Aye, Mustafa intended to besiege the Old City.

Climbing to the walls with Anastagi, Mezquita proposed that they inform the Vice Roy and the Grand Master at once.

"To what purpose?" replied the Captain with annoyance. "The only outcome of informing the Vice Roy that the City is besieged is that he will turn tail and refuse to land the relief. I say we just fire on the whore-mongers. The end of August has arrived. They cannot afford to stay long."

With no further argument, Mezquita opened fire on the Turks with all his artillery.

At the Turkish camp below, Yakhshi didn't like the looks of things. In the past three and a half months he'd never come this close to the city, but it didn't appear as weak as everyone said. Its walls commanded the plain from atop steep precipices, which they could never scale from this side. The ground on the other side was flatter, an assault might be possible, but more infidel defenders stood atop the ramparts than they'd expected. He saw no recourse but batter down the walls with artillery, and they hadn't dragged more than a few small pieces along. Now, while their colorful standards fluttered gaily, the infidel guns were battering them.

Finally, the engineers Mustafa had sent out returned with their advice. When Mustafa Pasha's screaming reached his ears, Yakhshi knew it must have been exactly what he himself would have told the Commander: Either bring up the siege guns, or retire.

With no warning to anyone, Mustafa gave the order to retire. As they marched back to the main camp at the harbor, Yakhshi cursed under his breath. This was all *sachma*. The time had long past to abandon this accursed island to the plague. Unfortunately, the raging Pasha was possessed by the Devil and the Devil had other intentions.

Balthazar once told me that the ancients put days at the end of the year that belonged to no time. The last days of August and first days of September were like that. The Turks embarked guns; they continued the bombardment. Mustafa marched on Mdina; Piyale's forces made ever more desperate attempts to mine Castille and Fort St. Michel. The azabs and Hasan's corsairs launched yet massive assaults in the sun; the rain poured down and they called them off. Were the Turks leaving? Were they wintering on Malta? Had we won? Had we lost? Glancing at the few soldiers about me, I found not the courage to say we had triumphed. Glancing at the condition of the Turks, neither would I concede them victory.

A constant suspense filled those days out of time. Uncertain of the whereabouts of the relief or of the enemy's intent, de Valette never relaxed his vigilance, for he knew that with so few defenders left, a single misstep could yet spell disaster. So we existed in the twilight that had settled over the siege. It was, truly, a twilight of the ancients. After Balthazar's death, I'd gone down to Fort St. Michel to be among my comrades and there lay on the ruined wall with a crossbow, while the foe attacked us with arrows.

"If they persist," I said to Balbi, crouched nearby me, "we'll be reduced to clubs."

Aye, he nodded. The troops were spent and the contest was now fully between Mustafa's will and de Valette's. With only a few stones separating us from the Turks, we might have shaken hands. We did trade jests and throw them melons, oranges and other fruits that grew on Malta, which astonished them because they thought we'd been starving.

All the while, it was so dangerous to show one's head that instead we mounted arquebuses atop lances, aimed downward. Raising them above the parapets, we fired them with matches which we also held on poles. Of course, we couldn't see what we were doing, but all the same managed to kill many of the enemy.

On the morning of the first or second of September, Balbi shook me awake and pointed up the hill. "Francisco," he said, "during our sleep a sorcerer has indeed carried us back to times of yore."

Before our eyes, the Turks were raising a wooden siege tower. This one, when it was finished, would be far taller than the tortoise of a week ago, taller than Fort St. Michel itself. And from such a tower the enemy could shoot the remaining defenders in the fort, then storm it.

"Siege towers and crossbows," I said, running down to find Eagle or Martelli. "It is meet."

By the time I got below, Eagle, Martelli and many others were already gathered, Pietru among them, and Girolamo Cassar with his carpenter brother Andrea. Andrea was proposing to repeat the plan of last week.

"Andrea," warned his brother, "if they come to the front of the fort, this time we shall have to dig a tunnel out through all the rubble that has fallen."

They had little choice and Eagle ordered them to get to it. And so, as the enemy lashed ships' spurs together above a colossal wheeled carriage, we raced to dig a hole thro' the wall of the fort and thro' the mountain of rubble beyond. We brought down every piece of wood or galley oar we could find to support the tunnel against the enormous weight above. Every hour someone would crawl in, saying that the Turkish tower had risen ten *braccia*, or that they had armored it with shields, or that it had four levels, each of which could support a dozen arquebusiers, or that they'd mounted muskets and falconets atop it. With each piece of news we dug ever more frantically, and twice the tunnel collapsed. Thankfully, no one was killed, and only one had his leg broken. At last the news came that the Turkish tower was finished. So were we.

The thing was enormous. Without putting our heads above the parapets, we could see it rolling slowly toward a breach, pushed from behind by slaves. No one needed to tell us the danger posed by the giant, from which some dozens of janissaries might pick off the last of us. To add to our misery, its platforms were closed up by walls to protect the arquebusiers within. All the while cannonading persisted from the Mandra and Corradino. We replied with crossbows, doing nothing but transforming the tower into a giant porcupine.

Andrea Cassar waited below in the tunnel, having loaded the same serpentine as before with chain shot. Moment by moment the engine creaked closer, and he waited. The wall shielding the top platform now came down, making a bridge to the fort and exposing the janissaries therein. At once they opened fire, killing one of our men after another. Pietru, at my side, asked me to wind his crossbow. I did so and placed a bolt. We took each other's arms and aimed at the leering foemen who shot at us from above with their arquebuses that never missed.

At the same moment Andrea Cassar told his mates to remove the final stones from the tunnel. The legs of the tower loomed directly in front of him, hardly five paces distant. He ordered his fellows out of the burrow and remained alone. For a final time he glanced at the supports we'd fashioned, he said a prayer and—he fired.

Those half-balls tied with chain roared out and crashed through two of the tower's legs. In the next instant the engine began to totter with a great twisting and splintering of wood. Everywhere, *yenicheriler* were screaming, attempting to jump from the platforms before they were crushed. Yakhshi, too, lunged for a spur but his hand couldn't grasp it as the platform tilted. Because of his wounds he had been waiting at a lower level; still he was thrown clear to the ground. Fighting to keep his senses, he scrambled away as quickly as his bruises allowed, praying to Allah. Shrieks, the cracking and groaning of wood filled his ears as the beast in its death throes collapsed and cast over the *yenicheri* a great cloud of dust.

As the gun roared, the tunnel began to buckle too, and Cassar ran for dear life before the whole weight of two months of bombardment buried him. The retort and quaking all around was terrific, a stone fell on his boot, but a miracle was granted and the tunnel held.

Those of us above, Ix-Xabaw, Balbi, myself and the others, stood with open mouths. We could do nothing more than watch as the great tower crashed into the ditch before our eyes, and with it, the Siege of Malta.

One Hundred Eleven

I went back to Birgu. I felt a sharp need for Balthazar's companionship, and was still wholly unable to accept his absence. Stepping off the floating bridge with the crossbow slung over my shoulder and now wearing a patch over my left eye, I walked through the crowded square where I passed Romegas. "Why are you not at your post?" he shouted.

"They have lost," I said and continued up the hill.

I picked my way over the rubble and corpses, seeking Isabella, Vigo, Flaminia—anyone. Suddenly, I realized I had not seen Flaminia for several days. I sped to her house near the creek to find it in ruins. "No!" I cried aloud, lifting stones like a madman and hurling them behind me. "Flaminia!" I shouted over and over without receiving a reply. At length some townspeople aided me in pulling away the remaining stones above the cellar and we found her father below in the cistern, dead, and the servants nearby, crushed. Of Flaminia or her daughter Francesca there was no sign.

I sat on a stone amidst the wreckage of her house and wept. At long last I felt a hand on my shoulder and turned to see Dr. Jean. He sat down on another stone beside me. "We have won," I croaked, thro' my sobs.

Vigo nodded with difficulty.

"How many wounded ... at the Hospital?"

The physician moved his shoulders in despair. "I cannot count them. Most will die, for we cannot treat them. We have lost two or three thousand soldiers. Of the people ... many more. Most crushed beneath ... " He did not finish.

"Why do you search for the living among the dead, Dr. Jean?" I asked, staring at him with wide, red eyes. He merely looked at me in a forlorn way. "Forgive me ... You had once spoken of curing the soul. You may have to begin with mine."

Vigo shook his head. "No, Francisco, you shall have to begin with mine."

Thereat we fell forward until our foreheads touched, and rested silently against each other as the Turkish guns continued to fire.

It was, he thought, the second of September when, standing on the poop of the Vice Roy's *capitana*, Rafael Salvago watched the tiny island of Linosa rise above the water. Don Garcia had, as he declared, made for Trapani, where the galleys were repaired and refitted in the space of a day. Between sunup and sunup, upon a thousand weary and ill soldiers took the opportunity to steal away. Cursing, but unwilling to tarry, the Vice Roy embarked the *gran soccorso* without them.

The weather had cleared some and the fleet made for Linosa to meet Gian Andrea as planned, but even as they approached the small harbor, Salvago felt uneasy; below the dead volcanoes, Doria's *capitana* was nowhere to be seen. Aye, but for the sea tortoises, the place appeared utterly deserted. "What do you think has happened?" Salvago asked, but Don Garcia had no answer except to order a boat readied to take them ashore.

As the small crew rowed into the harbor, Fra Rafael spied two sailors sitting on the rocks among some barrels. "Illustrissimo Eccellenza!" both of them shouted, jumping to their feet and bowing clumsily to the Vice Roy as he stepped onto the sand. The first of them handed His Excellency a letter with Doria's seal.

"What does Gian Andrea say?" asked Salvago, even before Toledo broke the seal.

Don Garcia motioned for the Knight to take a breath. "He says, 'Where are you?'—what do you think he says? He took Martinez to Gozo, then came to Linosa to meet us, and 'finding that the armada has not appeared, I suspect some misfortune has overtaken you.'" Toledo expelled the air from his lungs and handed Salvago the letter without another glance at it. "He has gone to Licata and says he will return hither to meet us."

"Licata," breathed Salvago. On the south coast of Sicily. "We can't wait for him."

"Of course not. But if Martinez is on Gozo we may proceed thither. And you, Salvago, may remember to address me as Eccellenza."

Don Garcia immediately ordered a small company of men ashore with bread and water for two weeks and instructions to await Doria's arrival, thence inform him that the armada had proceeded to Gozo.

Assuring the men that he'd ransom them if they fell into Turkish hands, he ordered the crew to shove off.

Only after I spoke to Vigo did it come into my head to search for Flaminia at the Hospital. I picked my way over those lying around the entrance and spied Isabella crouching in the courtyard near the fountain, tending the unnumbered wounded. She washed and bandaged fresh injuries, called for food, but could do little else without medicine. Screams emerged from the surgery. As I glanced around the courtyard, a Turkish ball crashed into the top of the building, sending more rocks upon those below. Isabella caught sight of me then and got to her feet. For a moment she resembled an ancient Roman statue, not entirely whole, standing in a villa no less ruined.

"Why do you search for the living among the dead?" she asked, speaking the same words as I had to Dr. Jean.

"We have won," I said, breaking into tears again.

Isabella regarded me as were I speaking gibberish, more, as if no words at all had come from my mouth.

"We have won," I repeated. "We have fulfilled our vow. We have survived."

Isabella stepped across to me, yet regarding me with a puzzled expression as the Turkish guns fired. Stiffly, she rested her head against my shoulder and began quietly to cry. At length she asked whether Parisot had declared victory.

I didn't know. She gently pushed me away and without a word went back to her duties. It was late in the day and the Grand Master himself soon appeared for his rounds. When I told him of the siege tower and said we had won, he regarded me without humor. "Monsieur," he replied. "Do you hear those guns? Have the Turks departed? Do you see any sign of the relief? Return to your post."

I'd only taken a few steps toward Galley Creek when de Valette called out from behind me, "God willing, you are correct, Señor."

As Rafael Salvago had two days earlier, Gian Andrea scratched his head when, on returning to Linosa from Licata, he saw only turtles floating beneath the volcanoes. The Admiral had yet to plant a boot in the sand when Don Garcia's men, who'd been fishing from the rocks, jumped up to greet him with bows and a letter. It took only a moment to read the missive: Don Garcia had proceeded toward Malta according to plan and wanted Doria to return with his galley to Zaragoza, where they would meet after the first troops had been disembarked. Gian Andrea collected the stranded men and their fish and set off again for Sicily.

The day after I saw her in the Hospital, Isabella spoke to de Valette on Birgu's square. From time to time the Turkish guns roared. With a voice devoid of expression, she asked whether we had won.

de Valette returned her question with an expression hardly less somber than the one he'd cast on me. "Isabella," he said. "They are returning from Comino with brush wood for more trenches and platforms, which can mean only that they intend to launch another assault. Listen." He cocked his head at the continuing crackling of arquebuses from Castille. Moments later a runner came up to the clock tower, reporting that some Maltese there had run forth and set fire to a small siege engine near the trenches.

But the Turks were withdrawing their guns, were they not, Isabella asked.

"Truly, the death throes of a giant are not quickly over," de Valette replied.

After regarding him long, Isabella said, "I want to know whether we can hope."

For an equally long time the Grand Master regarded her. "I have never lost faith that we would triumph," he said. "All hope was never lost, you knew that." She stared at him with some doubt, almost the first emotion that crossed her face. "Yes," he went on, "we can hope." He took her in his arms and embraced her.

Two nights after departing Linosa, as his fleet approached Gozo, Don Garcia ordered all the cocks aboard the galleys to be killed, that the *comiti* give orders only by whistle instead of drums or trumpets, and that the slaves not be allowed to raise their feet to the rests and rattle their chains. By the time the island came into sight, it was the fourth hour of the night.

"I don't see any signals," Don Garcia said needlessly to Salvago.

Martinez was to have lit one fire for each ten Turkish ships that appeared west of Malta, or no fires at all should no enemy ships be visible. He was also to have a man run with a torch in the direction of the enemy vessels. "Of course not," replied Salvago, also needlessly. "He must be on the east side of Gozo—he believed we were coming directly from Zaragoza."

The wet wind was up and the sea rising. "We've hit the Scirocco," the pilot wiped the drops from his face, "or it's hit us."

Don Garcia ordered them to circle around the island to the north, whence they should be able to see the signals, but Salvago pressed him to go straight through the channel as the quicker route.

It was with some surprise that Toledo regarded the Knight. "Fra Salvago, surely you understand that the Turkish fleet could easily be waiting for us."

Salvago pressed him again to go straight through the channel.

Alvaro de Sande stood by the pilot aboard the galley of Captain General Cardona, who was leading the rear guard of nineteen vessels. Darkness yet fully shrouded them and the sea had become rough under the winds. No one was getting any sleep as their destination neared, and all eyes were peeled ahead for the signals Martinez was to have placed. Of a sudden the pilot sent a boy to Cardona's cabin. A moment later the Captain General climbed to the poop and walked up to the pilot, who was pointing ahead. For a short while Cardona stood by him with his hand curled to his brow, then shoved his way to the forecastle. By the time he returned to the poop, de Sande had guessed what was apparent to all—

"By the Lord Christ!" cursed de Cardona. "The armada has vanished!"

"What do you intend to do?" de Sande said. "We have arrived at the place appointed for landing. Brave men await us."

"Don't you think I know?" Cardona replied angrily. Without losing another moment, he sent out a *fregata* one of the galleys had been towing into the channel to search for Don Garcia, thinking he might be at Comino. But as the sky slowly brightened, the *fregata* returned with the news that the channel was empty. At a loss, Cardona ordered his ships forward, where making their way slowly between Malta and Gozo, they espied neither Turk nor Don Garcia.

"Will you land us?" asked de Sande.

"Do you wish to put down fewer than half the men?" Cardona returned and the two men stared at each other.

There was nothing for it. By now morning of the fourth day of September had come. The rain had ceased and, later in the day, they spied the main body of the fleet standing some leagues out of the channel to the north.

As the Captain General's galley slid up to the Vice Roy's *capitana*, Cardona and de Sande stepped onto the *ballestriere* and climbed aboard. Don Garcia explained that he had circled around Gozo, not wanting to risk going through the Fliegu channel.

"But no one is there!" erupted Cardona. "Not a single Turkish ship!"

"We could not have known that," replied Don Garcia, taken aback at the impertinence of his own Captain General.

"Señor, you might have sent a *fregata*, as we did in search of you!" Toledo merely shrugged, refusing to apologize, but Cardona was fully beside himself, raging. "We've lost a perfect opportunity for landing the troops! Perfect!"

de Sande put in urgently that the troops must be landed now, before it was too late, but Cardona didn't hear him, so vexed was he. "We're already halfway to Sicily!" he shouted.

All was in vain, for Don Garcia's mind was made up. "It is already too late." Daylight was well upon them; the sea was high; the Turks would be prowling about. He could not risk the fleet. "For the moment we return to Sicily. And, Captain General Cardona, you shall remember to address me as Eccellenza."

Soon the fleet was proceeding again to Pozzallo. Late in the evening, as the wind brought them toward Cape Passero, Turkish ships discovered them but failed to give chase. Don Garcia told Cardona, who'd remained aboard the *capitana*, that his decision had been the right one.

It was, I think, the sixth of September, three or four days after I had last seen Isabella, when I came up from Fort St. Michel searching for supper. The siege's endless twilight persisted, but no assaults had been made for the past days and, as the enemy embarked ever more pieces, the bombardment slowly faded away. The quiet left in its wake was as none that any of us could recollect. Little food was to be had anywhere. At length I discovered Isabella sitting with a candle in her cistern below what had been her house, eating bread. I climbed down the ladder and sat beside her.

"Tell me again we have won," she said.

"Surely we have. Since the collapse of the tower, they've attempted almost nothing and the bombardment has been feeble—"

"Today they fired on Bormla with heavy guns."

I nodded at her blank face, softened only by the candle. "Yes, and on Martelli's Post, and on the galleon of the *Kapi Agha*." Throughout the siege the Turks had avoided firing on the great prize captured by Romegas, moored brazenly before their eyes. Today the Turks attempted to sink it, and nearly succeeded. "It is true desperation. They know they shall not have it back."

"Parisot has reduced the bread ration ... " Isabella said, handing me a piece of barley bread.

I nodded, accepting it. Her voice expressed hardly more feeling than of late, as were she utterly unable to comprehend all that had taken place. In that she was not alone.

" ... and today a renegado has warned him of another assault," she continued. This was also true. Rumors were about that a great, final assault loomed, that Mustafa had promised great rewards for bravery and five talents of gold to him who should first place a standard on the infidel walls. Isabella moved towards me and clutched my chest. At first she merely shook her head. "Say again we have survived," she insisted.

"We have struggled, and so we have triumphed," I said.

She began to cry, softly. I handed her her book so that she might write in it, but this time she did not take it from me and slowly fell asleep.

Explicitly following the Vice Roy's instructions he'd received on Linosa, Gian Andrea was making his way to Zaragoza, where he hoped to have direct news of the successful landing of the ground forces. As his *capitana* neared Cape Passero on the morning of September sixth, his galley Captain appeared at his cabin door. "Eccellenza," the Captain said, "I do not know how to explain this. The fleet appears to be anchored at Pozzallo."

With great perplexity, they rushed to deck, whence Gian Andrea immediately verified his Captain's observation and ordered him to put out a caique to discover what was afoot.

E'en well out in the water, Doria perceived that what was afoot had never entered his imagination. On the embankment, a great disturbance unfolded. Sicilian horsemen trotted back and forth beyond the docks, at moments breaking into a gallop; amongst them halberdiers stood, sometimes running this way and that, every one vainly attempting to keep the crowd before them at bay as angry shouts rose into the air.

By the time he stepped ashore under the circling gulls and grabbed a soldier, Gian Andrea was hardly surprised by what he heard.

"Don Garcia has no intention of taking us to Malta," the fellow said. "Rather he would us drift about the sea, like pieces of wood, washing up on one island after another. We are soldiers, not sailors. We want to be paid for our days and discharged."

The cavalry's presence showed that Don Garcia opposed such a plan. Doria asked the soldier where the Vice Roy was to be found, only to have that one exclaim, "The Devil if I know! No doubt hiding on his damn ship!"

Gian Andrea followed the soldier's raised chin to the Vice Roy's *capitana*, which was moored nearby. Boarding, he encountered a fierce dispute underway on the poop.

The Prior of Auvergne, who'd traveled from that place to join the relief, was pressing Don Garcia to embark the troops again without delay. "Can you not understand, Signore," the Prior said, voice sharp with urgency, "every moment lost brings the Religion closer to complete destruction."

"Sir," the Vice Roy answered, well exercised even before Doria had appeared, "do not take such a tone with me. Address me as Eccellenza."

Auvergne himself had already lost the humor for disputation. "Signore," he said, "provided we land on Malta in time to bring succour to the Religion, I will with all my soul give you the title of Excellency, Your Highness, or even Your Majesty. If you prefer, I shall nominate you as His Holiness, but let us *begone!*"

With a scowl, Toledo took to pacing the deck and waved his hands over the scene on the dock. "Ah! With all these worthless soldiers attempting to desert, we shall not be able to provide any relief to Malta. The entire undertaking is collapsing as we speak. How can we embark?"

"Eccellenza," interrupted de Sande, "the Grand Master of the Knights of St. John has been heroically battling a great Turkish force for nearly four months without the least help from anyone. I joined this expedition only with your solemn pledge that the undertaking would be carried out. What excuse can you offer for abandoning it so late in the day?"

Hereat, Doria himself finally interceded. Drawing up his slight frame to its full height, he said, "Eccellenza, I as well gave a solemn oath to support the ground forces. If you are not willing go to the aid of these heroic Knights, to whom all Christendom is in debt, I will take this fleet in hand myself, with your leave or without it, do you understand me? Eccellenza, reply!"

An exasperated Don Garcia once again waved his hand over the riot on the embankment. "Very well, if we have sufficient men, let us proceed."

"We will proceed," replied Gian Andrea, "if it is but Colonel de Sande and myself."

By nightfall, order had been restored, the galleys provisioned and watered. Alvaro de Sande watched the soldiers climb aboard the ships, understanding that more than a thousand had deserted this day, bringing the number of his troops down to eight thousand. What army awaited them twenty leagues south, he knew not, but with eight thousand, the *gran soccorso* again departed for Malta.

On the seventh of September, the eve of the Feast of the Nativity of the Virgin, we at St. Michel and Castille watched corsairs, janissaries and spahis gather below in the trenches. The assault we had been warned of was at hand.

"Who ever heard of such enduring love?" remarked Balbi, readying his arquebus

"I think rather it is fear," I answered, cranking the crossbow in my hands, "fear of the Sultan, fear of dishonor."

An armslength from us, Hasan of Argier was urging his corsairs forward and Mustafa himself to the last cajoled and threatened his troops.

Without warning, Pietru shouted, "Go away! We are tired of you!"

It was the only shot we fired. Peering over the wall, I convinced myself Yakhshi crouched below. Stupidly standing up, I hailed him. "Yakhshi!" I shouted in Turkish. "Didn't you hear? Go away! We're tired of you!"

Yakhshi or any of his comrades could easily have put a ball into my head. Instead, the janissary hailed me in return, then turned with a disgusted wave of his arm and climbed out of the trenches. At once a great discord arose among the troops and they all walked away.

One Hundred Twelve

Never did music sound so sweet to human ears as the peal of the town's bells did to ours on that eighth of September, the feast of the Nativity of the Virgin. On the eve of the feast, the bells remained reluctant to speak.

While we watched the Turks desert their trenches, the sentries at St. Angelo spied a Turkish galiot coming from the direction of Gozo. Soon after it landed at Rinella, a messenger jumped ashore in great excitement. A horse was quickly brought to him. He mounted it and fell to the ground. Enraged, he cut the horse's legs off with his scimitar and ran to Mustafa's pavilion on foot. Shortly after, three dozen Turkish galleys left Marsamxett to take up position at the mouth of the Great Port.

By that time I had walked again to Birgu, discovering Isabella at the Hospital, "It is over," I said as I had before. She stared at me with a slightly brighter smile than the last time, my words still incredible, but as we stood in the courtyard, the alarm bell atop St. Angelo began to sound, answered by the retort of a distant gun. All those in the courtyard who were able raised their heads. "Come," I said, taking her hand.

She would not leave the injured until she had found someone to take her duties, and then we ran to the fortress, climbing to the cavalier. From there we espied upon the sea the fleet of His Most Catholic Majesty, King Philip II of Spain. Each galley fired three blank charges in salute as it passed and then sailed on, in the direction of Sicily. I ran to the gun at the tower's edge, intending to fire it in return but the powder barrels were empty. Not entirely able to comprehend what was taking place, all of us atop the bastions of Fort St. Angelo began to wave, to cheer at the top of our lungs, to embrace anyone by them. Isabella and I fell into each other's arms.

The Grand Master, Romegas and the jester had just climbed to the summit. de Valette saw for himself the procession of galleys passing the Great Port, and for an instant I mistakenly thought I discerned a smile cross his face. When the sentries could not tell him whether the relief had actually landed, he remarked that if the Vice Roy had put the troops down, they would attack the Turks this night, but until then we must all remain vigilant.

He told those around him to make certain the men were provided with powder, shot and matches, should we have them, and crossbows.

"When will you believe we have won, Eminenza?" I asked.

"When the last Turk has left this island," he answered.

Yet, as we stood on the cavalier buffeted by the hot winds, the Turks, having also seen the armada, began to strike their tents on Salvatore in complete disorder and embark their remaining guns from Rinella. "On the other hand," conceded de Valette, "they appear to be declaring defeat themselves." This time he did smile.

As the sun rose the next morning, we saw the Turkish trenches deserted. But for some men guarding a big dismounted gun above Bormla, the troops were all at Rinella desperately embarking artillery and provisions, or on Sciberras doing the same.

"*Haqq!*" grunted Pietru. "If we'd gone out yesterday, we could have taken their pieces."

Soon, a renegado came over from the Turkish camp and said that a relief of thirty Christian galleys had landed at Mellieha Bay at the northwest of Malta. We immediately sent a runner to the Grand Master to give him the news and shortly thereafter the bells began to ring.

Never, I say again, did music sound so sweet to human ears as the peal of the town's bells did to ours on that eighth of September, the feast of the Nativity of the Virgin. For nearly four months those bells had sounded only alarms, but now they might have been the voices of angels on high and they rang without cease all day, thro' the Pontifical High Mass that the Grand Master ordered and which was celebrated with great solemnity as a thanksgiving to God and the Holy Mother for the mercy vouchsafed to us.

After the Mass, while the bells continued to peal, people surrounded the Grand Master on the steps of San Lorenzo, kneeling at his feet and weeping for joy. Many, though, remained short of water and did not know where to find it. "Why not let them take it from the cistern in the fortress," Isabella offered.

de Valette, gazing at the crowd below him, considered the request. "You may take water from the cistern only if you bring a Turkish cannon ball to the castle," he said.

Thereat the townspeople rushed headlong out the gates searching for Turkish ammunition. Within moments the stream of buckets and cast iron began to enter St. Angelo, and the balls began to pile up on the plaza by the empty mill.

Tho' we had no clear knowledge of it, at that moment the *gran soccorso* was disembarking at the other side of the island. Don Garcia had already departed to ferry more troops from Sicily, and de Sande's forces were trudging to Notabile with munitions and bisket, for Anastagi had written to della Corgna that the Old City lacked sufficient ovens to bake bread for the relief. To be sure, so heavy were the bisket sacks on each soldier's back, weighing almost as much as the armor the Knights wore, that many began throwing them to the ground until de Sande and Corgna put a halt to it. As the thousands of soldiers crossed the island for Notabile, Vincenzo Anastagi met them with horses and beasts of burden.

"As I promised," Anastagi said, holding out the reigns of two of the horses to Corgna and de Sande, "a pair of fine Berber stallions. Now let me guide you to some excellent lodging, Messeri."

"When do we get at the Turks?" de Sande asked, mounting his steed.

Anastagi waved his hand. "Ah, do not trouble yourself about that, Colonel. First, rest. By the time you awake, the Turks will have departed."

As the bells sang, people wandered throughout the town, greeting one another with bows or handshakes, weeping over their shattered homes, truly unable to grasp that today was the day of our deliverance. I stood at Flaminia's house, hoping beyond hope that she would miraculously appear from the rubble. She did not. Flaminia had been right; I had never loved her, but the hole left inside me from her loss was, after that of Balthazar, the greatest of the siege. The poor woman had never harmed a soul in her life.

While I stood in the wreckage a voice said to me, "She was only a whore."

I turned to see one of the townsfolk who was carrying the dead out beyond the city gates.

"She was not the only whore," I said and walked on.

Already people from Mdina had begun to appear at the town, as well as a company of soldiers to inform the Grand Master that the *soccorso* had truly landed. I hailed them as they passed and thanked them for coming to our aid. The Knights in the company scarce paid me any heed, so astonished were they at the ruins surrounding them, and the stench of the air, which made breathing near impossible.

One of the Knights, a beardless youth, who could have had no more than eighteen years to him, was saying to another that he had joined the expedition "just for the amusement of the thing."

For a heartbeat I regarded him, as he regarded me with a gay smile, then I laid low the Comte de Martinengo, as he turned out to be. The others lurched forward, but allowed the bandaged and filthy figure before them to stagger on.

Towards evening I agreed to accompany Isabella to Mdina to see her mother, but almost all Birgu's horses were dead. We went out on foot against all the people bringing in shot and any wood they could find to begin the repair of their homes. "I've heard they've stacked three thousand balls in the castle this day," Isabella said.

I had also heard.

For a time we walked in silence, picking our way over the deserted trenches, avoiding the corpses that had not been done away with. The Turks had made off with most of their weapons and burnt everything else. Little remained of consequence beyond the large gun above Bormla, which would be too heavy to easily move.

"I want to thank you, Francisco," Isabella said at length, "for helping me survive. For trying to save my soul."

"Those years ago, we said we were destined to be always with each other," I answered. "Perhaps it was for this purpose." I felt less certain of such portents now and whether we had survived, yet alone triumphed, I was unsure.

"The resurrection of Christ took but two days," Isabella said. "I fear our own will take far longer."

I nodded. Of all my sorrows, the keenest was truly that Balthazar had not lived to witness this day. "I cannot fathom the Almighty's design when one such as he should die and one such as Fuster should live, wounded tho' he may be." Balthazar had said all our questions would be answered by the siege. I no longer knew what he meant. "My only consolation is that he knew his time was past and was prepared to die."

"You shall take the best of him," Isabella pressed her hand to my chest, "and carry it always, here."

We walked on.

Troops were camped everywhere around Mdina, supping at the old windmills on the city's outskirts, or at the stables surrounding the walls. When we arrived at Isabella's house, Mezquita Anastagi, Alvaro de Sande, Acansio della Corgna, Pompeo Colonna, Chiappino Vitelli and Rafael Salvago were all gathered at the table. Lady Emilia did not at once recognize her daughter for the bandages wrapping her arms and her drawn and haggard appearance. When Emilia discerned that the gaunt woman standing before her was Isabella, she at once broke into tears and ran to her, wailing over and over again, "O my God! O my God! Madonna, what have the Turks done to you!"

"Mama," said Isabella, embracing her. "Shh. I am well. I am alive."

The servants made places for us at the table as introductions were given. "Colonel de Sande," I said, "you will certainly not recognize me, but I am Francisco de Barai, who was trapped with you at Djerbé five years ago and who, like you, was taken in slavery to Constantinople."

"Of course!" de Sande replied, grasping my hand.

"Old friends have gathered for their just reckoning," remarked Anastagi.

"The only reckoning has been God's," I answered.

Colonna and Vitelli asked how many men we had lost. I turned to Isabella; both of us moved our shoulders. "I know we have lost two hundred fifty or three hundred Knights, half of them during the siege of Fort St. Elmo. Three or four thousand soldiers have perished and mayhap another seven thousand of the common folk, a third part. Half the slaves, perhaps five hundred."

"And the enemy?" asked della Corgna.

Again Isabella and I shook our heads. "We are certain to have killed fifteen thousand," I said, "mayhap an equal number have died of sickness. I do not know."

della Corgna's eye bore into me with a fierce intensity. "Do you understand, Señor, what you have accomplished on this tiny island?" he said. I shook my head dumbly. "In the name of Almighty God, you have stopped the greatest army on the face of the earth! At Vienna, the Grand Turk merely retired after three weeks because of the weather as much as the defense. Never has he been so humiliated as here, right here. What has transpired here is the greatest victory of our age! You have saved Europe, Christendom. Señor, a toast to the invincible Grand Master Jean de Valette!" We all raised our glasses with the wine the *soccorso* had brought.

"À propos," put in de Sande, "the greatest army on earth yet resides on Malta, and we must decide forthwith how to quickly put a period to their sojourn."

At once the conversation turned to the best course of action. della Corgna proposed doing nothing. Now that the relief had arrived, the defeated Turks would surely depart of their own accord. Indeed, messengers from the Grand Master had already arrived, advising the *soccorso* not to attack the enemy from the Marsa because, as so many Turks had died there of fever, the air must be pestiferous.

"Sir," replied de Sande, "Philip and the Vice Roy might desire such a plan, but what will our men say, who have come from all corners of Europe, who been shipped hither and yon across the sea for weeks like these biskets, if they are not given the opportunity to confront the enemy?"

della Corgna remarked that the Colonel appeared more sanguine for revenge than he had been at Messina. To which de Sande replied only that Doria had fulfilled his sworn duty and, by God, he, Alvaro de Sande, would fulfill his.

Yakhshi had been ordering the men to burn everything—sacks, sails, ropes—anything that might be of use to the enemy, and stood watching the black smoke from the fires billow into the unearthly hot air of this accursed island. Even as the slaves and sappers loaded the artillery onto the galleys, most of the fighting men yet stood ashore, here on the Santarma island, or across the harbor where the gallows had stood. The disorder put into the men by the news that the Christian relief had arrived somewhere to the north astonished the *Boluk-bashi*, and everywhere they ran about like pigs. He spat on the ground, disgusted.

He watched teams of slaves haul one of the basilisks onto a barge at the foot of Santarma island. They were working too fast, carelessly. Yakhshi stumbled down to warn them that men were cheap but such guns rare. Late. As the slaves let up a huge cry, the barge tilted sharply and the great gun slipped off it with hardly a splash into the Marsamshet harbor. The *gumiler* were already screaming their heads off and flailing the dogs to within a whisker of their lives, but they would never be able to fish that behemoth from the water.

Nearby, in the open air where everyone heard the poison infecting their voices, the *Pashalar* were also screaming, at each other. With flailing arms Mustafa was again accusing Piyale, that had his galleys been patrolling the north of the island, the Christian relief would never have landed. But now, with such a large force preparing to march on them, they must leave the island at once.

Piyale, for his part, shook his head adamantly, saying that Mustafa was at fault for failing to take the island, though he had come with far more men than necessary. And now scouts told him the relief numbered only four thousand men. "O Mustafa," the *Kapudan* went on haughtily, "what excuse will you give to the Sultan for leaving the island without even having set eyes on the enemy? Will he not cut off your head? If you have not seen them, you cannot even say to the Padishah from what forces you have fled." Having recaptured some of his old daring, the *Kapudan* thereupon proposed that Mustafa march toward the old city to engage the relief while Piyale himself would take the fleet north to the bay of St. Paul and wait.

The order went around the camp. Yakhshi, having heard it, fumed to the *chavush* Abdallah, who he encountered on the hill. "I told you those Pashalar forgot that pride carries men off to Hell. Now it will carry us all off to Hell."

Aye, as His Majesty knows, his *Pashalar* mounted yet a further last attempt to save their honor, if not their enterprise. I needn't recount in detail the battle of Qala ta San Pawl, St. Paul's Bay. It was the eleventh of September, the hottest day yet of the siege. Mustafa, King Hasan and

Uluj Ali, who'd returned again from Barbary, advanced on Città Notabile as Piyale moved the armada north to the bay.

della Corgna yet advised to wait and receive the attack but de Sande, I think, only laughed. As he rode before the ranks brandishing his broadsword, the Colonel watched his soldiers gather their companies together and bring up the standards, and he knew that the point of no earthly sword could restrain them.

"For Christ! For Philip! For the Knights of St. John!" de Sande charged. Vitelli and della Corgna, Colonna and two thousand foot were behind him.

On that day de Sande received his long-awaited revenge, if that is what he sought. Tho' the sun was so hot that neither Christian nor Turk could stand from thirst and exhaustion, and tho' his horse was shot out from under him with an arrow to its neck, de Sande bloodied his sword to the hilt and his forces finally routed the enemy. Mustafa, seeing his troops completely broken, jumped from his horse and killed it. Thereat he placed himself at the head of his army to try to maintain order, in vain. As the Turks fled in terror to the waiting boats, de Sande's men pursued them, wading straight into the waters. Piyale had placed janissaries in boats, who kept up fire to protect the retreat, and neither did the *Kapudan* suffer the cannon of his galleys to remain silent. All for naught. de Sande's troops tore after them, killing the Turks with arquebus, lances or knives, even as they scrambled into the boats. By the time the fleet's oars dipped into the waters of St. Paul's Bay, another two or three thousand Turks covered the rock and sand with their blood.

Having watched the battle from Mdina's ramparts, Isabella and I among many others rode out to St. Paul to watch the Turkish galleys disappear over the horizon, but within a few days the stench at the bay became so unbearable that no one could go near it.

Epilogue

One Hundred Thirteen

Thus, Your Majesty, ended the Great Siege of Malta, if it could be said to have ended. Aye, as the story's finish may be everlasting, I shall not dwell on it. Three days after the battle of St. Paul's Bay, Don Garcia and Gian Andrea stepped off the Vice Roy's *capitana* at the Great Port, to be embraced by the Grand Master. Onlookers watched them retire to the Magisterial Palace for a sumptuous feast with provisions brought by the *soccorso*, and everyone marveled at the pyramids of cannon balls rising above St. Angelo. Within three days people had hauled in ten thousand and the stream showed no signs of diminishing.

The Grand Master bestowed great gifts upon the Commanders of the *soccorso*, giving Juan de Cardona and his successors the right to wear the habit of the Knights of St. John without payment of the customary fees, and Alvaro de Sande a piece of the True Cross. Likewise, he sent thousands of *scudi* to the children of Maestro de Campo Robles and those of Miranda and Medrano. At de Valette's intercession, His Holiness himself baptized the Turk Mehmed ben Davud as Philip de Lascaris, who received a perpetual appointment from King Philip in the Kingdom of Naples. Because the renegado Alfonso fought well and knew several languages, the Grand Master retained him in his service. The Vice Roy remained on Malta only a matter of days, then departed for Sicily, some praising, others cursing him.

For myself, the morning after we watched the Turks vanish from St. Paul's Bay, I knocked on the door of Matteo Falzon's house and was shown in by a servant. The master received me in the courtyard. "The siege is over, Signore Falzon," I said. "It is safe to walk the streets."

Smiling faintly, he asked whether I was certain, to which I shrugged. "You did not fight?" I asked.

He shook his head, proffering me a chair; instead I sat near the nymphaeum, on the low wall ringing the courtyard. "I told you I would never lift a finger for the Knights, and I did not."

That would be treason to most, but Falzon's stubbornness evoked some admiration from me. "I have come to ask from you another service," I said. As the servant brought wine, I recounted what had transpired with Cubelles and that he had threatened to exact vengeance once the siege was over. "It is over. My once mistress gave me a phial. I believed she intended to protect me with a potion, as was her wont, but inside I found instead this list of names." I handed Falzon the paper. "I thought you might know what they mean."

Falzon glanced at the names and nodded. "Have you ever wondered, Francisco, why I have not been judged more severely by Cubelles, given that my friend Gesualdo was burned at the stake?" The thought had once or twice crossed my mind. "Or why, with their hatred of one another, Cubelles has never openly attempted to ruin de Valette?"

After my midnight conversation with Cubelles, I had well pondered this, understanding how long ago Isabella's throwing me up protected her guardian, but not understanding what staved off Cubelles in subsequent years.

"I own the largest and most fertile tract of land on Malta. The Inquisitor intends to condemn me for heresy and confiscate my property, but the Grand Master also covets it, so he would prefer to see me not condemned for heresy."

"The Grand Master protects you?" I found this difficult to comprehend.

Falzon shook his head. "Consider me a cowardly battlefield. In exchange for calling off the torture those years ago, I gave the Bishop a deed for my land upon my death."

"Do you have a copy of this deed?" I blurted out in amazement. Such a document might be a powerful weapon against my adversary.

"I do, but will not reveal its location. In any case, the measure is no more enduring than the repairs you made during the assaults on St. Michel. When Cubelles attempts to confiscate my land, the Grand Master will write to the Pope, reminding him that Malta belongs to the Knights of St. John, not the Holy Office, and demand that the tract be ceded to him. The Inquisitor is powerful, but not invulnerable. The Grand Master has also undoubtedly for some years been prepared to wield the list of *familiari* you hold in your hand."

"*Familiari?*" I asked, wondering if they were the same as those employed by *El Santo Oficio* in Spain.

It appeared so. Cubelles, incorruptible as an Inquisitor must be, had surrounded himself with some dozens of bodyguards, priests, assistants— *familiari*—all of whom had received letters patent removing them from the law of the Grand Master and the secular authorities. *Familiari* were cursed as informants and rogues who never failed to use their privileges to their own ends. Half the Maltese people would kill for the letters patent, the other half would kill those who bore them.

"So," said Falzon, "you have in your hand the shield de Valette has used to protect himself from the Inquisitor. You may attempt to discover the crimes of these scoundrels wherewith you may suborn him. Your renowned mistress will be skilled in using this list."

She had disappeared in the bombardment, I told him.

"Then attempt to become one of the Grand Master's *familiari*, or if that road is closed to you—" Falzon looked at me knowingly—" the safest path is to leave Malta." He handed the list back to me.

I thanked Master Falzon for his counsel, which would undoubtedly prove useful, and departed, wishing him good fortune.

Immediately afterwards, Isabella and I borrowed horses and rode back to the Borgo. Isabella set off to the Hospital and I helped her servants begin clearing away the wreckage of her house. As we labored, Falzon's words came together with some of Flaminia's own and I walked to Blaij Vergã's house, where I found his mistress cleaning up what remained of it. I did not even know her name.

"You were a friend of mistress Flaminia's, weren't you?" I said to this dark girl, who stood before me as filthy as everyone else here.

She nodded.

"Tell me, did you gossip about these people with Flaminia?" I read her the names of the *familiari*.

"Oh *si*," she nodded. "I can tell you all about them."

For a price. After I paid her, the *quiraca* revealed everything there was to know about each of them and I wrote down every word. Before I left her, I put a question that just occurred to me.

"The *libelli* you posted with Flaminia about Blaij Vergã. You didn't write them to aid Balthazar or me. You were hoping to escape and wrote them because Blaij refused to aid you, planning to take Isabella Guasconi instead." I surmised that the girl nodded, but it may have been my imagination.

I never saw Flaminia again. Thousands upon thousands had been buried beneath the rubble during the bombardment. Almost certainly she and her daughter were killed and their bodies burned in a heap with the others whose names are forgotten by bards that sing the exploits of knights and princes. I was unable to fulfill my promise, to bury her and Francesca in consecrated ground, and for that I grieved. She had fought well for her land, a generous soul who had never harmed anyone, except mayhap with her worthless potions, but I prefer to believe that with the cleverness of a *quiraca* and the money of a rich one, that when things became finally desperate, Flaminia and Francesca discovered a way out of Birgu, mayhap to the Sultan's harem.

I found some sheets of paper and at the ruins of Isabella's house wrote a handful of *libelli famosi*. When Isabella arrived, I gave them to her. "If I am taken by the Inquisitor," I told her, "and not released the same day, post these."

Isabella gazed disquietedly on the sheets in her hand, and instantly secreted them away.

My encounter with the Bishop took place sooner than he or I expected. Toward vespers, as we labored at the house, Cubelles, gaunt and infirm, walked past with his *familiari*-bravi and, catching sight of me, ordered as on a whim that they seize me.

They brought me to the Bishop's Palace. Seeing that, like everything else in this quarter, the place lay half-ruined, I laughed. What sort of tribunal could take place here? But in his zeal the Inquisitor dusted off his throne and sat on it amidst the rubble, ordering his *famliari* to right the table and his scribe to find a quill. The old man, coughing and dripping with sweat, declared, as I had foreseen, that I'd been denounced for turning Turk and I proved it by freeing one. He would imprison me in the Palace dungeon—what remained of it—and put me to the question.

I replied by naming all the *familiari* by him and with what they would be accused should he detain me. At once, as if struck from Above, Cubelles fainted, collapsing wholly senseless against his throne. The *familiari* rushed to his aid and I walked away. It was the last time Bishop Cubelles troubled anyone. He never resumed his Inquisitorial duties and, to the sadness of many and the relief of some, died a year later.

If our own constitution was stronger than the Inquisitor's, neither Don Garcia's men nor we perceived it. While they gazed in stupefaction at the state of the towns, we accepted food from their hands and jested with them as walking spirits might. "How many soldiers fought here?" a fellow Spaniard asked. "Four thousand Maltese, a thousand Italians, some Germans and French, and a thousand soldiers," I answered. Would that we were half that now! Of the two hundred and some men who had at the siege's outset made up Romegas's flying *soccorso*, only seventeen remained capable of walking. Most of the men in the Hospital were on their death beds, leaving Vigo despondent. The three of us, Isabella, he and I, often took meals together during rest from our unceasing toil.

"I cannot save them," Vigo said when I came on him and Isabella at the Sacra Infermeria. He was applying oils brought by the relief to the wounds of the injured, while nearby surgeons whacked heads in the padded helmet before they hacked off greening limbs and Serving Brothers thrust clysters up the asses of those whose jaws were tied shut. "Even with herbs and digestives arriving, I cannot."

"Jean," I said as we stepped to the place near Kalkara Creek where biskets were to be had, "you must count those you have saved, not those you have lost. No man has done more than you during this siege to save lives ... "

" ... and perhaps souls," Isabella added, taking his hand and mine.

"We shall have to rebuild the Hospital," said Vigo, gazing up at the shattered walls behind us. "That is the Order's first duty. I hope someday those who live will be of a greater number than those who perish."

"It is a worthy dream," I replied.

Vigo rose and returned to work.

During the days immediately after the siege's lifting, Isabella prayed often. She made no complaint about all that faced us, but my jests that she had yet to be resurrected were met by a sad, stone face, and even my songs about Lucia hardly raised more than a faint smile before we fell silently back to work.

For some nights Isabella asked that I stay with her in the cistern, the only place we had to sleep, and she yet shuddered in my arms as if the guns were roaring, but after a week she said she wished to discover whether she might pass the night alone. I went to my room, which had not been hit, but in which slept six people.

Christendom took far less note of the rubble and corpses than of the glory. A few days after the arrival of the relief, de Valette himself decreed that the Borgo should be renamed Vittoriosa. Looking around at it, with scarce a stone upon stone, we hardly knew to call it Birgu, yet alone Vittoriosa. But e'en as the first wreckage-laden wagons lumbered out of Birgu, news of the Turkish defeat raced north to Europe with the speed of the wind. A week hadn't passed before a galley arrived in the Great Port with a report of jubilation in Naples and before another week went by the first sounds of bells in Rome reached us.

It took longer for word to return from kings and queens that we had triumphed in the greatest siege in history, and longer still for us to believe it, but as the weeks passed, ship after ship put into the Great Port laden with the most extraordinary tales of rejoicing throughout Christendom. Just as merchants and soldiers thirsted for each word we could give them about the past four remarkable months, so too did people gather at the docks of Galley Creek to learn how the news had been greeted in the capitals. Every traveler said the same: "No news of this century has been met with greater joy. Bells sound in every land, fires light the heavens, people dance in the street."

To our wonderment, it was all true. At Rome, His Holiness ordered a public festa. The whole city was shut down, artillery sounded and fireworks burst across the sky. In Paris, Madrid, even London, people flocked to churches where voices were raised in a *Te Deum*. From Venice, aye, we heard only a deathly silence, but e'en the nameless heretic who sat on the throne of England called for a thrice weekly thanksgiving to be celebrated for six weeks, and instead of "that obscure island of sandstone," Malta became "the island of heroes." One hero above all. On every pair of Christian lips was the same name, Jean de Valette, the invincible de Valette who had stopped the Turks, who had saved Europe.

Less than a month after the battle of St. Paul's Bay, the Papal Nuncio arrived at the Great Port and was escorted to the Magisterial Palace by Eminenza himself. Like everyone, the Nuncio stared speechless at the numbers of cannon balls that greeted his eyes. By now Fort St. Angelo overflowed, for well over one hundred thousand balls had been gathered, some said one hundred thirty thousand with the shot the corsairs had brought from Barbary. Whatever the number, stacks of iron became a common sight everywhere in Birgu, and people never ceased to discover balls in the ground or in the water for as long as I remained on Malta. I think they will never cease to discover them.

The Nuncio told of the festa in Rome and the outpouring of joy sweeping Europe. He told of Spaniards exulting that "one hundred thousand years from now, the great King Philip will still be worthy of praise and renown, and that God will have given him a seat in Paradise for having so nobly delivered so many gentlemen in Malta, which was about to follow Rhodes into enemy hands." The Pope, tho', during the festa, had refused to mention the King of Spain, the Vice Roy or the Captain General, and gave all credit for the victory to God and the Knights of St. John.

The Nuncio also brought a cardinal's hat for the Grand Master. Robles's jester, in his last remark while on the island, advised, "Two hats, one black, one red; one square, the other round, shall never sit in comfort on the same head." de Valette took the advice to heart and politely declined the office, saying that two such great stations would forever be in conflict with one another. "Wide brimmed and round," added the jester, "shields tired heads from the sun. Short and squat leaves one burned." That was also true.

de Valette did, tho', accept the diamond-encrusted gold sword King Philip sent him not long after, which the envoy admonished him to wield in the defense of Christendom.

Hats and swords were far from the only honors being bestowed on the Grand Master. Every poet and bard in every tavern across Europe took up his pen in praise of de Valette and the Knights of St. John. The torrent of sonnets, ballads, chansons and epics knew no end. Spaniards wrote how the Spanish Knights saved the island; Italians wrote how the Italian Knights saved the island. Most of the scribblers had never set foot on Malta. As for poor Balbi, he left the island shortly after the siege and published his book, but I do not believe he ever earned the praise for it he had hoped, or the gold.

"Listen to all the glad tidings," I said to Isabella one day while we sat
in a ruined tavern listening to a wandering musician sing of our epic
deeds. Such was his gusto in describing the exploits of Toni Bajada, who
swam from one end of the island under water, that we happily joined in,
singing the part of Bajada's guitar, "*don, don, don, diridiri don, don, don,*"
tho' I never heard him play one.

"It makes me believe we did not fight in vain," I said to Isabella,
laughing. "Milady, you must pen your own verses. You were here. You
saw."

"Truly they are glad tidings," she answered, smiling almost for the first
time since battle's end. Aye, the elation coming from all corners lifted
Isabella's spirits enough so that she did pen a handful of poems. They were
of a somewhat different color than many of those written from afar, but
she sent them to a printer in Florence and they were published, bringing
her praise:

Sento delle campane i lieti canti
gioir del fin della spietata guerra;
lodano il Re che le pregion disserra
e dan gloria ai cavalier, ormai santi.

Tra il fumo ch'al mio viso sta innanti
va 'l suon che giova la distrutta terra
e conforta' l cor che sì spesso erra;
ma tace là ove morte urla i suoi vanti.

Nostra voce un grido fino al cielo spinge,
onde vuol trovar di sue pene tregua
e chieder pace a chi Pieta' distringe.

Qual falcon trafitto che appen dilegua,
poi cade, ma'l cor fero risospinge,
così la speme nostra al ciel prosegua.

I render the same, poorly:

When I hear the joyous voice of the bells

Sounding everywhere across Christian lands,
Songs raised to Lord God our deliverer,
That fill the grandest cathedrals with light
And lofty praise sung to the valiant Knights,
They as if roll through heavy clouds of smoke
That shroud the inlets of my aching heart
And fall upon the crying graves of the dead.
We the half-dead cast our mournful laments
To the sky, hoping the sad cries take wing
And soar with the gladder songs of troubadours.
We watch their fierce struggle to gain on high,
Clutch our breaths, stifle our tears when they fail,
And cast them to Heaven once more with prayer.

No jubilation of any sort was to be found aboard the Turkish fleet as it neared Constantinople. After the battle at the bay, Mustafa ordered the *chavush* Abdallah-al-Waryagli ahead on a fast *kalyata* to Constantinople to inform the Sultan of what had transpired on the island that should forever remain nameless. When Abdallah delivered by his own hand Mustafa's dispatch, and His Majesty learned that onwards of twenty thousand men had been lost without capturing the rock, he flew into a rage the likes of which no one in the Sarai had seen during his long reign. Abdallah watched as the Padishah hurled the missive to the ground and stamped on it, crying, "The Sword of Islam is invincible only when it is wielded by my own hand! When the next season arrives, I will myself lead an expedition to that place and put every person alive to the sword!"

His Majesty, as I have said tho', was long steeled to the wayward path of Fortune. By the time the fleet arrived at the Golden Horn, he had declared victory. Mustafa and Piyale Pasha paraded through Constantinople in triumph, while horns and tambourines sounded and onlookers threw garlands at their feet. Although the city's people may have wondered why so many troops were lacking, Abdallah al-Waryagli and other officers had, as ordered, gave out that the island had been reduced and its inhabitants taken into captivity. In his wisdom the Padishah had decided not to garrison a barren rock at such a distance and had blown up all the fortifications instead.

Yet news of the disgrace couldn't be kept hidden. The returning soldiers told their stories and word quickly spread that the rock hadn't fallen, that the army had left behind twenty-five thousand, thirty or sometimes thirty-five thousand dead. The muftis publicly condemned the disgrace, riots broke out, thousands of homes were burnt. Once again Soliman forbade wine to Christians and Jews, and demanded from their churches and synagogues huge sums of money, which he said would finance the next expedition against the island without name. The Christians of Galata could not show their faces in public for fear of being stoned by the Turks, each of whom had lost a brother, a husband or a friend.

It is also told that His Majesty walked the streets at night disguised as a commoner to hear the curses rained on his head by the people. But I have said this before.

de Valette, as might be guessed, revealed little jubilation. He didn't rest a day, could be seen always at the Hospital or on the square, and soon enough was spurred to even more frenzied activity when word arrived from Constantinople: The Turks planned a new invasion. "It is to be expected," he said to Romegas in the shadow of the clock tower. "With the island in ruins and no defenses remaining, if Soliman invades in the spring, only six months away, he will succeed."

"Will we move the Convent to Zaragoza or Messina?" answered Romegas.

Counsellors everywhere had been advising it. The Grand Master, who'd once sought to return the Convent to Tripoli, or Rhodes, replied: "I would sooner be buried in the ruins of Malta than abandon this island."

What Balthazar would say about that, I wondered, but de Valette at once began laying plans for the long-dreamed city atop Mt. Sciberras and set about raising money to build it. With the prestige of the Knights higher than in five hundred years—and the understanding that they had saved Europe—vast sums of money quickly began to pour into Malta, money from Spain, France, Portugal, the Priories, from the Pope. Money, tho', would not prevent an invasion.

It was then, in the autumn, that de Valette called me to him in the Chapel of St. Anne. "I have heard from Isabella that you intend to travel to Constantinople."

Knowing I had lost Eminenza's favor, I nodded carefully, saying that I would leave only when permitted, to fulfill Balthazar's dying requests.

Before he uttered another word, de Valette swore me to secrecy on pain of death, forcing me to kiss the Holy Book. "Can I trust you and a few brave men," he said at length, "to get into the Turkish Arsenal and set it ablaze, to destroy the Turkish fleet and forestall a second invasion?"

For an infinite time I did not answer, and when I finally did, my words came with infinite slowness. "I cannot imagine a more perilous undertaking," I whispered. "E'en should I be able to enter unrecognized, the place is surrounded by janissaries who guard against mischief. Moreso, the powder stores are held at Tophane until needed by the fleet, in order to prevent exactly what you suggest. I see no means to accomplish this enterprise and, e'en were you to trust me, I could not promise."

"Great riches shall be yours, Esforzado."

Even the rewards failed to tempt me, so boundless was the risk. At last I agreed to reconnoitre the Arsenal, but would not swear to act. Yet such was the Grand Master's desperation to prevent another attack that he agreed to have Romegas ferry me and a few others who spoke Turkish to the Levant.

Isabella had already heard of the plans from de Valette's own lips. "If you do this," she said with rising color but pale desire, "Parisot shall surely give you my hand."

"It is always Parisot, isn't it?" I laughed somberly. "What do *you* wish?"

Isabella regarded me strangely, with a trace of her old haughtiness. "I wish as he does, that Malta be rebuilt."

"That is all?"

"Francisco," she said, taking my hands in hers, "until Malta is brought to life again, my own desires mean nothing. Forgive me."

With that we embraced with infinite sweetness and the infinite distance that had always separated us, and I made ready to leave for Constantinople, well understanding that Blaij Vergã had never been my true rival.

Before departing, I traveled to Gozo to say farewell to Pietru, who had already gone thither. I found him and Grezz on a small farm on the eastern side of the island. The wind was whistling and not another person was in sight, only some goats in a pen near the stone hut they'd built. Pietru's wounds were not fully healed and he left most of the heavy work to his wife. The sight of my old friend gladdened my heart and I stayed for lunch, eating goat's milk and cheese and barley bread.

"You have now fulfilled your vow to plant the island again," I said, looking around the green but empty place. "I fear you will have to plant people as well."

"We will try," he said, with a glance at Grezz.

We did not speak much—we never had—but of all the endings of the siege, the one that gave me the most joy was that these two souls might now take up their lives together, fifteen years after they had been torn asunder.

We embraced and I returned on a *luzzu* to Malta. The next day I set sail on Romegas's galley for Constantinople. I asked the him whether he regretted his capture of the old nurse but of course he said no.

One Hundred Fourteen

The remainder of the tale, Your Majesty, is yet more swiftly told. Romegas set our small band ashore at Crete and we reached Constantinople some weeks later. My first duties were to Balthazar. I found his lady and gave her the crucifix, and my deepest regrets that the Chevalier could not present it himself. I next sought out Giovan Barelli. I brought the Greek a chest of jewels that would make him fabulously wealthy and a letter from Eminenza that he was henceforth to be known as a Knight of Grace, the highest honor the Religion could bestow on a commoner. But the man who, perhaps more than any other after de Valette himself, had saved Malta, seemed more greatly rewarded when I passed on greetings from Balthazar, and more deeply grieved when I told him of that one's death.

"No more honorable death could have been wished," I said, "but I yet cannot think of him without tears."

We never set the Arsenal ablaze, Your Majesty. As I'd foreseen, it was heavily guarded, especially in the wake of the recent calamity, and my old fears of being recognized there returned. We simply failed to find a sure means to enter the place and destroy it. I do not know the author of the deed—or if there was one. I believe it to have been a spark, a divine one.

Natheless, such has been the danger to Christians in your city since the end of the siege, that once the explosions took place, the *yenicheriler* instantly set about rounding up anyone they regarded with suspicion. Thus I was seized the next night in one of the Galata taverns with my comrades. My only crime had been that when the thunder claps began, I along with every other person in Constantinople had rushed to the banks of the Golden Horn, wondering what new misfortune had been loosed from God's hand, and stood among the crowds watching the flames and embers shoot high into the night sky. But I and my men had nothing to do with the conflagration, which tho' not destroying the entire fleet, likely helped prevent a second invasion of Malta, as the Grand Master had wished.

The rest His Majesty knows. I was dragged to his feet at the Imperial Divan several months ago, whence I began to recount my history and that of the siege. I have omitted only one small thing—that the *yenicheri* who recognized me was Yakhshi.

"Pork-eater!" he exclaimed while I sat in my cell the first night, "we cannot seem to be rid of each other! You destroyed our army, now you have destroyed the Arsenal. You will lose your head for this."

"I may lose my head, but I did not burn your arsenal. I see you are limping. Did you not win a *timar* while on Malta? Why are you not farming it?"

"So many *yenicheriler* were killed that I have not yet been permitted to leave the city. After last night, I may have to wait longer." Thereat, the *Boluk-bashi* sat down outside my cell and we spoke of all that had taken place since I had last seen him, and he brought me greetings from Abdallah al-Waryagli. He asked whether there had been trouble after he escaped from me and Blaij Vergã and I said, yes, some trouble.

Thus I came before you, Your Majesty. I do not know how much of my tale the Padishah, Blessed by the Compassion of Allah, has believed. It is written that Allah is not ashamed to set forth any parable—that of a gnat even, or greater thing—and believers will know it for the truth, while unbelievers will be led astray by it. From the lips of a man it is certain even believers will fall into error.

But I am no relater of parables. For this reason I have merely told the tale. I perceive His Majesty's thirst for lessons and wisdom has gone unslaked, but as I warned him, I am no philosopher. Balthazar, surely, would have drawn more from the well. He foretold that all questions would be answered by the siege. Why of two fearless men, one flees to the enemy while the other plants his feet and dies. Why one man is marked a renegado and another is not. Why the Turkish forces, so much greater in number than our own, failed to take Malta in the greatest siege, whether it was arms or armor, the spirit of a Grand Master, the disputes of Pashas, the Whim of Fortune, the Will of God. I do not know whether Balthazar was right. I think everything happens in war. That is all. I have told my tale and leave the rest to others.

When I thus finished the story, I looked up at Soliman the Lawgiver, who had been lying before me on his bed, propped up on one arm. I quivered involuntarily, thinking that he would certainly be unconvinced, his recent disbelief at my story unabated and his anger unquenched. Surely, my life had reached the end of its road and I would shortly join Balthazar in Heaven. But at this juncture, Soliman merely nodded softly, closed his eyes and lay his head back on the pillow. As the roar of the cannon bombarding Szigetvár resumed in the night, I peered at him closely. The Great Sultan, Allah's Deputy on Earth, Refuge of All the People of the World, Shadow of the Almighty Dispensing Quiet on the Earth, had died.

At once I wondered whether my tale was the cause and in the same heartbeat feared for my head, for Grand Vizier Sokullu Mehmed, standing immediately outside the tent, would surely this instant demand it. When the physicians and servants understood that Soliman had sent his soul to God, there was immediate commotion and Sokullu incontinently rushed in. I needed no time to think. In the disorder, I slipped out of the tent. Yakhshi, standing guard, turned his back, and I disappeared into the camp.

Many months passed after that night of September sixth, *anno* 1566, before I regained Malta. Aye, by the time I at last sailed into Marsamxett harbor, 1567 was upon us. From the deck of the galleon, I saw an island transformed. The walls of the new fortress-city were already rising on Mt. Sciberras and as I disembarked I saw they would ring the entire peninsula. Work had been going on a full year. Before 1565 was out His Holiness had sent his military engineer, Michelangelo's student Francesco Laparelli, to design the works, and a few days after the beginning of 1556, on the twenty-eighth of March, the first stone of the new city, "la Valetta," was set in place. Laparelli had argued to abandon Birgu and Senglea, they had been so completely ruined, but de Valette objected and the two towns were also slowly rising from their ashes.

When I walked thro' the gates of la Valetta, I found the Grand Master sitting at a table amidst the carpenters and masons that everywhere swarmed around him, discussing the plans with Laparelli and his assistant, the same Girolamo Cassar whose ingenious schemes had helped save Fort St. Michel.

I bowed and kissed the ring. His Eminence was surprised to see me alive. He had assumed I had been executed with the others. "No," I answered, "that fate I escaped, but I cannot claim either to have carried out the mission you requested. The Turkish Arsenal went up in flames a year ago, but thro' no intervention of ours. Such things happen."

The Grand Master pondered this for a moment, replied that the Order was grievously short of money due to the building of the new city, but he saw the hand of the Almighty in this, and would reward me anyway. He ordered a sack of gold brought from the treasury.

Later in the day, I discovered Dr. Vigo at the Hospital in Birgu. "Truly, the place looks somewhat recovered from its condition two years ago," I said as we embraced.

"Much," the doctor answered. "It will be an age before these towns are whole again. A new Hospital is planned for la Valetta, which will be the greatest Christendom has known, but the first stones have not even been laid. While we wait, we toil here." He mentioned that the Knights had attempted to fish a huge basilisk out of Marsamxett harbor, to no avail. "It is very heavy," he said.

"Let it rest there," I said and asked after Isabella. "Is she to be found?"

Vigo shook his head. "She is in Florence this spring. Francisco, Isabella shall shortly be ... betrothed. She had little strength left. You were gone, thought dead. Parisot insisted—"

"Of course. And she obeyed."

I asked for the identity of the fiancé and Vigo said he was another Florentine. "Stefano Buonacorsi he is called. He comes from a ... noble family. The match is perfect." I remained silent as we began to walk together toward the square. "Francisco," Vigo went on, "Her spirit ... With her mother gone—"

"Lady Emilia dead?" I interrupted again.

Yes, after the siege her health declined rapidly for a last time. It was as if by staying on Malta she had carried out her duty to her daughter and Parisot, and once having performed her duty, she was ... released. "At least Emilia's death was a natural one, if hastened by worry." As we reached the square, the physician tore off a piece of paper from a door and handed it to me. A *libello famoso*. I read it, and could not believe what I read; the *libello* was directed against Grand Master de Valette himself.

"Yes," Vigo said, "all is not ... *well* here, Francisco."

"But he is the hero of Europe!" I exclaimed, utterly startled.

"He was. Come, you shall hear."

He led me to the same shingleless cellar where we ate of old, without a building atop it. Today rowdy and dissolute young Knights filled the place. They jested, drank and surely sang, but their songs were no longer of great victories. The patience of these men had been sorely tried by rumors of the new Turkish invasion and the huge expense of building la Valetta, and their songs, mean-spirited and mocking, attacked the deeds of the leaders who had fought two years ago. Nothing from their mouths, tho', was as vicious as the *libello* in my hands. It declared that de Valette had never run to the Post of Castille during the last great assault, that he had never fought with the valor sung of him. I cast my mind back to those terrible days. Truly, the chaos had been complete and the images in my mind remained jumbled. Reading this paper, I felt all certainty about what had taken place at during those terrible months slipping from my grasp.

I remained on Malta long enough to witness the outcome of this affair. de Valette, as occupied as he was directing the construction of the city named in his honor, would not let such defamations go unpunished. Instantly he set in motion an investigation by the full Council, whose suspicion quickly fell on some young Spaniards. As the Vice Chancellor penned their sentences, the accused burst into the Magisterial Palace itself, snatched the quill from his hand and threw the inkhorn out the window. The rebels flung themselves out of the Palace, dashed down to Galley Creek and made headlong for Sicily.

de Valette's wrath knew no bounds. With a demeanor not unlike that on the day he ordered me to fire Turkish heads across the harbor, he set his agents near and far after the criminals, arrested Knights and threw them into St. Angelo's dungeon, threatening to keep them there until they revealed the names of all the conspirators. When high-ranking Spanish Knights protested that there was no proof against those being detained, Eminenza defrocked two of them and threw two more into jail for good measure. Another, the same emissary who had carried the bejeweled sword from the King of Spain, de Valette sentenced to ten years in the Gozo castle.

I'd had my fill of *libelli famosi* and resolved to quit Malta. For a time I considered returning to Venice, for the air there pleases me, but decided after half a lifetime I must go first to Spain and discover what I might about the libels that had changed my life's course. I went to Granada and learned that my mother Anna had returned to our old house after the death of my father a few years ago. Assuredly, after sixteen or seventeen years, she did not at first recognize the scarred, one-eyed man standing on her threshold, and told the servants to see me gone. Only when I called out her name and mine did the veils of time part for her.

We sat for many hours. She told me that she and my father Fernando had, after some investigation, cleared our names. No taint of Moorish blood ran thro' our veins, to her enormous relief, and our family's reputation was restored. I was relieved to hear it as well, for the disgrace is too heavy for any Spaniard to bear. I told her, tho', that I had met a Moor and a Turk, as well as countless renegados, who had behaved honorably, mayhap with more honor than some of my own faith.

As to Blaij Vergã, Mother was uncertain, Fernando never having divulged any faithlessness, but she thought it might be true that Vergã was my half-brother. The idea that such a villain could share my blood disquieted me, but at times e'en I perceived that little would have been taken to put me on his path.

And so I did, after all, set eyes on my native land again. After some listless months in Granada, I returned to Venice, to discover whether I could make a life there. I yet carried Isabella's stained and bloodied kerchief with me, and disbelieving that she could possibly be getting married, I fancied that with my family's reputation restored, we would take the final step toward each other. Oh, how often have I cursed myself for not acting sooner! En route to Venice, I stopped at Malta at the end of August 1568, only to hear from Vigo himself amongst the worst and saddest news I ever received.

I was late by weeks. Isabella had married this Stefano Buonacorsi, but the criminal, on the pretense that she had been profligate and wanton before their betrothal, stabbed her and made off with her jewels. At hearing these words from Vigo, I flew into such a rage that the physician needed to restrain me. O God, for this had our destinies been so intertwined? I was beside myself, vowing at once to avenge her death on Buonacorsi. So impassioned were my cries that I scarce heard Vigo telling me how the de Valette, again putting the full might of the Council into motion, had himself attempted to apprehend the criminal. That act alone was extraordinary, for the Council never intervened in such secular affairs, never a Grand Master for a ward. But all proved for naught; Stefano's friends and relatives secreted the murderer off the island to Italy and thwarted the Grand Master's design.

de Valette was stricken thro' the heart. Weeks later, his parrot, then his falcon, then his lioness died. The people knew these for signs from God and were certain of it when multitudes of fish, larger than dolphins, appeared in Marsamxett and remained there. Yes, days before I arrived, on the twenty-first of August, 1568, those by him saw angels descend from Heaven to lift Parisot's soul to God, and the last Crusader departed, having lost the one true love of his life.

I went to the Church of San Lorenzo where Jean de Valette had been laid to rest and for a long time I stood before his coffin. Unbidden and unstoppable, tears flooded my eyes. I laid Isabella's kerchief on his casket. Then I continued on my voyage, bearing the souls of loved ones within me.

Acknowledgments

In deciding to undertake *The Course of Fortune*, I understood from the outset that I was embarking on a project for which I was in some ways ill equipped. I am neither an expert on the sixteenth century, nor proficient in the languages spoken by the Knights of Malta and their antagonists. And so I am heavily indebted to a number of people who gave graciously of their time and knowledge, without which the project never would have been completed.

I would first like to thank Maltese historian Arnold Cassola, who encouraged me to give it a try, and who provided me with an initial entry into the literature. My enormous gratitude goes to Inés Arribas, who got me started with Giacomo Bosio's history of the Knights, in an early seventeenth-century French edition. No less gratitude goes to Ron Martinez for providing authentic sixteenth-century renderings of Isabella's poetry. Many thanks as well to Andrew Patterson at the Bryn Mawr College library, who obtained for me many impossible-to-obtain documents; to José Pazo for acting as advisor on Spain and Spanish; to Pete Koelle, who provided some translations from Turkish and Spanish; to Enrico Lorenzini for translations from Italian; to John Guilmartin for tips on sixteenth-century warfare; to Dan Goffman for helpful information on Ottoman law and administration, and to Colin Imber for doing his best to answer impossible questions about sixteenth-century Turkish and slavery. Let me also acknowledge that the sonnet on page 400 is by Baltazar del Alcázar (1530-1606) as translated in *Treasury of Spanish Love* (New York: Hippocrene Books, 1999). The verses of Suleyman on page 694 are from Talat S. Halman, *Suleyman the Magnificent, Poet* (Istanbul: Dost Yayinlari, 1987). I have been unable to reach either publisher.

Above all I am grateful to be able to finally express my great indebtedness to former Justice of the European Court of Human Rights and Maltese historian Giovanni Bonello. With infinite patience and good cheer, Vanni freely shared his great knowledge of Maltese history, supplied material before publication, answered a never-ending stream of questions, read the entire manuscript, and checked facts—all for a complete stranger. It is safe to say I wouldn't have gotten anywhere without his help and encouragement. From the bottom of my heart, thanks, Vanni.

Afterword

Readers of historical novels invariably ask themselves, and often the author, what he has invented and what he hasn't. The rule I set for myself in writing *The Course of Fortune* was simple: not to consciously violate any known facts. Of course, the events forming the basis of the novel have now taken place four hundred fifty years ago. The only unimpeachable fact is that historical records of the early period of the Knights on Malta are at best fragmentary and always contradictory. Depending on the account you come across, you will probably believe that Turgut Reis was killed by a lucky shot fired from Castle St. Angelo—and a placard above the fort confirms it. But both fellows who were actually there write that the corsair's death was in fact due to an instance of "friendly fire." Hundreds of such examples lie about for the taking.

Any history, therefore, even a fictionalized one, must do violence to somebody's version. For the Great Siege itself, I have often gone with Francesco Balbi's day-by-day journal of events. As in the novel, Balbi was a Spanish-Italian arquebusier posted at Senglea, and his is the only known eyewitness account of the entire siege, excepting a less-detailed epic poem, *La Maltea*, written by the Knight Hipolito Sans. Throughout I have also relied heavily on the *History of the Knights of St. John* by the Order's official historian, Giacomo Bosio, because his book, originally published in 1588, is the earliest of the formal histories and infinitely more detailed than anything written after.[1] One senses he frequently had access to firsthand accounts.

All this means that readers familiar with modern retellings will be perplexed by many discrepancies. I leave it to the other authors to justify their versions. One thing, tho', becomes quickly apparent while researching the Siege: What has traditionally passed for a fact is, as often as not, simply an error propagated through the centuries. To forestall endless arguments, let me mention a few.

Students of the Great Siege will have noted two whoppers on my part regarding Jean de Valette. The first regards his name: Virtually any history of the Knights refers to him as "La Valette." Giovanni Bonello points out, however, that not a single document, medallion, signature, or anything else ever referred to him as "La Valette" during his lifetime. "La Valette" arose some decades after his death as a confusion with the city named after him, "la Valetta." The second matter concerns his age. Popular histories invariably give de Valette's dates as 1494–1568 because of the monument erected in his memory in 1591, twenty-three years after his death. This makes him seventy-one during the Siege. Arnold Cassola points out, however, that both Balbi and Sans clearly state that de Valette was sixty-seven at the time, and that the age of seventy-one is due to subsequent mistranslations. I have gone with Cassola's figure, tho' I understand it will cause ire among pretty much everybody.

Connoisseurs might also assume I have invented the stories about de Valette's arrests and exiles, as they are omitted in popular accounts. Nay; apart from the mild *settena* I give him in Chapter Fourteen, these are all part of the historical record. Interested readers may consult Bonello Volume II in the bibliography. Neither have I entirely invented the story of Isabella. Bosio writes:

"To the malcontents and upsets that disturbed and worried the spirit of the Grand Master, one must add a very awful and sad story that involved a beautiful damoiselle named Isabella. She was the daughter of a nobleman from Rhodes of Florentine descent, of the Guasconi family. The Grand Master, to satisfy some personal obligation to her father, had held her in baptism and had arranged to give her away in marriage. She was married briefly to a young man, also from Florence, called [Stefano] Buonacorsi."

The rest is almost exactly as I have related in the novel's denouement. Bosio goes on to recount how de Valette then fell ill and shortly died. Because Bosio does not give an age for Isabella, I have taken the liberty of assuming she was about thirty at the time of the siege, which, judging from the tenor of Bosio's remarks, makes her much too old.[2] And yes, according to Bosio, the Grand Master kept a pet lioness.

Regarding de Valette's speeches and letters, most of these are "genuine," being my rewrites of those found in contemporary sources. In particular, the letter from de Valette to Pedro Mezquita about the fall of St. Elmo is found in Curione and, as I have recently learned, Salazar. The letter from the Knights trapped in Fort St. Elmo has been problematic. My version is a further reworking of one given by Bradford, which is a good paraphrase of what historians say was in the letter; however, as the original document has never been found, one must conclude that Bradford's text is his own invention.

Regarding Romegas, the historical record is essentially mute on his early career. We know that he professed in 1547 at the age of eighteen. One account does put him at Zuara, "where three hundred persons were enslaved," but gives no date. His presence on Djerba in 1551 and activities during the 1551 siege are my inventions. The Knight's later exploits, beginning about 1555, on the other hand, are fairly well documented, in particular those precipitating the Siege, and I have attempted to follow them. Dates and details, however, are so elusive that I have once or twice combined episodes from different sources to create the Cocia-Cocia story.

As for issues such as numbers and types of ships, troops, armaments, etc., there is simply no consistency among historians. As a rule, defenders in heroic conflicts minimize their own numbers and maximize the enemy's. Both Sans and Balbi (in one place) indicate that nearly 50,000 Turkish troops and corsairs invested Malta during the Siege, plus at least thirty thousand oarsmen. In another place Balbi indicates 40,000 (before the corsairs arrived), and this figure is also given by de Valette himself in a letter to the Prior of Germany (see Curione), though it is unclear whether he includes the corsairs. (He also gives 250 ships for the size of the Turkish armada). All in all, I have found no serious evidence that there were fewer than about forty thousand Turkish troops and corsairs, as some historians maintain. (Vincenzo Anastagi [below], who had reason to "lowball" his estimate, does claim that only 22,000 Turkish troops arrived.) As for the defenders, Balbi gives precisely 6,100 total; Bosio 8,500. Sans says 3,000 Maltese were involved. A detailed comparison between the figures given by Balbi and Sans is presented by Cassola in *La Maltea*.

Finally, regarding the fire at the Turkish arsenal, which forms the frame story for the novel, the Abbé Vertot reports that de Valette successfully sent his spies to Constantinople to torch the Turkish fleet, but as Bonello points out (Volume I, below), the plan never materialized. Fires in Constantinople, as the Venetian Bailo reported, were nonetheless commonplace, and during my researches I did come across a claim that there was a fire in the year following the Siege that destroyed a large part of the fleet, which was however quickly rebuilt. Unfortunately, I have not been able to relocate this source, so perhaps I invented it. In any case, I have made use of this "coincidence" in framing the novel.

For determined readers, I now give a bibliography of the principal sources consulted while writing *Course of Fortune*.

Principal Sources

1. General History of the Knights of Malta

The earliest, and by far most complete history of the Knights of St. John is that of Giacomo Bosio, official historian of the Order. The original Italian edition is:

Giacomo Bosio, *Dell'istoria della sacra religione et ill'ma militia de San Giovanni Gierosolimitano* (Rome, 1588).

Unfortunately, at the time of the writing of the novel, no available copy of this edition appeared to exist in the United States. I therefore worked from a microfilm of the 1643 French version, *Histoire des Chevaliers de l'ordre de S. Iean de Hierusalem*, edited by J. Baudoin, which I received from the University of Minnesota library. Consultation with Bonello revealed significant omissions compared to the Italian editions. An early Italian edition is now available online from Google Books. Relying much on his predecessor but adding some new material and much confusion is:

Abbé de Vertot, *History of the Knights of Malta* (two vols., London: 1728; facsimile edition published by Midsea Ltd., Malta, 1989).

Of the modern histories, the most serious is:

H.J.A. Sire, *The Knights of Malta* (Yale University Press: New Haven, 1994).

Sire concentrates more on the structure than on the exploits of the Order. Recent biographies of two of the novel's characters are:

Carmel Testa, *Romegas* (Midsea Books: Malta, 2002);

Serge Elmalan, *Nicolas de Villegagnon ou L'Utopie Tropicale* (Favre: Lausanne, 2002).

As mentioned in the Afterword, little information exists about Romegas himself, especially in his early years. Testa's book is, however, useful as a succinct history of the period covered by the novel and utilizes rare archival sources. Elmalan's fictionalized biography focuses on

Villegaignon's voyages to Brazil, but several chapters concern Malta and the Knights.

Although relating to a slightly later period, indispensable for giving the flavor and escapades of the Knights has been:

Alonso de Contreras, *The Adventures of Captain Alonso de Contreras*, trans. by Philip Dallas (Paragon House: New York, 1989).

Contreras was the only plebeian ever made a Knight of Malta, and these astonishing memoirs detail his crimes and exploits after the year 1600. A popular and readily available introduction to the Knights is:

Ernle Bradford, *The Shield and the Sword* (Dutton: New York, 1973).

2. The Sieges

As mentioned in the Afterword, for the Great Siege we are fortunate to have a detailed day-by-day journal of a Spanish-Italian arquebusier, Francesco Balbi. Tho' his account is often confusing and sometimes inconsistent, all historians of the Siege, including Bosio, rely heavily on it. I have worked from two editions:

Francesco Balbi de Correggio, *The Siege of Malta 1565*, trans. by Henry Balbi (Gollcher: Copenhagen, 1961);

Francisco Balbi di Correggio, *The Siege of Malta 1565*, trans. by Ernle Bradford (Folio Society: London, 1965).

The latter is a somewhat smoother—and evidently looser—translation than the former. It omits some of Balbi's introductory material and his lists of Christian defenders, and makes other arbitrary cuts. On the other hand, it includes a translator's introduction and maps (some of which contain errors). Another account written shortly after the siege is:

Celio Secondo Curione, *De Bello Melitensi Nova Historia* (Basileae: 1567); The English edition is *A New History of the War in Malta (1565)*, trans. by Granville Pacha (Tipografia Leonina: Rome 1928).

Curione's is an "almost eyewitness" account that contains a few details lacking in Balbi and some dispatches from the Grand Master. Recently discovered has been cavalry commander Vincenzo Anastagi's report to the relief forces, which now takes its place among the important siege documents, and on which I have based Anastagi's observations in the novel. It can be found in Bonello Volume III (below). Of the modern histories, the most unusual is:

Albert Ganado and Maurice Aguis-Vadalà, *A Study in Depth of 143 Maps Representing the Great Siege of Malta of 1565* (Publishers Enterprise Group: Malta, 1994).

As its title implies, this is a rather extraordinary collection of one hundred forty-three maps of the Great Siege, many apparently drawn from on-site dispatches. The chronological ordering of the maps results in something of a day-to-day account of the siege. The most popular account of the Great Siege is:

Ernle Bradford, *The Great Siege: Malta 1565* (Hodder and Stoughton: London, 1961).

Virtually no Turkish sources on the Great Siege have come to light. The most notable—if not only—exception is:

Arnold Cassola, *The 1565 Ottoman Malta Campaign Register* (Publishers Enterprise Group: Malta, 1998).

Therein are reprinted documents and decrees relating to the Siege, an outline of the structure of the Ottoman military, details of the Turkish preparations, and a glossary of Turkish military terms. Cassola's argument for de Valette's dates, as well as a detailed discussion of the numbers of Turkish troops involved in the Siege, can be found in:

Arnold Cassola, *The 1565 Great Siege of Malta and Hipólito Sans's* La Maltea 1565 (Publishers Enterprise Group: Malta, 1999).

Details of the siege of 1551 and the fall of Tripoli have been largely taken from Bosio and Vertot. For the fall of Tripoli we are lucky to have a detailed eyewitness account by the Chamberlain and Geographer of the French Ambassador Lord d'Aramont:

Nicholas de Nicholay, *The Peregrinations of Nicholas Nicholay* (London, 1585; available through Early English Books online).

I have followed Nicholay and Bosio fairly closely. For the 1522 siege of Rhodes (and the earlier 1480 siege), a good modern account is:

Eric Brockman, *The Two Sieges of Rhodes* (John Murray: London, 1969).

The historian William Prescott apparently wrote that the sources describing the Djerba campaign were so contradictory that he defied the reader to reconcile them. I tend to agree. My account is a melding of Bosio's with those of Guilmartin in *Gunpowder* (below), Busbecq (below), Braudel (below), and Vertot, hopefully minus too many contradictions. The "almost successful sortie" and incident at Turgut's marquee, omitted in modern accounts, are described by Bosio. The tower of skulls existed until about 1825.

3. General History of Malta

The history of Malta is inextricably bound up with that of the Knights. Some works, however, concentrate on the social history of Malta. Of these the most revelatory have been the ongoing "microhistories" of Bonello. I have made use of four volumes:

Giovanni Bonello, *Histories of Malta*, Volume I, *Deceptions and Perceptions* (Patrimonju Publishing Ltd: Malta, 2000); Volume II, *Figments and Fragments* (2001); Volume III, *Versions and Perversions* (2002); Volume IV, *Convictions and Conjectures* (2003).

Helpful as well have been:

Louis de Boisgelin, *Ancient and Modern Malta* (Richard Phillips: London, 1805);

Victor Mallia-Milandes, editor, *Hospitaller Malta 1530–1798* (Mireva Publications: Malta, 1993).

The former is concerned mostly with the period after the time of this novel but is probably the most complete account of the natural history of Malta as well as the customs of the inhabitants. The latter is a fine collection of articles concerning Maltese society under the Knights. A useful book on the history of the Maltese Inquisition is:

Alexander Bonnici, *Medieval and Roman Inquisition in Malta* (Publishers Enterprise Group: Malta, 1998).

For slavery in Malta, the bible is:

Godfrey Wettinger, *Slavery on the Islands of Malta and Gozo, ca. 1000–1812* (Publishers Enterprise Group: Malta, 2002).

This tome is by far the most extensive treatment of slavery on Malta, and I have relied heavily on it for the description of the treatment of slaves, etc. The details of de Valette's slaving operations can also be found there.

4. Sixteenth Century Warfare

Indispensable for details concerning sixteenth-century galleys and naval tactics have been:

John Guilmartin, *Gunpowder and Galleys* (Cambridge University Press: Cambridge, 1974); *Galleons and Galleys* (Cassell & Co.: London, 2002);

Joseph Wismayer, *The Fleet of the Order of St. John 1530–1798* (Midsea Books: Malta, 1997).

The two great sixteenth-century works on metallurgy and military technology from which I have taken the details on metallurgy and cannon-founding are:

Vannoccio Biringuccio, *Pirotechnia* (1540; M.I.T. Press: Cambridge, 1959);

Georgius Agricola, *De Re Metallica* (1556; Dover: New York, 1950).

One of the few studies of Greek Fire is:

J.R. Partington, *A History of Greek Fire and Gunpowder* (W. Heffer and Sons: Cambridge, 1960).

Sources disagree widely on the details of the fortifications of Malta in the early period of the Knights and on the chronology of improvements. The most detailed study is:

Stephen Spiteri, *Fortresses of the Knights* (Book Distributors Ltd: Malta, 2001).

I have tended to go with Spiteri for descriptions of the fortifications of Malta and Tripoli as they would have existed in the sixteenth century. Testa (above) also gives details of the improvements made under d'Homedes. Details about the Venetian Arsenale have been taken almost entirely from:

Frederic Lane, *Venetian Shipbuilding and Shipbuilders of the Renaissance* (Johns Hopkins University Press: Baltimore, 1934); *Venice, A Maritime Republic* (Johns Hopkins University Press: Baltimore, 1973);

Robert Davis, *Shipbuilders of the Venetian Arsenal* (Johns Hopkins University Press: Baltimore, 1991).

A more conventional history of Venice, concentrating on doges and warfare is:

John Norwich, *A History of Venice* (Vintage: New York, 1989).

5. History of the Ottoman Empire

The indispensable eyewitness account of Suleyman's court is:

Oghier Ghiselin de Busbecq, *Life and Letters*, volume I (Slatkine Reprints: Geneva, 1971).

Busbecq was the Austrian Ambassador to Constantinople from 1554–1562, almost exactly the period covered by the novel. His book, written in the form of letters to a friend, gives detailed descriptions of Turkish customs, the royal household, and firsthand accounts of some episodes in the novel. Nicholas de Nicholay (above) also provides many firsthand descriptions, which I have pilfered. An older but detailed book on the Ottoman government is:

Albert Lybyer, *The Government of the Ottoman Empire in the Time of Suleiman the Magnificent* (Harvard University Press: Cambridge, Ma., 1913).

Two modern histories of the Ottoman Empire that have proven very useful are:

Daniel Goffman, *The Ottoman Empire and Early Modern Europe* (Cambridge University Press: Cambridge, 2002);

Colin Imber, *The Ottoman Empire* (Palgrave Macmillan, 2002).

The former concentrates on the Ottoman's association with Western Europe and the latter on institutional structures. Helpful popular books relating in whole or in part to Suleyman and his times have been:

André Clot, *Suleiman the Magnificent* (SAQI: London, 1992);

Raphaela Lewis, *Everyday Life in Ottoman Turkey* (Dorset: New York, 1971);

Philip Mansel, *Constantinople* (St. Martin's: New York, 1998);

Bernard Lewis, *The Muslim Discovery of Europe* (W.W. Norton: New York, 2001).

6. Medical Practices

The information about sixteenth-century medicine was gathered from divers sources. The more helpful books have been:

Paul Cassar, *Medical History of Malta* (Wellcome Historical Medical Library: London, 1964);

Edgar Hume, *Medical Work of the Knights Hospitallers of St. John of Jerusalem* (Johns Hopkins University Press: Baltimore, 1940);

A. Wear, R. French and A. Lonie, editors, *The Medical Renaissance of the Sixteenth Century* (Cambridge University Press: Cambridge, 1985);

Clifford Foust, *Rhubarb, The Wondrous Drug* (Princeton University Press: Princeton, 1992).

7 . General Background

The standard history of the Mediterranean at the time of the novel is:

Fernand Braudel, *The Mediterranean and the Mediterranean World in the Age of Philip II* (University of California Press: Berkeley, 1995).

A more popular overview of this period, with a chapter on Malta, is:

Jack Beeching, *The Galleys at Lepanto* (Scribner's: New York, 1982).

An excellent sourcebook on Renaissance thought is:

James Ross and Mary Martin, editors, *The Portable Renaissance Reader* (Penguin: New York, 1977).

The great account of the life of a galley slave, although dating from a later epoch and another country, is:

Jean Marteilhe, *The Huguenot Galley Slave* (1757; Leypoldt and Hold: NY, 1867).

Equally helpful in this regard has been:

Daniel Vitkus, editor, *Piracy, Slavery and Redemption* (Columbia University Press: NY, 2001).

This is a collection of firsthand accounts by sixteenth- and seventeenth-century Englishmen who were captured by the Barbary corsairs. Two books on Spain that have proven very useful are:

Henry Lea, *The Moriscos of Spain* (Greenwood Press: NY, reprint 1968);

Marcelin Defouneaux, *Daily Life in Spain in the Golden Age* (Stanford University Press: Stanford, 1979).

For Spanish curses and duelling stories I have naturally consulted Brantôme, but that would be telling.

---

[1] Since writing *The Course of Fortune* I have discovered a lengthy account of the siege that predates Bosio: *Pedro de Salazar, Hispania Victrix. Historia en la qual se cuenta muchas guerras succedidas entre Christianos y infieles assi en mar como en tierra desde el año de mil y quinientos y quaranta y seys hasta el de sestenta y cinco* (Madrid, 1570). Salazar's history is known, but has evidently never been translated and is never cited. It is now available online as a Google Book, as is Bosio's history.

[2] Since the writing of the novel, Giovanni Bonello has found documentary evidence that de Valette fathered at least two more illegitimate children.